ACCLAIM FOR
MAJIC MAN

"This eleventh entry in this stellar series—seven
have been nominated for the Shamus award—is a
typically intelligent, witty, and exciting examination
of a real-life mystery."
—*Booklist*

"Heller possesses a refreshingly gritty underside,
reflected in a past that encompasses a stay in a
psychiatric ward, perjury, and sensitive casework for
the highest levels of society and government.
There's magic of a literary kind here: full-bore
suspense coupled with an ingenious take on an
overworked pop-historical touchstone."
—*Publishers Weekly*

"In the latest in a remarkable series . . . Collins turns
real-life events into a cogent fictionalized mystery
plot and (even more difficult) real people into full-
fleshed fictional characters. The climax is a clear
homage to Collins's literary hero, Mickey Spillane."
—*Ellery Queen*

"As in all of his Nathan Heller series, Collins blends
fact and fiction, real people and fictional characters,
to provide a unique story with which to entertain
his readers."
—*Abilene Reporter-News*

Continued on next page. . . .

FLYING BLIND

"Buckle your seat belt and get ready for a journey into a world of intrigue, espionage, betrayal, and a rousing good time. Collins is at his best."
—*Mostly Murder*

"No one can twist you through a maze with as much intensity and suspense as Max Allan Collins."
—Clive Cussler, author of *Atlantis Found*

"A brilliantly realized conclusion to one of history's most spellbinding puzzles."
—*Kansas City Independent*

"Highly entertaining . . . snappy dialogue and jet-paced action."
—*Los Angeles Times*

DAMNED IN PARADISE

"Another writer who is a whole industry unto himself is Max Allan Collins. In this tale, Collins makes everything from the atmosphere in a raunchy rum joint to the unabashed prejudice among U.S. Navy brass as palpable as a palm tree's rustle."
—*San Jose Mercury News*

"An unprecedented seven Shamus nominations. That's how good this series is. A lovingly and often elegantly written novel, *Damned in Paradise* is marvelous entertainment and a 'must-read' for every fan of private eye fiction."
—*Mostly Murder*

"First-rate. . . . Collins's version of the real-life case is far superior to Norman Katkov's *Blood and Orchids*."
—*The Armchair Detective*

BLOOD AND THUNDER

"Riveting . . . abounds with colorful characters and roller-coaster plot twists. Collins masterfully blends fact and fiction into a compelling tale that transcends the historical thriller."
—Jeffery Deaver, author of *The Devil's Teardrop*

"As always, Collins's sense of place and time is unerringly accurate. A tough act to follow."
—*Publishers Weekly*

"The writing sparkles."
—*Richmond Times-Dispatch*

CARNAL HOURS

"Excellent. A Byzantine plot, rich atmosphere, and snappy, tough-guy narration—all qualities we've come to expect from Max Allan Collins."
—*Booklist*

"Fast, breezy fun . . . cleverly concocted."
—*New York Times Book Review*

THE MEMOIRS OF NATHAN HELLER:

MAJIC MAN

A Nathan Heller Novel

Max Allan Collins

A SIGNET BOOK

SIGNET
Published by New American Library, a division of
Penguin Putnam Inc., 375 Hudson Street,
New York, New York 10014, U.S.A.
Penguin Books Ltd, 27 Wrights Lane,
London W8 5TZ, England
Penguin Books Australia Ltd,
Ringwood, Victoria, Australia
Penguin Books Canada Ltd, 10 Alcorn Avenue,
Toronto, Ontario, Canada M4V 3B2
Penguin Books (N.Z.) Ltd, 182–190 Wairau Road,
Auckland 10, New Zealand

Penguin Books Ltd, Registered Offices:
Harmondsworth, Middlesex, England

Published by Signet, an imprint of New American Library,
a division of Penguin Putnam Inc.
Previously published in a Dutton edition.

First Signet Printing, August 2000
10 9 8 7 6 5 4 3 2 1

PUBLISHER'S NOTE
This is a work of fiction. Names, characters, places, and incidents either are the
products of the author's imagination or are used fictitiously, and any resemblance to actual persons, living or dead, events, or locales is entirely coinciden-
tal.

To Paul Thomas—
musical magician

Although the historical incidents in this novel are portrayed more or less accurately (as much as the passage of time, and contradictory source material, will allow), fact, speculation and fiction are freely mixed here; historical personages exist side by side with composite characters and wholly fictional ones—all of whom act and speak at the author's whim.

"... [A] comprehensive further examination of the so-called 'Roswell Incident' found no evidence whatsoever of flying saucers, space aliens or sinister government cover-ups."
—Captain James McAndrew
1997 U.S. Air Force
Roswell Report

"No quiet murmur like the tremulous wail
Of the lone bird, the querulous nightingale—
But shrieks that fly
Piercing and wild, and loud, shall mourn the tale. . . ."
—Sophocles, translated by
William Mackworth Praed

"I am a victim of the Washington scene."
—James V. Forrestal
America's first
Secretary of Defense

ROSWELL ARMY AIR BASE,
ROSWELL, N.M.
8 JULY, 1947 A.M.

The many rumors regarding the flying saucer became a reality yesterday when the intelligence office of the 509th Bomb Group of the Eighth Air Force, Roswell Army Air Field, was fortunate enough to gain possession of a saucer through the cooperation of one of the local ranchers and the Sheriff's office of Chaves County.

The flying object landed on a ranch near Roswell sometime last week. Not having phone facilities, the rancher stored the disc until such time as he was able to contact the Sheriff's office, who in turn notified Major Jesse A. Marcel, of the 509th Bomb Group Intelligence office.

Action was immediately taken and the saucer was picked up at the rancher's home. It was inspected at the Roswell Army Air Field and subsequently loaned by Major Marcel to higher headquarters.

—official U.S. Army Air Force
news release

PROLOGUE

WASHINGTON, D.C.
SEPTEMBER 1940

THE LEAVES WERE TURNING, but a humid summer heat hung on, a nasty, sticky reminder that our nation's capital—with its languorous "y'all" cadence, profusion of shade trees, and palatial private homes—was still a provincial Southern town, right down to the squalor of its colored slums. The strict segregation here made my Chicago look like a pillar of racial equality, and even worse, there was no air-conditioning.

Getting around Washington in my blue two-door rental Ford sedan was a mystery not easily solved even by Nathan Heller, President of the A-1 Detective Agency (corner of Van Buren and Plymouth in the Loop, second floor). Laid out like spokes on a wheel around the hub of Capitol Hill, the primary sections of the city were labeled after the compounded cardinal points of the compass—NW, SW, NE and SE.

But only that NW corner of the city seemed to count, everything interesting crammed into it, from movie palaces like Loew's Capitol to department stores like Garfinckel's, from restaurants like Olmstead's to hotels like the Ambassador, where I was staying. Along NW's 16th Street and Massachusetts Avenue were sixty or so embassies and chancelleries, not to mention various union headquarters and trade

associations. The closest thing to D.C. having a Main
Stem was NW's F Street where 14th Street crossed it;
but even there, any night including Saturday, the
lights were dim, sidewalks rolled up, most restaurants
closing by eight p.m.

The only action was the occasional cocktail lounge,
like the Ambassador's High Hat; first-class hookers
and bored government girls made it easy to get
cheaply and/or casually laid in that town; or so I understand (besides which, bubbly blonde Jeannie who
worked at the Farm Credit Administration has nothing to do with this story).

Many of the important politicians who didn't live
in suburban Virginia or Maryland lived in NW, including most congressmen, as well as the client who'd
summoned me here—James Vincent Forrestal, who
rented a big colonial house on Woodland Drive, behind the swanky Shoreham Hotel and overlooking
the leafy vastness of Rock Creek Park.

From a modest Irish Catholic background, Jim
Forrestal had stormed the Anglo-Saxon bastion of
Wall Street to become a key player at the powerful
investment banking firm of Dillon, Read & Company, eventually becoming president. In 1940 he
traded that million-dollar-a-year position for a one-
dollar-a-year job as one of President Franklin Roosevelt's administrative assistants. Not long ago
Forrestal had been appointed Under Secretary of the
Navy, and was currently applying his considerable
managerial skills to mobilization and production.

This was the second job I'd done for Forrestal this
year. The first one was a freelance Naval Intelligence
job, which even today is classified; despite that mission's failure, I had apparently impressed Forrestal to
the degree that he'd chosen to hire me again.

A butler tried unsuccessfully to take my hat and

showed me to a book-lined study, where Forrestal sat behind a massive mahogany desk, leaning back, smoking his pipe, a thick, brown-bindered document in his hands like a hymnal. The desk was littered with file folders and loose paper, as well as several stacks of imposingly thick books (*Outline of History* by H. G. Wells, *Abraham Lincoln: The War Years* by Carl Sandburg), mingling with a banker's lamp, framed family photos, pipe rack-and-humidor, candy jar, and ashtray.

Forrestal was as tidy as his desk was cluttered: three-piece Brooks Brothers double-breasted gray worsted, gray-and-blue striped four-in-hand tie. My navy-blue tropical suit from Sears was lightweight and, theoretically, cool; but I was working up a sauna sweat, the windows closed, the chamber stuffy with the memory of stale pipe smoke. Forrestal seemed aloof from such petty matters as climate.

I approached the waiting chair opposite Forrestal, who rose and flipped the binder onto the desk, extending his hand. Surprising power resided in the small man's grip, a fact he tried a little too hard to demonstrate. Standing perhaps five inches shorter than my six feet, Forrestal—slender, fit, late forties—draped himself in the controlled dignity of the statesman, but any air of elitist intellectualism was offset by the battered features of his spade-shaped face, with its broad flattened nose (he'd boxed at Princeton) and lipless slash of a mouth over a ball-like cleft chin.

"Thank you for coming, Nate," he said, fixing his intense blue-gray eyes on me.

"I wouldn't have," I admitted, settling into the hard captain's-style chair, "if your telegram hadn't specified this was personal."

His mouth seemed faintly amused around the pipe stem. "Not interested in government work?"

"No. And I hope this wasn't a ruse to get me back working for Navy Intelligence . . ."

He shook his head. "This is a private matter, Nate . . . though when we get into this war, I may call on you again—to serve your country."

There wasn't a war, not yet, so I just asked, "What sort of private matter?"

"My wife," he said, and he turned one of the framed photos toward me. "Josephine."

It was a rather exotic photo, dating I guessed to the late twenties or early thirties: a raven-haired beauty in an Oriental-pattern frock clutched a large reflective glass ball, like an absurdly oversize Christmas ornament.

"Well, she's lovely," I said.

And she was: a lanky, elegant woman with large dark eyes and bee-stung lips in an almond-shaped face, the dark hair bobbed in the Jazz Age fashion, a pale beauty in the manner of Louise Brooks or the early Myrna Loy.

"She's still quite lovely," he said, with all the warmth of a scientist describing a microbe. "Jo is an unusual woman. Unfortunately, at present, she's like a fine Swiss watch whose mainspring has been too tightly wound."

"I'm not sure I follow you, sir."

The gray-blue eyes stared blankly at me for a few moments, then he said, matter-of-factly, "Let me share a bit about her background."

In my business, I talked to plenty of husbands with cheating wives or otherwise troubled marriages, and no matter how hard they tried to suppress it, the emotion showed through. Not this guy.

"Jo's a Southern girl, and well-bred," he said, gesturing with pipe in hand, "but she's always had a rebel streak. She didn't finish college, rather became a Ziegfeld Follies chorus girl. The editor of *Vogue* met her at a party, was impressed by her wit and charm, and soon Jo was modeling, then writing a monthly column."

That explained the photo: it could easily have been snipped from those smart, pretentious pages.

"I met her at a party myself and, like that *Vogue* editor, was impressed," he said. "Witty, fashionable, sharp as a tack. . . . I'd never met anyone quite like her. Never have since."

Some admiration had crept in his tone now, but still no emotion or, for that matter, affection.

I asked, "How long have you been married?"

"Since nineteen twenty-five. We have two sons." He turned another of the framed photos toward me, displaying two handsome dark-haired lads perhaps seven and ten, wearing short-pants school uniforms with ties and caps, attire no more humiliating than getting tarred and feathered.

"Nice-looking boys," I said.

He nodded and turned the photo back his way, never mentioning them by name. To call this guy a cold fish was to give a dead mackerel a bad rap.

"Jo did much better when we lived on Long Island," he said, leaning back in his swivel chair, puffing at his pipe. "She's a wonderful horsewoman, a frequent prizewinner, and in Manhattan she was able to pursue her various other interests . . . theater, fabrics, flower arrangement, interior decoration."

"This was back in your Wall Street days."

He nodded, then shrugged, barely. "I was busy with my work and she was content to run with her circle, to '21' or wherever. Of course, even before I met her she had quite an array of unusual friends—George Gershwin, P. G. Wodehouse, Eddie Cantor, Bob Benchley, Jack O'Hara."

I tried not to look impressed.

"So you've gone your separate ways for some time now," I said, trying to lay the groundwork for the inevitable suspicions of infidelity I'd surely been summoned to confirm.

"Yes, and we've both liked it that way. The problem is . . . well, actually, Nate, there are two problems. The first is this town . . . Washington, D.C. It's been an enormous strain on Jo, trading in Long Island and Manhattan, horse shows and café society, for this dreary parade of politics."

This didn't seem to be heading where I expected.

Forrestal was shaking his head, somberly. "Such a different social milieu, here, such a narrow focus— the cocktail and dinner parties in this town don't dwell on the arts, it's all public issues and campaign talk."

"Noel Coward and Cole Porter don't come up much," I said.

"Not as regularly as Robert Taft and Wendell Willkie." This dry reply was surprisingly close to humor. "Jo's dislike of Washington has exacerbated her other problem . . . drinking."

"She had that problem before your move to D.C.?"

"Yes—only not to this degree. Not to where it was affecting her . . . mental capacities."

So that was it: Jo Forrestal was drinking herself into the laughing academy.

I asked, "How's all this manifesting itself?"

The slash of a mouth flinched in something that wasn't exactly a frown but sure wasn't a smile. "I'd prefer you speak to Jo and learn for yourself. She has a job for you."

I frowned. "*She* has a job for me."

He pointed with the pipe stem. "Yes, and I want you to take it, and take it seriously. If you don't investigate thoroughly, if we only pay lip service to her concerns, we would be courting disaster."

Now I was completely confused. "What concerns?"

But he would say no more; he wanted me to hear it from Mrs. Forrestal's lips.

And I did, the following morning, only not with her husband around. Forrestal was otherwise occupied, off rebuilding the Navy's fleet or something. The heat hadn't let up and I was looking like a tourist in my maize sportshirt, tan linen slacks and brown-and-white loafers as I made my way toward a specific picnic table in Rock Creek Park, as instructed.

On my way from where I left the rental Ford off the intersection of the parkway and New Hampshire Avenue, I passed a white marble statue of a heroic figure poised on tiptoes with arms outstretched, as if about to dive over the landscaped bank into the nearby river, where no boats—pleasure or otherwise—disturbed the glassy surface. A memorial to the victims of the *Titanic* disaster.

I was settling in on the bench at the rustic table, wondering if I'd just encountered an omen, when the gently building sound of hoofbeats announced the arrival of my client's wife. On the bridle path just below the slope of this picnic area, Jo Forrestal trotted up, or rather the black stallion she was astride did. She pulled back on the reins of the sleekly beautiful animal, bringing it to a stop, and swung her leg over, stepping down with the grace of a ballerina and the confidence of the experienced horsewoman.

Her white blouse with black scarf and black riding breeches and boots bespoke a chic simplicity, her black hair longer than in the vintage *Vogue* photo, and just as the horse was shaking its mane, she did the same with hers, the black blades of her hair shimmering into place at either side of her pale oval face.

Slender, regal, eerily reminiscent of cartoonist Charles Addams' Morticia, Mrs. Forrestal walked the horse to a nearby signpost that advised no littering, and tied it there; the stallion promptly deposited several road apples at the sign's base, whether a token of defiance or sheer illiteracy on the animal's part, who can say?

She strode confidently toward me, removing her black leather riding gloves, then extended a slender hand, which I took and shook. Like her husband, she had a firm grip, but she didn't try so hard.

"Jo Forrestal," she said. Her voice was low and melodious. "And you're Mr. Heller."

We were close enough that I would have caught liquor on her breath, if it had been there: nothing. Of course, maybe she was a vodka gal.

"Yes," I said. "But why don't we make it 'Nate.' "

"And 'Jo.' " A smile tickled lips that were wider than the Clara Bow rosebud of the *Vogue* photo.

"Step into my office," I said, gesturing across the picnic table. She sat opposite me, the wind whispering through the row of smoke-colored beeches that stood nearby, disinterested observers.

"Surprisingly cool here," I said, "for as hot as it's been."

She was a handsome woman of forty but looked every year of it; the dark, magnetic eyes had sunken, and drink had etched tiny lines in what was still a fine face.

"It's always cool in this park," she said. "Lovely year 'round." She gestured toward the colorful wildflowers hugging the feet of the beeches.

"Your husband said you love to ride," I said. "Must be a godsend to have this park so near your home."

She nodded. "Thirty miles of bridle paths, even a

practice ring and hurdles. Saving grace of this god-damned town."

"I gathered from Mr. Forrestal that you're not wild about D.C."

"I hate this fucking hellhole."

I was glad I was sitting down; such coarse language was unexpected from so refined and stylish a lady. Shit, what was I to think? On the other hand, she *was* a former chorus girl.

"Do you have a cigarette on you?" she asked suddenly.

"Sorry, no. I don't smoke."

"No bad habits, Nate?"

"Not that one."

She thought that over, then said, "Jim tells me you're from Chicago."

"That's right."

"I went to the University of Chicago—briefly."

I grinned at her. "So did I—the same way."

"When?"

"I don't know—'24 maybe? Kinda lost track."

"You were just after me, youngster. I think it was '20 when I ran off to New York. There was a town."

"Chicago or New York?"

"Take your pick. Either one is utopia compared to this shitbucket."

These occasional profane eruptions, from so chic a source, seemed calculated to me; she seemed to want my attention. Well, she already had that—her husband had paid for it.

"This burg does seem a little dull," I admitted. "There's more nightlife at a monastery."

Her eyes and nostrils flared. "You are so very right! No theater, no fashion, no art! No one to talk to, or anyway no one worth talking to. Nobody but these hypocritical fucking pompous politicians and petty fucking public officials with one hand in your pocket and the other on your ass."

From over at the signpost, the stallion whinnied, as if underscoring its mistress' displeasure.

"Okay, then," I said. "It's a dull town. We got that much established."

She laughed a little, mildly embarrassed. "Sorry. I guess I should've brought my cigarettes."

"What's really bothering you, Jo?" I asked gently. "Why do you need a detective?"

She swallowed and the confidence vanished; suddenly she seemed trembly as a bird, and the melodious voice took on an unexpected shrillness.

"It's my boys," she said. "Michael and Peter. They're going to kidnap my boys."

"Who is?"

"I'm . . . I'm not sure. This is going to sound crazy, Nate."

"Try me."

"Jim's made a lot of enemies. You know, everybody talks about the Nazis, Hitler this, Hitler that. But in the great scheme of things, they're nothing." She clutched my hand; squeezed. "It's the Reds we have to worry about, Nate—the Reds!"

"The Russians, you mean."

"Yes, but more likely their . . . minions."

"Have there been threats?"

"No, but they follow me. They listen to everything I say, they've tapped the phones, bugged our house. Why the hell d'you think I wanted to meet you in the fucking park?"

I thought, *Because your house isn't air-conditioned?* But I said, "Wise precaution."

She was shaking her head; the black scythe blades of hair swung. "But it's more, so much more than just the surveillance. . . . I've always been sensitive, Nate.

Do you believe in extrasensory perception? Psychic powers?"

"Sure," I lied.

The big dark eyes got bigger, brighter. "Well, I've had dreams . . . vivid dreams. And I have good intuition, I can sense danger, the way . . . an animal can. Like a horse knows when to rear up."

"Instinctively."

"Yes! And Michael and Peter, they're just boys, they're so helpless . . . Michael's thirteen, Peter eleven, they're off at private school, at Aiken School . . . that's in South Carolina."

"And you sense they're in danger."

"Yes. But not just them . . . me, Jim, my family, my friends . . . any way they can get to us. There's so much treachery all around us."

"What sort of treachery?"

She frowned, turned her thoughts inward. "I sense it, but also I catch them behaving suspiciously."

"Who?"

"The household staff, for one."

"I see."

"You need to investigate all of them! And Jim's assistants at the Navy Department, and I'll make you a list of my newer acquaintances . . ."

"Why them?"

Her eyes narrowed. "Isn't it convenient that they've suddenly become my friends at this particular stage? Doesn't that make your hackles tingle?"

My hackles were tingling, all right, but I just said, "You're right—make me that list, it'll be helpful."

"You may find that many of these people . . . perhaps even all of them . . . are working together to harm everything near and dear to me. The only person I trust is Jim—and that's why I asked him to bring somebody in from outside, someone that he trusted. You, Nate."

"I appreciate your confidence in me, Jo." I patted her hand. "And I promise you I'll give this my full attention. I'm not going to let anything happen to you or your boys."

"Or Jim!"

"Or Jim."

"Thank you, Nate . . ."

And she half-rose, leaning across the picnic table, and kissed me full on the lips.

She was gazing at me rather lasciviously, stroking my face as I said, "You're welcome," and then she stood, the nervousness gone, the confidence snapping back into place, and strode over to her horse, untied it, mounted and galloped off.

Now Jo Forrestal was clearly nuttier than a Baby Ruth bar, but her husband had come to the conclusion that the best way to snap her out of this was for me to take her fears seriously, and do a full, for real investigation. Forrestal figured that by demonstrating to her that her suspicions had no basis in reality, his wife would return to reality, herself. I didn't know whether I agreed with this approach or not, though I did agree with his thousand-buck minimum retainer.

"This business with the Reds is my fault," Forrestal admitted to me over the phone. "I'm afraid Jo has heard me rail on about the Communist threat to such an extent that it's entered into her alcoholic delusions."

So I spent a month doing full background checks on Forrestal's household staff, his assistants at the Navy Department and Jo Forrestal's new D.C. acquaintances. I also had the house swept for electronic bugs, and kept the place (and Jo Forrestal, and later Jim Forrestal) under surveillance for several days each, to see if anybody else was watching them. Finally I spent a week at the Aiken School in South Carolina where

Michael and Peter Forrestal were enrolled. I got to
know the boys—sweet, reserved kids—and the faculty,
as well. I knew all of this was wheel-spinning, but the
money was good.

And of course I discovered no kidnap plan, no
electronic bugs, no Reds under any beds, and nobody
conspiring against Jo Forrestal, with one notable, and
possibly irrelevant, exception. As a by-product of my
investigation and surveillance, I discovered that Jim
Forrestal was a first-class tomcat.

This guy went out with more good-looking women
than Errol Flynn, and his crowd seemed to know
about it, and accept it. He frequently took babes
other than Mrs. Forrestal to afternoon teas or cocktail parties, before heading downtown to one of several assignation hotels; where the Under Secretary of
the Navy was concerned, the fleet was always in. If Jo
Forrestal had been my client, and this a divorce case,
I'd have had the goods.

When I presented my detailed report to Forrestal
(which of course omitted his philandering), I gently
brought the subject up.

"I may be out of line, Jim," I said, "but your wife's
drinking, and her mental condition, might be her way
of sending you a message."

"I don't follow you, Nate." He was again seated
behind his big desk, puffing a pipe, looking wiser than
Sophocles.

"Hey, maybe I'm not qualified to make this call, I
mean I'm no head doctor . . . but if she feels threatened, maybe it's all the dames you're bangin', on the
side."

That impassive puss of his remained that way. Finally he said, quietly, "I've placed my trust in you,
Nate. I hope you don't plan to take advantage of my
faith in you with some cheap extortion scheme."

"Hell no. You're paying me plenty. It's just . . . you got a smart, good-looking wife. She's got herself in a mental jam. Maybe what she needs is some attention from the guy she married."

"You're right."

"That's okay . . ."

"You're not qualified."

I shrugged, and rose. "No extra charge for the unwanted advice. . . . You want me to present this report to Mrs. Forrestal?"

Perhaps my mentioning what I knew about his extracurricular activities colored his judgment, but at any rate he hefted my typed report and said, "No. This will be quite sufficient. Thank you, Nate."

Obviously, I'd had occasional contact with Jo Forrestal throughout the investigation, and we'd become friendly, though I'd kept my distance after that kiss she deposited on me, at our first meeting. So I wasn't entirely surprised when she showed up that night at my room at the Ambassador.

I also wasn't surprised she was drunk: I had discovered, during my tenure as a Forrestal employee, that the only time she didn't drink was when she went out riding.

She wore a classic black dress, side-buttoned and beautifully draped over her slender curves; the black arcs of her hair barely brushed her shoulders. Liquor didn't make a weaving wreck of her: the only major indications she was smashed were how hooded those big dark eyes were, and how exquisitely foul her mouth got.

Still in the doorway, she said, "I read that feeble fucking excuse for a report of yours."

I was in T-shirt and slacks, just getting ready to shave and go out for supper. "Jo, I did a thorough job. Nobody's trying to kidnap your boys; nobody's trying to hurt you."

"Yeah, yeah," she said, and brushed by me. I had a small suite, and the outer area boasted a couch and a few chairs, as well as a wet bar with a single bottle of Ronrico rum and some warm Cokes, and a table where I could work, my portable typewriter and various field notes still arrayed there. She went immediately to the bar, fetched the ice bucket and thrust it into my arms.

"Fill it," she said.

I went out and down the hall to an ice machine and filled the bucket and came back; fixed two water glasses of rum and Coke and ice, and joined her on the couch, where she sat, smoking.

"You disappoint me," she said, taking the drink.

"The Reds aren't out to get you. Honest."

"You didn't dig deep enough. You didn't look close enough."

"I dug. I looked."

She clutched my arm—my bare arm. Her nails, which were painted blood red, dug into my flesh. "They're insidious, Nate. You've got to stay on the case."

"There's no case, Jo. This town is just getting to you."

"Fucking town!" She gulped at the rum and Coke, then gulped at it two more times, finishing it. She stabbed her cigarette out and stalked over to the wet bar and was making another (with damn little Coke), as she said, "Jim's the only one I can trust. Jim, and you."

Why did *I* have her trust?

She settled in next to me, answering my unspoken question. "The same instincts that tell me who to suspect, tell me who to trust. And I trust you, Nate."

"Jo, nobody's after you. Really. Truly."

"Nate, you *have* to help me. . . ."

And she kissed me. There was urgency in it, and
something that might have been passion, and I felt
her arms slip around me.

"I need you, Nate." She pressed my right hand to
her small firm left breast. "Please help me."

This time she put her tongue in my mouth, and she
was a lovely woman, but she was drunk, and she was
nuts. Plus, she was my client's wife.

On the other hand, the asshole was catting around
on her, so it would serve the bastard right. . . .

"No," I said, pushing her gently away. "Jo, we're not
going to step over that line."

"You don't understand," she said, pressing against
me, slender fingers finding their way into my hair, a
giddiness working itself into her voice. "My husband
wouldn't mind—we've always had an open marriage,
Jim and I. We've both always been fiercely independent! Free spirits. . . ."

As free spirits went, Jo was in one hell of a cage,
and her pipe-sucking Brooks Brothers husband was
an unlikely candidate for tree nymph.

Besides, in shadowing both of them, I'd seen Forrestal score with half a dozen dames in under two
weeks, and Jo's assignations were strictly with booze
bottles.

So I pulled away, rose, poured her another drink,
and stuck to my story: nobody was after her or her
boys. An hour—and three drinks and six cigarettes—
later she seemed to be listening to reason.

She was shaking her head, staring into her sickness.
"But these dreams—what you say are *delusions . . .*
they're so vivid, Nate. The feelings seem so real."

"The feelings in you are real," I said, and took both
her hands in mine and looked right at her, made sure
she was looking back at me. "Listen—let me tell you
something about myself that I don't tell just anybody."

She smiled sexily; and she was sexy, bonkers or not, drunk or sober. "You'd share something personal with me, Nate? Something private?"

"Yes," I said, and I told her about my father killing himself with my gun.

"He was an old union guy," I explained, "and he hated the cops, he hated the system, but I managed to get myself on the police department, and it ate him up inside. Later on, when he found out I lied on the witness stand, for money, he used my nine-millimeter to blow his brains out. And I found him like that, at his kitchen table."

Her eyes weren't hooded, now. "Oh, Nate . . ."

"Anyway, I had some problems sleeping after that. I saw a guy, what they used to call an alienist."

"A psychiatrist?"

"Yeah. And it helped."

"You think . . . you think that's what I should do?"

"Yes. Talk to somebody like that, who can help you sort out the truth from the bullshit."

She just sat there quietly for the longest time; and suddenly the former *Vogue* model seemed like a little girl, a kid.

And in a kid's tiny voice, she said, "All right. I'll do it."

Then she kissed me again, and I might have reconsidered my noble stance where bedding her was concerned, but the truth is, I had just enough time to still make my date with Jeannie from the Farm Credit Administration (who maybe had a little to do with this story, after all). So if my conscience kept me from sleeping with Jo Forrestal, that conscience was blonde.

And that would have been the end of it, if it hadn't been the beginning.

ONE:

RED SCARE

WASHINGTON, D.C.
MARCH 1949

One

THE CHEVY CHASE CLUB was open for golf every day of the year, but the gun-metal sky threatened rain, a muted rumble of thunder promised the same, and only a madman would risk a round on a chill late March afternoon like this.

Make that a pair of madmen, and make me one of them.

I had an excuse, however; I was half of this ill-fated twosome because I was on the clock. No, not a caddy—a security consultant, as they said in the District of Columbia. Back home in Chicago, the term in use was still "private eye," even if these days I was an executive version of that ignoble profession.

After all, the A-1 Detective Agency was now ensconced in the Loop's venerable Monadnock Building on West Jackson in a corner suite brimming with offices, operatives and secretaries as well as a more or less respectable clientele. I could pick and choose which cases, which clients, were worthy of my personal attention, and those in that favored category had to be prepared to pay our top rate of a hundred dollars a day (and expenses) if they wanted the head man.

My golfing partner had wanted the head man, all right, but I was starting to think he needed a different sort of head man than the A-1's president. Specifically, the headshrinking variety.

Longtime client James V. Forrestal—immaculately if somberly attired in dark green sweater and light green shirt with black slacks and cleated black shoes—seemed the picture of stability. I was the one who looked unhinged, albeit spiffy, in my tan slacks, lighter tan polo shirt and brown-and-white loafers, having been encouraged to bring golf attire along, assured I was in for "perfect golfing weather." Then why were my teeth chattering?

Forrestal carried himself (and his own golf clubs—the caddies weren't working today) with a characteristic aura of authority, as well as a certain quiet menace; he would have made a decent movie gangster with his broad, battered Cagney-like features, and wide-set, intense blue-gray eyes that could seize you in a grip tighter than the one his small hands held on that three wood.

But on closer examination, the picture of stability started to blur. The athletically slim body had a new slump to the shoulders, his skin an ashen pallor, his short, swept-back hair had gone from a gray-at-the-temples brown to an all-over salt-and-pepper, and the eyes were sunken and shifting now, touched with a new timidity.

On the other hand, there was nothing timid about Jim Forrestal's golf game. After I'd hit my respectable two hundred yards, Forrestal strode to the tee and addressed the ball and gave it a resounding whack, then almost ran after it, all in about four seconds. Perhaps he was trying to beat the rain—God kept clearing His throat as we traversed the blue-green grass—but I suspected otherwise.

Forrestal played a peculiarly joyless form of golf, striking the ball in explosions of pent-up violence, expressing no displeasure at bad shots, no pleasure at good ones, as if the eighteen holes we were trying to get in were an obligation. He'd outdistanced my drive by fifty yards or so, and stood waiting with clenched-jawed impatience, foot tapping, as I used a two-iron to send my Titleist into a sand trap.

As for me, I hated golf—the game was something I put up with for the social side of business—and had no idea what the hell I was doing here, on the golf course or otherwise. I assumed, of course, this had something to do with Secretary Forrestal's rather unfortunate current situation. Politics never held much interest for me (the *Racing News* didn't carry coverage of the D.C. scene); but even an apolitical putz like yours truly knew what had been happening to Forrestal of late.

Plenty had happened in the nine years since I had done that "personal" job for Jim Forrestal. One of Washington's most powerful figures had, for the first time in a rather blessed life, suffered a humiliating fall from grace. This was the man who had built the vast fleets of the Navy from a mere four hundred to over fourteen hundred combat vessels; who had—despite his extensive administrative duties—made dangerous frontline inspection tours in the Pacific, landing under fire at Iwo Jima.

In 1944 he'd became Secretary of the Navy, and, following Roosevelt's death, President Truman appointed the highly regarded Forrestal the first Secretary of Defense, despite Forrestal having fought against the creation of such a position, in the belief that the Army, Navy and Air Force should each be their own boss. After Truman's unexpected victory over Republican Tom Dewey last November, Forrestal alone among Roosevelt's holdover cabinet members seemed likely to stay on for the peacetime duration.

Or anyway, that's what most of the pundits had

been saying, with a few key exceptions, specifically a guy who knew less about politics than I did—Walter Winchell—and, more significantly, Drew Pearson, the most powerful left-leaning muckraking columnist in the country.

In his various syndicated columns and on his national radio show, Pearson for over a year had been accusing Forrestal on a near-daily basis of everything from being a personal coward (by failing to stand up for his wife in a holdup, supposedly) and a Nazi sympathizer (because Dillon, Read & Company had done business with Germany in the twenties).

But from a political standpoint, most damning was Pearson's claim that Forrestal had secretly made a pact with Tom Dewey to continue as Secretary of Defense under a new administration that, obviously, never came to be.

James Forrestal's resignation had been made public on March 3, and that this action was taken at the request of President Truman was no military secret. Louis Johnson, a key Truman fund-raiser, would take over Forrestal's position two days from now, in a patronage tradition that was easy for a Chicagoan like me to grasp.

All of which added up to, I was golfing with the most famous lame duck in the United States.

Soon to be a wet one: the sky exploded over us while we were approaching the tenth tee, and Forrestal—the golf bag slung over his shoulder damn near as big as he was—waved for me to follow him back to the white-stone porticoed clubhouse. He'd moved fast, and so had I, lugging my rented clubs, hugging a tree line, skirting the tennis courts; we got drenched just the same. A colored attendant provided us with towels, but we looked like wet dogs seated in the clubhouse bar.

Save for the bartender, we were alone, which was one small consolation, anyway. Forrestal ordered a whiskey sour and a glass of water but I needed coffee, to help me stop shivering.

We sat at a small corner table by windows that provided a front-row seat on the rolling black clouds and white lightning streaks and sheeting rain turning the gentle hills of the golf course into a hellish surreal landscape. Forrestal, hair flattened wetly, sat back in his chair as if he were behind his big executive desk at the Pentagon, calmly sipping his whiskey sour. He looked like the elder of an elf clan, and a wizened one at that. He probably only had ten or twelve years on my forty-three, but looked much older.

"Nate," he said quietly, "they're after me."

I tried to detect humor in his medium-pitched, husky voice, and could find none; no twinkle in the blue-gray eyes, either.

"Well, uh, Jim," I said, and smiled just a little, "it seems to me 'they' already got you. You *are* out of a job."

"You can lose a job and get another," he said, and the slash of a mouth twitched in a non-smile. "But a man only has one life."

Thunder rattled the earth, and the windows; cheap melodramatic underscoring, Mother Nature imitating a radio sound-effects artist.

"Have there been threats?"

He nodded, once. "Telephone calls to my unlisted number at home. Cut-and-paste letters."

I gestured with an open hand. "But someone in your position always hears from cranks."

Now he leaned forward conspiratorially, whispering, "Didn't you wonder why I wanted to meet you here?"

"Hell no." I waved to the rain-streaked window

and the squall beyond. "Beautiful golfing weather like this?"

He dipped the fingertips of his right hand into his water glass, as if it were a fingerbowl, and then raised the fingers to his lips, moistening them gently.

Then he said, "My phones are tapped. Electronic bugs all through my house."

This wasn't making sense to me; I sat forward. "Why bring me in from Chicago? Why don't you call some of your friends in from the FBI or intelligence or something, and do a sweep?"

"That's who probably planted them."

I sat back. "Oh."

He began to shake his head, slowly, his eyes glazed. "We won the war, Nate, but we're going to lose the peace."

"What are you talking about, Jim?"

"I'm talking about Communists in government."

"Communists. In our government."

He nodded gravely.

"And that's who's 'after' you."

His eyes flared. "If I *knew* who wanted me dead, why would I hire you?"

"Who else could it be, Jim? Besides the Communists."

His whiskey sour glass was empty. He lighted up his trademark pipe, having to work a little to get it going. I was about to repeat the question when he said, "That prick Pearson, for one."

Lowering his pipe, which was in his left hand, he again dipped the fingertips of his right hand in his water glass and remoistened his lips.

"The S.O.B. made me out a coward, Nate." He was trembling; I'd never seen Forrestal tremble before, and I couldn't tell if it was anxiety or rage. "Told a pack of damn lies that made me out a yellow weakling who ran from danger when his wife was threatened! I wasn't even there, when that robbery occurred. . . ."

"Jim . . . Pearson's a newspaperman. All he's after are stories."

Forrestal's hand was clenching the bowl of the pipe as if it were a hand grenade he was preparing to lob. "Pearson is not a mere newspaperman. He's a crusader—a misguided one—and a pawn of the Communists. Hell, he may be a damn Russian agent; certainly it's no great stretch of the imagination to see him on Stalin's payroll."

"Maybe so. But you're still out of office."

His eyes narrowed and the thin line of his mouth almost curled into a faint smile. ". . . In four years I might assume another one."

"Under another president, you mean?"

An eyebrow arched. "I mean *as* president."

It seemed to me, despite my political disinterest, that I had read something about the Republican party courting Forrestal; but looking at this gray-skinned, sunken-eyed shell of his former self, a man seeing Communists under his bed and the FBI in his pantry, I found it difficult to picture his face on a *Forrestal in '52* campaign button. *In with Jim!* I didn't think so.

The real irony, of course, the aspect of this that was truly odd and even creepy, was the extent to which this circumstance mirrored that "private" job I'd done for Forrestal in 1940. The parallel was so glaring, so disturbing, I couldn't seem to find a way to bring it up, to point it out to Forrestal. . . .

In the aftermath of that earlier investigation, Forrestal had told me he'd taken the troubled Jo to see a New York psychiatrist, that she'd been hospitalized with a diagnosis of clinical schizophrenia. Shock treatment had been part of the therapy, and I hated to hear that, because I didn't believe in that snake-pit shit. I even felt a little guilty about telling her I'd seen a shrink myself; the story about my father killing himself with my gun was true, of course, and I still carried guilt for it. But I'd never lost a night's sleep and wouldn't have seen a psychiatrist if voices were telling me to paint myself blue and dance naked in Marshall Field's window.

And now, almost nine years later, in the bar of the clubhouse of the Chevy Chase Club, with wind and rain rattling the windows nearby, I was seated with Jo Forrestal's husband—the Secretary of Defense of the United States of America (for two more days, anyway)—who was telling me a story that seemed chillingly familiar.

"You're a Jewish fella, right?" he asked, out of nowhere, pointing with the pipe stem.

"My father was a Jew," I said with a shrug. "My mother was Irish Catholic, like your stock."

He waved that off. "I don't practice the faith."

"I wasn't raised in any church. What's that got to do with people trying to kill you, Jim?"

His eyes narrowed to slits. "If I was a Jew hater, if I was anti-Semitic, would I hire a Jewish detective? Christ, my secretary is Jewish!"

"I'm still not with you, Jim."

He wet his fingertips again and patted his lips, saying, "I stood against Palestine, for the sake of my country, and that makes me a Jew hater? It's bullshit, utter bullshit."

"The Jews are trying to kill you, too?"

He nodded; beads of water clung to the upper lipless mouth like sweat. "They could be. It could be the Zionists. Why aren't you writing this down?"

"I can remember it. Anybody else want you dead, Jim?"

Now the pipe stem jabbed at the air. "Is that sarcasm? I won't tolerate sarcasm. This is very real."

"No, it's not sarcasm," I said flatly. "Who else wants you dead?"

He pounded the table with a fist. "I don't know! I just know I'm being shadowed. I know they've got the house bugged, the phones tapped. You're the detective, Heller. Find out!"

"Okay." I sipped my rum and Coke, casually said, "Let's start with the other obvious question: *why* would somebody want you dead?"

"The obvious answer: I know too much." He dabbed more water on his lips. "Nate, I've done some bad things, trying to do good. Sometimes I'm afraid I've betrayed my country by trying to serve it. . . . Once I'm out of office, I'm a threat to all sorts of people."

I had a sick feeling in my stomach: fear. "If this is tied in with the intelligence community—what's this new branch called?"

Forrestal flinched a non-smile around the pipe stem. "The CIA."

"Yeah, a spook by any other name. Anyway, if that's what this is about, what do you expect a lowly private dick to do about it?"

He jabbed the air with the pipe stem again. "Don't do anything about it—just find out who the hell is after me! I can call in favors once I know who it is, whether it's the Zionists, the Russians, American Commies, or that bastard Pearson . . . and the list goes on!"

"The suspect list, you mean?"

"Call it that if you like." Forrestal reached behind him for his wallet and withdrew a check.

He held it out so I could see it: a three-thousand-dollar retainer for the A-1 Detective Agency.

"Nate, find out who wants me dead."

I took the check. "Jim . . . this is awkward, but

there's something I have to raise. Doesn't all this seem a little—familiar, to you?"

He blinked. "What do you mean?"

"That job I did for you, before the war—for your wife? She thought 'they' were out to get her, too, from the Commies to the household help."

"That is an interesting coincidence," he said, nodding somberly. "Of course, there's a major distinction."

I was putting the folded check into my wallet; mine was not to reason why, mine was but to keep my business afloat. "Which is?"

He shrugged. "My wife's a lunatic."

And he dipped his fingertips in the water glass and patted the moisture on the thin dry lips.

TWO

Back when the rest of the District of Columbia was swampland, Georgetown—in the city's furthermost NW section—was a booming colonial seaport. Despite the lovely landscaped acreage of Georgetown University in its midst, the village had declined into a run-down near-slum by '33, when FDR's New Dealers and Harvard brain trust types had arrived on the scene, looking for lodging. These pillars of social conscience soon displaced much of the village's Negro populace, and ramshackle former mansions that had housed ten or twelve colored families were renovated into suitable quarters for one wealthy white clan. Negroes were driven out of their timeworn wooden frame houses and crumbling stone cottages and weathered brick former slave quarters, which were quaintly though elaborately remodeled into dwellings befitting liberal white folk.

Now, in 1949, Georgetown was Greenwich Village gone to graduate school: within these reconditioned slums dwelled professors, artists, congressmen, and cabinet members.

But what these latter-day carpetbaggers hadn't anticipated was the ancillary impact of this transformation: tourists. Picturesque postwar Georgetown's once sleepy streets (some of which were still cobblestone) now bustled with tour buses and the sidewalks (some of which were still brick) teemed with Kodak-wielding explorers, seeking signs of their country's bygone days.

In from the hinterlands on safari, Mr. and Mrs. Frank Buck (and all the little Bucks) trekked through a jungle of shaded streets, seeking the big game of formal mansions on tree-flung manicured lawns, and the smaller game of cozy cottages set flush against sidewalks. In the commercial section—mostly M Street and Wisconsin Avenue—Great White Hunters from Nebraska and Idaho could take a breather from the chase and duck into cozy cafés or charming little antique shops or bookstores in ancient houses with brand-new storefronts.

The hordes of rubberneckers were undoubtedly a pain in the ass for the locals, but manna from heaven for yours truly. Though late March was hardly the height of tourist season, there were plenty of out-of-towners gawking at Georgian mansions, refurbished stables and antebellum houses for a detective on stakeout to blend in with on this sunny Saturday. The thunderstorm that yesterday had pummeled the Chevy Chase Club's golf course was now a few puddles, replaced by blossoming honeysuckle and magnolia announcing spring and welcoming visitors.

I tooled my dark green rental Ford down M Street, where I left the car in a parking garage near the Francis Scott Key Bridge; I walked away humming "The Star Spangled Banner," jaywalking across to 34th Street and—pausing once to take in the dramatic view of the canal and the Potomac at my back—trudged up its steep hill.

Washington was a suit-and-tie town if you were a native, but I was a tourist in a pencil-stripe blue rayon short-sleeve shirt, darker blue garbardine slacks and a tan felt fedora. Falling in behind a honeymooning couple from Dubuque (eavesdropping is second nature to the paid snoop), I turned left onto Prospect Street; the lovebirds and I crossed to the right-hand side of the street. The bride was a curvy little brunette, by the way; the groom . . . I don't remember.

Their destination—and that of any number of other Washington wayfarers—was a weathered gray-painted brick colonial house with white trim and shutters and authentic period decor. Tours were available and a gift and coffee shop was inside, a stone bench outside. When I wasn't on foot, scouting the neighborhood, the coffee shop and the bench were my home for the surveillance.

The coffee shop in particular was perfect, with its generous window view of the big house cater-cornered from here. The plump fiftyish colonial-costumed gal who managed the coffee shop (and who cheerily negotiated me up from a sawbuck to a double sawbuck for the privilege of hanging around most of the day) informed me that 3508 Prospect Street was known as Morris House, built in the 1700s and once owned by a naval commander of that name.

Another naval commander—the former Secretary of the Navy, in fact, who was the current Secretary of Defense—lived there now. Forrestal and his wife had only been in that Woodland Drive house near Rock Creek Park a year or so before moving into this impressive, dignified near mansion with its trim brick walls and exquisite Georgian detailing. The front was well-proportioned, sitting above the sidewalk on a low, stone basement story, and the west wing had been turned into a garage; but its most distinctive feature was an octagonal tower that had no doubt once allowed the naval commander named Morris to keep watch on his fleet.

In back of the house were well-tended terraces

that fell toward the Potomac, a view that could be en-
joyed from New Orleans–style balconies whose iron
grilles and leaf-and-grape design were sheer French
Quarter. Beyond the terraces, hugging the waterfront, were the ramshackle shacks of some of
Georgetown's remaining colored residents; I
doubted the tour buses pointed these out or that
many Brownie snapshots got taken.

Of course I couldn't see the rear view of the Forrestal house from my window seat in that coffee
shop, or the bench out front, either. Periodically I
walked the area, as the point of this exercise was not
to maintain surveillance on Forrestal but to ascertain
whether he was the subject of surveillance. This
meant a careful, surreptitious assessment of any ped-
dlers, vagrants, street cleaners, laborers or other invisible members of the landscape; plus checking out
second-floor or higher windows, and parked cars.

Throughout a long Saturday morning, neither my
periodic reconnaissance of the neighborhood nor my
across-the-street observation turned anyone or anything up. Despite my suspicion that Forrestal's fears
were a stress-induced unconscious imitation of the
symptoms of his wife's earlier mental breakdown, I
operated from the assumption that he really was
being watched. I took him seriously. Or anyway, I
took his three-grand retainer seriously.

This was an atypical day for Forrestal. Any other
Saturday, he would have been at his Pentagon office;
he was a fourteen-hour-a-day, seven-day-a-week
workhorse and what little leisure time he had was
spent on the golf course at Chevy Chase or Burning
Tree, or in the company of women other than his wife.
It seemed to me if somebody was trying to kill him,
the husbands of the married women he slept with
were more likely candidates than Zionists or the CIA.

Today, however, my client was home. There was no work to do at the office because tomorrow was his last day as Secretary of Defense. His wife wasn't home, either—she was at their farm in Duchess County, New York; this was not atypical, as they'd been living more or less separate lives for some time now. But Forrestal indicated he and Jo would be "meeting up" at the Island Club resort in Hobe Sound, Florida, later in the week, for a "post-retirement wind-down."

"You'll come to Florida with me," Forrestal had told me yesterday in the Chevy Chase parking lot when the rain had let up, "as added security. Hobe Sound's a perfect place for them to do it."

"Do what?"

"Kill me!"

"Oh. Right."

Which gave me today and tomorrow to determine if my client was being watched.

Just after one o'clock, Forrestal came out the front door, in golfing attire, and was picked up in a black Lincoln with a white chauffeur—Forrestal was chauffeured everywhere by government limo—and, per plan, I walked back to M Street, got my car, caught up with the Lincoln and hung a loose tail on it.

The driver headed out Wisconsin Avenue, toward Bethesda in nearby Maryland, where Forrestal was to meet a friend from New York—investment banker Ferdinand Eberstadt—at Burning Tree, a private, men's-only country club. This excursion would allow Forrestal to relax a little (if that grim brand of golf of his could be considered relaxing) and give me the chance to see if anybody else was tailing him.

Nobody was. After Forrestal got dropped off at the two-story stone clubhouse, I followed his chauffeur to a movie theater in nearby Rockville where the chauffeur (and I, though he didn't know he had company) caught a matinee of *Undercover Man,* Hollywood's version of how the feds sent Capone away. Glenn Ford didn't remind me much of either Elmer Irey or Frank Wilson, the real IRS agents on that case, and my pal Eliot Ness and his squad of Treasury agents were nowhere to be seen. Not that it mattered, as I was paying more attention to the chauffeur than the silver screen, waiting to see if anybody made contact with him.

Nobody did. So it was back to Georgetown, with no one following Forrestal's limo but me, and back to the bench and the coffee shop and periodic bouts of foot surveillance. The coffee shop was my salvation because it provided cold sandwiches, hot coffee and a men's room. But the place closed at eight p.m., just after dark, when the streets were beginning to thin of tourists, so after a brief stint on the bench, I went back to the parking garage for the car and parked on 35th Street, where I had a reasonably good view of Morris House.

I was on the same side of the street as sprawling Georgetown University Hospital, which took up the entire block between Prospect and N Street. I sat in front, behind the wheel, seat reclined as far as possible, to where I could see just over the dashboard, fedora tipped forward and almost covering my eyes, arms folded casually, as if I'd pulled over for a rest. The key to this is sitting very still—passersby rarely notice you, and if they do, think nothing of the sight of a guy grabbing a quick nap. Plus, the proximity of the hospital made my presence commonplace.

With the tourists gone, and the traffic eased, the neighborhood grew quiet, its carriage-house-style gaslamps casting a golden patina over the elegantly historic homes with their deep-red brick walls, black

wrought-iron trim, burnished brass doorknockers. It
was not difficult to imagine the likes of John Adams
or Aaron Burr walking these streets, or to summon
the ghostly clip-clop of hoofbeats, or the sound of
children singing "Yankee Doodle" when it was still a
new tune.

Or maybe I'd just been on stakeout too long.

It had been a long day and I was about to hang it
up when an attractive young mulatto woman, in her
mid-twenties, exited a side door of Morris House,
near the garage. She had a nervous manner: nothing
extreme, just occasional furtive glances as if afraid
somebody was watching her.

Which of course somebody was.

I recognized her, because I'd questioned Forrestal
about his small household staff; this would be Della
Brown, the maid. The others were a colored cook,
Leon Parker, a Filipino houseboy (Remy something),
and a white butler, Stanley Campbell, all live-in help.
The Brown woman, who had this evening off, looked
prepared to step out on the town, a milk-chocolate
Veronica Lake in her clingy pink-and-black dress
with pointed collars and keyhole neckline and bright
nosegay at her waist; high heels and black patent
leather clutch purse, too.

So why was she looking around like a kid sneaking
down a rainspout?

A dish like this, going out on Saturday night, surely
had a date; but nobody was picking her up. Maybe
that was frowned on in this white neighborhood, a
colored boy picking up a colored gal after work.
Whatever the reason, she was on foot, crossing
Prospect Street at the moment, and walking directly
toward where I was parked.

I remained motionless as the Lincoln Monument,
in my feigned nap, and she walked on by, pretty legs

flashing under the pink-and-black dress. In my rearview mirror, I could see her rear view and it was like watching kittens wrestle in a burlap bag. If she was trying not to attract attention, she needed to find a whole new way of walking.

At the end of the block, she cut right, onto N Street, and when she'd disappeared around that corner, I followed; the night was cool and I'd thrown on a tan sportcoat. With so little traffic on the street and no other pedestrians, I could have been spotted by Helen Keller, so I had to play tiptoe anarchist and keep to the bushes and duck behind trees, staying a good half block behind her, on the opposite side of N Street as she made her way down, her high heels clicking like castanets. Fortunately, there were plenty of trees on this well-shaded street with its handsome Federal-style townhouses, but it was an endless block and made for nerve-racking work, particularly since she was glancing behind her now and then.

Finally she turned onto Wisconsin Avenue, leaving the residential neighborhood for the heart of Georgetown's commercial district, where cafés, restaurants and bars were courting the remaining tourist trade. Now I had pedestrians to blend in with, storefront windows to catch her reflection in and otherwise conduct a normal tail; and before long she had headed into Martin's Bar, which surprised me some.

I knew, from previous jobs I'd worked in this town, that Martin's was Georgetown's favorite political watering hole—more New Deal policy had been made over beers in this unpretentious joint than at cabinet meetings. What was Forrestal's maid doing, dropping by the place where Tommy the Cork and Harry Hopkins changed the world while Georgetown students got boisterously blotto around them?

In Chicago, New York and Hollywood, barroom walls are festooned with photos of movie stars, stage actors and recording artists. The dark-paneled walls of Martin's, like those of any respectable D.C. gin mill, were adorned with framed presidents, generals and cabinet officers.

The place was not hopping—this wasn't a Saturday-night kind of bar, even lacking a jukebox—and for a moment I thought Miss Brown had made me, and ducked in here to slip a quick exit through the alley door. But then I spotted her, sitting in the farthest back booth, opposite a young guy in a brown suit, yellow tie and white skin.

Georgetown was looser than the rest of Washington about coloreds and whites mixing; but this was fairly bold. The emptiness of the bar was in their favor—in other booths, a few couples were having a drink after dinner or before a show, the bar stools empty, except for the one I perched myself on.

Was this the reason for Miss Brown's furtive manner? A date with a white guy, a well-dressed, respectable-looking white guy at that. . . .

I watched them in the mirror behind the bar. The red-vested bartender, a pudgy thirtyish guy with thinning brown hair and a name tag that said Tom, came over to take my order.

"Coke," I said.

"Living dangerously, huh?"

"Not as dangerously as some."

Tom caught on that I was watching the mixed-race couple in the back booth.

"Hey, we mind our own business around here." But he had a gentle tinge of Southern accent that called his comment into question.

Tom went away to get my Coke and I watched the couple in the mirror. There was nothing lovey-dovey about it; the man—his face was an intelligent, not unpleasant oval dominated by a strong nose—seemed to be asking questions and Miss Brown seemed to be answering them. Their expressions were equally blank, though occasionally Miss Brown shrugged and her companion leaned forward and tightened his eyes and tried again.

The bartender brought my Coke and said, "Anyway, it's not what you think."

"It isn't?"

He was whispering; and I was whispering back. That was how it was done in D.C.

"Naw. That guy's a straight arrow. Hell, he's a damn Mormon. Notice he's not smokin', plus he's drinkin' what you're drinkin'."

"Mormon, like in multiple wives?"

The bartender smirked. "He's engaged to a nice white gal. . . ."

"Just one?"

"You know who that is, sittin' over there?"

"Lena Horne?"

"I mean the guy."

"No. Who?"

"That's Jack Anderson."

"Who's Jack Anderson?"

Tom shook his head and half-smiled. "You *are* from outa town. He's Drew Pearson's legman."

"Oh, the columnist, you mean."

"Yeah. The colored babe's probably just a source. Anderson talks to all sorts of people, in here—generals, congressmen, you name it."

"And usually on Saturday night, I'll bet."

Tom frowned a little. "How did you know that?"

"It's the only night this joint isn't crawling with politicos—also, Pearson's weekly broadcast is Sunday night."

Now he gave me the other half of the smile. "Maybe you're not from outa town."

Anderson was handing Miss Brown an envelope. She tucked it in her purse and exited the booth without a goodbye; he watched her go with the thin, world-weary smile of a priest exiting a confessional. Through the front colonial bay windows I watched her pink-and-black dress hike pleasantly up as she raised an arm to hail a taxi; soon she headed off to her real date, with some lucky colored fella, no doubt.

Drew Pearson's man was still in that back booth, with his notebook out and pencil in hand, doing what many a good investigator does after a sensitive interview: taking down his notes afterward.

I took my Coke with me and wandered over.

Flipping his spiral notepad shut, he glanced up with a guarded blankness and, in a rich baritone that had some edge to it, asked, "Do I know you?"

I was leaning against the side of the booth. "No, but we have a mutual friend . . . or anyway a mutual boss."

His eyes were a deceptively placid light blue, the cool blue of a mountain stream; they fixed themselves on me, unblinking. "Do we." It wasn't exactly a question.

"I did a job for Pearson in Chicago a while back," I said. "When he did that rackets exposé. My name's Heller."

The thin skeptical line of his mouth curved into something friendlier. "Nate Heller. . . . Drew's mentioned you."

"And you'd be Jack Anderson."

He was nodding as I extended my hand, which he took and shook, firmly but not obnoxiously.

"Mind if I sit with you for a few seconds?" I asked. "I know you're probably up against deadline, getting ready for the Sunday broadcast . . ."

His smile was almost boyish as he nodded and gestured for me to take the seat across from him in the booth. "Yeah, I'll really be burnin' the midnight oil. I'm tied up with church all day Sunday—like every Sunday—and have to get my work done tonight, to make sure my contribution to the show's up to date."

Settling in across from him, I saluted him with my Coke glass. "You must be good, if you don't work Sundays and Pearson hired you anyway. Either that or you work cheap."

He grinned. "Little of both. What brings you to Washington, Mr. Heller?"

"We'll make it 'Nate' and 'Jack,' if that's okay with you."

"Sure," he said, still somewhat guarded; he was young, but he was a newsman.

I said, "I'm doing a job for Jim Forrestal."

His grin froze, then melted a little; something around his eyes tightened. "Really. What sort of job?"

"I don't know if I should be giving Drew Pearson's man that information. I mean, for months now, your boss has been dragging poor ol' Forrestal by the short hairs behind your 'Washington Merry-Go-Round.' "

Which was the name of Pearson's syndicated column.

Anderson thought that over; for a young guy, he had a lot of poise. Finally he asked quietly, with just a hint of menace, "Does Jim Forrestal realize he's hired an investigator who once worked for Drew Pearson?"

"Probably not. And I didn't think it was . . . 'politic' is the word, isn't it? Politic for me to mention it."

Those light-blue eyes were examining me like X-rays. "Why did he hire you? Guy from Chicago like you. Why not somebody local, with Burns or Pinkerton?"

"Why not just use the FBI, if you're Jim Forrestal? No, Jack, this job requires an outsider."

A tiny nod. "Sometimes an outsider's the only kind of man you can trust." There was a hint of sarcasm in his tone.

I sipped my Coke. "Do you think Forrestal can trust me, Jack?"

He sipped his Coke. "According to the boss, you're a man who likes money."

"That Scrooge you work for thinks anybody who wants more than a cup of gruel is a greedy bastard."

That made Anderson chuckle. "Sometimes I do feel like Bob Cratchit, at that."

"You think Forrestal's getting a fair shake from Pearson?"

For the first time Anderson's gaze dropped, his eyes avoiding mine; his voice sounded troubled as he said, "The boss says Forrestal's the most dangerous man in America."

"What do you say? Ever interview him yourself?"

Anderson nodded. "I'd call Jim Forrestal a genuine public servant, dedicated, with an enormous expertise; we were lucky as hell to have him, during the war. And the inside word is he has a capacity for firm, clear judgment, that he can appreciate the complexity of any situation. They say he's never fallen prey to the ruthlessness that this town almost always engenders in the powerful."

Like the sort of ruthlessness Drew Pearson indulged in.

I said, "Sounds like you admire the guy."

Anderson shrugged. "I don't admire some of what he stands for."

"Like what?"

"The boss calls him 'the archrepresentative of Wall Street Imperialism.' "

"I thought we were talking about your opinion."

He flinched a frown. "Hey, I'm like you—I'm just a paid investigator."

"Yeah, but you spend Sunday in church. I'm more likely to sleep in with a chorus girl. What's so dangerous about Forrestal?"

Anderson ticked the topics off on his fingers. "His anti-Israel stance, his ties to Big Oil, his anti-Russian sentiments . . . hell, his investment firm practically bankrolled Hitler!"

"Yeah, if you believe what you read in your boss's column."

Anderson laughed once, harshly. "What, are you my conscience, Nate? From what I hear about you, you make an unlikely Jiminy Cricket."

"I'm not your conscience, Jack. I'm just the guy who tailed that cute colored maid of Forrestal's to this bar and saw an information/money exchange transpire."

The blood drained from his face.

"What, did you think I just happened into this place, at this moment? Shit, you're not young— you're a fuckin' fetus."

Suddenly Anderson seemed to be tasting something foul. He said, "You know I can't work out anything financial with you without the boss's approval."

"I don't remember asking for money."

His fingers drummed on the spiral notepad. "You gonna tell Forrestal about his maid?"

"Maybe not. Why would I want a good-looking kid like that to get in trouble, lose her job or something?"

Anderson smiled again but it was nasty, this time. "Well, then, why don't you negotiate with her, directly?"

I laughed. "Don't believe everything Pearson tells you about me. He's still pissed off that I squeezed a fair wage out of him."

"What *do* you want?"

"I want you to tell your boss I'm in town—at the Ambassador. Have Drew call me there, so I can set up a meet with him."

His eyebrows were up. "So you can sell out Forrestal?"

"Now you're *my* conscience. Look, kid—I know you must be pretty good or Pearson wouldn't take you on. But listen to the voice of experience—don't meet with a colored girl in a white joint, unless you think attracting attention is a good thing for investigative work. Don't be interviewing your sources in Georgetown's favorite political gathering place, either, even if it is Saturday night—that bartender gave me your life story and all I did was buy a damn Coke from him. Listen to your Uncle Nate and maybe you'll last in this town . . . but I doubt it."

From the look on his face, you'd think I'd passed gas. Hell, maybe I had. Anyway, he didn't say anything as I got up, deposited my empty Coke glass on the bar, tossed Tom the bartender a half dollar, and trundled out of the place.

Out on the street, I pondered whether to take a cab to my car in that M Street parking garage, or just hoof it; I was fairly well beat, though feeling pretty good about myself. I had discovered the leak on Forrestal's staff and found where it led—no murder plot, just good old-fashioned betrayal of your employer mixed in with sleazy yellow journalism, All-American stuff.

And I had determined, to my satisfaction, that neither Uncle Sam nor the Zionists, not even the Commies, were staking out Forrestal's place, for purposes of assassination or anything else, for that matter.

I was just raising my arm to hail a cab when the finger tapped my shoulder.

Thinking it was probably Anderson, I turned and started to say something wise, but nothing wise or otherwise got said: I was staring into the coldly businesslike mug of a guy perhaps thirty in a nicely tailored dark gray suit with a dark blue tie; his hair was black and trimmed military short, and he had a blandly handsome face with hard dark eyes.

"Secret Service, Mr. Heller," he said, holding up his wallet with five-pointed silver star and photo-credentials for my perusal. "If you'll just come with me, please."

He was whispering, but there was nothing soft about the grip on my arm as he shoved me past the yawning door into the backseat of the black sedan that waited at the curb to take me away.

Because, after all, that's how it's done in D.C.

Three

A S WE ROLLED down Pennsylvania Avenue at night, the White House loomed to our right, bathed in spotlights like a theater hosting a premiere, only the star here was the structure. Was the Executive Mansion where these Secret Service boys were taking me? Perhaps the President of the United States wanted to consult the President of the A-1 Detective Agency; you know, maybe Harry wanted me to see if Bess was shacked up at the Rockville Shady Rest with Ike or MacArthur or somebody.

My escorts hadn't bothered sharing any information with me. They sat in the front and I sat in the back, like an obnoxious kid getting his questions ignored by the grown-ups—*Am I being charged with anything? Do I need a lawyer? Don't you guys have any counterfeiters you can go bother? How many more miles, Daddy?*

But our destination proved to be just past the White House, flanking it on the east, at Pennsylvania Avenue and 15th Street: a gray granite Greek Revival–style structure that rose five stories and consumed two blocks. I'd been here before—the Treasury Building—on various visits to Elmer Irey and Frank J. Wilson, the Capone case IRS agents I'd seen Glenn Ford playing a composite of, this afternoon. Both Irey and Wilson had risen in the government, Irey eventually overseeing the Treasury Department's various law-enforcement agencies, including the Secret Service, of which Wilson had become chief in 1936.

Despite a few adversarial situations, the two men were friendly acquaintances of mine, but I couldn't hope to lean on them tonight: Irey had passed away last year, and Wilson recently retired.

My Secret Service escorts left the black sedan in an outdoor, "United States Government Employees Only" lot and ushered me up a broad flight of stone steps to a colonnaded portico, then through the high-ceilinged, imposing West Lobby; my shoes had surveillance-suitable rubber soles, but the shiny Secret Service shoes created footsteps that echoed off the marble floor like small-arms fire. We moved past an exhibit called "Know Your Money," featuring methods of detecting counterfeit bills and forged checks, and onto an elevator that stopped at the fourth floor.

They deposited me in a small, rectangular conference room that seemed designed around a small, rectangular dark-varnished oak conference table where I was directed to take the nearest of half a dozen wooden chairs. The walls were a smooth, cream-color plaster occasionally broken up by framed exhibits of damaged money that Treasury experts had managed to identify despite (their prominent labels said) charring by fire, nibbling by mice or shredding by streetcar wheels. The dark-haired, dark-eyed agent who'd showed me his badge stood along a wall without leaning, arms folded, with the expression of a state trooper waiting for you to get your driver's license out.

"Are you going to tell me what this is about?" I asked him.

"No," he said.

Well, that was more than he'd said on the way over.

Down at the far end of the table, a single window, tall and narrow, was hidden by barely slitted-open venetian blinds, but behind them the window was open and a cool breeze rattled through, flapping the metal shutters like a stiff flag.

Ten or twelve minutes later, when the door opened and a lanky, thin-lipped, poker-faced guy about my age ambled in, the agent unfolded his arms and stood even more erect. Oddly, this new arrival—however much immediate respect he commanded from my chaperon—was not in suit and tie, but a blue-and-green Hawaiian-print sportshirt, brown slacks and brown sandals with socks; he looked more like Bing Crosby than a Secret Service man—all he lacked was Der Bingel's pipe.

The only official-looking thing about him was the thick manila file folder in one hand. He turned a penetrating gaze on the younger agent. "Have you spoken with our guest?"

His voice was a pleasant second tenor.

"No, sir."

"Leave me alone with him."

"Yes, sir."

The young agent went out, yanking the door shut: the sound was like the pistol shot at the start of a race.

The superior officer in the Hawaiian shirt turned his clear-eyed gaze on me. "Baughman," he said by way of introduction, sticking out his hand.

Shaking it, I asked, "*Chief* Baughman?"

"That's right."

This character in an explosion-at-the-paint-factory shirt was Chief of the Secret Service. I was being interrogated by the top guy.

"Mr. Heller," he said, chuckling with what seemed to be mild embarrassment, "you'll have to excuse my informality ... I got the call while my wife and I were at a barbecue."

He was standing looking down at me; he was tall enough that I had to crane my neck back to look at him.

"What call would that be, Chief Baughman? The call to drop your 'Don't Mess with the Chef' apron and grill me personally? Instead of another cheeseburger?"

His thin lips formed a smile; it was like a cut in his pasty face, a wound that opened with the words, "They were shishkabobs, actually—lamb. . . . You live up to your reputation, Mr. Heller, for having a smart mouth."

"Is that in my file?"

"Actually, yes ... in so many words."

The breeze-fluttered blinds were making unmelodic metallic music.

I asked, "Why would the Secret Service keep a file on me?"

His non-answer was: "I had a chance to read up on you, on the way over."

So a chauffeured government limo had been sent to pick him up; and somebody had seen fit to send along a file on me for U. E. Baughman, Chief of the Secret Service himself, to read.

Fanning the air absently with the file, Baughman wandered toward the end of the table, where he sat with his back to the fluttering tone-deaf wind chime of the venetian blinds, putting some distance between us. Possibly this was to allow him to peruse my file away from my prying eyes.

"Am I being held for anything, Chief Baughman?"

"Certainly not. I hope no one indicated that you were. I don't condone violation of rules or regulations by any agent."

"False arrest and kidnapping fall within acceptable guidelines, I take it."

The piercing gaze in the deceptively bland face bore through me. "You weren't arrested. And I believe you were asked to accompany the agents."

"I was shoved bodily in the back of a Buick."

"Would you like to lodge a complaint about undue force?"

"No. I'm from Chicago, where the cops throw you in the back of cars just to express their affection."

The thin lips pursed; it was like a crinkle in paper. Then he said, "You're welcome to leave, Mr. Heller."

But I just sat there. The son of a bitch knew my curiosity was up.

He began flipping through the file. "You've had a rather checkered career, Mr. Heller . . . friends and enemies in high and low places. It says here you once spoke 'disrespectfully' to Director Hoover."

I shrugged. "I just suggested he do to himself what Clyde Tolson does to him behind closed doors—is that my FBI file? As a taxpayer, I'm gratified to see the various branches of the government rising above their petty differences to cooperate in running roughshod over the rights of the individual citizen."

"You had some dealings with the Secret Service back in '32, in Miami. . . . This *is* impressive—Mayor Cermak's bodyguard at the bandshell when Zangara tried to assassinate Roosevelt?"

"It would be more impressive if Cermak hadn't been killed."

He paged through the file, slowly, savoring its contents. "When you were with the Chicago Police Department, you went to New Jersey to serve as their liaison on the Lindbergh kidnapping case, working with both Frank J. Wilson and Elmer Irey, two of my former bosses here at the Service. Both apparently have a . . . guardedly high opinion of you and your abilities. In particular, Chief Irey cites your good work for him in the IRS inquiry into Huey Long and his confederates. . . . My! So you were *Huey Long's* bodyguard as well. Didn't he also get killed?"

"I'll do the jokes, if you don't mind."

"No, actually it's a very unusual, even noteworthy file. When Eliot Ness was with the Treasury Department in Chicago, and later with the Alcohol and Tax Unit in Ohio, you aided him on several government matters. Then later when he was safety director of Cleveland, you worked with him on several successful investigations . . ."

"Listen, I know all about my life. I've been busy living it for over forty years now."

"Patriotic, too. Shaved a few years off your age to get into the Marines. Guadalcanal, Silver Star, Purple Heart . . ."

"Battle fatigue, malaria, Section Eight."

Baughman shut the manila folder and then lifted it in one hand, as if weighing it. "One of the most curious aspects of your FBI file, Mr. Heller, is that it's incomplete."

"In what way?"

"It notes that before the war you on occasion worked for Navy Intelligence, but that your service in that regard is still top-secret. Classified. You know, usually information doesn't elude J. Edgar Hoover."

"Maybe I was off in the South Sea Islands looking for Amelia Earhart."

"I almost believe you." He tossed the file on the table. "It also says you 'cooperated favorably' with British Naval Intelligence on a matter in Nassau in 1943, shortly after you left the military. But no details."

I leaned back in the hard chair, crossed a leg over

a knee. "Well, I'm pretty impressed with me, so far. Why do you suppose I'm not famous?"

Baughman nodded toward the closed file. "Oh, you've had your share of press, and there are a good number of clippings here to prove it. . . . When you left the Chicago Police Department in '32, to form your A-1 Detective Agency, it was under a cloud of scandal, and since then you've been a known associate of mobsters—Al Capone, Frank Nitti, Meyer Lansky, Sam Giancana, Benjamin 'Bugsy' Siegel, quite a rogues' gallery."

"You must be mistaken. There's no such thing as the Mafia. I heard J. Edgar Hoover say so on the radio."

The thin mouth formed another smile: a nasty one. "With your ready wit, that's where you belong—on the radio, or the television. Uncle Miltie, maybe."

"Listen, I didn't come to Washington to be insulted. I can get that back home."

The penetrating gaze narrowed. "Why *did* you come to Washington, Mr. Heller?"

Now we were to it.

"I wanted to be here in time for the cherry blossoms."

"You can do better than that, Mr. Heller."

"No, not really. That's about as clever as I get."

"Why did you spend today maintaining a stakeout on Secretary Forrestal's house on Prospect Avenue?"

"Is that what I did?"

"Except when you followed him to Burning Tree golf club, and when you tailed Secretary Forrestal's maid—Della Brown, is it?" He removed a small notebook from the back pocket of his slacks, flipped it open. "Della Sue Brown, yes. You followed her to Martin's Bar on Wisconsin Avenue in Georgetown."

"It sounds to me like I was just another tourist

hanging around a touristy part of town, except when I took that jaunt over to Maryland to catch a matinee. . . . You left out where I went to see *Undercover Man* in Rockville."

"When you followed Secretary Forrestal's chauffeur, Ted Hertel, you mean."

"Now you have more information than I do; his name's Ted Hertel, huh? What do you know. I didn't much care for the movie, if you want to jot that down."

"What did you and Secretary Forrestal discuss at Chevy Chase golf club yesterday?"

So much for my prowess at spotting somebody else's surveillance in progress.

I said, "Jim Forrestal's an old friend; we just played a round of golf."

"And talked in the clubhouse for two hours."

"There was a downpour we were waiting out."

Baughman twitched a smile, sighed and folded his hands atop the closed folder. "Mr. Heller . . . I'm well aware that, as a professional investigator, you have a certain code of ethics—"

"Are you sure you read my file?"

"I understand your . . . reluctance . . . to betray the confidence of a client. But I must ask you—is Secretary Forrestal in fact your client? And, if so, what have you been hired to do?"

"I told you, Chief Baughman . . . I'm just a tourist."

"Does your . . . friendship with Secretary Forrestal date back to these classified jobs you did before the war, for the Navy Department? When he was Secretary of the Navy?"

"Let me get this straight—the head of the Secret Service is asking me to share government secrets? Is this like where they show a kid a picture of a farmyard and there's a pig upside down and he's supposed to spot it?"

Baughman ignored that, and an edge came into his mild voice. "We know you did a job for Secretary Forrestal in 1940, when his wife had her mental breakdown—"

"What does Secretary Forrestal have to do with protecting the president, or catching counterfeiters?"

A sharp knock at the door made me jump.

"Jesus!" I said, undermining my stance as a cool customer.

Baughman, raising his voice, said, "Yes?"

The door cracked open and the dark-haired young agent peeked in. "Chief Wilson is here, sir."

"Good," Baughman said. "Send him in."

"He's just signing in, sir, down the hall. It'll be a moment."

Baughman nodded, and the door closed.

"Not *Frank* Wilson?" I asked. "I thought you were the big cheese around here, now."

He arched an eyebrow; his tone was arch, too: "Haven't you heard that expression, Mr. Heller? Too many chiefs and not enough Indians? That's Washington to a tee."

"A tee-pee," I corrected.

He gave me only half a smile but it was completely condescending. "I knew you could be more clever if you tried."

The door opened and Frank J. Wilson, former Chief of the Secret Service, stepped inside. Baughman stood, out of respect for his onetime boss; and I stood, too, surprised to see this old friend—or anyway, friendly adversary.

"Been a while, Nate," Wilson said, and there was nothing halfway or condescending about his smile, always a surprise in that dour, jug-eared, round-cleft-chin countenance of his—almost as unexpected as the long feminine lashes of the keenly alert dark blue eyes under thick black slashes of eyebrow behind round, black-rimmed glasses.

No Hawaiian shirt for Wilson: he wore a dark blue suit with a blue-and-red striped tie that, against his white shirt, invoked Old Glory. He was not a big man—perhaps five eight, possibly 180 pounds—but he had considerable presence; his dark hair was almost entirely gray now, and his forehead had receded to Baltimore.

We shook hands—a firm quick clasp from this one third of the triumvirate of Ness, Irey and himself who had brought down the notorious Scarface Al (Snorkey, to insiders)—and he gestured for Baughman and me to be seated. We sat, at our respective ends of the table, the wind still ruffling the blinds while Wilson, unbuttoning his suitcoat, sat next to me.

"Well," Wilson said pleasantly, in his businesslike baritone, placing his palms flat on the smoothly varnished table, "where are we?"

It was like somebody who'd come into a movie late, asking what he'd missed.

"Mr. Heller says he's a tourist," Baughman said dryly. "He claims that yesterday he was golfing with his old friend Jim Forrestal, strictly social, and today he was taking in the sights of Georgetown."

"I see," Wilson said.

"I don't," I said. "Frank, I thought you left the Secret Service over a year ago."

His face had a little less expression than Buster Keaton's. "I did."

I leaned forward. "Or were you asked to leave? I know Elmer saw the handwriting on the wall."

Wilson's longtime associate Elmer Irey had retired in '46 after putting political boss Tom Pendergast away—Pendergast of course having been Harry Truman's political godfather.

"Everyone thinks Elmer stepped down for political reasons," Wilson said. "But really there were health concerns—obviously."

"A lot of vital men die when their work gets taken away from them."

He leaned back in his hard chair. "I've never had a conflict with the Truman administration. In fact, I'm still working for them."

"Not with the Secret Service."

"No," Wilson admitted. "I'm a security consultant, attached to the Atomic Energy Commission, at the moment."

I tried to digest that.

Baughman said, "Frank was nice enough to stop by and take a hand in this, because of your past relationship."

"A hand in what?" I asked, worry spreading in me like a rash. "Frank, don't tell me I've wandered into A-bomb country here. . . ."

"What are you involved in, Nate?" Wilson asked, eyes narrowing behind the round lenses. "Secretary Forrestal hired you to do something. What?"

"Frank, if your assumptions are right, then Forrestal's my client. I'm protected by the same client privacy privileges as an attorney."

"No you aren't," Wilson said, "not unless you're working *through* an attorney. There are national security issues involved here, Heller. Or would you prefer talking to Hoover's people?"

Baughman picked up the file folder. "I neglected to mention, Mr. Heller, the two FBI agents who were hospitalized in 1937—in Burbank, California? Broken nose, severe concussion . . ."

"Surely they're out by now," I said, but I sounded cockier than I felt.

"Nate," Wilson said, leaning forward and, in a gesture oddly personal for him, placing a hand on my right arm, "we've learned that Secretary Forrestal believes he's being followed. That he thinks his phones have been tapped."

I removed Wilson's hand like a scab I was picking. "How did you learn that, fellas? By following him, and having his phones tapped?"

Wilson dropped his gaze. "Secretary Forrestal is under a . . . protective watch."

"Then he's not paranoid—he *is* being followed."

"Paranoia is a self-fulfilling prophecy, Nate. Forrestal had these feelings before he actually was under surveillance."

Baughman said, "The president himself asked us to investigate—that's why this inquiry is in the hands of the Secret Service. I began with the assumption that if a man of Secretary Forrestal's acumen feels he's being followed, then in all likelihood he *is* being followed, and we wanted to know who by, for obvious national security reasons."

"But he wasn't," I said.

"That's not entirely true," Baughman admitted. "As you discovered yourself, today, Drew Pearson's people are actively, continually investigating, even hounding, Secretary Forrestal."

"Nate, we'd like your cooperation," Wilson said.

"Why?"

"Let's begin with you telling us what you're doing for Secretary Forrestal. After all, we've been forthcoming with you."

And they had been.

So I told them, since—what the hell—they'd figured it out anyway and just needed my confirmation. Then I complimented them on the Secret Service's expertise, because I sure hadn't seen any signs of their surveillance.

"We thought perhaps you had," Baughman said with a wry little smile.

"Why?"

Baughman laughed, once. "Because at one point you fell in right behind Daniels and Burnside, and seemed to be monitoring their conversation."

I frowned. "Who the hell are Daniels and Burnside?"

"Male and female team of agents. They were posing as honeymooners."

"Yeah . . . yeah, I thought they seemed a little wrong."

"No you didn't," Wilson said.

"No I didn't," I admitted. "Listen, could Forrestal really be in danger from, say, the Zionists?"

"Unlikely," Wilson said. "His anti-Israel stance becomes more or less irrelevant when he steps down from office."

"More or less?"

"Well, he *is* a potential presidential candidate . . . but try to kill him? The Israelis are lobbying for American support, raising money, building an image. Would they risk an assassination of a respected, admired American like Jim Forrestal?"

Baughman snorted. "It's absurd."

I asked, "What about foreign agents?"

"Reds, you mean."

"Yeah, or maybe American members of the Communist party, in bed with the Russians."

Baughman shook his head. "The secretary's suspicions are unfounded. There's very little evidence of espionage activity by the Russians in this country, and what there is certainly doesn't include assassination. Again, Forrestal's a moot point now—unless his political future should blossom."

I looked from Baughman to Wilson. "Is that Truman's interest in Forrestal? As a potential political opponent in the next presidential election?"

"No," Baughman said firmly. "Truman doesn't always agree with Forrestal, but he admires the man, and appreciates what he's done for this country."

"Nate," Wilson said, almost gently, "Secretary Forrestal has occupied . . . at this moment, still does occupy . . . an extremely rarefied position of power in our government. He is privy to information, secrets, knowledge that only a handful of living Americans share."

"And if he's cracking up," I said, finally starting to get it, "that makes him dangerous."

Baughman, speaking slowly, as if to a child, said, "This is a man who controls . . . or at least has controlled . . . weapons of enormous destructive capacity."

"You mean planes loaded with atomic bombs. Is this where you and the Atomic Energy Commission come in, Frank?"

Wilson ignored that. "Secretary Forrestal is a great man. A public servant with few peers, a patriot of historic distinction. His government wants to help him, if in fact this is his hour of need."

Wilson seemed sincere, but I knew horse hockey when I heard it.

"Mr. Heller," Baughman said, "what we tell you stays in this room."

"Understood."

"Secretary Forrestal has become exceedingly nervous and emotional . . . afflicted with insomnia and loss of appetite."

"You've learned this from surveillance?"

Baughman hesitated, glancing at Wilson, who shrugged and nodded; then Baughman said, "That maid . . . that same maid Jack Anderson was speaking to tonight, in Georgetown . . . also spoke to my people. She told us that Mr. Forrestal has become so overly suspicious that whenever the doorbell rings, he goes to a window and peers out secretly, to see who's there."

"So does everybody in Chicago."

Baughman's brow furrowed. "Does everybody in Chicago wander around the house with their hat on, apparently forgetting they have it on? Does everyone in Chicago look directly at their uniformed maid and ask, 'Where's my maid?' "

I shrugged. "He's under great stress, gentlemen. He worked fourteen hours a day, seven days a week, from before the war till today . . . and now he's losing a position that was his whole life."

"We know," Baughman said gravely. "We also know that, last week, he went to an attorney and made out his last will and testament."

"And," Wilson interjected, "he got a prescription for sleeping pills, and filled it to its entirety . . . enough pills to put an army to sleep—forever."

"Now you're saying he's a potential suicide."

"I'm convinced," Baughman said, "that he's had a total psychotic breakdown, characterized by suicidal features, yes."

"Are you a psychiatrist?"

"No. But our field data was interpreted by our top staff psychiatrist, and these are his findings."

"Without this shrink actually talking to Forrestal."

Baughman shrugged an admission, then said, "Please understand that this is . . . treachrous, and embarrassing, turf. We can't ask the Secretary of Defense to submit to such an examination."

"Why the hell not?"

"It . . . it just isn't done."

"Oh, so you fire him to hell and gone, instead. Hey,

that'll clear up any of his suicidal tendencies in a hurry."

Wilson sat forward, saying, "Nate, if the press gets wind of this—"

"Gets wind of this! What do you think Pearson will be talking about on his broadcast tomorrow night?"

"Pearson isn't the news. He's a phenomenon unto himself. People listen to him, but they don't take him as seriously as the front page, or even the editorial section."

"You trying to convince me, or yourself? What do you guys want from me, anyway?"

Wilson glanced at Baughman, who nodded.

"Have you had dinner?" Wilson asked.

I frowned. "Dinner? No."

"Grab your hat. Uncle Sam is buying."

Following Wilson out reluctantly, I informed him, "Don't get the idea if you feed me, you can fuck me. I'm just not that kind of girl."

"Really," Wilson said. "I heard you were easy."

Four

FRANK WILSON AND I rode in back of another black sedan with another young agent for a driver. Chief Baughman did not come along, having to get back to his barbecue; besides, he wasn't "dressed for it." He didn't say dressed for what, and on the way to wherever we were going—skirting Lafayette Square, to head up Connecticut Avenue, D.C.'s version of Fifth Avenue—Wilson spoke not at all of Jim Forrestal, making small talk instead.

"Sorry to hear your marriage didn't work out," he said.

"Funny, isn't it?"

"What is?"

"With my randy reputation? And she was the one running around."

"Hell of a thing."

"Piece of advice for you, Frank—never screw around on a divorce dick."

"Yeah?"

"Got pictures of her and that married jerk. . . . Gave 'em to his wife."

We were passing the shade trees of Farragut Square.

Wilson sat caught in the awkward moment for a while, then asked, "How's your boy doing?"

"Fine. His mom treats *him* right, anyway. For the child support and alimony she's getting, she should."

"What's his name?"

"Nate, Jr. Want to see a picture?"

Wilson said sure and I got my wallet out and showed him.

"Mine are grown," he said. "But I got grandkid pictures."

He got his wallet out and showed me.

Then the limo slowed and pulled up in front of the huge Mayflower Hotel, on the southeast corner of De Sales Street and Connecticut; only it turned out we were going to the nearby Harvey's, one of the city's best-known, most popular restaurants, seafood a specialty. Wilson led me through the nondescript but packed dining room—where it didn't seem likely we'd be seated until maybe next Wednesday— toward a teensy elevator behind a velvet rope guarded by a massive colored samurai of a head-waiter.

"Evening, Mr. Wilson," the burly headwaiter said with a wide, white smile that made him no less menacing. "Been some time, sir."

"Yes it has, Pooch. We're expected on the third floor."

"So I understand, sir," Pooch said, and unclipped the velvet rope for us. We stepped aboard and there was just room enough for the two of us and the ancient colored elevator operator, who said, "Evening, Mr. Wilson."

"Evening, James."

As the elevator groaned and wheezed its way up, Wilson said, "You're lucky, Nate—J. Edgar's out of town this weekend."

"Why, is this a favorite spot of his?"

"The third floor is; he and Tolson have a regular table."

When the elevator door slid open, even an unin-

formed oaf like me was able to recognize a good
share of the faces seated in the spare, simple dining
room with its old tables and chairs and black-and-
white tile floor: my late client Huey Long's son, Rus-
sell; Estes Kefauver, who'd got his picture in the
national press by campaigning in a coonskin cap (he
was bareheaded tonight); the radio and TV commentator Edward R. Murrow.

While there were wives sprinkled here and there, it
was mostly men, eating in groups, and the air was
laughter-filled and as smoky as those legendary political smoke-filled rooms, though the aroma was only
partly cigarette and cigar smoke, the scent of sizzling
meat and barbecue sauce mixed pleasantly in. Wilson
led me past an open charcoal grill, where a Negro
chef prepared steak, fish and ribs (Baughman in his
Hawaiian shirt might have fit in at that). Diners were
selecting their own lobsters from a tank, or steaks
from a butcher-shop-style counter, and helping themselves to gumbo and oyster crackers at a huge cast-
iron cauldron in the middle of the room.

We were headed toward the back, past some tables
that had been left empty, to a table near the wall
where a small compact man in his sixties sat with
three younger men, another man standing behind the
older man, in the same manner that bodyguards used
to watch Frank Nitti eat.

No one at this table seemed to be dining except the
older man, who was dunking into the butter the last
bits of what must have been a two-pound lobster, the
shell and various other remnants of which were on a
platter; also on the table was a basket of sliced white
bread with butter pads, a pitcher of water and a bottle of Old Fitzgerald and a glass.

The older man's hair and double-breasted suit
were neat and gray, though a snappy red bow tie en-

livened his ensemble, set off by a perfectly folded five-pointed handkerchief in his breast pocket; his gray-framed glasses magnified his gray-hazel eyes, slightly. Thin-lipped but with a ready smile, pleasant features dominated by a prominent, almost hooking nose in an egg-shaped face, he sat as erect as if a steel rod had been implanted in his spine. His jaunty manner had a birdlike, almost roosterish quality, and the younger men around him said little, hanging on his every word and movement, possibly because they were Secret Service and he was President Harry S. Truman.

This man had been (in this order) a farmer, an artillery battalion commander, a bankrupt haberdasher, an obscure county judge, the chief patronage man in the U.S. Senate for the corrupt Kansas City Pendergast machine, and Franklin Roosevelt's final—and largely ignored—vice president. Dismissed as an inept, stodgy mediocrity by not just his enemies, Harry Truman was fooling everybody as a strong-willed, decisive president.

I felt butterflies gathering in my stomach as Wilson led me to the leader of the free world, who jumped to his feet and thrust a hand toward me to shake, like a javelin.

"You must be this Heller fella I been hearing about," he said in that familiar dry Missouri twang, as he pump-handled my hand.

"I'm Nathan Heller, Mr. President," someone's voice said. Mine, presumably.

"Sit, sit," he said, gesturing to the open chair beside him, and I did, and so did he. "I meant to wait for you, but the hunger got the best of me. I have never gotten accustomed to eating at such an ungodly goddamn hour—six o'clock still seems late to me, but then I'm a Midwestern boy like you. Do you eat lobster? I know some Jewish fellas abstain from shellfish, but my partner back in Kansas City, he's a Jewish fella, and he'd eat the asshole out of a pig, so you never know, do you?"

He said all this in about three seconds. The machine guns at the St. Valentine's Day Massacre had nothing on Harry.

"I like lobster," I allowed.

"Boy!" Truman called out, and a colored waiter—a "boy" of probably fifty-plus years—hustled over. Truman said to him, "Cut up a two-pound lobster for my friend Mr. Heller, here."

"Yes, Mr. President."

Truman turned his magnified gaze on me; the bug eyes made a cartoon of him. "May I call you 'Nathan' or possibly 'Nate'?"

" 'Nate' is fine, sir."

"Nate, I'd ask you to call me 'Harry,' but the one ceremony I stand on is respect for the presidency. So you'll have to refer to me in a proper manner, and that may seem like horseshit to a Chicago boy like you, but so be it."

"Not a problem, Mr. President."

Suddenly Truman noticed that Wilson had assumed a position against the wall, and said, "Frank, what the hell are you standing there for? Join us. You want a lobster?"

Wilson sat next to me. "I've eaten, sir, thank you."

Truman grinned at me; it was infectious. "I ran the fanny off Frank and his boys, you know. FDR spoiled 'em; how the hell hard is it to keep up with a fella in a wheelchair? I put 'em back to work, didn't I, Frank?"

"You certainly did, sir," Wilson said with a small smile.

"I understand you're a combat veteran," Truman said to me.

"Yes, sir."

"Guadalcanal—rough damn action you saw. I'm a veteran myself." He flicked a finger toward the World War One service pin in his lapel. "How's your friend Barney Ross?"

Barney had been wounded on Guadalcanal and his treatment had led to an addiction to morphine.

"Completely clean, sir. He went through the government program at Lexington, Kentucky."

"I'm pleased to hear that." His concern seemed genuine; if this was political bull, it was a variety I'd never encountered. "What a great boxer that boy was. Do you know who the Secretary of Defense is?"

Was the sudden shift of subjects meant to blindside and throw me off guard? Or did this amazing man's mind just move that fast?

"Certainly, sir. It's James Forrestal."

"You're wrong." He speared some lobster, dipped it in butter, nibbled it from his fork and said, "*I'm* the Secretary of Defense. For weeks on end, Jim was calling me ten times a day to ask me to make decisions that were completely within his competence. It got burdensome, Nate. I don't have time to be Secretary of Defense. And that's why I asked Jim to resign."

"I see."

"No offense, Nate, but I doubt you do. Everybody thinks I'm one tough old crusty son of a bitch, but I'm a softy, really I am, hate like hell to fire anybody; talented people giving their lives over to government service, goddamnit, they deserve better. And with that cocksucker Winchell, and that S.O.B. Pearson, blackening Jim's name, shit! I really hate this, Nate, I really do. To dismiss Jim while he's under fire . . ."

He dropped his fork, shook his head. His jaw tightened; his face reddened.

"No fucking columnist tells me who to hire or fire

as members of my cabinet or my staff. I name them myself, goddamnit, and when it's time for them to move on, I do the moving—nobody else."

My lobster arrived, the meat removed from the shell. Timidly I began to eat it.

"Good?" Truman asked. He poured me a glass of water.

"Delicious."

He took another buttery bite of his own lobster, then said, "Nate, you may hear things about me wanting to shove Jim out to make room for Louis Johnson, who worked so hard on my whistle-stop campaign; but it's horseshit. Jim's gone toe to toe with me more times than any other member of my cabinet—over Palestine, over civilian control of the A-bomb, and lately he didn't think a measly fifteen billion dollars, a fucking third of the federal budget, mind you, would be enough to keep the military in bullets and khaki. I would have every right to fire him over any one of those issues, Nate, but a man who won't listen to intelligent, informed opinions contrary to his own has no business being president." He sighed. "This is strictly a health matter."

"I understand, sir—really I do."

"I believe you do, Nate, I believe you do. Jim's weary, he's troubled. He's worked himself into a frazzled state of mind where he's imagining things, like some poor son of a bitch in the desert crawling toward a water hole that isn't there, or some pitiful bastard with the d.t.'s trying to round up a buncha pink elephants. Will you help me, Nate?"

I blinked. "Help you how, sir?"

"You're working for him. He trusts you. He's hired you to find out who's . . ." Truman laughed humorlessly. ". . . trying to, Jesus H. Christ, kill him. I want you to stay close to him. If he worsens, if leaving office does not remedy his wearied state, if full collapse ensues . . . I need to know immediately."

"What will you do in that case, sir?"

"We will help him. I don't give a damn if Pearson and Winchell make a scandal out of it—Truman's Secretary of Defense goes bughouse! Well fuck them and the newspapers and radio stations they're in bed with. We need to help Jim, and protect the interests of this great country."

He was staring at me now, with those intense gray-hazel eyes, large behind the thick lenses; he was waiting for my response.

So I gave it to him: "Whatever you need, sir."

"Now I won't insult you by offering you money."

I risked a smile. "I don't insult all that easily."

He chuckled. "Well, there's no money in it for you, just the same. Just the satisfaction of helping your country, and knowing you have a friend in the White House . . . for a few more years, anyway."

"That could come in handy."

"Eat your lobster, Nate, 'fore it gets cold. What are you drinking?"

"I wouldn't mind a rum and Coke . . ."

"Boy! Rum and Coke for my friend, here! . . . You know, Nate, they're always yelling to me from crowds, 'Give 'em hell, Harry! Give 'em hell.' "

"Yes, sir, I've heard of that."

"Well this time, we'll give 'em Heller."

And he winked at me, and poured himself some Old Fitzgerald.

Five

A STAIRWAY FROM 14TH AND H STREETS led up to
the Casino Royal, which was not, strictly speaking, a casino at all: there were illegal gambling joints
within the D.C. environs, but this wasn't one of them.
It was instead one of Washington's two principal
nightclubs (the Lotus being the other) and with its
prom-night glitter, popular prices and endless dance
floor—a poor excuse for a Chicagoan's Chez Paree
or a New Yorker's El Morocco.

Still reeling from the surrealistic experience of eating lobster with Harry Truman, I had been dropped
off at the Ambassador Hotel by Frank Wilson, who'd
handed me a slip of paper with both his and Chief
Baughman's numbers, "should anything interesting
develop." It was barely after ten p.m., but exhilaration and exhaustion were fighting within me, and exhaustion was winning. Cool sheets and a soft pillow
awaited. . . .

But so did another slip of paper, at the front desk,
a handwritten note left in my mailbox, reading: "I'll
be at the Casino Royal until midnight. Please come if
you want the real lowdown. We have mutual
friends—F.S. and the late Ben S., among others.
Teddy K."

I had no idea who "Teddy K." was, but F.S. was a
certain boy singer I'd done a few jobs for, at the re-

quest of friends of his in Chicago, and "the late Ben
S." was Benjamin "Bugsy" Siegel, who I'd worked for
in the early days of the Flamingo Hotel in Las Vegas.
Sinatra was indeed a friend, as had been Siegel,
though in both instances I'd sometimes wished
otherwise.

Having no idea how I was supposed to identify
Teddy K., I swam the Casino Royal's sea of tourists,
navigating through a fog of cigarette smoke, searching for an empty table along the periphery of the
packed dance floor, where couples were swaying to
"On a Slow Boat to China."

"Maybe that's the boat that brought Dick Lamm
over," a thick, middle-European-accented baritone
voice beside me said.

I glanced at the stocky, bucket-headed figure at my
shoulder. In his late thirties, spiffy in a three-button
light blue glen plaid sportcoat and a maroon tie with
big blue amoebas swimming on it, the guy had a
blond thatch of Brylcreemed hair, quizzical eyebrows
high above small sharp dark eyes, a sweet-potato
nose and narrow lips in a fleshy, friendly face.

"Who's Dick Lamm?" I asked.

"Chinaman that runs the joint. Used to run the
China Doll in New York. He's got uptown manners,
but, brother, he sure knows what the hicks want."

"Really."

He extended a blunt-fingered, almost pudgy right
hand. "I'm Theodor Kollek, but everybody calls me
Teddy. You prefer Nate or Nathan?"

I shook hands with him, warily; he looked like a
very successful bookie. "Nate's just fine, Teddy. Who
the hell are you?"

Kollek grinned and his eyes disappeared into
pouchy slits. "Nate, you ain't had time to absorb
who Dick Lamm is, much less Teddy Kollek." He

gestured rather grandly. "They're savin' a back booth for us."

I followed him. An announcer was shooing the crowd off the dance floor; just as we were settling in our booth, a thin spotlight cut through the cigarette smoke to fix upon a small stage with a six-piece band. A drumroll and an announcer introduced Jack "Jive" Shaffer, the plump, bald, tomato-faced comedian/bandleader, who buck-and-winged his way to the microphone in a blur of pink and green apparel, rhinestone cuff links catching the light, both they and Jack winking at the applauding crowd.

"Hey," he said into the microphone, looking toward the rafters whence his spotlight came, *"can't you find a light with some hair on it?"*

That got a pretty good laugh, considering how lame it was, and Kollek said, "Kind of sad, what passes for entertainment in this town, ain't it?"

His speech had an educated, even cultured tone that told me the scattering of ain'ts were an affectation.

"Of course, I'm spoiled," Kollek said, lighting up a cigar with a hand laden with gold and diamond rings. "Till a few months ago, my office was over the Copa—in the Hotel Fourteen, off Fifth Avenue?"

"I know where the Copacabana is."

"Yeah, I guess you do get around, but I figured you bein' from Chicago and all—"

"That where you know Frankie from?"

"Yeah, matter of fact it is." He blew a fat smoke ring, then frowned and said, "Hey, I don't mean to be rude—you want a Cuban?"

"No thanks. I don't smoke."

"In this joint, you might as well." Whenever Kollek smiled, which was often, it was a wiseguy, Leo Gorcey–style half-smirk. "Frank's a nice fella. Hotheaded, impulsive, but heart of pure gold."

"I don't know if his wife would agree with you."

"Yeah, this Ava Gardner thing is a pity; kid's career is goin' to hell in a handbasket."

At a postage-stamp table nearby, a young couple—who'd apparently had enough entertainment for one night—rose to leave and almost bumped into a husky young guy in a well-tailored blue suit, who was quickly taking their place, despite the empty glasses and tip awaiting a waitress' attention.

"I got that information about Dick Lamm pretty well absorbed by now, Teddy, if you'd like to tell me who the fuck you are."

He patted the air with a palm; cigar smoke swirled around him like the aftermath of a magician's trick. "Don't get testy, Nate—we're gonna be great friends. Couple of Jewish joes like us."

"I'm not all that Jewish, Teddy."

Finally a grin showed some teeth: big white ones. " 'Heller' sure as hell ain't Scottish."

I leaned on an elbow and gestured with a thumb at my face. "Take a look at this Irish mug of mine; my mom was named Jeanette, she went to mass and she didn't exactly keep kosher."

"Did you go to mass, Nate, or synagogue?"

"I wasn't raised in either church. If there's a God, He keeps out of my way and I stay out of His."

Kollek shrugged. "I grew up in a religious home, but I never been a regular synagogue-goer myself. When someone tries to force me to behave a certain way, I don't like it."

"I'm the same, Teddy. Which is why you have about twenty seconds to convince me to hang around."

"Hey," the red-faced comic was saying, *"how about these new government deductions, these new 'pay as you go' taxes, the President calls 'em? But after you pay, where can you go?"*

Polite laughter rippled; the crowd, denied dancing, were mostly talking among themselves, and drinking. Not far from where we sat, though, somebody was laughing a little too loud, I thought, trying a little too hard: the husky guy who'd taken that postage-stamp table. Like Kollek, he was blond, in his late twenties, with the blank, barely formed features of a fullride-scholarship jock; hell, he was big enough to play tackle in the Big Ten. . . .

Kollek casually asked, "Ever hear of the Haganah, Nate? That's not a word you necessarily have to go to synagogue to run into."

The Haganah, which had been around since after World War One, was an underground defense organization controlled by David Ben-Gurion's Jewish Agency for Palestine and a high command of Palestine's Jewish leaders. There were Zionist terrorist groups of course, but Haganah wasn't one of them: their policy was *havlagah*, self-defense.

"Is that still around, now that Israel's a state?" I asked.

Kollek just smiled and puffed his cigar. He was about to say something when a waitress came around to ask us if we wanted drinks. He ordered Jack Daniel's on the rocks and I ordered rum and Coke.

"What's a poor young nation to do," Kollek said, not exactly answering my question, "when a great patron like the U.S.A. decides to ration its goodwill the way it used to ration gas and meat?"

"What you mean is," I said, "the U.S. won't 'ration' you any arms or military supplies."

An arms embargo was in effect: neither side of the Arab-Israeli war could have American weaponry—legally.

Kollek shrugged and said, "I'm a fund-raiser, Nate, workin' through the UJA."

United Jewish Appeal.

" 'Just' a fund-raiser, Teddy?"

"Well, also I'm a recruiter. I look for influential American Jews who can give *more* than money—who can provide leverage—like Eddie Jacobsen, President Truman's old business partner."

"I hear he doesn't keep kosher either," I muttered.

"What was that?"

"Nothing."

"You know, a big part of my job, Nate, is I'm always on the lookout for guys like you."

"What kind of guy would that be?"

He gestured to me like I was a Cadillac on a showroom floor. "American Jewish war veterans, with combat experience, willing to volunteer for the Israeli army—over half our volunteers come from America, y'know."

"One war was plenty for me, thanks."

A waitress finally cleaned off the tackle's tiny table; he ordered from her, without even looking at her, a good-looking little brunette, though on occasion he was still sneaking peeks at our booth.

"Hey," Kollek was saying, shrugging, "you were a long shot, but it couldn't hurt to ask. Anyway, it's not like we're beggin' for leads on ex-soldiers ripe for recruitment."

"You're not?"

"No . . . we're supplied with names and personal details of potential recruits by our friends on the inside."

"The inside of what, Teddy?"

He shrugged, exuding friendliness and cigar smoke, then dropped his bomb: "The Pentagon."

". . . This is about Forrestal, isn't it?"

Kollek laughed, again ignoring my question. "You know, Nate, it's the last thing I ever expected to be involved with. . . . I was one of the lucky Jews, you know, the lucky few the British allowed to move to Palestine in '35, before Hitler started gobbling up Europe. I started a kibbutz on the shores of the Sea of Galilee—can you picture it?"

I had to smile, hearing this from the Damon Runyon character seated across from me.

"Galilee, that's where they say Jesus walked on the water. Easier for him doing that than me being a farmer. Oy! They said, 'Teddy, you're a worldly man, you have charm, people meet you and they like you . . . we'll send you to godless New York.' . . . You know, these are people that admire the Soviet-style economy, socialists that view America as materialistic, superficial, pointless. Me, I took to New York immediately—Sinatra, Louis Armstrong, and those jazz musicians from Harlem, hot damn!"

"What did you mean, Teddy? What was the last thing you'd ever expected to get involved with?"

He rolled the cigar around in his mouth, giving me a sly look. "What do you think I'm talking about, Nate?"

"Arms smuggling," I said. "Intelligence gathering."

Up onstage, Jack "Jive" Shaffer was singing an effeminate version of "Nature Boy" in a pageboy wig, prancing, mincing, getting some laughs—though not from the tackle at the postage-stamp table.

Kollek's cigar had gone out; he relighted it. "Let's just say I won't deny I've developed contacts, informers, assistance of various kinds in the Pentagon."

"Why are you telling me this?"

"I promised you the lowdown; Teddy Kollek delivers on his promises. Sure you won't have a Cuban?"

"No thanks."

"First Cuban I ever smoked, Ben Siegel gave me, after one of his Havana trips. Ben, God rest him, was

one of our biggest contributors—better than fifty
grand. Meyer Lanksy, Mickey Cohen—you know
them, too, don't you?"

"Acquaintances, not friends."

"Well, they're *my* friends, generous ones, and not
just in terms of money, no. Jewish and Italian gangsters can be helpful in so many other ways."

"Like linkups with waterfront unions, if you're trying to smuggle guns and money, you mean?"

Again Kollek didn't answer me directly, saying,
"They're crazy, those guys. Do you know Lanksy suggested I draw up a hit list of 'enemies of the Jewish
people'?"

"Take him up on it?"

"No, it was tempting, but I declined—respectfully."

Using the same tray, the cute brunette waitress
brought us our drinks, then took the tackle his: a bottle
of 7 UP and a glass of ice. Maybe he was in training.

"Okay, Teddy. You got friends in the mob, you got
friends in the Pentagon. What's your point?"

Kollek leaned forward, the eyes again disappearing into the slitted pouches. "Haven't I made it? Your
pal Forrestal thinks we're trying to kill him. Why, to
get information we're already getting from sources
all around him? Hell, a phone call to Meyer Lanksy,
I could have that fat cat snuffed out like a candle. But
that's not how I operate—not that the son of a bitch
wouldn't deserve it."

"So, any American official that doesn't back Israel
deserves to die, Teddy?"

He was shaking his head, cigar smoke swirling
around him like a wreath. "That's what I don't get
about you, Nate—you're Jewish, you're a combat veteran—how can you work for that Nazi bastard?"

Up onstage, the drummer hit a rim shot, punctuat-
ing Jack "Jive" Shaffer's latest joke—and Kollek's.

"Oh," I said, "so now Forrestal's a *Nazi*? I see—Roosevelt's Secretary of the Navy, a Nazi, sure, that makes sense; Truman's Secretary of Defense a Nazi. Teddy, this may come as a shock to you, but not everybody who opposes Israel is a fucking Nazi."

The quizzical eyebrows raised even higher. "You mean, maybe James Forrestal doesn't have a corner on the paranoia market? Don't you read Drew Pearson? Nate, your friend Forrestal's company Dillon and Read helped *finance* Hitler!"

I sipped my rum and Coke, refusing to get caught up in his hysteria. "A Wall Street firm doing business with Germany after World War One, before Hitler's rise, doesn't make Forrestal and the rest of Dillon, Read & Company a nest of Nazis."

"Bullshit! They loaned hundreds of millions to the German cartels that formed the backbone of Hitler's war machine. Hell, Forrestal's on the fuckin' board of directors of General Aniline and Film, the American arm of I. G. Farben, the drug and industrial trust that created Auschwitz!"

Kollek was getting really worked up; it was all the tackle at the postage-stamp table could do not to just pull up a chair at our booth.

"You got a lot of passion, Teddy, but you're as full of shit as a Christmas goose. Jim Forrestal's a patriot."

"In his twisted view of it, I'm sure he is. And you're right, I'm overstating, he's no Nazi—he's just one hell of a capitalist. I mean, Chase National Bank, General Motors, ITT, Ford Motors, Standard Oil, they've all been in bed with Germany since long before the war."

"Hey, this is all way over my head," I said, but I had a sick feeling in my stomach and it wasn't the lobster mingling with his cigar smoke.

Kollek waved a blunt-fingered hand; the diamond and gold rings on it seemed at odds with his patronizing view of capitalism. "Yeah, what the hell, Nate—these guys were just protecting themselves—and their great country—to make sure that, after the war, the same fraternity of all-American business bigwigs still had their holdings."

I held up a palm: stop. "Teddy, I'm way out of my element, here. . . . I'm just a private eye with a client who thinks somebody wants to kill him. You say your group isn't a likely suspect, then you give me hundreds of reasons why you oughta be on top of the goddamn list!"

Kollek blew another fat smoke ring; raised his eyebrows, set them down. "Not the top, maybe. But why bother killing the bastard? Forrestal's on his way out, isn't he? And even if he *was* staying, he'd just be one of many."

I frowned, shook my head. "Many what? Nazis? If I believed what people were telling me lately, half the government's Communist, and the other half is fascist. Back where I come from, we call them Democrats and Republicans."

Now he held up a palm; in fact, he held up two of them. "All right, okay—fine. Dismiss everything I say as biased, alarmist, Zionist bullshit. But know this: if your friend Forrestal is in danger, it's more likely from his own people than mine."

This time it was Forrestal's voice echoing in my head: *I know too much.*

"Have you heard about these new brassieres?" the comic was asking the crowd. *"The Salvation Army bra uplifts the fallen, the Communist bra supports the masses, and the Drew Pearson bra makes mountains out of molehills!"*

That one got some real laughter—not just titters—

and Jack "Jive" Shaffer knew when to get off the stage, the six-piece band returning to dance music, starting with "Little White Lies"; the floor was soon flooded with couples. This left the well-groomed tackle all alone in a sea of empty tables, a shipwreck survivor on a desert island; the exposure didn't stop him from occasionally stealing glances at our booth.

Kollek swirled the remains of his drink in its glass and said, too casually, "Has Forrestal ever mentioned Operation *Nachtigall* to you, Nate? Operation Nightingale?"

"No."

He sipped the drink, smiled his half-smile. "I'm not surprised. We have solid information that U.S. intelligence agencies—even while they were rounding up, shall we say, sacrificial wolves for the Nuremberg tribunals—were at the same time actively recruiting Nazis and Nazi collaborators for what Forrestal and others in your government see as the coming war on Communist Russia."

"Oh, please . . ."

The smile evaporated and he leaned deep across the booth. "You can't imagine how many scientists fresh from factories run by concentration-camp labor, and doctors right out of 'research facilities' where Jews were human guinea pigs, are on Uncle Sam's payroll, now."

"That's ludicrous. If that were true, and the public found out—"

"Which is exactly why Forrestal is in more peril from his friends than his enemies. These efforts go beyond gathering up top Nazi minds, understand— Operation Nightingale, for example."

I sighed. "You seem to want me to ask, Teddy, so I'll ask: what the hell is Operation Nightingale?"

He sat back in the booth; his glass was empty, his

arms folded, the cigar sending up smoke signals from an ashtray before him. He spoke very softly: "My sources indicate that the NSC . . . that's the National Security Council, a body formed at Forrestal's urging . . . is secretly financing and arming underground resistance movements in the USSR and its Eastern European satellites."

I thought about that, translating it for myself. "Funding the overthrow of Russia from within, you mean."

"Yes. Operation Nightingale is one of those efforts, a recruiting of right-wing Ukrainian militia members who during the war were among the Nazis' most eager lapdogs, perpetrators of atrocities beyond comprehension. They not only rounded up thousands of Jews for the Nazis, they performed the mass executions themselves—after the women had been raped, of course. These barbarians, these purveyors of modern-day pogroms, your friend Forrestal enlisted in the service of anti-Communism. These monsters were even brought here, to your great country, and trained for their mission."

"If this is true—"

"And not just Zionist propaganda? Then what, Nate?"

"That's my question—then what? Why tell me all this? So I'll quit working for Forrestal?"

The eyebrows flew up, the small eyes widened. "Hell, no! We want you to stay as close to him as possible. See what you can learn. If Forrestal is suffering from pangs of guilt, as our sources indicate, he might come forward with what he knows."

Now I gave him a smirk. "And think of how much money you could pry out of indignant rich American Jews, if he did—how pissed off they'd be over their country's Nazi collaboration . . . oh, and how much money they'd cough up for *your* country's cause."

Kollek shrugged with his eyebrows. "I won't deny that's one motive. Simple goddamn justice is another. Everything we know about Operation Nightingale, and other efforts to employ Nazis and Nazi collaborators, is hearsay; our sources won't take the step of stealing or microfilming top-secret and classified materials."

"Maybe they don't want to get shot by a firing squad for treason."

Kollek pointed his cigar at me. "I'll tell you about treason and firing squads: if a man of Forrestal's power and stature came forward with this ugly story, it would tear the dome off the Capitol. These goddamn Nazis would be flushed out of their lucrative new government positions and tried for their war crimes. And the traitors in government who hired them might see those firing squads, as well, or imprisonment, or at the very least disgrace."

I laughed softly, shook my head. "Teddy, you're a very persuasive man, for a lunatic. But I already have a client."

Who was also a lunatic, but never mind.

His expression had fallen. "I'm very disappointed in you, Nate."

"I suppose I'm on your Nazi collaborators list, now."

"No. But whether you like it or not, you're a Jew— and that puts you on a lot of other lists, all of 'em shit lists. . . . Damn, that drink went right through me. I'm gonna use the can—you still be here when I get back?"

"You want me to be?"

Kollek put out his cigar, his smile turning gentle. "Please. And no more serious talk, tonight. This place is gonna close up pretty soon—if you wanna hear some good Negro jazz, I'll take you over to the Hide-away Club, in Georgetown, after-hours joint."

"What's this, the soft-soap portion of your recruit-ment process?"

"Stick around and see."

He trundled off toward the john and, moments later, the tackle got up from the postage-stamp table and headed after him; it was about as subtle as the Ritz Brothers doing their Snow White routine. I took the last sip of my drink, and decided I'd use the men's room, too, seeing as how the tackle had gone in on Kollek's heels.

I pushed the door open and found myself in a medium-size men's room—two urinals, two stalls, two sinks, two men on the floor, tussling, missionary-style.

The tackle was on top of a squirming, wriggling Kollek, whose arms were pinned by the guy's massive thighs; the tackle was bringing his arm back, and as that arm had a canned-ham-size fist on the end of it, I figured he was planning to rearrange Kollek's features.

Kollek saw me come in, brightening at the prospect of rescue, and the tackle looked my way, too, but not in time to stop me from grabbing with both hands onto his fist and arm and tug-of-warring him off Kollek, enough for Teddy to squirm free and get to his feet, his spiffy green sportcoat wrinkled and mois-ture-spotted, some of it piss, probably, some of it sink water, some of it blood: Kollek's nose was bleeding—he'd already taken a punch. The tackle's face was contorted in reddened rage.

I let go of the guy's arm, retreated a couple steps, held out my palms and said, "This doesn't have to get any uglier than it already is . . . there's two of us . . . now back off."

Kollek, breathing hard, had already backed off, by the far, high-windowed wall. His eyes were wild and scared shitless above the palm cupping his bloody nose.

On one knee, the tackle, still grimacing fiercely, reached inside his suitcoat and, before he could bring a gun out, I kicked his balls up inside him; his anguished cry echoed in the tiled room, like an animal that had taken a spear.

As every man knows, the son of a bitch should have been paralyzed by that pain, but—amazingly, frighteningly—he instead got quickly to his feet while simultaneously swinging a massive fist at my face, narrowly missing as I ducked it, then threw myself at him, tackling the tackle, driving him into the door of a stall, through that door and into the stall, where the stool caught him in the back of his legs, sitting him down hard, not for a dump, but for two fast right hands, interspersed with a fast left, a one-two-three combination that knocked him out, leaving him sprawled on the pot, head against the wall where it said "For a good time, call Irene."

He may have had brass balls, but his goddamn jaw was glass.

I checked inside his suitcoat for the gun, and there was a gun, yes, but not in a shoulder holster where I thought it would be, and not on the side of him where he'd reached: a .38 snubnose Colt in a cross-draw holster on his belt. What the hell had he been reaching for, then?

His wallet, maybe?

"Oh shit," I said, knowing.

His credentials.

The tackle's name was Gary W. Niebuhr and he was employed by the federal government; he was, in fact, an FBI agent. If he'd gotten a good enough look at me, this might wind up yet another glowing entry in one of J. Edgar's favorite files.

"What the hell have you got me into?" I snarled at Kollek, who was at the sink, wetting a paper towel for his nose.

"I didn't ask for your help," he said.

"What, were you resisting arrest?"

Kollek nodded.

I suggested we scram, and—leaving Agent Niebuhr in his stall, sleeping soundly—we scrammed, just as another patron was heading in, seeking relief, a sentiment I could well understand.

As we moved quickly down the stairs to the street, an embarrassed Kollek said, "That's why I had to shut down the office over the Copa. The FBI had our phones tapped; I been under surveillance for months. Somehow we aroused the Bureau's suspicions."

"Do you suppose it was the arms smuggling and hanging out with gangsters?"

He looked sheepish as we reached the sidewalk. "Most of my network's already been arrested."

"Thanks for saving this information for last."

"No hard feelings. . . . I could use a man like you, Nate."

"Give it up, Teddy. I'll take a raincheck on the Hideaway Club."

I was moving through the pleasantly cool evening toward where I'd parked my car.

Kollek was jogging off in the opposite direction, disappearing into the shadows, but calling out: "I'm afraid I can't give you a number where I can be contacted!"

"Somehow I'll manage to get over that," I said, got in my car and got the hell out of there.

Fucking zealots, anyway.

Six

T HE "MOST FEARED and hated man in Washington, D.C."—as the *Washington Times-Herald* had termed him, with neither affection nor irony—lived in a typically dignified Georgetown townhouse so evocative of bygone days that you might expect to see a gloved gent in stovepipe and muttonchops stroll down the steps to the cobblestone lane where a horse-drawn coach awaited.

But on this sunny Sunday afternoon on Dumbarton Avenue, you would instead have seen only a gloveless guy in a tan fedora and dark blue shantung suit going up those steps, and trying the polished brass knocker at the door of the home/office of Drew Pearson.

Speaking of knockers, it would have been more fun trying those of the healthy young woman who answered—a buxom lass of perhaps twenty with big blue eyes in a heart-shaped face.

"Who is, sir?" she asked, in a middle-European accent similar to, but much more fetching than, Teddy Kollek's.

She stood at attention in a crisp, streamlined white dress with thin vertical blue stripes (well, as vertical as they could be, considering her figure) and white collar and cuffs; she looked like a nurse in one of my dirtier dreams.

"Would you tell your boss his overdue account from Chicago is here?"

She frowned, full red-rouged lips forming a pouty kiss. "Excuse, please?"

So English was her second language; still, I'd wager her job description read "Secretary." Clearly she was the latest office "fair-haired girl," as Pearson's veteran employees dubbed them, "cutie-pies" as the boss described each lucky girl singled out for such special services as enlivening cocktail parties and accompanying him on out-of-town speaking engagements.

"Just tell the big cheese Nate Heller is here."

"Big . . . ?"

"Nate Heller, honey."

"Very busy today." She frowned again and shook her shimmering golden locks; it was cuter than a box of puppies. "Mr. Pearson see no one on broadcast day."

I dug out one of my cards and handed it to her. "Just give him this—I'll wait."

Soon she was back, equal parts solicitude and pulchritude, smelling like lilacs (or anyway lilac perfume), hugging my arm, yanking me into an entrance hall that fed both the residential and office areas of the house.

"I am too sorry, Mr. Heller," she said, batting long lashes, putting the accent on the second syllable of my name.

A modern living room was straight ahead, down a couple steps, and to the left, also sunken, was a formal dining room with a kitchen glimpsed beyond.

"Honey, I'm almost over it," I said, taking off my hat.

That confused her for a second, but then she grinned, showing crooked teeth I was perfectly willing to forgive, and lugged me down two steps to the right, through a doorway into a book-, paper- and keepsake-arrayed study where the air was riddled with the machine-gun rat-a-tat-tat of typing. To one side of a wide, wooden desk, at a typewriter stand, his back to us, a large (not fat) bald man in a maroon smoking jacket was hammering away at the keys.

The blonde looked at me gravely and held up her hand, in case I was thinking of speaking: the boss was not to be interrupted while he was creating.

A window fan was churning up air. Off to the right of the fairly small room, visible (and audible) through the open doorway, a desk-cluttered workroom bustled with two men and a trio of women typing or talking on the phone or attending the clattering wire-service ticker or putting something in or getting something out of one of the endless graysteel filing cabinets lining the walls. While these secretaries were not unattractive, they—unlike my blonde escort—had the businesslike apparel and bespectacled, pencil-tucked-behind-the-ear manner of professional women. Depending on the profession, of course.

Drew Pearson's profession was journalism, or anyway a peculiar variant of his own creation. At one time just another Washington newspaperman covering the State Department for the *Baltimore Sun*, Pearson had taken the gossip-column style of New York's Walter Winchell and Hollywood's Louella Parsons and grafted it—to use a fitting term—onto the Washington political scene.

The column—"The Washington Merry-Go-Round"—initially had not been solely Pearson's. The *Christian Science Monitor*'s D.C. correspondent, Robert S. Allen, had come up with the idea for a hard-hitting book that would expose both the per-

sonal peccadilloes and political chicanery of our
country's leaders, particularly those in the Herbert
Hoover administration.

Bob Allen did most of the writing, but brought his
pal Pearson aboard as a collaborator for a few chap-
ters because Drew knew the social scene, his mother-
in-law being the powerful newspaperwoman and
socialite Cissy Patterson. The book, published anonymously in 1931, was a huge best-seller and made
tidal-type waves that started in Washington and
splashed across the nation; the pissed-off President
sicced the FBI on the case, to ferret out the identities
of the contemptible authors.

Exposed, Allen and Pearson were fired by their papers, but Pearson—giving himself top billing—took
the notion of the book to a newspaper syndicate,
United Features, which snapped it up. The column
was a sensation, and Pearson hogged the spotlight,
and became the country's best-known crusader for
liberal causes. With World War Two imminent, Bob
Allen left the column to enlist in the Army; Pearson
took that opportunity to remove his partner's name,
refusing to pay Allen, or his wife, a dime while he was
away. When Allen returned, a colonel who'd lost an
arm in combat, he found he'd lost his column, as well.

The man at the typewriter stopped typing, yanked
the page out of the machine and, without turning,
tossed the page on the desk, on which paper-filled
wooden intake boxes were lined, a regal black cat
sleeping quietly in one of them.

"Get that added to the script, Anya," he commanded in a rather harsh, clipped baritone. Pearson
had trained himself to sound like a more dignified
Walter Winchell when "Washington Merry-Go-
Round" had become a radio show as well as a column.

"Yes, sir!" The blonde leaned over to snatch up the typed page, and the plump globes of her behind under the blue-striped nurse's dress tilted up invitingly.

"That's a good girl. Now shut the door behind you."

"Yes, sir!"

And she scampered out.

He scooted over on his chair till he was behind the big desk, and twisted around like a kid on a soda fountain stool, to where I could see him. His rather large head was shaped like—and had only a little more hair than—an egg; his eyes crowded a strong, prominent nose and his mouth was no wider than his well-waxed, pointed-tipped mustache. A white shirt and maroon-and-black tie peeked out from under the smoking jacket.

"What a cutie-pie," Pearson purred, looking toward where Anya had exited.

The sleeping cat echoed him with its own purring.

"You lucky bastard," I said.

He stood, rising to his full six three, and extended his hand over the messy desk and the tidy cat. "Nice to see you, too, Nathan. Jack said you were in town."

"I hear he's a Mormon," I said, shaking his clammy hand. "Is he a Mormon like you're a Quaker?"

Raised in that faith, Pearson only used the "thee" and "thou" routine at dinnertime with family, and while he didn't smoke, he had a reputation for hard drinking.

He lifted an eyebrow, as he sat back down. "You understand this is broadcast day. I can only give you a few minutes."

Ignoring that, I prowled his office. The dark-painted plaster walls wore framed original newspaper cartoons featuring Pearson, and photos of him with various political figures, including the last two presidents. A primitive rural landscape in oil—a relative's work, apparently—hung near a portrait of a man who might have been his father; snapshots were lined up along the mantelpiece of a working fireplace, and the windowsills were piled with books and papers.

"Why don't you buy yourself a new typewriter?" I asked, nodding toward the battered Corona on the typing stand. "Live a little."

"That machine was given to me by my father"— and he nodded toward the portrait, confirming my suspicion—"in 1922. It's my pride and joy; take it with me on trips, and nobody touches it but me."

"How do you get away with that?"

"When it breaks down, I simply get it fixed at a certain small machine shop—"

"I was talking about the blonde." I shook my head. "Right under your wife's nose?"

His wife, Luvie, was an elegant, model-thin blonde; his second wife, actually—he'd stolen her, like his column, from a close friend.

"Well, she's at the farm today," he said, "but she doesn't mind my dalliances. Boys will be boys. She understands my appetites."

"Does she have a sister?"

"Who? Luvie or Anya?"

I pulled up a chair and sat. "Where's the blonde from, anyway? Transylvania?"

"Yugoslavia. War refugee."

"You are a public-spirited son of a bitch. And open-minded by not insisting that your secretary speak or write English. You're in arrears three hundred bucks, by the way."

Pearson tilted his chin and looked down his considerable nose at me. "Your expense account was outlandishly out of line. We'll call it even—or you could always sue, though you'd have to take a number." He was smiling; he smiled a lot, a smile that creased his eyes into slits.

"Didn't do General MacArthur much good, did it?"

"None whatsoever," Pearson chuckled. He had a quiet, gentlemanly manner, and the chilly, aloof bearing of an ambassador to some unimportant country. "By the way, does your current client know of our past association?" He posed this mildly, sitting forward, stroking his cat, its back arching.

"No," I admitted.

In the mid-thirties I'd done a few jobs for Pearson, having been recommended to him by another former client of mine, Evalyn Walsh McClean, wife of the publisher of the *Washington Post,* owner of the Hope diamond, and a prominent if eccentric D.C. socialite and party-giver. Evalyn was a friend of Pearson's first wife and her mother.

The initial work I'd done for the columnist had been so long ago, it well predated my relationship with Forrestal, and had apparently not made my FBI file, or Baughman would have rubbed my face in it, the other night.

And the government apparently wasn't aware that, as I'd mentioned to Jack Anderson, I'd done some work in Chicago for Pearson, not long ago, despite swearing I never would again, as he really was the cheapest son of a bitch on the planet. He negotiated you down to nothing, then took forever to pay.

"Your client's ignorance of our past history," Pearson said, "puts you in a delicate position, Nathan— and me at an advantage."

"Sure it's not the other way around," I asked, "since I know how you're getting inside info from Forrestal's house? If I tell Jim about that colored maid, he'll fire her . . . but then, of course, maybe you could hire her as your next secretary."

He just smiled, corners of his mustache up, eyes lost in slits. "For a man who's been in your tawdry profession for as long as you have, Nathan, you have a less than firm grasp of blackmail."

"Well, hell . . . then I'll defer to the master."

That didn't seem to offend him in the least. Amid the mess on his desk was a glass jar filled with small chocolate chip cookies; he lifted the lid, plucked one out and began nibbling it. "Would you like one, Nathan? Anya made them."

"How much are they?"

"Now that's unkind. I pride myself on being a gracious host. You're the one charging fees; you're the tradesman."

"And knowing your politics, Drew, I'm sure you mean that in the nicest way, friend to the working-man that you are."

He took a last bite of cookie, chewed it and swallowed before speaking. "How do you think Jim Forrestal—in his current delicate mental condition—would react to the news that his trusted investigator has done numerous jobs for his archnemesis—yours truly?"

Obviously, it would further fuel his paranoid delusions and I'd be out on my ass.

But I said, "Jim knows I'm not terribly particular about who I work for."

Pearson selected another cookie. "And does he know your loyalty is to the dollar?"

"Now *you're* being unkind. But then that's your stock-in-trade, isn't it?"

He bristled a little, leaned back in the chair. "My stock-in-trade is telling the truth, and letting the chips fall where they may."

Chocolate or otherwise.

"Telling the truth, Drew, like that story about Forrestal running away from robbers who stripped his wife of her jewels and money? The truth is, Jo Forrestal was on her way home from a party, with another man, and Forrestal wasn't even at the scene. You knew that and printed the lie, anyway."

He shrugged, rocking gently, nibbling his cookie. "It could have been worse—I could have told the real truth: that he and his wife live a sham marriage."

I laughed, once. "You can say that with a straight face, while Miss Yugoslavia 1946 is out in the other room buttering your scones?"

He frowned and his close-set eyes almost crossed. "*I'm* not a public official."

"Jesus, Drew—can you imagine, a proud guy like Forrestal, responsible for the safety of his country, how a false accusation of base cowardice could affect him?"

The smile returned; he looked like your rich uncle. "Please, Nathan. You don't wear moral indignation very well. Come on, man! People forget that I'm trying to do something for my country, and the world."

"By lying to ruin a man's reputation?"

"In politics, questionable actions are often employed for desirable goals."

"The ends justify the means, you mean."

"Isn't that how you operate? I'm well acquainted with your mode of operation, Nathan."

I sat forward. "What the hell's the idea of putting all your muscle behind destroying an able, dedicated guy like Jim Forrestal?"

"Sure he's able," Pearson huffed. "Of course he's dedicated. But to what? He's a man who lives only for himself. He's broken his word, turned his back on his friends . . ."

This was rich, coming from the guy who stole "Washington Merry-Go-Round" from Bob Allen.

". . . and he's driven by one ambition and one ambition only: to be top man, first of Wall Street, then the cabinet, and now he's got his eye on the presidency. And were he president, with his worldview that the godless, evil Soviet Union is on the verge of invading us, we'd find ourselves in a catalysmic world war. He has to be stopped. I *have* stopped him."

"You've crushed him, Drew."

"Then good for me." Pearson was shaking his head. "He's been a law unto himself, Nathan, and behavior like that can't be countenanced."

"From a public official, you mean. It wins columnists Pulitzers."

"Listen, my friend, Jim Forrestal has nurtured, has created, this nightmarish Central Intelligence Agency, and mark my words, America will suffer the consequences for decades. And before he had that charming organization up and running, peddling its counterintelligence and counterinsurgency around the world, he would step in himself, raising huge funds from his rich friends to pay off railroad strikers in France, to buy off politicians in Italy—"

"Save it for the broadcast."

He arched an eyebrow. "All right. Since you seem disapproving of my campaign—*successful* campaign—to induce Harry S. Truman to remove James V. Forrestal, I have to ask: why did you want to see me today?"

"Why were *you* willing to see me?"

The smile turned sly again; he stroked his purring pussy and said, "Well . . . I thought, as someone who's spent time with Forrestal . . . who has his ear, his trust . . . you could, you might, let me know just how far around the bend he is."

"Why, so you can put it on the radio tonight?"

"Yes," he said, with no shame. "It appears to me that Forrestal has gone off his rocker. That he's mad as a hatter. And if I could say that, with confidence, on the air, it would be a great service to our country."

"Jesus! Suppose the guy *has* lost his marbles . . . and I'm not confirming that, mind you . . . what purpose does it serve humiliating him further? You won, Drew! Isn't that enough?"

"You don't think the country has a right to know that its Secretary of Defense is a madman? I want to know how long he's been demented, I want to know what orders, policies, security breaches might be ascribed to his mental state! If a raving lunatic has made government policy, mightn't we want to undertake a critical review of those policies?"

"Well, I hate to disappoint you, but I haven't seen a 'raving lunatic'—just a man battered down by years of hard work for his country, and maybe buckling a little under your barrage of bullshit."

He rocked gently. "I ask again, Nathan: why did you want to see me today?"

"To ask you, out of common decency, not to broadcast any speculation about Jim Forrestal's mental condition. He's quitting tomorrow—give him a chance to go out with a little goddamn dignity."

Both eyebrows lifted. "This is unexpected, Nathan."

"What is?"

"The milk of human kindness in one so monetary."

"Why don't you surprise me, Drew, and behave like the liberal lover of mankind you pretend to be: give the guy a fucking break."

He thought about that, as he scratched his cat's neck. Finally he said, "All right. But if Forrestal gets back into the political fray, all bets are off."

I hadn't expected it to be this easy; frankly, I hadn't expected him to go along with me at all.

"Understood," I said.

"But . . . I need a favor of you, in return."

So much for the milk of human kindness.

"What kind of favor?"

"Your presence in Washington is fortuitous, Nathan."

"It is?"

"Yes. I'd like you to do a job for me. Today. This afternoon."

". . . What kind of job?"

He folded his hands prayerfully on the desktop. "I want you to talk to somebody for me. I don't want to be seen talking to this individual myself, and I don't even want my staff knowing about this particular . . . subject matter."

That didn't surprise me. Pearson had a conspiratorial managing style, never letting an investigator or legman know what each other was up to.

I asked, "What subject matter is that?"

He spoke very softly: "In researching your client, Secretary Forrestal, I stumbled onto some information that is either the biggest story of the century . . . or an attempt to make such a fool out of me that I would be discredited, once and for all."

"All right. You've got my attention. But, favor or no favor, my fee is a hundred a day."

Immediately, he reached in a desk drawer, withdrew a checkbook and began filling out a check, asking, "You want that made out to the A-1 or to yourself?"

"A-1 will be fine . . . but make it four hundred, to bring your account up to date."

Pearson shrugged. "All right."

My jaw dropped. "Now you *really* have my attention. . . ."

He handed the check across to me, its black ink

glistening wetly. "No further expenses, though . . . for right now, this is a one-day affair, and you can buy your own damn meals."

"Fair enough. Who do I talk to, and on what subject?"

He rocked back, folded his arms. "Let's start with the subject. Nathan . . . what do you know about flying saucers?"

I winced. Weren't Commies, Zionists and Nazis enough? Must I add spacemen to the list?

"Nathan, please . . . answer the question."

Money was money. "Well . . . last year or two, there have been a lot of sightings of flying saucers, flying discs, flying cigars, whatever, some of 'em by fairly reputable types. I figure it's some kind of postwar hysteria—like the gremlins pilots in the war talk about seeing. I saw 'em myself."

"Really?"

"Yeah, in Bugs Bunny cartoons."

Pearson shuffled through some manila file folders on his desk, came up with a thick one, folded it open and began thumbing through; I hoped it wasn't my FBI file again.

"The first published report of a saucer sighting was in June of '47," he said, "by an air rescue pilot—Kenneth Arnold, of Boise, Idaho—who said he saw nine flying saucers flying at twelve hundred miles per hour over the Cascade Mountains in Washington State, in formations, shifting positions like . . . what's it say, here, where is it . . . 'like the tail of a kite.' This seemed to trigger sightings, with saucers spotted in Texas, New Mexico, Oregon, Idaho, Missouri, Colorado, California, Arizona, Nebraska . . ."

I nodded. "Yeah, for a few months there, if you wanted to see your name in the paper, all you had to do was just call in and say you saw an unidentified flying what's-it."

"Your attitude mirrors my own, essentially; but some of these sightings are from credible sources—a United Airlines pilot, a National Guard captain— and I've learned that the U.S. Air Force is studying and cataloguing these sightings."

"Or pretending to—after all, these 'saucers' could be some new experimental top-secret aircraft or weapon of ours. The kind of thing a civilian might easily misconstrue."

Pearson nodded. "And the inquiry into 'saucer' sightings could be a military screen of 'black propaganda'—lies. In any case, that effort—whether sincere, or simply cosmetic—started in December '47, as Project Sign, but it's evolved into something called Project Grudge."

"That sounds like the code name for your Forrestal crusade."

He arched an eyebrow. "Well, Secretary Forrestal *is* involved in this matter."

"You're kidding."

"Not at all. As I said, I came across this information in my investigation of Forrestal. . . . Take a look at this, Nathan."

Pearson handed me a photostat from his folder; it was of a single sheet of stationery, rubber-stamped at the top: TOP SECRET/MAJIC EYES ONLY.

White House stationery.

The date was September 24, 1947, and the contents were as follows:

MEMORANDUM FOR THE
SECRETARY OF DEFENSE

Dear Secretary Forrestal:

As per our recent conversation on this matter, you are hereby authorized to proceed with all due speed and caution upon your undertaking. Hereafter this matter shall be referred to only as Operation Majestic Twelve.

It continues to be my feeling that any future considerations relative to the ultimate disposition of this matter should rest solely with the Office of the President following appropriate discussions with yourself, Dr. Bush and the Director of Central Intelligence.

And it was signed, with a flourish: "Harry Truman."

"This doesn't say anything about flying saucers," I said.

"Indeed it doesn't. But a Pentagon source has informed me that Operation Majestic Twelve is a government research and development project formed with exploring the 'flying saucer' problem as its mandate."

I reread the letter, then asked, "Who's this Dr. Bush?"

"Dr. Bush is, with Forrestal, one of the twelve—the 'Majestic Twelve'—that is, key government, scientific and military figures. Bush is former dean of MIT; he led the development of the atomic bomb, radar, the proximity fuse, the analog computer, and much more. The top government science mind."

I tossed the photostat back on his desk. "Do you believe your source?"

"You know what they say—in Washington, if your mother says she loves you, get a second source to corroborate it."

"Glad to see you checking your facts, for a change."

He sighed rather heavily. "Nathan, as I said, I suspect this may be an effort to make a colossal boob out of me. But if what I've been told does prove correct, our government may have in its possession technology from another planet, which they are intending to capitalize upon for military purposes."

"I'm gonna vote for the colossal boob theory on this one."

Pearson was shaking his head. "I know, I know—it sounds incredible, even bizarre . . . but it all seems to stem from one incident—the crash of an unidentified flying object in Roswell, New Mexico, in July of '47."

I shifted in my chair. "Not a sighting—a crash. . . ."

"Yes—a crash by an alien spacecraft."

"And Forrestal is nuts? Drew, you thought about trying a smoking jacket that buttons up the back?"

"The Air Force base at Roswell—the 509th Bomb Group, who incidentally are the only squadron in the world armed and ready to drop atomic bombs—issued a public statement to the effect that a flying saucer had crashed, and its wreckage been recovered . . . a statement that was, within hours, withdrawn by the powers-that-be."

"You're making this up."

"No. I'll give you my clipping file to take with you, on your way."

"My way where?"

"To talk to the Air Force major who says he found the saucer. Sure you won't have a cookie?"

Seven

DUE WEST OF THE WHITE-MARBLE TEMPLE of the Lincoln Memorial, and bordering the low-slung but formidable granite-and-concrete Arlington Bridge, yawned a convex arc of granite steps known as the Water Gate. A couple hundred feet wide at the top, fanning out gently to maybe another thirty feet wide at bottom, these steep steps formed an ornamental buttress between the bridge and the roadway ramp angling from the memorial toward Rock Creek Park. The Water Gate was designed, in part, to serve as an outdoor amphitheater; in the summer, a barge outfitted with a band shell would be anchored at the foot of these forty or so steps as a stage for concerts by the National Symphony Orchestra, among others.

But late March was too early for the band-shell barge and the only stage that stretched out in front of the scattering of Sunday-afternoon loungers seated there was the sun-shimmering gray-blue Potomac itself, where pleasure boats—mostly canoes streaking by—were the featured attraction.

He was easy enough to spot, as I came down the steps: seated alone, a third of the way down, a small, even mousy-looking man in a light tan short-sleeve sportshirt with a wide pointed collar and brown corduroy slacks. His hair was dark brown and cropped short, his forehead high, and—I noted when he turned to see who'd sat down next to him—his eyes were buggy, nose beaky, chin rather weak.

Major Jesse Marcel would have been unimpressive if I hadn't read the material in the file folder Pearson had given me, a combination of newspaper clippings and background check, which I'd perused when I parked the rental Ford over by Honest Abe's memorial.

Marcel had entered the U.S. Army Air Force in 1942; he had both studied and taught at the Air Intelligence School at Harrisburg, Pennsylvania, where his civilian experience with Shell Oil, making maps from aerial photographs, soon developed into a much-valued expertise in mapping, and photographic reconnaissance and interpretation. His duties in the South Pacific had included serving as squadron intelligence officer as well as flying several combat missions in B-24s, winning two Air Medals.

Promoted to group intelligence officer and transferred stateside, Marcel was involved with radar navigation study at Langley Field when his unit, the 509th, dropped the bomb on Hiroshima. Shortly thereafter he was named intelligence officer for the bomb group; his first assignment: observer at the atomic tests at Bikini.

Right now Major Marcel was assigned to Strategic Air Command headquarters here in Washington: the officer in charge of the War Room, Intelligence Branch Operations Division, AFOAT-1. Apparently this mousy little guy was head of something called the Long Range Detection Program, intended to alert the U.S. to any atomic explosions elsewhere in the world, in particular the Soviet Union.

This latter information was probably classified, at least, and possibly top-secret; and I had to wonder if Pearson had gotten it from Marcel himself—and why a guy so tied to intelligence work would share it with a muckraker like Pearson.

Also, my neck was getting prickly with apprehension at atomic bomb stuff turning up again, even in this sidebar to the Forrestal investigation: first Frank Wilson of the Atomic Energy Commission, and now SAC's atom bomb watchdog, Major Marcel.

Who said, in a husky tenor, "Jesse Marcel, Mr. Heller. You *are* Mr. Heller?"

His tan sportshirt was a print design of cartoony representations of vacation spots: Miami, Cuba, Rio, palm trees, volcanoes, hotels.

"Nathan Heller, yes," I said, shaking the hand he offered.

His smile was friendly but nervous. "Mind if I see some identification?"

"Not at all." I got out my wallet, showed him my Illinois private operator's ticket.

"No offense," he said, and sucked on the stub of his cigarette. "Can't be too careful. Swell day, huh? Nice breeze—my wife and son are over at the park, so we should have plenty of time to talk."

"Major," I said, slipping my wallet back in my hip pocket, "I read the newspaper accounts about the incident at Roswell, but considering the inconsistencies . . . I'd really like to hear your version of it."

"Call me Jesse," he said, dropping the spent cigarette to the granite, heeling it out. "We seem to be pretty much by ourselves here, but let's keep it unmilitary, all right? You prefer Nathan or Nate?"

"Nate'll do. Jesse, if you're planning to reveal anything of a classified nature, I'll have Pearson send somebody else over to talk to you."

He shook his head, as he plucked a Camel out of a half-used pack. "Smoke?"

"No thanks."

"None of this is classified, Nate, or top-secret or anything. But it's military matters just the same, and I'm in intelligence, and I might get a tit in the wringer if it was known I was a damn source for 'Washington Merry-Go-Round.' "

"Understood. I just have no desire to see the inside of Fort Leavenworth."

"You're comin' in loud and clear on that one." He fired up his Camel with a silver Zippo, which he snapped shut. "No, they clamped the lid on this thing, but oddly, I never got any kind of serious debriefing or orders to clam up or anything. But, understand, this deal blew over real quick."

And it had. One day the headlines were trumpeting AIR FORCE CAPTURES FLYING SAUCER ON RANCH IN ROSWELL, the next ARMY DEBUNKS ROSWELL FLYING DISK AS WORLD SIMMERS WITH EXCITEMENT and GENERAL RAMEY EMPTIES ROSWELL SAUCER. These had been the headlines of Roswell's own *Daily Record* and *Dispatch,* but the story had been carried via the Associated Press and United Press, and spread worldwide—the Pearson file had clips from Rome, London, Paris, Hamburg, Hong Kong, Tokyo—creating a momentary sensation, only to be laughed off as a fluke of the flying saucer "craze."

"So what really happened at Roswell, Jesse?" I was getting out my small spiral notebook.

"No notes, Nate. We're just two pals chatting, okay?"

"Sure." I put the spiral pad away.

He plucked tobacco flakes off his tongue. "I can only tell you my part of it; I've heard of some fantastic things that other people witnessed, but I'm not gonna pass that along to you. If you're interested, you can go talk to 'em in Roswell; I'll even give you, or Mr. Pearson, a list of names. Make some calls for you pave the way. But I'm in the intelligence game myself, Nate—and I'm not going to insult *your* intelligence with hearsay."

"Fair enough. What's your story, Jesse?"

Laughter echoed across the water, as pleasure boaters glided by; the afternoon sun was turning the surface of the Potomac a glimmering gold.

Marcel drew on the cigarette, held the smoke in, blew it out through his nostrils, dragon-style. "It was the first Monday after Independence Day weekend, what—two years ago. I was just sittin' down to lunch, at the officers' club, when I got called to the phone. It was Sheriff Wilcox, saying he had a man in his office tellin' him something real strange."

"This is the sheriff in Roswell."

"That's right—Chaves County sheriff, to be exact. Anyway, Wilcox says this rancher from over by Corona has come trampin' into his office, yammering about a flying saucer crashing on his property. Well, as you can imagine, the sheriff took this with a big ol' grain of salt, but this rancher—Mac Brazel, your typical dusty ol' cowboy, not the owner of this ranch, just a guy running it for an absentee owner—had come three and a half hours over rotten roads and he wasn't about to stand for the bum's rush. Seems he had a few pieces of debris of this supposed saucer out in his pickup truck, which he shows the sheriff."

"And this prompts the sheriff to call you."

"Well, Sheriff Wilcox called the Army airfield and got put through to me, as Intelligence Corps officer. So the sheriff fills me in a little, and then he puts the rancher, Brazel, on the line, who says he's found something on his ranch that crashed down either yesterday or the day before; didn't know what it was— just that there was rubble all over a pasture of his, 'bigger than a football field,' he said, and that the grass looked like it had got burnt underneath."

Despite the cool breeze, the sun was warm enough for me to slip out of my sportcoat, and drape it over the granite step beside me. "So you headed over there."

"After I finished my lunch, I did. I wasn't in any rush. You know the papers were full of this flying saucer baloney around then, and somebody or other, I don't know, some radio station I think, was offering a reward to anybody who found one. I figured this might be a weather balloon—we had a lot of those come down—or some experimental thing from over at White Sands, which is nearby."

"Or did you think it was a hoax, maybe? With a reward at stake?"

He shook his head, sucked some more on his cigarette. "That's not the kind of thing that would occur to a guy like Mac Brazel; he was just your typical New Mexico salt-of-the-earth shitkicker."

"So you went to the sheriff's office."

"I did, and I saw the stuff in Brazel's truck, and it was pretty weird—there was this parchmentlike substance, extremely strong, so brown it was almost black, only more like a rough plastic than paper but it didn't seem to be either one; and some scraps of this shiny, flexible metal, like tinfoil, only it wasn't tinfoil, it was as thin as that, but much stronger. Here's what was really peculiar—you could bend that stuff, and if you put some muscle in it, even kind of wad it up . . . but it would then assume its original shape—without a bend, without a crinkle."

"Is that possible?"

"I would say no, if I hadn't seen it, held it." Marcel took his Zippo lighter from his shirt pocket. "I tried to burn the stuff with this very lighter—held the flame under a piece, and it wouldn't burn. You couldn't pierce it with a sharp knife, either!"

This subject clearly made him nervous, and he was drawing on the cigarette constantly, and on this beautiful sunny fresh afternoon, I was sitting in a swirl of smoke.

"So you saw these . . . samples of debris, in the rancher's truck. What then, Jesse?"

He shrugged. "I thought the matter was certainly worth reporting, so I called Colonel Blanchard at the base, commanding officer, and he asked me to bring some of the debris back for him to take a look at. I told Brazel and the sheriff I'd come back in, in an hour so, asked 'em to wait for me, and I met with Colonel Blanchard at the base. I showed him a piece of that shiny shit and asked him what he'd advise me to do. He looked it over carefully, and got the gist of how curious this stuff was, and he asked me how much debris was at the ranch, and I said, according to this Brazel character, plenty. I told the colonel, 'I believe we have some kind of downed aircraft of an unusual sort.' Then he said, 'Well then, I'd advise that you drive out to that site, and take one of our three counterintelligence agents along with you for support.' "

"And did you?"

Marcel nodded, sucking on the cigarette; he was almost ready for another. "I took the highest-ranking man we had, a CIC captain named Cavitt, who drove a jeep carry-all from the base. We took two cars—I was in a staff car, a prewar Buick—and we met up with Brazel at the sheriff's office, and followed him out to the ranch."

"The sheriff didn't come with you."

"No. He'd tossed the ball to the military and that was fine with us. Anyway, it was a long, hot, bumpy ride, and it was five p.m. before we got out there. Brazel had some of the debris stored in a shed, more of the same plus some rods, maybe two and a half inches in girth, in various lengths, none of them very long."

"What, metal rods?"

He shook his head. "I don't know what the hell they were made of. They didn't look or feel like metal, more like wood, and light as balsa wood."

"Plastic, maybe?"

"If so, the toughest damn plastic I ever saw—kinda like that stuff, whaddyacallit, Bakelite? Anyway, you couldn't bend it or break it."

"These were just little pieces?"

"Well, later we saw bigger ones, but right then, in the shed, no—although there were large pieces of the shiny stuff, and of the parchmentlike material, as big as ten feet in diameter."

"Jesus."

"Colonel Cavitt—I don't remember his first name, we just called him 'Cav'—he says, 'This could be radioactive,' and I says, 'Well, we'll find out right now.' I'd thrown a Geiger counter in the Buick trunk, so I got it and held the sensor near the pieces and got no radiation reading. 'Whatever this is,' I told the fellas, 'it's not dangerous.' By this time it was gettin' dark, no point going out to the pasture till morning. So we dined on canned beans and crackers and slept in sleeping bags in an empty shack, a hired hands' bunkhouse."

"Sounds quaint."

"We turned in early—this was a sheep ranch, understand, no radio, no phone—but we did sit and talk awhile. Brazel said he'd heard an odd explosion, during an electrical storm, night of the fourth, but that he hadn't paid it any heed, figuring it was a clap of thunder, or somethin' getting hit by lightning. Next morning he found the wreckage."

The gleeful screams of children playing echoed across the water.

"So Brazel didn't report finding the debris immediately?"

"No. That first day he went into Corona—smaller town even than Roswell, closer to the ranch. Place was buzzing with talk about flying saucers; in late June and early July of that year, people all over New Mexico were spotting all sorts of strange lights and objects in the sky. Almost hate to admit it, but I had what they call a 'sighting' myself."

"Sighting of what?"

He smirked, sighed, letting more smoke out. "A few days before the July Fourth holiday . . . must've been around eleven-thirty at night . . . Major Easley, the provost marshal, called me all excited and said, get out to the base—I lived in town—and he wouldn't even say why. On my way there, in my car, on a straightaway, I spotted a group of lights moving north to south, bright lights flying a perfect V formation, movin' like a bat out of hell. I mean, it was visible for maybe three or four seconds from overhead to the horizon. We didn't have any planes in the air that night, not that any of 'em could've traveled at that speed; maybe they did at White Sands or Alamogordo."

"The provost marshal saw what you saw?"

"Yeah. So did several other GIs and MPs. . . . Anyway, when Brazel went into Corona and heard all this saucer talk, it got him thinking, and somebody probably told him about that reward for finding a flying saucer, which I think was pretty good money, like three thousand or somethin', so he decided to report it."

"Why did he go to Roswell to make his report? Because that's where the county sheriff was?"

"Exactly." Marcel stopped to light up another cigarette, saying, "Sure you don't want a coffin nail? Mr. Pearson said you were in the service . . ."

"Marines."

"Guadalcanal, right?"

"That's right."

He grinned as he slipped his Zippo back in his breast pocket. "I thought everybody came back from overseas with a two- or three- or four-pack-a-day habit."

"I did smoke, on the island," I admitted. "But I managed to leave the habit there. So, uh—the next morning?"

He nodded, drew in smoke, exhaled it, saying, "Next morning, right after breakfast, right around seven o'clock, our rancher host starts saddling up horses. Now Cav was originally from Texas, so that was no problem for him; but I'd never sat a horse before and told 'em I'd follow 'em in the jeep. Besides, we could start loading up the debris that way, save some time."

"So the debris wasn't near the ranch house?"

"No, it was maybe three or four miles north of the house. Funny, bouncing along in that jeep, middle of nowhere, all that emptiness stretching to the horizon, and then, wham—all of sudden, as far the eye could see, that weird wreckage."

"There was that much of it?"

His buggy eyes bugged further. "Hell yes, spread over a wide area, three quarters of a mile long, two hundred, hell, *three hundred* feet wide. From the way the stuff was scattered, I had the feeling no aircraft had hit the ground, you know, bounced on the ground or anything."

"More like a midair explosion?"

"Yes, like something must have exploded in the

sky just over the pasture and strew this shit all over . . . although there *was* this deep scorched gouge, maybe five hundred feet long, and that could've been where something touched down and skipped along."

"And then, what, bounced up in the sky and exploded?"

He sighed out more smoke. "Who knows? Maybe some kind of craft had an explosion and kept going a ways before finally crashing. I learned later that north of Roswell, they found something else."

"What?"

"That I can't say. I only know what *I* saw, and what I saw was enough."

"The debris, was it just more of the same as in the shed?"

"Pretty much, just a *lot* more of the same, bigger pieces in some cases. A ton of that blackish-brown parchment material, from scraps to sheets. And we found a piece of that foil-like metal about two feet long and maybe a foot wide, so thin, so light it weighed practically nothing. But back at the base, we couldn't tear it or cut it, we even tried to make a dent in it with a sixteen-pound sledgehammer. Nothing."

"Not a dent?"

"Well, it made a dent, but then the damn stuff went back the way it was. It was right out of Ripley—you could bend it but you couldn't crease it. But you know, those rods were just as weird as the magic tinfoil."

"Rods?"

"Yeah, that stuff I told you about, that was light as balsa but didn't seem to be wood? They ranged in length from a few inches to a yard. Flexible stuff, but hard! We couldn't break that shit or burn it; didn't even smoke!"

The same couldn't be said for Marcel; my eyes were burning from his Camels.

"But the truly bizarre thing," he said, and I was certainly glad we were getting around to something bizarre, "was the markings on them, the writing."

"Writing?" I had to smile. "Outer space writing, Jesse?"

"I don't know what it was, symbols, maybe numbers . . . but not our numbers. It reminded me of hieroglyphics only without any animal-like characters: purple and pink embossed writing on the inner surface of the rods, which were kind of like I-beams."

"Maybe it was Chinese or Japanese or Russian . . ."

"No, I have some familiarity with those. That's not what it was."

"You saw nothing you recognized as man-made?"

Marcel shook his head, smirking humorlessly. "You know, I'm interested in electronics and kept looking for something that would resemble instruments or electronic equipment, 'cause then we'd know what the hell we were dealing with. But I came up empty on that front, though Cav found a black, metallic box, several inches square. There was no apparent way to open it, so we threw it in with the rest of the stuff. I don't know what became of it, but it went along with the rest of the material back to the base."

"Did you gather up all the debris?"

The buggy eyes bugged again, eyebrows climbing his high forehead. "Hell, no! We worked all morning and most of the afternoon, loading up the jeep carry-all and transferring it to the Buick staff car's trunk and backseat, then filled the carry-all again."

"So how much were you able to haul?"

He shrugged. "A fraction. But after we got back to the base, Colonel Blanchard took a look at the wreckage, then the next morning sent Cav and Major

Easley back, to cordon off the field. Thirty men cleared it."

"How did the press get ahold of the story?"

He grinned, which made his weak chin seem weaker. "It was a press release straight off the air base! Walt Haut, the lieutenant who was public information officer, was kind of an eager beaver, and it would've been like him to jump the gun."

"You can hardly blame the guy. It's not every day the Air Force finds a flying saucer."

"Yeah, but when I asked Walt about it, he claimed Colonel Blanchard personally dictated the press release to him, that same morning, and instructed him to hand-deliver the release to the two newspapers and the radio stations, there in Roswell."

"Why would your commanding officer have done that?"

"I understand word about the saucer was getting around town, and Blanchard prided himself on good relations with the community, and keeping 'em informed. Or maybe he wanted some glory. They say he always resented he didn't fly the *Enola Gay*."

"But within twenty-four hours, it was all retracted."

Marcel's eyes flared. "Hell, that same day the colonel ordered me to fly to Fort Worth and make a personal report to General Ramey. A B-29 was loaded up with all of the wreckage, most of it boxed up, the bigger pieces wrapped up in brown paper; damn plane was stuffed like a Thanksgiving turkey with that debris. When we got to Fort Worth, the wreckage was transferred to a B-25, which I heard later was flown to Wright Field in Dayton, Ohio. Me, I was taken to General Ramey's office, with a box or two of debris, which I showed him, making my report. He listened, politely, nodding, and I left the samples of debris behind when we went to the map room, 'cause the general said he wanted me to show him on a map where we found the wreckage. After we had dinner at the officers' mess, there was a press conference, and I was instructed to keep my mouth shut, let the general answer all the questions, while I bent down and smiled for the camera with the debris . . . only it *wasn't* the debris."

I'd seen the newspaper wire photos in Pearson's clip file: Marcel had posed with the crumpled remains of a weather balloon and its trailing radar target—aluminum foil, balsa wood, burnt rubber. Only a total chump would have mistaken this stuff for something from outer space.

"I was the fall guy," Marcel said, grinning like a skull, "the Army Air Force major who 'goofed,' who mistook a weather balloon for a flying saucer. Big joke."

Now I knew why he was talking to Pearson, intelligence officer or not; like most soldiers, Marcel would have been willing to die for his country, but it's much harder to play the fool for it. To play the sap.

"What do you think that really was out in that pasture, Jesse?"

The eyes tightened and weren't buggy, anymore. "It wasn't a goddamn weather balloon, I'll tell you that much. I was familiar with every kind of gadget we used in the Army for meteorological observations, and was in fact fairly familiar with everything in the air, at that time. Not just our own military aircraft, mind you, but other countries', too."

He pitched the still-burning butt of his latest Camel down the granite steps and it trailed sparks like a dying comet.

Then he said, flatly, "That was not a terrestrial object. It came to earth, but not from this earth."

Laughter echoed gently across the Potomac.

I put a hand on his shoulder. "What was found north of Roswell, Jesse? What were you hinting at, earlier, when you said I should talk to other people?"

He was lighting up yet another Camel. "No hearsay, Nate. I told you that."

"For Christ's sake, Jesse, we've come this far. At least point me in the right direction."

Marcel exhaled a mushroom cloud of smoke. "Well, that would be northwest, wouldn't it? Where they say the craft itself came to rest. Where they found the four little bodies."

And suddenly, as we sat there on the steps of the Water Gate, I was fresh out of questions.

Eight

ON MONDAY MORNING at the Pentagon, as a matter of good form, James V. Forrestal attended the swearing-in ceremony of his successor, lawyer Louis Johnson—chief fund-raiser for the Truman campaign—as the new Secretary of Defense. Custom had it that the outgoing cabinet officer would then proceed to the White House for a final exchange of respects with the president, a task Forrestal—being a creature of protocol—dutifully performed.

At the White House, however, the former Defense Secretary was surprised by President Truman with an assemblage of government dignitaries, including the entire cabinet and the military's Joint Chiefs of Staff. Reading from a presidential citation, Truman honored Forrestal for "meritorious and distinguished service," pinning the Distinguished Service Medal on Forrestal's lapel.

Flustered, Forrestal said, "This is beyond me . . ."

And Truman warmly clasped the deposed secretary's shoulder and said, "You deserve it, Jim."

God knew what Forrestal read into that remark.

After much applause, and many impromptu tributes, Forrestal did not make a thank-you speech. The papers, reporting this event, found Forrestal's tight-lipped non-response in keeping with the innately emotional complexion of the occasion.

While Forrestal was busy getting honored (having already been fired), I spent the day with two key people in his life: his wife and his archenemy.

I met Drew Pearson at ten a.m. on the third floor of the Metropolitan Club, a venerable, subdued bastion of respectability on Connecticut Avenue. A colored waiter in a starched white coat served us eggs Benedict; the dark-paneled room was sprinkled with selected bankers and executives doing business over breakfast.

"At noon this place is jam-packed," Pearson said, sipping a glass of orange juice. He was immaculate in a well-cut gray suit with gray-and-blue tie, the tips of his mustache waxed, sharpened. "You can't turn around without bumping into a former Secretary of State or a top diplomat."

"How is it that you're a member?"

I knew an exclusive club when I saw it; this reminded me of Chicago's Tavern Club.

"Oh I'm not," he laughed, his smile turning his eyes to slits, as he took my dig in stride. "They draw the line at only two types of members: Negroes and journalists. But I'm on the approved permanent guest list."

"I heard your broadcast last night," I said, sipping my orange juice. "Thanks."

Pearson had kept his word: no mention of Forrestal's unstable mental condition; no mention of Forrestal at all, in fact.

"I held up my end of the bargain," Pearson said, buttering a muffin. "What did you learn from Major Marcel?"

I told him Marcel's story, reading from notes I'd taken after the interview. As the fantastic aspects of the tale accelerated, Pearson's expression shifted from amused to absorbed to astonished.

"What do you make of all this?" he asked.

Our breakfast had been cleared away; we were having coffee.

"Marcel seems sincere enough," I said, "and he did not appear to be deranged, or deluded. And he was reluctant to give me any secondhand information. All of that is a plus."

"Do I detect, in your tone, the presence of a minus, as well?"

I nodded. "The guy's in intelligence work, for one thing, which makes him a ripe candidate for carrying misinformation. He's awfully high-placed to be spilling his guts like this."

"But he has credible motivation to talk," Pearson said. "If he's being truthful, then his government ordered him to go along with a deception that made him look an utter fool who mistook an ordinary weather balloon for the wreckage of a flying saucer."

"Listen to yourself, Drew. Think about your own credibility, using a term like 'flying saucer' in a sentence as if you take the possibility seriously. Major Marcel is a skilled intelligence officer, remember, fresh out of a war where propaganda and misinformation were common currency."

And yet his eyes glittered with the possibilities. "But if it's true, Nate, why . . . this is the biggest story since Jesus Christ . . ."

"What does your nose tell you?"

Pearson's motto, famously, was: "If something smells wrong, I go to work."

Now his eyes had hardened, studying me, deadly serious, even though his smile was wry. "You're a professional bloodhound, Nathan. What do your olfactories tell *you*?"

Our waiter returned to refill our coffee cups, the rich aroma drifting up.

"I'm just not sure," I said, stirring some sugar in. "The guy seems legitimate to me. If he were telling me a story that didn't have all this Buck Rogers shit in it, I'd buy him wholesale. Hell, retail."

"If the government recovered an aircraft from outer space," Pearson said melodramatically, "it might have access to new technology that could make the atomic bomb look like a popgun."

"Quit writing your column out loud; you're jumping to a preposterous conclusion."

His eyebrows climbed his chrome dome. "Am I? Suppose, as Marcel indicated, there were aliens found, as well? Do you know the implications, the ramifications? Social, political . . . religious?"

"Print that, why don't you? See how seriously you're taken, after."

He sighed and nodded. "And, as we both know, that could well be what this is all about: discrediting me."

"The only thing you might do," I said with a shrug, sipping my coffee, "is send me to Roswell to poke around a little. Talk to these other sources that Marcel mentioned."

His eyes slitted again. "How much would that cost me?"

"Who cares, if it's the biggest story of the millennium? A hundred a day and expenses."

He frowned, staring into his coffee cup. "I'll consider it." Then he looked up, arching an eyebrow. "You know, Nathan, if this is true—if there is a Majestic Twelve group in the government, that Forrestal is a part of—it could go a long way toward explaining the man's mental state."

"How so?"

"What if he's been faced with a threat from the skies?"

I smirked. "Little green men to join the Reds he's already frightened of?"

Pearson painted a picture in the air with a splay-fingered hand. "Think about it: a recovered flying saucer, advanced technology—maybe he thinks creatures from outer space are trying to kill him. Maybe they are!"

I laughed, grinned. "Definitely put that in your column. You'll be in the padded suite next to Forrestal's."

He shook his head, returning my laughter. "It does sound ridiculous. . . . Let's just put it aside, for now at least. But, uh, should I decide to explore this further . . . you are willing to make the Roswell trip?"

"As long as it's in a train or a plane," I said, sipping at my coffee cup, "and not one of these."

And I tilted my saucer.

We left it at that, and to Pearson I'm sure I seemed indifferent about whether he sent me to New Mexico or not; but in truth my curiosity was piqued.

And Pearson was right: if the government had recovered—and covered up—technology from beyond the stars, the possibility that Forrestal's condition was related to that remarkable discovery could be very real. Considering that the guy was under stress anyway, suffering from a world war's worth of physical and nervous exhaustion, being confronted suddenly with the existence of creatures from another planet just might be . . . taxing.

I didn't mention the subject to Jo Forrestal, however; she seemed only marginally more stable than her husband, as she prepared for their trip to Hobe Sound, Florida, and I supervised a sweep of their home for electronic bugs.

My A-1 Agency and Washington's Bradford Investigations supported each other in their respective cities, and two of their men took much of the day combing the big house from basement to watchtower, garage to garden. Electronic surveillance was never my specialty, though, and I spent more of my time with Jo Forrestal than with the Bradford boys.

The Filipino houseboy, Remy, had let me in, and informed me that the bug hunters had beat me there.

"Men in kitchen," the skinny little man said. He seemed kind of wild-eyed, put out by the intrusion.

I moved past half a dozen suitcases that were lined up next to the second-floor stairway—for the Florida trip, no doubt—and padded on into the kitchen, which was fairly small for such a big old house, and had been remodeled a gleaming white, cupboards and all. The two Bradford dicks were searching high and low, to the displeasure of the Negro cook, who was pacing out back, smoking and muttering.

Bob Hasty, whose last name was an inaccuracy, looked up from the black-patterned white linoleum where he was on his hands and knees, checking the floorboards, looking like a cat after a mouse. Both he and Jack Randolph, who was standing on a kitchen stool, checking the light fixture, were dressed in tan jumpsuits that looked vaguely military.

"Bowing and scraping in my presence isn't really necessary, Bob," I said. "A respectful tone will do. You could avert your eyes, maybe."

"Blow me, Heller," the round-faced Hasty said with a grin.

"Seems to me you're in a better position for that."

His lanky partner Randolph, checking the light fixture, was cackling over our witty exchange.

I asked him, "How's it going, Jack?"

"Clean so far," Randolph said. "If I get electrocuted, by the way, it's gonna cost you."

"Time and a half," I said.

Bob, who had gotten to his feet, was brushing himself off. "Nothing so far. I swept the house with a field-strength meter . . . clean as a whistle. Jack checked all the phones."

"Checked at the junction for a black box," Randolph said, "came up empty. Phones themselves seem clean—no inductive pickups, no 'suckers,' no replaced transmitters . . . but we're still at it."

"If there are bugs present," I said, "they could be very sophisticated—espionage quality."

"We're going over every floorboard," Hasty said, "every electrical fixture in the place. But I think we're on a fool's errand."

I put a hand on his shoulder. "And nobody's better at that than the Bradford agency."

"Go to hell, Heller," Hasty said with a grin, which then faded. Whispering, he said, "Say, what's the deal with the lady of the house?"

"What about her?"

"Well I think for breakfast she put a little orange juice in her vodka."

Randolph, still up on his stool, looked down at me wide-eyed. "She told us if we fucked anything of hers up, she'd have our balls. In that very language."

"She had her hand on my ass at the time," Hasty said.

So they had met Jo Forrestal.

"Well, Bob, it is a very cute ass."

And I left them to their work.

She was coming down the front stairway, so slender she seemed tall—which she wasn't—looking quietly elegant in a white blouse and black slacks. One hand casually stroked the banister as she came, the other hand held a tumbler of clear liquid and ice that I doubted was water. More than ever, she reminded me of the hostess of the house in the Charles Addams cartoons.

"Nate Heller," she said, cheerfully. "You fucking bastard."

"Nice seeing you again, too, Jo," I said.

When she reached the bottom of the stairs, I added, "You're looking lovely as ever."

She did and didn't: the pale oval of her face, the large dark eyes, the handsome features, were all still in evidence, but more pronounced, as if time had made a caricature of them; and though she hadn't gained much weight, she had the double chin that years can give anybody. Her hair was still black, but artificially so, soft curls clinging to the side of her head, the length in back hairnet-held.

"Why thank you, Nate," she said, and beamed, and slapped me, hard.

Then she clip-clopped past me, in her black high-heel sandals, into the spacious living room with its Duncan Phyfe furnishings, where she plopped into a textured cotton-and-silk-damask blue-green lounge chair and curled her legs up under her, sitting like a teenage girl.

I plodded in, rubbing where my face burned, and asked, "What did I do to deserve that greeting?"

She shrugged, sipped at her tumbler. "Maybe it's because I trusted you and took your advice, and ended up getting shock treatment. Y'suppose that could be it?"

I sat on the nearby plump beige sofa. "I'm sorry about that. I just thought they'd have you talk to a shrink; I didn't know they'd go the Frankenstein route."

"Do you have to work at it?"

"What?"

"Talking like Humphrey Bogart in some cheap movie?"

I tossed my fedora on the coffee table. "Well, first of all, he's trying to talk like me. Second of all, Bogie doesn't make cheap movies."

That made her laugh a little, then she frowned and said, "Stop that. I've decided not to like you."

"When are you leaving for Florida?"

She sipped her drink. "I'm going today. Jim can follow me down whenever he likes, or not at all."

"Why aren't you going down together?"

Her hooded-eyed, fluttering-lashed expression included a smile that had very little to do with smiling. "We don't do anything together, Nate, remember? Jim has some banquet tonight, for that horse's ass replacement of his, Johnson, and then some meeting tomorrow morning. And he wants to make himself available throughout the week, in case he's 'needed.' Do you think they'll give him shock treatment, too? Or is that just reserved for the ladies?"

"I guess I can't blame you for being bitter, but I think your husband really does need some help. Or anyway, a good long rest—and maybe a little understanding."

She laughed, once. "Excuse me while I fucking puke, Judge Hardy! I like you better when you're doing Bogart. Jim made his own bed; let him fuck and lie in it."

"Did you ever consider maybe he really is under surveillance?"

Her eyes and nostrils flared as she leaned forward. "You mean, like I was? By the Reds? See, that's typical; typical! A *woman* says that, and she's a goddamn maniac! A man, a *powerful* man like Jim, well there's either something to it, or maybe he just needs a little resty-bye. And understanding."

"Jo, it's not Jim's imagination that Drew Pearson's been out to get him. Is your maid working today?"

"No. It's her day off."

"Make some excuse and fire her. The girl's feeding information to Pearson's guy, Jack Anderson."

"What? Fuck!" She flew to her feet and hurled her glass against the wall, narrowly missing a framed Currier & Ives, taking a chunk out of the painted plaster. It wasn't anywhere near me, but I ducked reflexively, anyway.

"That little nigger bitch!" she shrieked. "And to think I treated her like a daughter!"

The Filipino houseboy, summoned by the crash of glass, peeked his head around the corner, observed the cursing Mrs. Forrestal, and disappeared like a turtle into its shell.

She raved and ranted as she crossed the Axminster carpet to a liquor cart, building herself a martini, surprisingly heavy on the vermouth. Then in mid-rant she stopped, turned and said, with no apparent irony, "I don't mean to be a shitty hostess. Can I get you something to drink, Nate?"

"No thanks."

"You think I won't drink alone?"

She was drinking before I got here, but all I said was, "Just a little early in the day for me. Don't let me stop you."

"I'd like to see you try to stop me," she said acidly, strolling back to her chair, sipping from the tumbler. "That fucking Pearson, anyway. You have a gun, don't you?"

"Not on me."

She sat again, tucking her legs back under her. "Well, you're on the job—why don't you go get it and do the world a favor and shoot that evil cocksucker."

"That's extra."

She laughed hysterically at that, tears rolling down her apple cheeks.

"It wasn't that funny, Jo."

"I know," she said, and her laughter stopped cold, like a switch had been thrown. Her face tightened with rage, but she was controlled as she said, "Do you know what that son of a bitch Pearson said about me? That I was a snob for enlisting Mainbocher! A snob!"

"Who's Mainbocher?"

"You are hopelessly unschooled, aren't you? Mainbocher is only one of finest purveyors of fashion in the world, you dumb fucking cluck. And I got him to help me design new uniforms for the Waves! Which are so much more chic than those Wac rags; but that bald bastard Pearson has the balls to *criticize* me for it!"

I was vaguely aware that Forrestal had attempted to involve Jo, to make her feel she had a role in Washington, and the war effort; and it didn't surprise me that Pearson had crucified her for it.

Her eyebrows rose and the big eyes got huge. "You know what I was being paid to be a consultant to the Waves? Nothing! Not a red fucking cent! So I quit.... I told Jim he could fight the goddamn war by himself, and Pearson and the rest of the columnists could kiss my ass!"

"Was that columnists or Communists?"

Her expression froze, and then she broke out into brittle, near-hysterical laughter. Holding her stomach, rocking in the easy chair, laughing. I was a riot today. Maybe Jack Benny needed a new writer.

"Oh, I could use you around here, Nate. You would definitely cheer me up. You wanna go to Florida with us?"

"Jim wants me to, but I'm not sure . . ."

"We have separate bedrooms down there, just like up here. You can slip into my room late, and fuck me till my eyes pop out of my head."

"Well, that's nice to know . . ."

"And no one the wiser, not that anyone would give a shit." She rose and wobbled over to me and sat in my lap. "Of course, there's always right now—upstairs. Jim won't be home till after that banquet tonight, and I'll be long gone, on my way to Florida."

She was long gone now.

Her hands were locked behind my neck as she wiggled her bottom into my lap. "Or are those awful little men of yours still snooping about?"

The scent of Chanel No. 5, and her still slenderly appealing figure, almost made it tempting, no matter how drunk she was. But in a way I still thought she was bluffing: those years of "open marriage," with Forrestal banging half the good-looking broads in D.C., were a one-sided affair. That was my instinct, anyway.

"Jo, you're a lovely woman," I said, not exactly lying. "But let's not rush things."

"Why? Which of us is getting younger?"

I kissed her, tenderly, and it wasn't half bad. "Let's wait for a better moment."

She shrugged. "All right," she said, in a small voice, slipping off my lap. But once she got on her feet, she bellowed, "It's your fucking loss!"

Then she wheeled and pointed a finger right at me; remarkably, it didn't tremble at all. Auntie Jo wanted me.

"Did it ever occur to you, shithead, that maybe I had the idea people were after me because my husband *made* me think that? He's been nuts longer than I have! He was the one who saw Reds under the bed! I just caught the sickness from *him*, I just didn't wear it as well as he did . . . still waters running deep and all. Because I'm a little more *outgoing* than he is, because I'm a mother and got concerned about my children being kidnapped, because I believed the paranoid rambling fucking delusions of a man who was supposed to be a goddamn fucking tower of strength, a powerful man who oughta know whether somebody's out to fucking get us or not, well then . . . what was the question?"

"I don't think I asked one."

"Don't mind if I do."

"Don't mind if you do what?"

"Have another drink."

And she ambled over to the liquor cart and built herself another one; again, the vermouth outdistanced the gin, but that didn't help much, as many as she was throwing down.

"So," she said, falling into the chair but not spilling a drop, "is anybody *really* trying to kill the great former Secretary Forrestal?"

"I don't believe so, no. . . . I, uh, think I'm gonna see how my men are doing."

"You do that. You do that."

I did that, and when I came back, she'd fallen asleep in the chair. Her tumbler—which was empty— I plucked from her hands and set on the coffee table.

When she woke up, a little over two hours later, with a kind of spasm, eyes snapping wide open, she asked, "What time is it?"

"Three-fifteen," I said, checking my wristwatch.

I was sitting on the sofa, reading an old issue of *Time* with her husband's picture on it. Bob Hasty and Jack Randolph had pronounced the residence free of bugs—at least the electronic kind—and were fifteen minutes gone.

"Shit!" She slapped the arms of the easy chair. "Why didn't you wake me?"

"Was I supposed to?"

She jack-in-the-boxed to her feet, glaring at me. "My flight's in an hour; cab'll be here any minute."

She hustled off, almost ran up the steps, and came down several minutes later, with a flowing black jacket over her white blouse and black slacks; she'd added some jewelry—black-and-white round earrings, a jeweled brooch, some rings—and had freshened her makeup. It wasn't hard to remember that she had once been extremely beautiful, enough so to pose for *Vogue*.

I met her as she reached the bottom of the stairs. "You look swell," I said.

"Thank you." She had a watch on now, and was winding it. "I'm, uh . . . sorry if I seemed rude, earlier. I have a bad habit of speaking my mind—particularly to people I like."

"I thought you'd decided not to like me."

She touched my face with a slender hand. "I changed my mind. Would you see if my cab is out front? I have to leave some instructions with Remy."

"I haven't seen him since you tossed that glass."

Her tiny smile was an odd mix of embarrassment and pride. "He retreats to his rabbithole when I'm on a rampage."

The cab indeed was waiting, and I went out and told the cabbie his fare would be along shortly. In the meantime, I carried out her bags and the cabbie helped me load them in his trunk, though they wouldn't all fit; a few had to go in the backseat.

Inside, I found her snugging on some white gloves; a big black patent-leather handbag was slung over her shoulder, and she looked rather stylish—as chic as a well-dressed Wave.

"Have a good trip," I said. "I'm making a full report on my investigation to your husband, tomorrow. Any message for him?"

"Just that I hope he'll join me soon."

"Is that concern I hear?"

"I love Jim, in my way, as I'm sure he loves me in his." She kissed my cheek, tickled the side of my face with gloved fingertips. "You're really a very sweet man."

"You know, you haven't cursed in something like five minutes; it makes me uneasy."

She laughed and this time it lacked the brittle hysteria. "Well, then, Nate, why don't you go fuck yourself."

"That's extra, too."

She laughed some more and, as if she were a duchess on her way to the ball, I escorted her to the cab and waved as she drove off. She waved from her backseat window, and smiled, but if I'd ever seen a sadder expression, I couldn't remember when.

My day's work was done; I'd be leaving Washington tomorrow, I'd decided. The evening was mine, and I had a date with Anya, the blonde in Pearson's office, who in that wonderful accent had requested I not tell her boss.

Well, if she insisted.

Anyway, it was nice to know Drew Pearson wasn't on top of everything that went on in this town.

Nine

THE DAY AFTER he reluctantly stepped aside as Secretary of Defense, James Forrestal was honored by a rare special meeting of the House Armed Services Committee, at which he was lavishly praised by committee chairman Carl Vinson and ranking minority member Representative Dewey Short. Forrestal was presented with a silver bowl, "engraved with our names in testimony of our regards—a regard also indelibly inscribed in our hearts."

The flustered Forrestal of the day before, struck dumb by surprise and emotion, was replaced by a prepared, dignified statesman who delivered several brief, gracious speeches.

Also attending—and celebrating Forrestal's accomplishments in public life—were his successor, Louis Johnson; Secretary of the Army Kenneth Royall; Secretary of the Navy John Sullivan; and Secretary of the Air Force Stuart Symington. The press made much of the kind words the latter said about Forrestal, and vice versa, as the onetime friends had become bitter adversaries over matters of budget, among other things, with the Air Force Secretary's disloyal, harsh criticism of Forrestal in a notorious *New York Times* interview almost getting Symington fired.

The warmly positive press coverage of Jim Forrestal and the honors bestowed him on that Tuesday morning held no hint of the bizarre, even tragic turn the rest of that day would take.

My appointment with Forrestal, to report on my investigation, was in the afternoon, three o'clock, and shortly before that time I rang the bell of Morris House on Prospect Street. A light, pleasant breeze ruffled my lightweight tropical suit and my hat was in my hand when the Filipino houseboy, Remy, again wild-eyed, answered; but this time Remy was not annoyed, but visibly upset.

"Mr. Heller," Remy said. "So glad to see you."

"What's wrong?"

"Please come in."

I did. The house was dark—every light was off, all the blinds drawn.

" 'Cept for cook, I am alone of staff," Remy said. "Mrs. Forrestal give Miss Brown, Mr. Campbell week off. Because of Florida trip."

Stanley Campbell was Forrestal's butler/valet, a trusted right-hand man.

Turning my hat in my hands, I asked, "Where's your boss?"

Remy pointed a tremulous finger, toward the living room. There, seated in the same easy chair Jo Forrestal had curled up in yesterday, sat Forrestal, but on the edge of it, rigidly erect. He was wearing his hat, and looked small in his well-tailored gray suit, which was only a slightly darker gray than his complexion; he seemed even thinner and more haggard than he had in his golfing attire, collar hanging loosely from a creped neck. His hands were on his knees, his eyes staring straight ahead, unblinking. He might have been a statue; he might have been dead.

Before him on the coffee table was the engraved silver bowl.

Then I realized he was saying something—muttering—though the thin line of his mouth barely moved.

"Hello, Jim," I said, taking off my hat, moving into the room.

Now I could hear him. "You're a loyal fellow," he was saying, with no inflection whatsoever. "You're a loyal fellow."

I pulled over a fan-back chair and sat opposite him, with the coffee table between us; his eyes showed no sign of registering my presence.

"We had an appointment, Jim," I said. "I need to make my report. I think you're going to be pleased."

He blinked, once, and now his eyes seemed to land on me, instead of look right through me.

But he still said only, "You're a loyal fellow."

Was he talking about me, or himself? Had he discovered my affiliation with Pearson, and was this a sort of shell-shocked sarcasm?

Remy was standing in the archway between the living room and the entry hall; he called out, "Mr. Forrestal! It's Mr. Eberstadt again! He says you must come to phone."

Forrestal's head turned slowly on his neck, like a well-oiled moving part.

"No," he said.

Then just as slowly, his head returned to its forward staring position.

"Just a second, Remy," I said. "I'll take it."

The phone was on a stand in the hallway, but out of Forrestal's earshot, so I was free to talk.

"This is Nate Heller, Mr. Eberstadt," I said. Investment banker Eberstadt was one of my client's oldest, dearest friends; I'd seen them playing golf together at Burning Tree, Saturday.

"You seem to know who I am," he said, in a commanding baritone. "Who the hell are you?"

"I'm an investigator Jim hired to see who was trying to kill him."

"Oh, my God," he groaned. "I hope by now you know the real nature of his problem."

"I'd say I do. Right now he's sitting in the living room with his hat on muttering about what a 'loyal fellow' he, or somebody, is."

"What's your appraisal of the immediate situation?"

"I'd say he's about two inches away from falling off Catatonic Cliff."

"Damnit." A weary concern colored Eberstadt's tone. "I got a similar report from Marx Leva, his assistant at the Pentagon. Seems James was fine at the ceremonies honoring him this morning, but when he returned to his office, he just sat and stared at the wall . . . with his hat on. I think it may have been that goddamn Symington's fault."

"Symington?"

"James was supposed to go back to the Pentagon, not to his old office, but another one that's been set aside for him, so he can deal with the nice letters that've been coming in from all over. Symington apparently went out of his way to give Jim a ride back over there."

"That sounds like a friendly gesture to me."

"I don't think it was. Leva said Symington told Jim, emphatically, 'There's something we must talk about.' "

"So what did they talk about?"

"Leva doesn't know; Symington insisted on privacy. But James was a different man after that ride— Symington must have said something that shattered whatever remained of James' defenses, that double-dealing son of a bitch."

A crazy thought flitted through my mind: Symington, as the Secretary of the Air Force, would surely know about the Roswell incident. Could that "something important" he had to discuss with Forrestal have had to do with a recovered flying saucer and the bodies of little green men?

And, having had that thought, who the hell was I to question Jim Forrestal's sanity?

Eberstadt was saying, "I'm really worried about James. Can you stay there with him?"

"Sure."

"You know, this assistant of his, Leva, called me over at the Capitol, had me paged, really concerned. After sitting there for an hour or so, like you're witnessing—just staring and muttering, 'You're a loyal fellow'—James finally asked Leva to call for his car; he wanted to go home. And that was a problem."

"Why?"

"James doesn't have an official car, anymore. It's Louis Johnson's now; and Leva was afraid if he called a cab, it might upset his boss. So I got Vannevar Bush to send over his chauffeured limo."

"Who?"

"Bush, Vannevar Bush."

Christ—Bush was one of the Majestic Twelve! That atom bomb scientist Pearson mentioned who, with Forrestal, was part of the top-secret research and development group supposedly investigating the "flying saucer problem."

Maybe Jo Forrestal was right: maybe paranoia *was* catching.

"I can't get away for half an hour, at the least," Eberstadt was saying. "Will you stay with James, till I can get there?"

"Won't let him out of my sight."

"Good man."

I hung up, went back into the living room, where Forrestal's posture hadn't changed.

"Take off your hat and stay awhile," I said, gently.

He gazed at me, gray-blue eyes in a gray face; there was something lizardlike about it.

Gently, I removed his hat, tossed it next to mine on the coffee table. Then I sat opposite him and said, "I need to make my report. Jim, are you listening?"

He blinked, several times. "Nate Heller," he said, obviously noticing my presence for the first time.

"Hi, Jim. All right with you if I let you know what I came up with?"

His nod was barely perceptible.

"You're aware that we did a full sweep of the house for electronic surveillance, yesterday? You got the note I left to that effect?"

Another barely perceptible nod.

"Well, I used the best men in the city; they didn't find a damn thing. On the other hand, I have learned that Pearson was bribing one of your household staff—Della Brown—for any tidbits of personal gossip; I told Jo yesterday, and, obviously, recommended firing the girl."

He said nothing; but at least he did seem to be listening.

"Now, I've learned that the Secret Service has been keeping your home under surveillance. That's not because they wish you ill, quite the opposite. They learned of your fears that someone was trying to 'get' you, and—much as I have—they investigated."

His eyes left my face, dropping to the silver bowl, where he could stare at his reflection, and it could stare back at him.

"So, you were right, Jim—you were being watched; and your suspicions about Pearson were, to some degree, well placed. But I've found no indication at all that your life is in any danger."

The single line of his mouth twitched in something

that was almost a smile. "Really?" He rose, as fluidly and slowly as Bela Lugosi waking up in his coffin. He crooked his finger. "Come with me."

I followed him to the window across the room; he parted a blind and said, softly, "On the corner."

On that same bench I'd inhabited not so long ago, in front of the weathered gray-brick colonial house with the tours and the coffee shop, sat a couple of pasty-faced kids in their early twenties wearing colorful but soiled T-shirts and dingy jeans and tennis shoes. They were either out of work or avoiding it, and when the next cop came along, they'd no doubt be told to shove off.

"Russians," Forrestal said ominously, and let the blinds snap shut.

"I kind of doubt that, Jim," I said.

His head swiveled and he fixed narrowed eyes upon me. "They were waiting for me when I got home."

The doorbell rang and he jumped; but hell, so did I.

The houseboy, moving quickly, went to answer it. Couldn't be Eberstadt already, could it?

"I know you mean well, Nate," Forrestal said quietly, taking me by the arm, "but you haven't found the truth. They're after me, they're still after me."

"Who?"

"All of them. All of those I've opposed."

"A conspiracy, you mean?"

He squeezed my arm. "Exactly. Commies, Russians, Jews, as well as certain . . . parties in the White House. That's why they've fooled you: you're looking for one villain. But it's all of them—in concert."

Maybe I could start my new investigation at the Water Gate band shell.

"They've united against me," he said, "their common enemy."

I could hear the muffled sound of the houseboy dealing with somebody at the front door.

Still latching onto my arm, Forrestal whispered into my ear: "They're probably in the house right now, some of them."

"They're not in this house, Jim."

"Keep your voice down. Don't you know this house is wired?"

"It's not wired. My men went over it, I told you, stem to stern."

His eyes tightened and so did his grip on my arm. "If you don't lower your voice, I'll be forced to ask you to leave."

Remy stood nervously at the archway. "There is a man want to see him."

The houseboy was addressing me, pointing to his boss.

Forrestal clutched my arm, desperately. "I won't see anyone."

I extricated myself, gently, saying, "I'll talk to him, Jim. Just take it easy."

The man on the front stoop was short, plump, with a receding hairline, wire-frame glasses, and though it was a cool afternoon, sweat beaded his round face. He wore a crumpled-looking brown off-the-rack business suit and a blue-and-red tie and carried a battered briefcase.

"I need to see Mr. Forrestal," the man said in a thick Southern accent.

"That's impossible right now."

"I'm Phil Dingel—from North Carolina?"

Oh, well, hell—that changed everything.

"Look, sir," I said. "Mr. Forrestal is not available."

"But he knows me—I was an alternate delegate from North Carolina . . . at the convention in '48? And Mr. Forrestal promised he'd throw his support my way for my appointment to postmaster, back home."

"You want to be postmaster, huh?"

"Why, yes!"

"Then write him a letter," I said, and shut the door in his face. Fucking political worm.

In the living room, Forrestal was watching at the window, blinds again parted; his face was clenched. "See! You see, Nate?"

I took a look. The plump would-be Podunk postmaster, who had worse timing than a pregnant teenager waiting for her period, had stopped to talk to the two unshaven vagrant kids on the bench.

"You see, he's one of them," Forrestal said excitedly. "They're everywhere!"

"Let me check into it," I said easily.

Soon I was cutting across the street, approaching the boys on the bench. They were both skinny with greasy hair, bad complexions, and worse attitudes.

"What did the fat guy want?" I asked.

The skinnier of the two sneered. "What's it to ya, pops?"

Knocking their heads together might have agitated Forrestal, so I got out my wallet and flashed my Illinois private investigator's badge; that usually works.

They both sat up straight, like kids reprimanded in school, and the other one said, "Guy just wanted to know if this was a bus stop. I said no, but he could catch a trolley over that way."

I still had my wallet out. "How would you fellas like to earn a five-spot each?"

The skinnier one sneered. "Who do we have to kill?"

His pal laughed at that; they didn't know how funny it really was.

I said, "Just find another bench to park your butts on."

They looked at each other and shrugged; the skinnier one said, "Okay, pops."

So I peeled off a couple of fives, and the kids got lost. Strange how cheap Russian agents could be bought off, these days.

When I went inside, Forrestal was not in sight, but I could hear a racket upstairs. The houseboy was at the foot of the stairs, wringing his hands.

"What's going on, Remy?"

"Mr. Forrestal, he looking." And he gestured to an open closet door near the entrance, where coats and hats, among other things, had been scattered about.

"Looking for what?"

"Somebody hiding."

I found him in his own bedroom, a warmly masculine chamber of walnut furnishings, wood-tone floral Axminster carpet, dark woodwork and cream-painted plaster. He was searching in the dark. This was obviously a room that had been fastidiously shipshape, even down to the neatly stacked half a dozen formidable volumes on the nightstand—light reading like Nietzsche, Proust and Kafka—or anyway it had been until its occupant had scoured the walk-in closet, leaving the door open, clothes and other belongings strewn as if by a careless burglar. Right now he was on his hands and knees, looking under his double bed.

It had come to this: Forrestal literally looking for Reds under his bed. Not to mention Jews and traitorous White House types.

"There's no one under there, Jim," I said, and helped him to his feet. His body was like a bag of loose bones.

"We have to search the whole house. I have more closets to search!"

There was no stopping him, so I didn't try to. He emptied every closet in the house; he ransacked the basement and the garage, and I accompanied him. Finally the effort began to wear at him, and the frail former Secretary of Defense stumbled back into his living room and into that same chair, with the silver bowl before him, gleaming, empty.

"They were here," he said. "They must have heard me come in. Got out the back way."

I sat down again. "Jim, I think you ought to get out of here. Your wife's down in Florida. You said you have friends down there waiting for you. Relax . . . unwind."

"You don't understand how insidious they are. I've been chosen; I've been marked."

"Chosen? Marked, how?"

"I'm not the number one target—just the first to be liquidated. Because I tried to alert America to the menace."

"What menace, Jim?"

He was trembling all over. "The Kremlin plans to liquidate all our top leadership in Washington; the Reds are planning an invasion as we speak. The first wave, the secret wave, is already here!"

I had to ask; at this point, what would it hurt to ask?

"Jim . . . what about Roswell, Jim?"

His eyes widened and flickered, as if I'd lighted a flame in them. "How do you know about Roswell?"

"You mentioned it," I lied.

". . . I've done a bad thing." He shook his head. "I've done a bad thing. Sometimes you do bad things, to try to do right, don't you?"

"Sure, sure . . ."

The flames in his eyes flickered out. He sighed and his body seemed to deflate. His face had a flatness,

like a frying pan, his wide eyes like fried eggs clinging
to it. "Do you know what it's like?"

"What what is like?"

"Being a complete failure? Failing your family,
your country, yourself?"

"Stop it, now."

"My life's a wreck. A shambles. I know terrible
things; I did terrible things, allowed terrible things to
be done.... Have you ever considered suicide, Nate?
If there was a button I could push, and end my life,
I'd push it. Why should I give them the satisfaction of
ending my life, when I can do it myself?"

"You've been through the mill, Jim. Things look this
way because of your overwork. You're exhausted ..."

He shrugged, just a little. "That's probably because
I haven't had a full night's sleep in months. My teeth
ache ... my intestines are all out of whack ... all my
normal bodily functions are breaking down. I'm not
even a man, anymore. Do you have your gun?"

His wife had asked me the same thing, only she'd
been joking, and wanted Pearson's hide; I knew, with
cold certainty, that if I handed this man a gun, he'd
shoot himself, right in front of me.

The doorbell rang.

Remy ran for it, and thank God, it was Eberstadt.
Relief flooded through me, as I went to meet him.

"You're Heller?" he asked, stepping inside, a tall,
well-tailored, square-jawed handsome man of
around sixty with the look of a former athlete and
hair the color of burnished steel.

I said I was Heller, and we shook hands, and I took
him aside and whispered, "He's talking suicide. I'm
out of my depth here, Mr. Eberstadt. He's your
friend—help him."

He nodded gravely, said, "Thanks for standing
watch."

From where we stood, we could see into the living room where Forrestal sat, having again lapsed into a sort of trance, now holding the empty bowl in his hands, staring into it.

"Where's his valet?" Eberstadt asked.

"Has the week off, 'cause of the Florida trip. The houseboy's around somewhere."

"Would you find Remy and have him pack a bag for James, some sports clothes and the like, maybe round up his golf clubs. I'm going to get him to Hobe Sound, where he can rest in the sunshine, in the company of close friends."

I shook my head. "Anything you say, but I think he's a little past the vacation stage. He needs medication, and he needs supervision—away from sharp objects."

"I appreciate your advice, but please do as I ask."

"Sure," I said, and I found Remy in his quarters and sent him on his mission. Then I slipped into Forrestal's study, got out my wallet, found the slip of paper I'd been given by Frank J. Wilson and used the phone.

"Chief Baughman," I said to the head of the Secret Service, "you wanted me to call if something interesting developed?"

Ten

My call to Chief Baughman set several things in motion. Within half an hour, at Morris House, Eberstadt heard by phone from Louis Johnson, Forrestal's successor, expressing grave concern about Forrestal's condition.

The President was providing an Air Force Constellation, Eberstadt was told, to facilitate the former secretary's much-needed vacation; and by early evening Forrestal had arrived in Florida, where a formidable circle of friends—including banker (and former Under Secretary of State) Robert Lovett, Douglas Dillon of Dillon, Read & Company and playwright Philip Barry—took him under their wing.

Jo Forrestal was staying at the Jupiter Island Club, but Forrestal was soon in a private home where he was attended day and night by Eberstadt and others, including Dr. William Menninger of Topeka's Menninger Clinic. The presence of Menninger, the country's preeminent psychiatrist, was Eberstadt's doing.

Ironically, Menninger had been invited to the Pentagon just months before, to aid in a Forrestal-directed study of combat fatigue; Forrestal and Menninger had spent a morning together, discussing the subject, at which time Menninger apparently noticed nothing of a similar (or any) malady in the behavior of the Secretary of Defense.

Nonetheless (Eberstadt told me on the phone), this brief contact and casual acquaintanceship had made Forrestal willing to at least talk with Menninger.

But, at the same time, the government sent down their own man, Captain George N. Raines, chief psychiatrist at the Bethesda naval hospital. This may have reflected President Truman's natural humanistic concern for a great public servant in a time of dire need; or it may have indicated the administration's desire to contain the incident and handle the manner in which the press and public learned that a crazy man, until a day or so ago, had been their Secretary of Defense, holding his fingers to the nation's atomic pulse.

I had intended to return to Chicago that same evening Forrestal made his Florida trip; but the Secret Service "requested" that I stay in Washington for "debriefing," and at both Treasury and Justice I was questioned by Baughman himself, and Frank Wilson, and several other agents whose names I did not know (and which were not offered to me). This exercise in repetitiousness took three days, and the government was kind enough to pick up my hotel check for my extended stay—one of the rare times my tax dollars came back to me.

I was frank about what I'd witnessed regarding former Secretary of Defense Forrestal's mental breakdown, and filled them in on my own meager investigation, from the maid leaking to Anderson to the unproductive sweep of Forrestal's home for bugs; but none of my dealings with Pearson came up, specifically no mention of Roswell or Majestic Twelve. Had they asked me, I would have been forthcoming (because if they asked, that would indicate knowledge on their part, possibly stemming from sur-

veillance of myself and/or Pearson); but they didn't
ask. And I didn't tell.

Friday afternoon marked the final stop of my debriefing tour, which took me tooling through the suburban slumber of white cottages and brick bungalows
that was Bethesda, and beyond into the flat, green
countryside of Maryland. Just when I thought I'd misunderstood the directions, easing the rental Ford up
over a little rise in U.S. Route 240, a nineteen-story
white tower rose out of nowhere like an *art moderne*
apparition; it was as if the Empire State Building had
sprouted in a pasture.

The National Naval Medical Center sprawled over
some 265 acres, the central tower flanked by L-
shaped four-floor wings, a complex at once utilitarian
and starkly beautiful, modern and timeless, its struc-
tural steel faced with white-quartz-aggregate concrete panels, dark spandrels between windows
creating an effect of massive square columns.

On the periphery of the endless parking lot were
many squat temporary buildings, so this facility—
which had seemed so vast during the war—was already experiencing growing pains. The bustling lobby
was lined with three colors of marble, and the corridors were a soothingly cool terra-cotta; the naval nature of the place was evident by not only the gob and
jarhead patients, but the sailor-style attire of nurses
and attendants, and the uniformed doctors.

While Bethesda—a site supposedly chosen by
Roosevelt himself, because biblically Bethesda had
been "the pool of healing"—was primarily a naval
hospital, medical and dental schools were also a part
of the complex. So was the Naval Medical Research
Institute, a separate building I was directed to, where
I was to meet with Dr. Joseph Bernstein, Chief of
Psychiatric Research.

Not a military man himself (not all the doctors at Bethesda were, particularly in the research area), Bernstein had a compact, linebacker's frame wrapped in a white smock jacket; his blue tie bore a Star of David tie tack. Perhaps fifty, he had short-cropped blond hair going white, though the difference was negligible, and he had eyes so light blue they were almost gray, and eyebrows so light they disappeared. This gave him an eerily albino cast, that his handsome features—Roman nose, dazzling smile, and square jaw—did not quite dispel.

Standing behind his desk in a small, spartan third-floor office, he offered a hand for me to shake, which I did. Firm but not showy.

"I appreciate your willingness to speak with me," he said, in friendly but clipped manner, with an understated middle-European accent. "I take it you're Jewish, Mr. Heller?"

"Sort of."

Dr. Bernstein settled into his chair as I took the one opposite him. "And what does that mean, 'sort of'?"

I explained, and he said, "I have never been religious, either, but I hope one day to go to Palestine, myself."

"Oh?"

He folded his hands on his desk, prayerfully, on a manila file folder; they were large, thick-fingered hands and I was glad he wasn't a surgeon. "Most of my relatives died in concentration camps, Mr. Heller. I was fortunate to leave Germany in the late twenties, and establish a practice in Zürich."

"Yeah, well, that's sure shrink country, isn't it?"

That stopped him for a moment, but then he laughed, once—politely, I thought.

He raised an invisible eyebrow. "You have a rough-hewn wit, Mr. Heller."

"That's one way to describe it, I guess. All right if I ask you something?"

"Certainly."

"Why the nickel tour through your background, Doc? No offense, but I don't give a flying, rough-hewn fuck. Uncle Sam has bounced me from here to there, for three days, asking me questions, and now I have to spend the afternoon at a head clinic. Not my favorite tourist spot."

His smile was small and casual, but his eyes were studying me; he unfolded his hands and picked up the manila folder. "Would that be because you were once a patient at such a facility yourself?"

"Not here. I was across town at St. Elizabeth's, or do you know that? Is that my file?"

Everybody had a fucking file on me.

He tossed the folder to one side of his tidy desk. "You had amnesia induced by combat fatigue. You recovered your identity, through hypnosis therapy, but your condition was deemed serious enough not to return you to combat. You were discharged on a Section Eight."

"Now we know both our life stories. Is there anything else, Doc?"

His expression turned somber. "I shared my background with you because I understand that you are Mr. Forrestal's friend."

"He's my client. We're friendly enough, but it's a business relationship."

He gestured with an open hand. "I wanted to be frank about my background, and my . . . support for the new state of Israel . . . because if you were to learn that background from someone else, you might assume I'd been less than forthcoming in an area sensitive to this patient's case. You are the first representative of the Forrestal family that I've spoken to—"

"I don't represent the Forrestal family. I work for them, or I did. I've completed the assignment, and plan to submit my bill. Please tell me insanity isn't grounds for nonpayment."

That made him smile, a little. "Perhaps my concerns were misplaced. I thought you should know that my politics will not be a conflict of interest in my involvement with Mr. Forrestal's case."

"Oh. Okay, I get it: you're not one of the Zionists out to get Forrestal, 'cause of his anti-Israeli tendencies. Well, I'd worry more about convincing Forrestal of that."

"Captain Raines will be the primary physician on this case," he said. That faint accent combined with his impeccable English somehow added weight to his words. "I will be a consultant, an adviser; in fact, if Captain Raines were not still in Florida, with his patient, you would be speaking to him and not me."

"You're more in research, is that it?"

"Yes. Like Dr. Menninger, who is also involved in this case, I'm delving into operational fatigue, that is, combat fatigue and related battle neuroses . . . and certainly Mr. Forrestal's case—like yours—touches upon that area. He shows that the casualties of our recent world war are not confined to combat."

"Fine. Swell. I'm here to cooperate; what do you want to know?"

He asked different questions than the feds, but got the same answers: everyone wanted to know what Forrestal had been saying, how he'd been behaving. It didn't take as long to fill Dr. Bernstein in, however, because—unlike the Secret Service and the FBI—he had no interest in my own investigative efforts.

When we'd come to the end of his questions, I asked Bernstein one of my own: "Do I gather you're bringing Forrestal back to Bethesda?"

A tiny shrug. "It's no secret: he'll be flown here tomorrow."

I had called Eberstadt in Florida, the day after Forrestal had been flown down there, and he'd indicated Dr. Menninger was the doctor in charge, that Captain Raines was only consulting.

So I asked, "Why isn't Forrestal going to the Menninger Clinic, in Topeka? That's the best psychiatric facility in the country, I understand."

His response was faintly defensive: "The treatment here at Bethesda is among the best available, anywhere. Also, treatment this close to home will make Mr. Forrestal feel at ease, and his family and friends will have convenient access to him, providing support he'll need to recover."

"Does Dr. Menninger agree with this?"

"Frankly, no . . . but the general consensus is that Mr. Forrestal will be better served here, in a general hospital, than in a psychiatric clinic."

"Why?"

Dr. Bernstein twitched a non-smile. "Committal to a mental hospital would be an embarrassment to a public person like James Forrestal—"

"An embarrassment to the government, you mean."

"The stigma of mental illness in so public and powerful a man might engender a feeling of hopelessness, even despair . . . *in the patient.*"

I leaned back in my chair, gestured expansively. "Hey, I don't blame the White House for wanting to control this. How would the country respond to knowing that, till last Monday, its national security was in the hands of a fruitcake?"

"Your flip manner does not fool me, Mr. Heller. I know you are deeply concerned about Mr. Forrestal."

" 'Deeply' overdoes it, Doc, but the question is, are you? Keeping him here will make it easier to isolate him, screen visitors, keep out the press, maintain strict security. All of that's great for the government. What's it do for the patient?"

Both invisible eyebrows lifted this time. "He's suffering from a form of combat fatigue; where better to receive treatment than a naval hospital?"

"He doesn't have combat fatigue, Doc; he worked long hours and suffered stress, but he didn't have bullets flying around his head and Japs with bayonets in his lap, and as a bona fide star-spangled combat-fatigue graduate, with a Section Eight for a diploma, I resent the term being bandied about."

Bells were quietly ringing outside; time in this naval hospital was told by ship's bell system.

The handsome near-albino combined a patronizing smile with a regal nod. "Mr. Heller, you're quite right. Mr. Forrestal is most likely suffering from a depressive condition common to middle-aged men: involutional melancholia. In such cases, the mental faculties become less acute, there's a tendency to bemoan past mistakes, a feeling takes hold that the future holds no promise. Doubt, indecision, fear, anxiety manifest themselves. And there are physical effects, also: the internal secretion glands begin malfunctioning, resulting in a general overall lowering of bodily health."

"Maybe you do know your stuff."

"Maybe I do." His eyes narrowed, his brow tensed, which caused his eyebrows to show up better. "I do know your friend . . . your client . . . will not survive long without hospitalization and around-the-clock care. The reports from Florida are disturbing, to say the least."

"I know."

I'd spoken to Eberstadt again, yesterday, and heard a harrowing tale of suicide attempts and constant supervision. In the early-morning hours, not long after Forrestal arrived, a fire engine had gone by, its siren wailing, sending the former Secretary of Defense bolting from his bed, running in his nightshirt into the street, screaming, "The Russians are attacking! The Russians are attacking!"

Dr. Bernstein stood, a cue for me to do the same, which I did.

He said, "I can assure you, Mr. Heller, that both Captain Raines and I will do everything in our power to see that Mr. Forrestal's stay at Bethesda is as short as possible."

"Didn't mean to give you a hard time, Doc," I said, and handed him my business card. "I'll be back in my Chicago office tomorrow morning, if there's anything you need."

"Thank you, Mr. Heller." He ushered me to the door, and smiled almost shyly. "And if I'm not being too personal, as one rather nonreligious Jew to another, I hope one day you will come to embrace your Jewish side, as I have."

"Yeah, well I plan to start with a pastrami and Swiss cheese sandwich in about half an hour."

From my room at the Ambassador, I made one more call to Florida, again talking to Eberstadt.

Eberstadt said that he and Dr. Menninger were against the Bethesda decision, but had been overruled.

"Who by?" I asked.

"Jo Forrestal and President Truman."

"What? How the hell—?"

"Jo is adamant about protecting James' reputation from the 'stigma of mental illness,' which she felt would be inevitable if he was admitted to such a famous psychiatric clinic as Dr. Menninger's. She talked it over with Truman, on the phone, and he agreed with her and put the Bethesda plan in motion."

"And you think it's a mistake."

"Hundreds of cases of operational fatigue have been successfully treated at Topeka. But what can you do? She's his wife."

"And he's our president."

"Don't blame me," Eberstadt said, "I voted for Dewey."

That night I returned to Chicago, and the next day Forrestal was admitted to Bethesda. (When his plane landed, he had refused to disembark until the airport had been cleared of "all Air Force men and Jews," a request that was not fulfilled.) On April 11, the newspapers finally reported the former Secretary of Defense was under treatment at the naval hospital for "nervous and physical exhaustion." In covering the explosive story, the press showed restraint, for the most part.

With the exception of Drew Pearson, who made a feast of the news, distorting Forrestal's behavior in Hobe Sound into hourly suicide attempts and constant raving about the Reds. Forrestal was a "madman" who'd had access to atomic bombs, and Pearson wondered in his column and on his radio broadcast just how gravely the secretary's insanity had jeopardized national security.

It was typical Pearson: bombastic, overstated, cruel . . .

. . . and a damn good question.

TWO:

BLUE SKIES

ROSWELL, NEW MEXICO
APRIL 1949

Eleven

SOUTHEASTERN NEW MEXICO, this part of it any-way, was not what I had expected. I was beginning my trip to Roswell with a detour, heading up Highway 70 in yet another rental Ford (a green one), but cutting over at Alamogordo, maybe an hour and fifteen minutes out of El Paso, to take Highway 82 with a village called Cloudcroft as my destination. I was in the foothills of the Sacramento Mountains, and on the winding eighteen-mile drive, past roadside produce stands peddling apples and cider, I climbed five thousand ear-popping feet, scenic overlooks frequently presenting themselves, views of sprawling desert dotted with sagebrush, yucca and cacti from a forest thick with pine, blue spruce and aspen; it was like seeing Mexico from Canada. From certain overlooks, the glittering white sands that gave White Sands its name were in amazing evidence, as if snow had fallen in the desert.

The more typical drive to Alamogordo—at one point crossing through a plateau-bounded basin—had been hot and dry, my cotton knit yellow-and-brown T-shirt and brown tropical worsted slacks sticking to me like flypaper (the T-shirt a Navajo pattern purchased at Sears in Chicago, to help me fit in out here in the wide open spaces). The brim of my straw fedora was snugged down, but the sun hadn't bothered me—I wasn't even wearing the sunglasses I'd brought along, enjoying the endless skies, which were a clear, rich, unthreatening blue, the occasional clouds looking unreal, like an artist's bold brush-strokes. The lack of glare, however, didn't keep that dry heat from turning the Ford into an oven, even with the windows down.

Now, up in these mountains, I found myself rolling the windows up; it was getting chilly, the shadows of evening creeping in like friendly marauders. I had to slip my tan notch-lapel sportjacket on when I pulled over by the road to watch the setting sun paint the desert more colors than an Indian blanket—a gaudy one, at that.

It had taken Drew Pearson almost a month to decide to send me to Roswell looking for flying saucers. I'd been back in Chicago, running the A-1, with both Washington and Outer Space filed under Bullshit in the back of my mind. My agency was doing fine; after a postwar lull, divorces were on the upswing again and personnel investigation was holding steady, while our retail credit work for suburban financial institutions remained the backbone of the business.

"I figured when I didn't hear from you," I told Pearson, "you were taking a pass on the little-green-men mission."

"I received a document relating to that matter."

"Could you be a little more vague, Drew? I almost understood you."

"I can't be specific on the telephone, you know that!"

"I thought you were calling from a pay phone."

Which was Pearson's usual habit.

"I am. But I suspect every pay phone in Washington is tapped."

"Say, I understand there's a nice room open next to

Forrestal in Bethesda, if you want that paranoia of
yours looked at."

"I'm fortunate you don't charge per witticism,
Nathan."

"What you pay is already pretty funny. So what got
you off the dime?"

". . . I've received a document that appears to be a
briefing to the President on the formation of that . . .
magic group."

"You mean, Majestic Twelve."

". . . Yes. Nathan, please . . . a little discretion."

"See, Drew, once you mention receiving a briefing
document for the President, this whole discretion
thing kinda goes out the window."

Pearson sighed, but when he continued, he
dropped the coyness if not his imperious manner: "I
have all twelve names, now, and they're all credible—
people like Admiral Hillenkoetter and General
Twining, commanding general at Wright Field."

Hillenkoetter was head of the CIA, and Wright
Field was significant because that was where Marcel
had said the wreckage of the saucer had been taken.

"If this is a hoax," Pearson said, "we have a very
knowledgeable practical joker at work."

"So you want me to investigate Major Marcel's
story," I said.

"Yes. In particular, I'd like you to talk to the witnesses who claim they saw the crashed craft and the
bodies of the crew."

"Isn't that the part of the country where they
smoke locoweed?"

"Well, there's smoke, all right, Nathan, but not necessarily from locoweed. And where there's smoke,
there's—"

"Mirrors. . . . What's the latest word on Forrestal?"

"Making good progress, they say."

"Don't sound so disappointed."

Defensiveness edged his tone. "I don't wish the man any ill, personally. Just politically."

"Then why don't you let up on him?"

"What I write and say isn't having any effect on Jim Forrestal's state of mind. My sources inside Bethesda tell me he isn't allowed to read newspapers or listen to the radio and all communication from the outside is strictly controlled. He may be insane, but I'm confident the nation is strong enough, stable enough, to hear the truth, to have the answers."

Pearson had been asking the questions in his column and on the air: *Why had Forrestal's malady not been detected or acted upon sooner? Who in our government was responsible for concealing this danger to our national security? And to what extent was Forrestal's medical treatment being compromised by public relations considerations?*

Now dry sarcasm colored his voice. "Do you know where your former client's room is?"

"No."

"The sixteenth floor of the Bethesda tower. Doesn't that sound like just the ideal place to keep a potential suicide?"

"More like the ideal place to help keep him away from the press," I admitted.

"Or maybe they're isolating him for yet another reason."

"What would that be?"

"Who knows what drugs they're pumping into him, or what sort of mind-control magic they're up to? That hospital is a hotbed of CIA shenanigans, you know."

"Bethesda."

"Yes. And if my sources are to be believed, the CIA—Forrestal's own 'baby,' which is a nice irony—

is doing research with drugs, electric shock, hypnosis. . . . Nathan, I just want you to understand—I'm not the villain here."

"Neither is Forrestal."

An operator's voice came in to let Pearson know that he needed to feed in some more coins to keep this conversation going.

After the music of the dropping coins had ceased, Pearson said acidly, "You're already costing me money. Will you go to Roswell and do this job?"

"Sure, but I want a five-hundred-dollar retainer, in advance, nonrefundable."

"What if you only work three days?"

"It's a minimum fee, Drew. I never chase flying saucers for under five cees."

". . . All right. I'm going to send you a list of names that Marcel has given me, with some rudimentary background information. It'll come Special Delivery, with your retainer check, and your plane tickets. Can you go out there next week?"

I could, and I did. Of course that miserly son of a bitch sent me the cheapest way he could: on a charter flight of retired schoolteachers going to Carlsbad Caverns. At El Paso, the charter group boarded a bus and I rented the Ford. It was a wonder Pearson didn't expect me to tag along with the teachers and then hitchhike to my first stop.

Sleepy little mountain-nestled Cloudcroft (pop. 265) had the near ghost-town look of off-season, its downtown storefronts no different than in an Illinois or Iowa hamlet; but from a perch overlooking this slumbering resort community loomed a wide-awake ghost of another sort.

The hotel known as the Lodge seemed to have been transported from another time—say, Queen Victoria's—and another place—the Swiss Alps,

maybe. The grand old railway inn was an architec-
tural aberration, a rambling three-story gingerbread
chalet—wooden, not adobe, painted gray, trimmed
burgundy, with gabled windows, glassed-in verandas
and a central copper lookout tower. The shape of the
structure was distinct against the New Mexico sky,
which at night was a deeper blue but no less clear,
with stars like tiny glittering jewels set here and there
in its smooth surface, purely for decorative effect, the
full moon casting a ghostly ivory luster upon the
mansionlike building, whose windows burned with
amber light.

Lugging my Gladstone bag, I moved through the
covered entryway, pushing open double doors decorated with stained-glass windows, and entered into a
two-story lobby that was at once cavernous and cozy,
its dark woodwork highly polished, its hardwood
floor worn, plants and flowers everywhere, from pot-
ted to freshly cut, a world of elegant antiques and
hand-beveled glass and sepia lighting; it was as if I
had walked into a daguerreotype.

"We have your reservation, sir," the assistant manager said numbly, at the check-in counter. He was a
guy in his late twenties with short-cropped prematurely gray hair and a scar over his left eye; he was
pleasant enough but had an all-too-familiar look, the
postwar equivalent of what we used to call the thou-
sand-yard stare.

"Which theater?" I asked.

"Huh?" He flashed a nervous smile. "Pacific."

"Me too. I helped remodel Guadalcanal."

"At least you had some ground under you—I was
on a carrier."

"Listen, Mac, you got any suites available?"

"Just one; we're underbooked, and even off-season, the suites get snapped up."

"But you do have one?"

"Yes," he said, but shook his head, no. "The Governor's Suite. It's pretty expensive—it's where Pancho Villa, Judy Garland, Conrad Hilton and Clark Gable've stayed."

"Together?"

That made him chuckle; he looked like he hadn't chuckled in a while.

Pushing my hat back, I scratched my head. "I have to do some interviews and I'd rather not do them in a public place, like your bar or restaurant—"

"It's fifty a night."

"Christ, I just want a room, not stock in the joint. Never mind—my cheapskate boss would stick me with the bill. I'll muddle through with my five-dollar room . . ."

". . . It's just the one night?"

"Yeah."

"Take the bastard," he said. He had a tiny smile as he handed me the key. "You gonna eat first?"

"Think so."

"Leave your bag. I'll get it to your room."

"Thanks, Mac."

"A warning, though . . ."

"Yeah?"

"The Governor's Suite is Rebecca's favorite room."

"Who's Rebecca?"

He raised the shrapnel-scarred eyebrow. "Our resident ghost. She was a chambermaid, murdered by her jealous lover here, back in the thirties."

"No kidding. Was she . . . is she . . . good-looking?"

"They say she's a gorgeous redhead."

"What the hell—I always wanted to lay a ghost."

I tipped my hat to him and headed over to where leather armchairs were grouped about a large

carved-wood-and-stone fireplace; New Mexico or
not, it was chilly enough for a fire, flames lazily lick-
ing logs. Only two of the comfy chairs were taken, by
a couple I'd spotted when I came in. The glow of the
fire lent the pair a golden patina that made them
seem a part of that old photo I'd walked into.

They were seated next to each other, but not saying anything much, watching the fire like a disaf-
fected married couple watching television. These
were obviously my interviewees: they fit the descriptions Pearson had provided, although the woman's
didn't do her justice, as she'd been pronounced
merely beautiful.

In her late twenties, a petite, painfully pretty thing,
sitting with her hands in her lap atop a small black
patent-leather purse, Air Force nurse Maria Selff
looked a little like Dorothy Lamour only better, and
instead of a sarong she was wrapped up in a simple
but shape-hugging short-sleeve powder-blue frock
with Spanish-style white embroidery on the bodice.
Her heart-shaped face was blessed with large, lumi-
nous, long-lashed dark blue eyes, a strong yet feminine nose, and full, cherry-lipsticked lips, stark against
her milky white complexion, starkly lovely next to the
lustrous black hair of her shoulder-brushing pageboy.

This is what the boys overseas had been fighting
for, what pilots had painted on the nose of their
planes, what dogfaces had pinned up in their barracks
and foxholes, what Varga and Petty had imagined and
God had finally accomplished. And yet her manner
was shy, even demure.

Her male companion was out of his league, but then
most men would have been, even those that weren't—
as Glenn Dennis was—a mortician. Smelling of Old
Spice, which was better than formaldehyde, Dennis
was of medium height, slender, twenty-five maybe,

with short brown hair, heavy streaks of eyebrow lending the only distinguishing feature to a pleasant, oval
face; he struck me as rather mild and unassuming, a
rather typical small-town merchant, even if he was
dealing in death. He was duded up in a Western shirt,
tan with brown trim and cuffs, with a bolo tie and
crisply pressed stockman's slacks—trying to be worthy
of her, the poor sap.

"Mr. Dennis?" I asked.

He looked up sharply, stood, nodding, extending
his hand. "Yes, sir. You must be Mr. Heller."

"I must be," I said, shaking the hand, and motioning for him to sit back down. "Miss Selff? Nathan
Heller."

"Oh my," she said, looking up at me like a frightened child, covering her mouth with a hand. She
began to tremble, and averted her eyes from mine.

Usually I have to work at it awhile, before getting
a reaction like that out of a woman.

"I'm sorry," I said. "Is something wrong? Did I—"

She was shaking her head, still turning away from
me, holding up a hand, calling a momentary halt. "No,
no . . . you didn't do anything . . . I'm the one who's
sorry . . ."

Goddamn, she was crying! Fumbling with her
purse, finding a hanky, she dabbed at her eyes, snif-
fled, and regained her composure.

"You . . . you just reminded me of someone, that's
all," she said. "It's a rather startling resemblance, and
I'm afraid it just . . . threw me a little." She smiled, embarrassed. "Please sit down, Mr. Heller."

I nodded to her as I took the chair beside Dennis.
She got her compact out of her purse, checked her
makeup—it was fine—then returned it to her purse
and her purse to her lap and her folded hands to their
patent-leather altar.

"I appreciate your cooperation, Miss Selff . . . Mr. Dennis," I said. "I know this was a difficult decision . . ."

"I'm afraid I've made a terrible mistake," she said. Her voice was a fluid alto, still quivering slightly from the odd emotional outburst. "I'm putting all of us in harm's way, here."

"Now, Maria," Dennis said, his voice higher-pitched than hers and as flat as hers was musical, "that's nonsense. It's been almost two years since the trouble."

"We were followed," she said gravely, her distressed gaze starting on him, landing on me—and holding.

"Were you?" I asked him.

Dennis shook his head, no, insistently. "Highway was darn near empty. One farmer in a beat-up old pickup went roarin' around us, like to have his fenders fall off. That wasn't any government man."

"They have devious ways," she said.

Her melodrama was at once silly and disturbing.

"I'd like to interview you, individually," I said. "But first, let's get to know each other a little. Why don't we have dinner? I'll admit to being starved; I haven't eaten since Chicago."

"I could eat," Dennis admitted.

She shrugged. "Fine."

Just off the lobby, the dining room was called Rebecca's (after the gorgeous ghost, whose image in stained glass adorned several windows) and we had the place pretty much to ourselves. Despite the Victorian trappings, the menu included plenty of traditional New Mexican dishes, and I tried the green chile stew—which made first my mouth, and then my eyes, water—while Dennis had spareribs with *chauquehue* (cornmeal and red chile) and Miss

Selff a small bowl of soup, Anasazi bean with lamb, which smelled so good I had the waitress bring me a cup.

I used small talk to get information out of them and, I hoped, put them at ease. Dennis, it seemed, was not a full-fledged mortician at the Ballard Funeral Home in Roswell, but an assistant, serving a sort of internship.

"I graduated in '46, from the San Francisco Mortuary College," he added cheerfully, cutting meat off a bone. He said it as if he were looking forward to the class reunion.

Miss Selff had been a nurse since 1945, only it wasn't "Miss."

"Actually," she said, "it's Mrs. Selff. My husband was a pilot, Army Air Force."

I drank some ice water; those green chiles were getting to me. "What does he do now, Mrs. Selff?"

"His B-17 went down over Dresden."

"I'm sorry." That was a tough break: only a handful of planes were shot down in the devastating raid on the so-called Florence of Germany. "Do you have any children, Mrs. Selff?"

"No. We didn't have much time together—just one leave."

She looked like she might start crying again, so I dropped the subject.

The mortician, however, picked it up. "After the tragedy, Maria decided to dedicate herself to her husband's memory, and stay in the service." He beamed at her. "I really admire her for that."

This, understandably, seemed to embarrass her.

She pushed her barely touched bowl of soup away and leaned forward, the big blue eyes wide enough to dive into. "Is it possible, Mr. Heller, that we could talk more privately than this?"

"I've arranged a suite for that very purpose, Mrs. Selff. But I would like to interview you separately."

Dennis frowned. "Why? Our stories kinda dovetail, you know."

"That's the problem." I sipped my ice water. "I really need to hear your stories independently. It's not good investigatory technique to allow interview subjects to interact. . . . The result can be a collaboration that doesn't truly represent what either party saw."

"I'd really like to get away from this public area," she said, scooting her chair away, wadding her napkin and tossing it on the table, with an air of finality. "I don't want to be seen."

I got the room key out of my pocket. "Why don't you go ahead to the suite, and wait there? I can interview Glenn downstairs, in the bar."

She worked up a tiny smile, but on those luscious lips it was monumental; I wasn't quite in love with her yet—at this point I'd only steal for her: we were hours away from murder. "Could you walk me to the suite, Mr. Heller? I'd feel more at ease."

"Certainly."

The mortician started to rise, but the Selff woman gave me a quick, narrow-eyed glance that sent a message: she wanted to speak to me, alone.

"Glenn," I said, with a familiarity generally reserved for close friends, "why don't you settle up the bill for me—just charge it to my room, Suite 101. Then go on down to the bar and find us a nice private booth."

"Sure," he said, but he obviously sensed something. "See you in a little bit, Maria."

She smiled and nodded to him, rather stiffly.

Then she and I were on our way to the suite, moving together down a wide empty hallway. We'd

walked silently for maybe a minute when Maria
planted her tiny black-pump-shod feet on the carpet
and swiveled toward me, clasping her hands tight before her like she was trying to keep a lightning bug
from escaping. Her voice trembled as she said, "I
need your help."

"Name it."

Her eyes tensed. "Glenn . . . he's a problem."

"How so?"

She sighed and her bosom strained at the embroi-
dered bodice and, as I tried not to pass out, she
looked away from me and began walking again,
slower; I tagged along.

"We were dating," she said, "back in '47, at the time
of . . . you know, at the time of all this . . . strangeness.
We'd just gone together a few weeks, a month at
most, and then when the strangeness began, I . . . I
told Glenn it was better we didn't see each other."

"And not just because of the 'strangeness,' I take
it."

She nodded, smirking with chagrin. "I'm afraid I
used that as an excuse to break it off with Glenn. He
was moving way too fast . . . I'd only just started dating again . . . after Steve died, for the longest time,
I . . ."

"I understand."

"Anyway, now, almost two years later, against my
better judgment, I agree to talk about what happened, and suddenly it's thrown Glenn and me back
together—I allowed him to drive me down here."

"I see. And he's trying to rekindle a spark you
never felt."

She stopped again, looking up at me with an expression that was not without compassion. "Yes.
Glenn's a nice man, but he thinks 'no' is a three-letter
word."

"Nice men usually spell better than that."

The expression darkened, she shook her head and began walking again, more quickly now. "I don't want to ride home with him tonight. I don't trust him."

"Hey, you wouldn't catch me dead, riding with a mortician."

That made her smile, just a little; she started walking again. Did I mention she smelled of Evening in Paris perfume, ever so delicately?

She was saying, "I'm enough of a nervous wreck without having to worry about those clammy mortician hands of his. . . . Would you drive me back to Roswell?"

"Tonight?"

"No, tomorrow morning. . . . I'll get a room or something."

Normally a letch like me would take this as an opening; but something wasn't right about it, and I said so. "I thought you didn't want to be seen with me. That was the whole point of meeting away from town—"

"I left my car in a parking lot at Bottomless Lake, southeast of Roswell. That's where Glenn picked me up. You can drop me there. No one will see."

"You should have just come separately . . ."

Abruptly she stopped, and clutched my arm: a tiny hand with surprising power. "I needed to talk to him about what happened; I needed to try and make him understand how dangerous this is. I need to do that with you, too, Mr. Heller."

Then she let go of my arm and began to walk again, slowly, saying nothing.

Soon we were at the door to Suite 101. I asked, "Do you want me to tell Glenn you're not going back with him?"

She beamed at me and it was like watching one of

those speeded-up movies where they show flowers
blooming. "Will you handle it, Mr. Heller? I'd be very
grateful."

That voice . . . she talked like Dinah Shore sang. . . .

"Sure," I said. "Which is a four-letter word, by the
way . . . but don't worry about it."

That got another little smile out of her, and she
handed me my key, and I unlocked the door for her,
and she slipped into the suite, the first pretty girl who
ever figured my hotel room was a safe haven from
wolves.

In the basement of the hotel was the Western-
themed Red Dog Saloon, with timbered fake-adobe
walls, an intricately carved mahogany bar and wanted
posters of Billy the Kid, Jesse James and Black Jack
Ketchum. A bartender in a red vest and a barmaid in
a dancehall dress were entertaining a handful of couples sipping beers or cocktails at tables and booths.
This seemed to be—in the off-season, anyway—a
place for couples, not necessarily married ones, to get
quietly away.

Glenn sat in a back booth, sipping a glass of beer.
I slid in across from him.

"She's a little high-strung," I said, arching an eyebrow.

"No kiddin'! She was weird all the way down here.
You know, we used to go out, a little, you know—
date? Hell, I know that's over but I don't see any reason we shouldn't be civil to each other."

"She wasn't civil?"

"More like sullen. She's really got herself worked
up over this." He sighed. "Not that I blame her. If she
saw what she says she saw, it'd give anybody a permanent case of the willies."

"Glenn—is it all right, me using your first name?"

"Sure. You go by Nathan or Nate?"

"Make it Nate. Glenn, you don't share Mrs. Selff's fears about reprisals?"

The heavy eyebrows lifted. "Well, hell, Nate, maybe she's right—there were all kinds of threats and even some strongarm tactics . . ."

"By the military?"

"So they say, and I witnessed a little of it, myself. Anyway, there was enough of that nonsense that I can see Maria bein' spooked. But that was almost two years ago, and—speaking for myself—there's been nothin' since."

I got out my spiral notepad. "Why don't you tell me your story, Glenn? Do you mind if I take notes?"

He didn't mind. Back in '47, on the afternoon of Saturday, July 5, Dennis had been "minding the store" at the Ballard Funeral Home in Roswell. Ballard's, "the biggest firm of undertakers in town," had a contract with the RAAF (Roswell Army Air Field) for both embalming and ambulance service.

So it was no surprise to Dennis, receiving a call from the RAAF's mortuary affairs officer.

"This fella," Dennis said, cradling his beer in both hands, "Captain somebody, don't remember his name, he was more an administrator than a technical specialist, and didn't know the ins and outs of handling corpses."

The officer had asked Dennis if Ballard's had any small caskets available, child- or youth-size, and if those caskets could be "hermetically sealed." The assistant mortician had said there wasn't much call for the latter, but as to the former, the funeral home had one kid casket in stock, and could call the warehouse in Amarillo and have more in by the next morning.

Dennis had asked, "Has there been some kind of crash, or accident, Captain?"

The Ballard Funeral Home had handled as many

as twenty bodies at a time, from crashes out at the base, and had invested in building a special chamber next to the embalming room specifically for such emergencies.

But the captain had said, "No, no ... we're, uh, having a meeting and discussing provisions for, uh ... future eventualities. ... We'll let you know when and if we need a coffin."

"Well," Dennis said, "if you need a bunch of little coffins quick, I gotta get the call in to Amarillo before three, and that's just a couple hours from now."

"At present I'm only gathering information," the mortuary officer said, thanked the mortician and hung up. Dennis shrugged off the peculiar call and was in the driveway, washing one of the hearses, when the phone rang again. Running in to answer it, Dennis found the mortuary officer on the other end of the line.

"Glenn," the captain asked, "how do you handle bodies that have been exposed out in the desert sun?"

"For how long?"

"Four or five days. What happens to tissue when it's laid out in the sun like that?"

"Are you just gathering information, I mean is this a hypothetical situation, or do you need to know specifically how Ballard's goes about it, what chemicals we use and suchlike?"

"It's a hypothetical, but we want to know Ballard's procedure. For example, what chemicals does your embalming fluid consist of? And what would you do if you didn't want to change any of the chemical contents of the corpse? You know—not destroy any blood, destroy anything that might be of interest, down the road. Also, could holes in a body be sealed over, holes made by predators, I mean? What's the best way to physically collect remains in such a condition?"

"That's a whole lot of hypotheticals, Captain. . . ."

"Well, let's start with the steps you could take not to change the chemical contents of the corpse."

"Well, we usually use a strong solution of formaldehyde in water, and that's damn sure gonna change the composition of the body. Of course, if a body's been sunnin' out on the prairie in July for four or five days, it's already gone through some changes, lemme tell you, gonna be in real sorry shape. In a case like you're describing, I'd recommend packing the body in dry ice and freezing it, for storage or transport or whatever. . . . Look, Captain, I can come right out there and help—"

"No! No thank you, Glenn. This is strictly for future reference."

And the mortuary officer had hung up.

"Of course I knew right away," Dennis told me, smiling as he sipped his beer, "that something big had happened, some VIP got killed or some such, and they weren't ready to release it. But I might have forgot all about it, if an airman hadn't got in a fender-bender that same afternoon."

In routine Ballard's business, Dennis had transported an airman who'd broken his nose in a minor traffic accident out to the base hospital. At about five p.m., Dennis—who was well known around the base, and had rather free access because of the funeral home's contract with the RAAF—pulled around back to escort the injured airman in the emergency entrance.

But the ramp was blocked by three field ambulances, so the mortician parked alongside and walked the patient up and in, on the way noticing that standing near the rear doors of each of the boxy vehicles was an armed MP. The back doors of one vehicle stood open and Dennis glimpsed a pile of wreckage—thin, silver-metallic material, with a bluish cast.

"One piece was formed like the bottom of a canoe," he told me, "and was maybe three feet long, with writing on it, about four inches high."

"What kind of writing?" I asked him. By now I had my own beer to sip.

"Not English. It reminded me of Egyptian hieroglyphics."

"You ever talk to Major Marcel about what you saw?"

"No. Anyway, I just glanced in and kept goin'—I had this patient to deliver, and I took him to Receiving and did the paperwork. There was a lot of activity in that emergency room, I'll tell ya, a real hubbub, not just doctors either, I knew all of them—big birds I never saw before."

He meant high-ranking Army Air Force officers.

"Anyway, I wandered down toward the lounge, to get a Coke, kinda hopin' I would run into Maria. We were dating then, you know."

"Nobody stopped you?"

"Anybody who knew me would've made the natural assumption I'd been called out there. This one MP, who I didn't know, stopped me in the hall and I told him the mortuary officer called me, which was true, and he let me pass. I went on to the lounge, and got my Coke and kinda stood where I could see what was goin' on, out in the hall . . . and that's when I spotted Maria, comin' out of an examining room, holding a cloth over her mouth."

The mortician had also caught a glimpse of two doctors, also covering their lower faces with towels standing by a couple of gurneys, but not of who was on those gurneys.

Nurse Selff had been shocked to see him.

"How did you get in here, Glenn?" she'd asked him, lowering the cloth, looking "woozy" to him.

"I just walked in," the mortician had shrugged.

"Well, my God, you've got to leave! You could get shot!"

"Don't be silly . . ."

"Listen to me—get out of here as fast you can."

Then she'd slipped into another room, just as a captain was coming out; Dennis didn't know this captain, who was in his mid-forties and prematurely gray.

"Who the hell are you?" the captain had demanded. "What are you doing here?"

"I'm from the funeral home," Dennis said. "I run the ambulance service—just delivered a guy at the emergency room, and now I'm havin' a Coke. Hey, I can see you had an air crash, I saw some of the debris—can I help?"

The captain had glared at Dennis and pointed to the floor. "You just stay right where you are."

"Sure."

The next thing Dennis knew, two MPs were grabbing onto his arms and were in the process of hauling him bodily out of there, when another voice called, "We're not through with that S.O.B.! Bring him back here—now!"

And the young mortician had been dragged back to a second captain, "a redhead with the meanest-looking eyes I ever saw," who said, "You didn't see a thing, understand? There was no crash here. You go into town, shooting off your big mouth about what you saw, or that there was any kind of crash, and your ass is gonna be in a major fucking sling. Do I make myself clear?"

"I'm a civilian, mister," Dennis said. "Where do

you get off, talkin' to me like that? You can't do a damn thing to me!"

The redheaded captain gave the mortician an "awful" smile, and said, "Don't kid yourself, kid. Somebody'll be picking your bones out of the sand."

"Go to hell!"

The captain nodded to the MPs. "Get his scrawny ass outa here."

Then the MPs had dragged Dennis out to his ambulance and followed him all the way back to the funeral home, in Roswell.

"About two or three hours later, at home, I got a phone call, just a voice . . . I think it was that redheaded bastard . . . sayin' if I opened my mouth, I'd get thrown so far back in the jug they'd have to shoot pinto beans in my mouth with a pea shooter to feed me. It was a stupid threat and I just laughed at it, and hung up on him; but a couple days later, my pop heard from the sheriff—Sheriff Wilcox—that I was in some kind of hot water out at the base. The sheriff told my father to tell me to keep my mouth shut about what I saw out there."

"Why would Sheriff Wilcox be the one to convey that message?"

"Maybe because he and my pop were old pals. The sheriff said military personnel came around asking about me and my whole family, including my brother, who's an Army fighter pilot. The implication was, my whole goddamn family was in trouble 'cause of me."

"Anything come of it?"

"No. I heard about people getting threatened, and even hauled out to the base and questioned; but me? Nothing. I'd have probably forgot about it—except for being called an S.O.B., which I don't think anybody much likes—if Maria hadn't told me what she told me, the next morning."

"Did she call you, or did you call her?"

"She called me. She said, 'We need to talk.' Urgent, upset. We decided on the officers' club, and we met out there around eleven Sunday morning, had the place pretty near to ourselves. She was crying, very distraught. She looked . . . different, like if you said 'boo,' she'd go into shock. I asked what had happened out at that base last night, and she said she'd seen something no one else on this earth ever had."

"Tell me what she said she saw."

And he did. I would be hearing this firsthand, from her lips; but it might be helpful to compare the story she had told Dennis to the one she would tell me. Too many inconsistencies could indicate she was "remembering" a delusion, possibly unconsciously enlarging and enhancing it; no inconsistencies at all could mean her story had been learned by rote, government misinformation being fed, first to the mortician and then to me, a cover-up of some other incident and/or an effort to discredit Drew Pearson by planting a false, ridiculous story.

So I took it all down in my spiral notebook, and Dennis concluded with, "You think she really saw that, Nate? Or is she insane?"

"What do you think, Glenn?"

His frown drew the two thick dark streaks of eyebrow into one. "It was real weird out at that base hospital, that night; something big happened that afternoon, no question about it. And Maria saw something strange, no question about that, either. You know, bodies that been exposed to the elements for days on end, to predators and everything else out in the desert, they could look pretty darn weird."

"Yeah," I said, putting my pen down, "but could they grow suction cups on their fingertips?"

Twelve

As cooperative as Roswell's friendly neighborhood mortician had been, I felt almost guilty, giving him the bum's rush with a side of baloney.

"Pity about Maria," Glenn Dennis said, as I walked him out into the Lodge's moonswept parking lot, the cool night air pungently tinged by the surrounding pines, whose silhouettes made a decorative pattern against the deep blue sky. "If she don't feel good, she can stretch out in my backseat and I'll get her back to Roswell, lickety-split."

I figured getting stretched out in the mortician's backseat—lickety-split or otherwise—was exactly what Maria wanted to avoid; but I didn't tell him that.

"She's feeling nauseous," I said. "Having all these unpleasant memories stirred has really upset her. And the idea of a long car ride is something she just can't handle."

He nodded, chin crinkling. "Maria *is* kind of delicate . . . sensitive. You know, she was raised in a very religious family. She told me she's going to become a nun, when her tour of duty's up."

That was disappointing news, but then again, maybe that had been her way of trying fend off the mortician's advances.

"Well, Glenn," I said, "I'll get her a room, and then

drive her back to her car, at that lake, first thing to-morrow morning."

"I'd stay and help you out," Dennis said, as we reached his car, a blue Buick, "but I gotta be into Ballard's by nine. We got two big funerals tomorrow."

"It's a living," I said.

He laughed gently. "That's one thing about my trade—you never run out of customers."

We shook hands. He seemed like a nice enough guy, and I had a hunch Maria had misread his natural friendliness for lechery. On the other hand, who knew what any man might be tempted to do, at night, in the desert, with Maria?

He drove off, kicking up gravel dust, and I headed back inside, stopping at the front desk for a word with my pal the assistant manager.

"You have any little complimentary toiletry kits," I asked him, "for guests who got separated from their luggage?"

He raised the shrapnel-scarred eyebrow. "Male or female?"

"Female."

He smiled just a little, said, "I'll have housekeeping stop by with what you need."

"Thanks."

"Uh, it doesn't include Trojans."

"It's not like that. Really. Anyway, I'm a Sheik man."

I knocked at Suite 101, and her musical alto said, "Mr. Heller?"

"Yeah, it's me, Maria. I'm alone."

She cracked the door open, sneaking a peek at me—she didn't know me well enough to recognize my voice, I guess—and then let me in.

"He's gone?" she asked eagerly, hands clasped to the lucky white embroidery decorating her bosom.

I nodded, taking off my hat, holding it over my heart briefly. "To another, better place." I tossed the straw fedora onto a coffee table as I took in the joint.

The Governor's Suite was really something—even more steeped in Victorian ambiance than the lobby, with just as high a ceiling, and an open stairway leading to a balcony off which the bedroom could be glimpsed; tucked under the stairway was a wet bar and the bathroom. The rest of the downstairs was a sitting room, or a living room, really, with a cozy scattering of mahogany and satinwood antiques; the lighting was subdued—she'd turned on a single amber-shaded table lamp—and a golden hue suffused the handsomely appointed suite, with its yellow-and-white brocade wallpaper, white marble fireplace overhung with gilt-framed desert landscape, and green-and-yellow-and-gold floral carpet.

Maria noticed me taking in this opulence—the clue may have been my mouth hanging open—and, glancing up, she said, "There's even a chandelier."

There was; a crystal one.

"Not very big," I said. "Still, it's one of the larger chandeliers I've run into in a hotel room."

She laughed at that, just a little, enough to show me that her laughter was as musical as her voice.

"Thank you for . . . getting rid of him."

I shrugged. "Glenn doesn't strike me as such a bad egg. Seemed genuinely concerned that you weren't feeling well."

Now she seemed mildly embarrassed. "I probably overreacted . . . but the way he looks at me, things he says, I know he's holding out hope for something that's . . ."

"Hopeless?"

She nodded, shivered, and sat in the middle of a floral-upholstered love seat angled toward the fireplace, smoothing the skirt of the powder-blue dress, both feet on the ground, knees together, prim, proper . . . provocative. I moved to an easy chair opposite her, similarly angled. She sat hugging her bare arms.

I nodded toward the fresh wood in a brass bin. "Want me to make a fire?"

"I do feel a chill."

As I built the fire, we made casual conversation. I asked her if she'd gotten herself a room.

"No. You don't think there'll be a problem . . . ?"

"Not as underbooked as they are. I stopped by the desk, to get you some complimentary toiletries. Somebody ought to be around with 'em, soon."

Her expression was warmer than the fire I was lighting. "Are you always so thoughtful, Mr. Heller?"

"Unfailingly . . . except around Christmas, when I get distracted—you know, all that stopping by orphanages handing out toys, and hitting hospitals, caroling."

She didn't laugh this time, but she did smile, and it was a surprising smile, one that made her little-girl vulnerability disappear; she had rather large teeth, very white, a smile almost too big for her face, an overpowering smile, not unattractive exactly, but turning her into someone else, momentarily.

"It's a defense mechanism, you know," she said, as her smile dissipated and the big blue eyes again became her dominant feature.

The fire was going now; I sat in the easy chair across from her. "What do you mean?"

"The jokes, the wisecracks. You hide behind them."

"Everybody hides behind something."

"Why is that, d'you suppose?"

"Well, the alternative is being seen as we really are—and nothing frightens us more than that, does it?"

The fire, cracking and snapping to life, was casting its dancing shadows on us, throwing warmth and color, tinting her a burnished amber. "You're surprisingly deep, Mr. Heller."

"I was trying for refreshingly shallow."

"I'm surprised. I didn't expect to like you."

"Why?"

"I don't know . . . Mr. Pearson is kind of . . . smarmy."

"Ever meet him?"

"No. Just talked to him on the telephone."

"Well, it's worse in person. So, you figured anybody working for him had to be a jerk?"

"I guess."

"Then why cooperate with him?"

"I can't say."

"Why not?"

Her expression darkened. ". . . I gave my solemn oath to Mr. Pearson."

That meant he was paying her—a journalistic taboo that probably got violated about as often as your average parking meter. Judging by this girl's apparent conservative nature, I figured she probably had some family problem, a mother with a bad heart, father in an iron lung, brother in a wheelchair, that only money could cure. Even a prospective nun can fall into the end-justifies-the-means trap.

"We should probably get started," I said. "You mind if I take notes?"

"No . . ." Her brow furrowed. ". . . but Mr. Heller, let's get something straight between us, right now."

That had already happened, a couple of times; she just didn't notice.

She was saying, "I'm not going to tell you anything unless *you* take a sacred oath, too."

"About what?"

"That my name will never be mentioned."

"That's fine with me," I shrugged. "Have you broached this subject with Mr. Pearson?"

"He's given me that assurance. Can I trust him?"

"On this score, yes. One person he won't betray is a source; I believe he'd go to jail for contempt first."

"Well, I could get into a lot of trouble . . . I was warned to forget everything I saw. There's still pressure—talk of a transfer, and I *like* it at the base. Anyway . . . think how I'd look."

"Look?"

She folded her hands in her lap. "Mr. Heller, I'm going to tell you my story, and before this evening is out, you'll wonder if I'm a liar, or a lunatic. And those may seem to you the only reasonable choices . . . and there's not a thing I can do about it."

This was setting a ponderous, even foreboding tone that would not be conducive to a good interview; something had to be done.

I leaned forward, gave her my most ingratiating, unthreatening smile. "Mrs. Selff . . . would it be all right if I called you 'Maria'? And you maybe call me 'Nate,' or 'Nathan'? I feel like we're hitting it off pretty well, and this 'Mr.' and 'Mrs.' stuff is for the birds."

"That would be nice . . . Nathan."

"Before we get started, would you like something to drink? I can call room service."

She perked up. "Don't bother—there are soft drinks in the little refrigerator behind the bar; I'm afraid I snooped a little, before you got here."

"For shame."

"Shall I get us something? To drink?"

"Please."

Then she was back behind there, calling out, "Coca-Cola or 7 UP?"

"Coke."

"You know, I think I noticed an ice machine down the hall . . ."

Soon I'd returned, handing Maria a brimming bucket of ice and a small plastic bag of toiletries.

Accepting them like awards, she asked brightly, "What, are you a magician, Nathan?"

Out in the hall, I'd intercepted the maid delivering the complimentary toiletries.

"Yes," I said.

The ice was broken, or anyway cubes of it were floating in our respective glasses of Coke, and we returned to our seats in the warm orange glow of the fire, and I got out my spiral notepad and pen.

"I'm not going to be shocked by what you tell me, Maria, and I promise I won't be judgmental, either. I've already heard our mortician friend's account, including what you told him at that officers' club, over lunch, the morning after."

She smirked, humorlessly. "*Over* lunch is right . . . I couldn't eat a bite. You know . . . it's funny. I don't think I've eaten right, or had a decent night's sleep, since it happened."

"I need you to tell me about it, Maria. Tell me what happened at the hospital—on the evening of Saturday . . . July fifth, is it?"

"Yes," she said. "Day after Independence Day. But the Fourth of July couldn't compare to those fireworks. . . ."

Maria Selff said that she had been performing perfunctory duties in the emergency room when she entered an examination room, to get some supplies from a cabinet, only to stumble onto a bizarre tableau. Two doctors were performing preliminary autopsies under rather makeshift conditions; she didn't recognize either of the medics, and she certainly didn't recognize the three bodies they were working on, "foreign bodies," laid out on gurneys. But even before the strangeness of the corpses could fully register, the first thing that hit Maria was the overwhelmingly foul odor.

"Such a horrible stench . . . you just immediately gagged. It was hot in there, because the air-conditioning had been turned off—the smell was so terrible, the doctors were afraid it might spread throughout the hospital. It was almost impossible to stay in that room and work . . . I didn't last long, and some of the doctors staggered out of there, too—at least one passed out in the hall."

"You called them 'foreign' bodies, Maria . . . but you don't mean they were foreigners, do you?"

She frowned. "You know I don't. Glenn told you."

"Please. Don't think about Glenn's story; give me your account of the events, as you remember them."

"I tried to turn around and run out of there—I don't know what kept me from screaming, unless that stench immobilized me. . . . Then one of the doctors told me to stay and assist them, and take notes . . . but I didn't take many notes. About all the doctors were saying were things like, 'This isn't like anything I've ever seen,' and 'There's nothing in the textbooks like this.' "

"What did the 'foreign' bodies look like, Maria?"

"I never saw anything so gruesome in my life. Two were badly mutilated, mangled, dismembered, probably by predators . . . one was mostly intact; I think he may have survived the crash, but died of exposure—all three bodies were black, but it wasn't pigmentation, I'd say prolonged exposure to the sun."

"What did they look like, Maria?"

"I worked as long as I could, but finally it got the best of me, the nausea, that all-pervasive odor. The doctors were having as much trouble as I was; finally they put the bodies in body bags and packed them in dry ice for shipment to Wright Field. And that's . . . that's all I know."

"Maria—what did they look like?"

Her eyes narrowed as she stared into her memory. ". . . Three and a half feet, four feet tall. Small, fragile, no hair. If they looked like anything human, it'd be an ancient Chinaman. Their heads were large for their bodies, larger than ours . . . noses didn't protrude, more concave, with two little slits. Where the ears should be, just slight indentations, with little flaps, like lobes. Deep, sunken eyes—concave eyes. Slit for a mouth, no lips at all . . . one thing the doctors said, something I do remember writing down, was that there was heavy cartilage instead of teeth, like a . . . like a piece of rawhide. Their bones were like cartilage, too, pliable, the head like a newborn baby's, nothing like the bone structure of a human being. Could I . . . could I please have some water?"

"Sure." I got up and went to the wet bar and poured her a glass of water over ice, brought it back to her, returned to my seat as she drank it as greedily as if she had been lost out in the desert.

"Go on, Maria."

"There were some basic anatomy differences. . . . For example, the distance between wrist and elbow was longer than the distance between elbow and shoulder. Oh, and they didn't have thumbs, but four fingers that were long and slender, almost like tentacles . . . and on the fingertips—they had no fingernails, by the way—on the fingertips were little hollowed pads, like suction cups."

"Did they have any sex organs? Were they men, or women, or something else?"

"I think probably something else. There were no signs of sex organs, or secondary sexual characteristics, either. But then that's the sort of tissue predators go after, first, and also the first thing that decomposes, so how can we be sure?"

"Did they have any kind of clothing on? Had the doctors removed any garments . . . ?"

"I don't think so. I don't remember seeing anything like that, but frankly, it was all so horrible and gruesome, and I was so overcome with nausea, and the desire to get the hell out of there, I just didn't pay the close attention I should've."

"I think you did just fine. You came out of there with more details than most people could ever have managed."

"Well . . . maybe my nurses' training came through for me, a little. Nathan . . . are you humoring me?"

"What do you mean?"

"Pretending to believe all this, while you think it's nonsense?"

"Maria, I don't know what you saw, but I believe you saw something."

"Glenn thinks they're from outer space. He thinks the debris he saw was from wrecked 'escape pods.' "

"What do you think?"

She frowned, searching inside herself. "I try to make those bodies into humans, possibly human children . . . features distorted because of long exposure to the high desert . . . or maybe monkeys. There are rumors of missiles being shot off, at White Sands, with animals—dogs, monkeys. . . ."

I sat forward. "Could they have been monkeys, their hair burned off in a crash? I'll bet dead monkeys that've been out sunnin' in the desert could smell pretty ripe."

"I want to believe that's what I saw. But the anatomy was all wrong . . . and it was consistent from corpse to corpse." She shook her head, in frustration.

"All I know for certain is it was the most horrible thing I've ever seen. Do you think I'm insane, Nathan?"

"No."

"I wish I were as confident of that as you are," she said, and collapsed into tears.

I went to her, gathered her in my arms—she was trembling all over, bawling like a baby, and I cradled her in my arms, patted her back, rocking her, saying, "It'll be all right . . . it'll be fine . . . don't you cry . . . shush . . . shush." She whimpered and sobbed for quite a while, as I held her, and finally it abated, and she relaxed, face against my shoulder, as I kept rocking her.

She was feather-light, when I carried her up the stairs like Rhett Butler whisking Scarlett O'Hara away, only my Scarlett was sleeping, snoring even, a very unfeminine snore that made me smile. The bedroom was decorated in an Early American style, centering around a four-poster double bed with a quilted comforter. I eased her onto the bed, slipped her black pumps off her tiny feet, made sure the pillow was cradling her head comfortably, then eased out of there, switching off the light, padding down the stairs.

Since I hadn't even bothered to take my bag upstairs, I camped out on a couch downstairs—a Duncan Phyfe number whose carved mahogany and light blue tapestry-style upholstery looked too elegant to be comfortable. I took off my shirt and my shoes, but decided to sleep in my T-shirt and trousers, for decorum's sake. I threw some more wood on the fire, got it going again, then stretched out on the couch, whose plump cushions proved my expectations nicely wrong; on my back, elbows winged out, I watched the walls and ceiling where flames and shadows did a mocking dance.

Was I just humoring her? For those blue eyes, what

couldn't I convince myself of? For that Dorothy Lamour figure, what wouldn't I pretend to believe? I mean, could I really be taking seriously the prospect of outer space creatures with big heads and big eyes and tentacle fingertips, taking a right turn at Pluto and heading for Roswell, New Mexico? What, they could navigate all those asteroids and meteor showers, they could make it safely to earth from the other side of the Milky Way, but those Roswell July Fourth fireworks really threw them, and they panicked, and slammed on the brakes. . . .

Yet within a day or so of when the Army Air Force may have been out recovering those "foreign bodies" from some unknown desert crash site, Major Jesse Marcel was salvaging pieces of strange debris at a nearby ranch. *Something* had crashed in the desert; something important enough for Uncle Sam to go around scaring the bejesus out of those citizens unlucky enough to be witnesses, coercing those good Americans into a terrible silence.

The fire was dwindling, and I was nodding off, when a tiny noise drew my eyes to the stairway and the ghostly figure coming down; in the faint dying glow from the fireplace, throwing long shadows, she moved slowly, as if in a trance, the powder-blue dress wrinkled from her sleeping in it, hiking up a little, her knees and even her thighs showing.

She crossed tentatively toward where I lay on the couch, whispering, "Nathan? Are you awake?"

"For a minute there," I said, moving onto my side, leaning on an elbow, grinning, "I thought you might be Rebecca."

She sat on the edge of the couch; the raven's-wing hair was fetchingly tousled, an improvement on the severity of her pageboy. "Who's Rebecca?"

"The ghost."

"What ghost?"

"The one the restaurant's named after—some chambermaid who was killed by her lover, years ago. This is supposedly her favorite room."

She smiled a little, but nervously. "You're just saying that. You're teasing."

"No. That's the story. You know, it's just nonsense to keep the tourists entertained."

She seemed oddly troubled by the silly tale, and began hugging her arms again. "That's so *bizarre....*"

"You're cold—I'll feed the fire."

Thinking that this girl had run into more bizarre occurrences in her time than a stupid ghost story, I went over and put a few more logs on, got some heat and glow going, then returned to the couch, where she was sitting, now; she'd left room for me, and I took the liberty of putting my arm around her.

"We'll warm you up," I said, and she snuggled close. "I don't mean to be fresh...."

But she lifted her face up and her dreamy expression, and her parted lips, gave me permission to get a little fresh, anyway; specifically, to kiss her.

It was a soft, warm, sweet, almost chaste kiss. Almost.

She drew away from me, gazed at me earnestly. Her voice was husky as she said, "It's so strange . . . I came down here because I thought . . . I thought I *sensed* something in that room up there. A presence. Maybe an . . ." She cut herself off, laughed ruefully. "Now you *will* think I'm crazy."

"What?"

". . . I thought maybe it was an . . . evil presence."

"I think Rebecca's supposed to be a friendly ghost."

She shuddered. "Well, I don't want to sleep up there."

"You want the couch? I'll go risk the bed . . ."

"No!" She hugged me tight. "Stay down here, Nathan. Stay with me—all night."

"Well ..."

"Maybe it was dredging up all those . . . awful memories, maybe that's what's got me spooked. But the one thing I know for sure is, I don't want to be alone tonight."

"All right. You take the couch." I gestured toward the easy chair by the fireplace. "I'll pull a couple of chairs together and ..."

She patted the couch. "There's room for us both, don't you think? I'm not very big."

Some places she was.

"Okay," I said, and I lay on my side, against the back cushions, and she lay next to me, her back to me, and we were like spoons, as she nestled her bottom into my favorite place, and I looped an arm around her waist, held her next to me and she snuggled; oh how she snuggled.

"Funny," she said. Whispering. Maybe she didn't want Rebecca to overhear. "When I first saw you, I thought *you* were a ghost."

"Me?"

"Yes."

"Whose ghost?"

She didn't say anything. Then I realized she was crying again. Not bawling like before, no racking heaving sobs; just quietly weeping.

Gently I turned her around to face me. "What is it, Maria?"

Emotion tugged at her face. "You look so much like him."

"Who?"

". . . Steve."

Her husband. Late husband.

Then she was crawling on top of me, kissing me

with an urgency that was contagious, and I was on my back as she writhed around on me, the curves of her molding, pressing themselves to me, my hands moving across the back of her, over her rounded bottom, up the curve of her spine, to the buttons.

"Undo me," she whispered.

With far less fumbling than you'd imagine, I unbuttoned the dress, and she sat atop me and peeled it off the upper part of her, the garment gathering at her tiny waist, revealing a formidable white bra into which considerable engineering had gone, and she asked me to undo that as well, and I did, and none of that engineering had been necessary because the full breasts were capable of standing up for themselves, large nipples dark against the pale rounded flesh, puffy soft nipples that got crinkly and hard under my kisses. I kissed her and kissed her, her salty face, her lips, her neck, her shoulders, and she let me do most of the kissing, as if basking in the affection; then she eased herself off me, and the couch, onto the floor, and stepped out of the dress, a pool of powder blue at her feet. She wore no nylons, no garter belt, no girdle, simply sheer panties, the pubic triangle vividly dark beneath the fabric.

I managed to say, "I'll . . . I'll get something."

She shook her head. "No. It's a safe time. It's safe . . ."

Maybe she was a Catholic at that, though the nun part was starting to sound doubtful.

Then she tugged down the panties, and the blackness of the untamed tuft between her legs against the creamy flesh was startling. She was a stunning woman, petite but with that Botticelli body, and she stood there with the reflection of flames and shadows flickering crazily on her flesh, a campfire dancing around her.

"Now you," she said.

I stood and yanked off my T-shirt, got out of my trousers, stepped out of my drawers. I started to take my socks off but she stopped me.

"Leave them on," she said, with a new wickedness. "It's dirtier that way."

This nun concept was definitely flawed.

We did it on the carpet, near the fire, with me on top, with her on top, and then she stuck that heart-shaped bottom in the air and had me finish her from behind, me saying "Oh God," again and again, her saying "Yes" over and over, building from a whisper to a scream.

And that was just the first time.

"You were wonderful," she said, as we lay on the couch; she was back in her bra and panties, and I was in my skivvies.

"You . . . you're not so . . . bad . . . yourself." I was pretty winded; we won't go into our respective ages.

"Of course, I don't have much to go on," she said, suddenly pixieish.

"Oh? You seemed to know what you were doing."

"Really? Gee whiz. You're only the second man I was ever with."

Then, having kicked me thusly in the head, or somewhere, she fell asleep, leaving me to ponder whether it bothered me or not, playing substitute for that late fighter pilot husband of hers. Had I taken advantage of her, in her distraught state? Gee whiz— was *I* the evil presence she sensed in the room?

Had she mistaken my natural lechery for friendliness?

"Naw," I said to myself, and fell asleep with her in my arms.

Thirteen

IF NORMAN ROCKWELL were looking for a classic American small town to represent the Southwest for his next *Saturday Evening Post* cover, he could do worse than Roswell. Under cotton-candy clouds and ball-of-butter sun in a sky so clearly blue that Hollywood simply had to be involved, Roswell and its thirteen or so thousand inhabitants (mostly white, maybe ten percent Mexican and Indian) nestled in a setting of sprawling desert and majestic mountains.

Right down to the manure-rich aroma wafting in from surrounding ranchlands, this was a typical farm community, though distinctly modern, with wide paved streets and flourishing industry (meat-packing plant, flour mill, creameries), and oddly similar to the District of Columbia in its preponderance of shade trees, handsome public buildings and flower-filled parks. Of course in Roswell, it was not granite, but adobe; not cherry trees, but cottonwoods; not memorials, but playgrounds. There was even a Pennsylvania Avenue, with a few Federal-style houses, though mingled with Queen Anne, Tudor, Prairie and more.

In fact, Maria her-Selff (who this morning I had dropped off at her car parked at the recreation area of Bottomless Lake) lived on Pennsylvania Avenue. But I had orders not to come around her place unless it was after dark and she knew I was coming and I left my car parked at least four blocks away and slipped in back. I knew an invitation when I heard one, and—what the hell—it wasn't like this was the first time I was a back-door man.

Right now, however, the sun was high and hot, the air still and dry, and I had people to see, starting with the sheriff of Chaves County. A risky proposition, walking right up to the local law and introducing myself; wasn't this the sort of tumbleweed town where they didn't cotton to my kind around these here parts? Where the man with the badge gave prying strangers a choice between the noon outbound stage or a one-way ticket to Boot Hill? The only proposition riskier would be *not* seeing the sheriff, first.

The Chaves County Courthouse, on Main Street, was a neoclassical tan brick structure dating to 1912, the year New Mexico joined the Union. A green-tiled dome loomed imposingly over a massive entryway, and the interior sported equally impressive Greek-key-design tile floors, brass chandeliers and ornate plasterwork. But the adjacent office of the sheriff proved as shabby and nondescript as is customary, bulletin boards sporting Mexican, Indian and white suspects in unprejudiced array.

I wanted to keep things casual and unthreatening, so I'd dressed like a tourist, in a two-tone shirt—tan with blue collar and sleeves—and lightweight blue twill slacks and two-tone brown-and-white shoes. Taking off my straw fedora and slipping my sunglasses in my breast pocket, I checked in with a thin, young, dark-haired deputy—his name tag said REYNOLDS—and asked if I could see the sheriff, telling the kid briefly who I was.

"If this is a bad time," I said, "I can make an appointment. I plan to be in Roswell for several days."

"In all the way from Chicago, huh?" the deputy

said. He had bright eyes and a ready toothy smile. "Fly into El Paso?"

"Sure did. Pretty drive up here."

"Get a load of them white sands? That's as close to Christmas as it gets around here."

"Never saw anything like it. Low crime rate around these parts?"

He snorted a laugh. "About as exciting as pickin' a flea off a dog."

I had figured as much, as long as this was taking. Finally, the chatty deputy scooted his chair back, rose and checked with the sheriff, who saw me right away.

Sheriff George Wilcox stood to shake hands behind his tidy desk in his doorless cubbyhole off the main office, which was taken up by the booking area and his two deputies at their desks. In a short-sleeve khaki shirt with a badge and Apache-pattern tie, Wilcox was a sturdy-looking, square-headed, jug-eared lawman of maybe fifty-five; his dark white-at-the-temples hair rose high over dark careless slashes of eyebrow, and his large dark eyes were somewhat magnified by wire-rim glasses; blunt-nosed, with a wide, thin mouth, Wilcox had a no-nonsense manner, gruff but not hostile.

"What's the nature of your business here, Mr. Heller?" he asked; his baritone was as sandswept as his county's terrain.

I had already shown him my Illinois private investigator's license and my Cook County honorary deputy sheriff's badge; neither seemed to impress him much.

Settling into a wooden chair no harder than the expression the sheriff was giving me, I said pleasantly, "I'm doing some background research for a nationally known journalist."

"Who would that be?"

"My client requested I keep that confidential."

"Why?"

"Frankly, he's got a controversial reputation and he doesn't want people to be put off." That was about as candid as I could afford to be.

Wilcox rocked back in his swivel chair, digesting that. Then he said, "What's the nature of the article? You're too late for Rodeo Days."

"Sounds like that would've made a fun story, but this one's fun, too. You know, this flying saucer fad, in all the papers a couple years now—my client's doing a kind of wrap-up, sort of a postwar hysteria angle. Looking into the better-known of the so-called 'sightings.' "

Wilcox said nothing; his eyes had gone cold, their lids at half-mast.

I pressed on: "You know, Roswell has a special significance—it's the only time the Air Force officially recognized the existence of saucers; they even put out a press release saying the wreckage of a disk had been recovered."

Wilcox was studying me the way a lizard looks at a fly.

"Anyway," I said, shifting in the chair, crossing my legs, "I've come to see you for two reasons. First of all, I didn't want to go poking around your town without you knowing."

"Appreciate that," he said, nodding slowly.

"Second, I'm hoping I can interview you, for the article. I understand this rancher, Mac Brazel, brought in some samples of the oddball debris, and that you're the one who called in the Air Force. . . . You mind if I take a few notes?"

I was taking my small spiral pad from my right hip pocket.

"Put that back, son," he said, waggling a thick finger.

He wasn't all that much older than me, not enough to be calling me "son," anyway; but he made me feel about fifteen, in the principal's office, just the same.

"Sheriff, if you don't want to be quoted," I said, the notebook still in hand, "I could still use some background information . . ."

"Mr., uh—Helman, was it?"

"Heller."

"I'll let you take a few notes, and you can use my name, too. This won't take long."

"Thank you, sir."

"The Air Force said that thing was just an air balloon. That first press release . . . three hours later, they said it was a mistake."

"Well, uh, Sheriff, mistake or not, there was quite a fuss you had to field phone calls from all around the world, I understand."

He nodded again. "I sat up all night, taking calls from Germany, London, France, Italy, all kinds of places, and probably every state of the Union. I told 'em what I'm telling you: talk to the Air Force."

"That what you're advising me?"

"No." His tone was firm but not unkind. "My advice to you would be, move on to the next flying saucer story on your list."

"Why is that?"

He nodded toward the notepad in my hands. "Now I am going to insist you put that thing away."

"All right."

"Don't quote me. Don't paraphrase me."

"Certainly."

Wilcox sat forward and placed both his hands on the desk; his tone shifted to a flatly ominous one that would have seemed ridiculous if it hadn't been chilling. He said, simply, "Don't look into this or you're going to have real trouble."

"Trouble from you, Sheriff?"

"Not from me."

"Who from?"

"That's all I have to say, on or off the record. Do yourself a favor, son—move on."

"But, Sheriff, my understanding is that you saw some of this strange debris, even handled some of it. Was this stuff really as weird as has been reported? Thin metal that goes back to its original shape, if you wad it up? Unearthly hieroglyphics?"

Wilcox stood, slowly, smiling as benignly as a Buddha. "I appreciate your courtesy, Mr. Heller, stopping by to let me know about your inquiry."

There's a stage out of town at noon; be on it.

I sighed, stood, sticking my pad in my back pocket, nodding to him. "Thank you for your time, Sheriff."

On the way out, the chatty deputy called to me, "Mr. Heller! Where are you staying, should we need to get in touch with you?"

I went over to his desk. "I'm at the El Capitán Hotel."

"Over the drugstore downtown," Deputy Reynolds said, nodding, writing it down. "Thank you, Mr. Heller."

Then he extended his hand and I shook it, and felt a piece of paper there. His bright eyes narrowed and communicated something, and when I withdrew my hand, I tightened it over the note he'd passed me.

I didn't look at it until I was out of the courthouse and onto the street: "Clover Café, two p.m."

But right now it was barely ten, so I headed for the next stop on the list Major Marcel had provided Pearson; with the exception of the sheriff, everyone else was either expecting me or at least a chum of Marcel's, and should be a friendly witness.

On the third floor of the Roswell equivalent of a

skyscraper—a four-story brick building on Main Street—down on the left of a wood-and-pebbled-glass hallway, black stenciled letters on the door announced the HAUT INSURANCE AGENCY. I knocked, and a flat, midrange voice called, "Come on in!"

It was a single office, not very wide, and not very long, either, barely big enough for the ceiling fan that was lazily whirling, like a propeller warming up; no receptionist—no room for one. By an open window looking out on Main Street, at a work-piled rolltop desk, a boyishly handsome blue-eyed blond young man—maybe twenty-six, in shirtsleeves and a red-and-blue tie and blue slacks—was on the phone, talking life insurance with a client.

He waved me toward the hardwood chair alongside his desk and I sat, removing my straw fedora. The blond kid smiled at me, motioned that this call wouldn't take long. It didn't.

"Walter Haut," he said affably, without standing, extending his hand, which I took and shook. "And you are?"

"Nathan Heller," I said. "I believe Jesse Marcel warned you I'd be stopping by."

"Oh, oh, yeah—sure! Glad to see ya. But, uh . . . you mind if I check your i.d. first?"

"Not at all." I showed him the Illinois license and the honorary deputy's badge.

His grin was affable and embarrassed. "You'll have to excuse the less than lavish digs . . . I'm just getting in the insurance game . . . independent agent. I was in your field till about two months ago."

"Investigation?"

He rolled his eyes. "Collection agency. I don't know how you guys stand it."

"My firm doesn't do repo or skip tracing. Ugly work."

"I agree." He leaned an arm on his desk, leaned forward. "You know, I like people—I'm a member of the chamber of commerce—and the last way I want to make my living is doggin' folks for a dollar. So . . . let's make it 'Nate' and 'Walt' and skip the formalities. Any friend of Jesse's is a friend of mine."

"I don't want to overstate my case, Walt. I've only spoken to Jesse once. But my feeling is he's pretty bitter about taking the fall for Uncle Sam."

Haut's head bobbed up and down. "He got a bum shake, all right. Which is why I'm willing to talk . . . off the record, of course—confidential source, that kind of thing?"

"You got it. Mind if take notes?"

"Feel better if you would. Only thing . . . if my phone rings, I have to take it . . . one-man agency, you know how it is."

"Actually, I do. I spent almost ten years that way, myself. When did you leave the service, Walt?"

"I left last August. I never intended to make a career of it. Were you in the service, Nate?"

I nodded. "Marines."

"Overseas duty?"

"Guadalcanal."

He blew an appreciative whistle. "Then you can understand how good civilian life looks to a guy who flew thirty-eight combat missions against the Japs."

"Not a pilot, I take it."

"Bombardier and navigator."

Pen poised over the pad, I said, "Your postwar position out at the air base, I understand, was public relations officer?"

Haut leaned back in his chair, put his hands behind his head, elbows winging. "Yeah, it was a pretty uneventful ride—except that Tuesday after the Fourth, in '47. You gotta understand my job was kind of a

funny mix—there was a lot we kept the lid on. Very
tight security out at that base—keep in mind, you're
talking to the guy who dropped glass-gauged instruments smack dab into the Bikini explosion, and yet
even I couldn't get near aircraft with atomic bomb
configuration."

"Tightly run operation."

He nodded vigorously. "Secure areas fenced off,
MPs on twenty-four-hour guard—not only do you
need a pass to get on that base, you need a further
pass to even get near those aircraft."

"Understandable."

Haut sat forward again. "At the same time, for all
of that, we wanted to foster good relations with the
local community. Colonel Blanchard's first duty out
of West Point was same as mine, a public relations officer. So he had a real thing for building good feelings
between the town and the base. Anything we were
doing that was newsworthy, I was to let the two newspapers and two radio stations in on it. We let 'em
come out and take pictures, whenever and whatever
they wanted—long as they didn't try to snap pictures
of the B-29s."

On the morning of July 8, 1947, Haut told me, he'd
been called into the base commander's office.
Colonel Blanchard dictated a statement to his public
information officer for immediate release to the local
press acknowledging the 509th Bomb Group being
"fortunate enough to gain possession" of a downed
flying saucer (I had read the clipping in the file Pearson gave me).

"Around ten-thirty that morning," Haut said, "I
drove to town and made the rounds, dropping off the
release at the radio stations, KGFL and KSWS, then
over at the *Roswell Daily Record* and *Roswell Morning Dispatch*. The *Record*'s an evening paper, and

they're the ones that had the headline story, that night—I just barely beat their deadline." He shrugged. "Then I had lunch."

"You didn't think anything of it? Another day, another captured flying saucer?"

"Hey, it was lunchtime, so I ate lunch. I didn't give it a second thought; when a superior officer said, 'This is what it is,' that was what it was. I went back to the base, to my office, and nothing much happened the rest of the afternoon, except the phone was ringing pretty heavily for a couple hours, there."

"The press?"

"Oh, yeah, from all over the world!" Haut laughed, shaking his head, struck by a funny memory. "First call I got was from London, this very proper English accent asking me how the 'chap' who found the saucer had known how to fly the 'craft' back to the base! I had to explain it was just wreckage that was found."

"Walt, you and I both know how cautious, and secretive, the military usually is. Here's the first instance of the Air Force capturing a flying saucer . . . obviously, an event with national security implications, and international repercussions. Do you think Colonel Blanchard could have issued that press release on his own authority?"

Haut rocked in the chair, thought about that. "Well, the Old Man could put out just about anything he wanted, short of information about the atomic weapons on the base. Things of a secret nature, that'd have to be cleared with the Eighth Air Force, and probably further up the chain of command. . . ."

"Don't you think a flying saucer would fall into that category?"

The insurance agent sighed, nodded, mulling some more. "Come to think of it . . . I honestly don't think

Colonel Blanchard did authorize that release. My feeling is it went to General Ramey and probably on to higher headquarters."

"Why would they sanction something this sensitive?"

An eyebrow lifted. "I can hazard an informed guess, if you like."

"Guess away, Walt."

Haut sat way forward, eyes narrowing. "That same afternoon, remember, word from General Ramey came down that the wreckage wasn't from a flying saucer at all. And all of a sudden, we're sending out pictures of Jesse Marcel holding up fragments of your everyday garden-variety weather balloon, looking like Public Idiot Number One."

I was shaking my head, confused. "Why would the brass do that? Issue a statement about a flying saucer, then a couple hours later contradict themselves?"

Haut's smile turned sly. "I believe they knew the cat was out of the bag ... the rumors about a recovered saucer were flyin', around here. So the best cover-up is to announce a saucer's been found, attributing it to Major Screwup, then have the much smarter, more knowledgeable general say, 'Oh no, you children got it wrong—it's just a weather balloon.' And the incident gets laughed off and forgotten. It was a real sleight-of-hand trick, typical disinformation."

"Disinformation?"

"That's an intelligence term, Nate—same as 'black' propaganda, purposeful misinformation issued by the government to confuse its citizens. And as a guy who put his ass on the line for his country, that ticks me off. I mean, America's supposed to be in the truth business."

"You believe a saucer *was* found."

The boyish features tightened. "I believe Jesse Marcel knows a weather balloon when he sees it. And did you hear about that weird tinfoil shit?"

"Yes. Did you see any of it?"

"No. I saw nothing—no wreckage, no outer space creatures, none of it. A public relations officer is kept away from things that the public isn't supposed to know; that's a practice I was accustomed to."

"But you believe Jesse Marcel."

"We were friends. My wife and I would go play bridge with the Marcels; we rode to work together. He was rock-steady, and hell, they kept him on as intelligence officer for something like a year after that. Then he was transferred to a job of even higher responsibility!"

"You mentioned 'outer space creatures' . . ."

Haut raised a hand. "You need to talk to Glenn Dennis about that."

"I have."

"Well, Glenn's a friend, too, and I can tell you, he's not a nut; if he tells you something, you can give it credence. Now, I don't know much about this military clampdown that supposedly went on, and nobody threatened me or anything—but you might want to talk to Frank Joyce, over at the radio station."

Which was my next stop, an adobe storefront operation with a small neon reading RADIO STATION, in small letters, over KGFL in large ones, above a sunfaded canvas awning. In a small control booth, I talked with Joyce, a sturdily stocky brown-haired kid in his mid-twenties, who ran a one-man operation on his afternoon show, reading the news, spinning records, doing live commercials and serving as his own engineer. I sat at the little table used for on-air interviews and we chatted sporadically, while discs spun—not flying ones, the kind with Crosby and Perry Como on them.

Joyce had Mickey Rooney-ish features clustered in the midst of his round face, making his rather large head seem even larger; he might have been young, but he had the no-nonsense attitude and manner of a seasoned reporter.

Doing twelve things at once on his control panel, he said, in his announcer's mellifluous voice, "Late morning, Monday after the Fourth, I was making my usual calls, before the noon news, looking for any late-breaking items. . . . When I checked with Sheriff Wilcox, he put this rancher, Mac Brazel, on. Never met the man, and wasn't sure I wanted to."

"Why?"

"Well, this bizarre wreckage he described made me pretty skeptical; flying saucer talk, I mean, really! Little green men, that sort of thing. I asked him to put the sheriff back on, and recommended they call the RAAF, since they were the experts on everything that flies."

"Did you put the story on the radio?"

"No. This was Monday; that story didn't break till Tuesday."

"I see."

"Anyway, having been in the military, I knew they'd frown on something like this getting out—assuming there was anything to it. We're just a little station, and we were just starting out, then—we didn't need to alienate the local air base. Funny thing is, my pal Walt Haut was the p.r. officer out there, and I'd been giving him a hard time about putting me last on his list, whenever a story broke. Guess what story he brings to me, first, to make it up to me?"

"And that's when you put it on the radio."

"Yeah, but the funny thing is, I was still reluctant. I

mean, I find myself readin' this press release about the Air Force saying it has a flying saucer, and I say to Walter, 'Wait a minute! I know this story—*I* sent this guy Brazel to you!' And Walt says, 'Oh, well, thanks,' and I say, 'I don't think you oughta release this story.' Like I said, I know how the military works, and I could see the top brass havin' a shit fit. But Walt says, 'It's okay, Frank, the Old Man has cleared it, and it's okay for you to put the story on the air.' "

Since it was close to airtime, Joyce had flown out the door to reach the Western Union office, two blocks away, to wire the release to the United Press in Santa Fe, knowing he had hold of a "once-in-a-life-time" story.

"You're the one that spread the news, then," I said.

Joyce nodded, getting the next disc ready on his second turntable, cuing it up in earphones that left one side uncovered, so we could converse. "By the time I got back here, the phones were going crazy, AP, UP, every big and little paper in the Southwest, hot for confirmation and more details." His mouth tightened under the mustache. "Then I got the first of the threatening calls."

"Who from?"

"A Colonel Johnson, in Washington. He cursed me out, told me I was going to get in a lot of trouble, and I told him I was a civilian and a member of the press, and he couldn't treat me that way, couldn't tell me what stories I could put on the air. And he says, 'I'll show you what I can do,' and hung up."

This made a kind of skewed sense. If Walter Haut was right, the point of the exercise had been to release the flying saucer story locally—where rumors were rife—and then quell it a few hours later with an official retraction and the new "weather balloon" explanation. Having the story spread over the wire, nationwide and worldwide, focusing instant and intense attention on Roswell and its purported flying saucer, may have been more than the brass bargained for.

"A day or so later," Joyce said, a new platter spinning, a Peggy Lee, "two soldiers escorted that rancher Mac Brazel into this very station. They sat him down in that chair you're sitting in and he offered to do an interview. I said, 'Fine, but you boys'll have to wait outside,' and the soldiers, they waited out on the street, by the jeep they brought him in."

"And you interviewed him."

"Yes, but I didn't bother putting it on the air. How could I? The story he told this time was completely at odds with what he first said."

"He backed up the military's weather balloon tale."

"In spades. *Now* Brazel said that what he found on his ranch was rubber strips, tinfoil, paper, Scotch tape and sticks. Like a big kite had crashed. No writing on it, either. All the debris could be tied up in a little bundle weighing less than five pounds, he said. And he told the same story at a press conference for the AP, among others."

"Did you get a sense of why he lied? You figure he was threatened, too, and caved in?"

"Well, there are two schools of thought on that. One is based on the fact that ol' Mac somehow came into a considerable amount of money—a fella so poor he couldn't rub two nickels together suddenly shows up in town in a brand-new pickup. Then he buys his family a new house, at Tularosa, and a cold store at Las Cruces. . . ."

"That sounds like the Chicago school of thought," I said. "What's the other one?"

"Money may have been part of it, but this is one of your old Wild West, dirt-in-the-pores cowboys, and I could see his quiet anger, how coldly p.o.'ed he was. He'd been bullied, pushed around and threatened."

"Is this something you surmised, or . . . ?"

"I had a moment with Brazel here in my ugly little announcer's cabin, and I said to him, 'You know that this story doesn't have a damn thing to do with what you told me on the phone, the other day.' And he says, 'Look, son—best keep that to yourself. They told me to come here and tell you this story, or else.' 'Or else what?' I ask. 'I open my mouth, I'm in the federal calaboose. Or breathin' sand.' "

That was not the end of it, not of the threats anyway. Joyce told me that his boss, the owner of the station, had received a call from "someone in Washington, D.C.," who made it clear that if KGFL aired an uncensored story about Brazel's two differing accounts "the station's license would be in jeopardy."

"So you never aired the story," I said.

"No. And whenever I run into Mac Brazel, here in town, we don't speak."

The Roswell Fire Department was a new buff-brick building with room for three trucks in as many stalls, but only two were taken up. I checked in at the front office with the receptionist, who fetched fireman Dan Dwyer for me.

Dwyer, a big brown-haired man in his thirties, asked me what I wanted and I suggested we talk outside; he didn't object, and when I brought Major Marcel's name up, he responded warmly.

"Jesse's a nice fella," the husky fireman said, hands in the pockets of his jumpsuit. "How's he like Washington?"

"I think he's happy. But I'm pretty sure he feels his reputation at SAC is tainted, because of the ridicule heaped on him, in that 'saucer' incident."

The fireman's friendliness evaporated. He studied me through slitted eyes. "Is that what this is about? Who are you?"

I told him, was showing him my i.d., when he held up a hand in a stop fashion.

"I have nothing to say about that situation."

"Jesse seems to think you witnessed something, Mr. Dwyer. Didn't you respond to a call in early July of '47? Was there wreckage of some kind of flying craft, possibly bodies of—"

"Stop. I told you, already. I'm not talking."

"We can keep it discreet. Your name won't be used. We're just trying to determine what happened, and whether the military got out of line in the way they—"

"I'll tell you about the military getting out of line. How about threatening to stick my wife and kid and me in Orchard Park?"

"What's Orchard Park?"

He threw his hands up. "That's all I got to say, mister. And anybody asks me, I didn't say *that*."

Then turned and all but ran into the station.

The Clover Café made no attempt to serve the native cuisine; its Blue Plate Special was meat loaf, peas and gravy, and worth every bit of fifty cents. At two o'clock, the lunch crowd was gone; you could have fired a cannon off in the place and not hit anybody. I sat in a back booth, finished off the wholesome fare, and waited to see if Deputy Reynolds would show. He did, about two-fifteen. We spoke over Cokes and a radio's country-western music.

"Sorry I'm late," the slender deputy said. "We were bookin' a guy."

"What happened to your low crime rate?"

"This drifter tried to rob the Conoco station in broad daylight. Wanted everything in the cash drawer." He laughed. "Manager's an ex-Marine who gave him a wrench alongside the head, instead."

"Stopped his drifting, anyway. Say, Deputy—what's Orchard Park?"

"Former POW camp, for the Japs, out in the desert—why?"

"Nothing important."

"Look, Mr. Heller, we need to make this quick. This joint is pretty dead after lunch hour, so it's safe enough. But I don't want to take any chances."

"Why are you?"

"What, taking a chance? Because it pisses me off how the strongarm's been put on a lot of good citizens by their own goddamn government. In particular, pisses me off, what the sheriff's been subjected to."

"Like what?"

"You wouldn't know it, from talkin' to him today, but Sheriff Wilcox is an easygoing, even gregarious fella. Progressive, too—he was the first one in the state to separate juvenile offenders from adults."

"He wasn't oozing warmth and compassion this morning."

"Not after what he's been put through. Do you know he's talking about not running again? Best sheriff we ever had, best boss I ever had. He hardly says anything about what happened, though I have heard him say he's furious with himself for bringing the military in. Once they showed up, and claimed jurisdiction, we got completely cut off. I heard him say, if he had it to do over again, he'd call in the press, first. Give 'em carte blanche."

"Deputy . . . what's your first name, anyway?"

"Tommy."

"Tommy, call me Nate. Listen, were you there from the beginning?"

"From when Mac Brazel stumbled inta the office, just a cowboy in faded jeans and scuffed boots and a week's worth of dirt and dust caked on him, yes I was."

"Then you saw the saucer debris?"

"Yes—but not the bodies."

"Bodies?"

"I'm gettin' ahead of myself. Look, I saw that thin metal you'd crumple that'd then uncrumple itself; and I saw some little I-beams with hieroglyphics. Saw samples of all that stuff. Sheriff sent me and Pete Crawford out to the ranch—"

"Wait a minute . . . this was *before* Major Marcel went out there?"

"Yes, sir. We didn't see the debris, but we saw this patch of blackened ground; it looked like somethin' big and round and hot had sat itself down. We come back and reported in to the sheriff, and he called the air base, and there was no new news, and then things settled down for a bit."

The next morning, Tuesday, things got unsettled, and unsettling, in a hurry. Deputies Reynolds and Crawford drove back out to the ranch and found it had been cordoned off by the Army; they were not allowed passage, lawmen or not. Armed sentries and Army vehicles were stationed at ranch roads, crossroads, everywhere. Annoyed and frustrated, the deputies returned to the sheriff's office, where Wilcox was fielding phone calls from all over the world.

"We still had a little box of that strange debris," Reynolds said, "off in our side room. Day or so later, just when things had kinda gone back to normal—the weather balloon story had calmed things down—the military landed on us like fuckin' D day, excuse my French."

"Landed, how?"

"Two MP trucks showed up and they came in and demanded the box of wreckage, and the sheriff handed it over, with no protest. But they were belligerent as hell, anyway. These MPs gathered all of us, deputies and Sheriff Wilcox, and told us to keep quiet about recent events and direct all inquiries to the base. The sheriff said, well, that's what he'd been doing. And the MP, a colored sergeant, real menacin' fella, said, well, if any of us had any other ideas, there'd be 'grave consequences,' was what he said. I didn't take kindly to that, and said something to the effect, what do you guys think you're doing, threatening officers of the law like that? And this black bastard, he says, cold as ice, he says, 'We'll kill you all, and your families, and your goddamn dogs, too.' "

"Sounds like you're taking a hell of a chance, telling me this."

"I don't like being threatened. And ... look, there's something I haven't told you."

"What's that, Tommy?"

"I kinda got a personal stake in this. I date the sheriff's daughter, have been, off and on, for a couple years. Threatening me is one thing; threatening my girl's life, well those guys can go fuck themselves!"

We listened to a staticky Hank Williams singing about a cheating heart, then I asked, "You said something about bodies?"

"I didn't see anything, but I think the sheriff did. I think it's part of why he's so shook up, why his health has failed and everything else. My girl, her father wouldn't answer any of her questions, and her mother told her to stop asking him ... but that night she heard him talking to her mom, heard the sheriff say that three little bodies had been found, little guys with big heads in silver suits. Found 'em in a burned area with metallic debris and the crashed saucer."

"When was this supposed to've happened?"

"I don't know. Hell, maybe my girl imagined all this, or heard snippets of conversation and wove 'em into somethin'. But I know the military got to Sheriff Wilcox, browbeat him, threatened him, maybe even took him for a stay in that same 'guesthouse' where they held Brazel."

"What do you mean, 'guesthouse'?"

"Some kind of place where they hold unofficial prisoners for questioning, out at the base. Brazel was there for a week, I hear. I don't know, maybe you could ask him yourself. Maybe he's ready to talk, after all this time has passed."

"Yeah, I was thinking of driving out to his place, later today."

"Hell, don't bother—he's in town!"

"What?"

"Yeah, Brazel comes in every now and then to sell some wool."

"Where can I find him?"

"My guess is, if you park yourself at the bar next door, your man'll come to you, before too very long."

The bartender at the Trading Post Saloon knew Mac Brazel and—for the assurance I wasn't a process server, and a consideration of one dollar—agreed to point him out to me, should the rancher decide to stop by for a drink.

On a bar stool, I nursed a beer and went over my notes, trying to decide what I made of all this; I wasn't convinced that a flying saucer had really crashed, but the military's misbehavior in these here parts seemed undeniable. My back was starting to hurt, and I was about to move to a booth, when the door opened, sunlight slashed in, and in strode a tall character in a beat-up Stetson, dirty faded jeans and an equally dirty, even more faded denim shirt.

The bartender gave me a barely perceptible nod, but I think I could have saved myself a dollar: who else could this long, tall New Mexican be but Mac Brazel? His face was spade-shaped, his eyes wary slits, mouth a wider slit, skin as dark and leathery as a saddle.

He settled onto a stool two over from me, and in a low voice requested a Blatz.

"Mr. Brazel?"

He glanced at me; his face was like something an Indian had carved out of wood. "Do I know you?"

"I'm a friend of Major Marcel."

He turned away, but I caught him looking at me in the mirror behind the bar; I looked back at him in it, and said, "I'd like to talk to you about what happened out at your ranch July before last."

His bottle of beer arrived, with a glass. "I don't talk about that."

"You know, you're an American citizen, Mr. Brazel. The military can't tell you what to do and what to say, or what not to say."

Brazel was pouring the beer. "I'm not so sure about that."

"What did you find, Mr. Brazel, out in that field?"

He sipped the beer, savored it, then—speaking so slowly it would have irritated Gary Cooper—said, "I'll tell you one thing, mister. It sure as hell wasn't a weather balloon."

"What was it?"

Several swallows of beer later, he responded—sort of. "If I ever find anything else, it better be a bomb, or they're gonna have a hard time gettin' me to say anything about it."

"Even if you find more little green men?"

He took a last swallow of his beer, and then that leather face split into a strange grin. "They wasn't green."

And he tossed a fifty-cent piece on the bar, climbed off his stool and ambled out.

I'd been running a tab, and had to take the time to pay for two beers before I could follow him, and by the time I got back out to Main Street, the rancher was climbing into a recent-model Ford pickup truck, across the way. I might have made it to him, before he pulled out, if that hand hadn't settled on my shoulder.

"Mr. Heller," a crisp young voice said in my ear. "Would you come with us, please? Colonel Blanchard would like to see you."

Then a white-helmeted MP was at my side, a wide-shouldered kid of twenty or so, no bigger than your typical starting college fullback; he took me by an elbow and walked me to an open-topped jeep at the curb, where a second MP—a big colored sergeant—was behind the wheel.

I saw Brazel's new pickup heading north, out of town, as we headed south.

Toward the air base.

Fourteen

Rustic Roswell slipped away and scrubby desolation took over, the two-lane ribbon of well-worn concrete stretching endlessly ahead. In the open-air jeep, jostling along, I held on to my hat, figuratively and literally. I didn't ask any questions, because getting my ass hauled out to the former Roswell Army Air Field was about the only way I might hope to actually talk to Colonel William H. Blanchard. And the two white-helmeted MPs, both of whom sat in front, had nothing to say to each other, let alone me.

Five minutes outside of town, the base was signaled by a sign with the words WALKER AFB in a proud deco mushroom cloud that rose above its horizontal base, smaller letters spelling out HOME OF just below, with 509TH BOMB GROUP and 1ST AIR TRANS UNIT boldly emblazoned left and right, respectively. The field had been renamed after the Air Force had broken off from the Army into its own entity, something which Jim Forrestal had initially opposed, incidentally.

Then through heat shimmer, like a desert mirage, the sprawl of the air base revealed itself: first the tower, then hangars, one- and two- and three-story barracks and other buildings, fenced-off areas, far-flung tarmacs where planes were taxiing, taking off and landing, even green landscaped grounds complete with trees. The main gate wasn't terribly impressive, however, sitting like a brick tollbooth in a vast, unfenced paved area, the words WALKER AIR FORCE BASE curving above, black letters on white. For all the talk of security, Walker seemed fairly accessible; I mean, hell—they let me in, without a pass, merely on the word of the two armed MPs who'd kidnapped me.

We pulled up to a two-story white clapboard building and, over the rumble of airplane engines and churning propellers, I was told to follow the colored MP while the white one trailed behind me. We trooped through a bustling bullpen where aides and secretaries were at work at desks, typewriters clattering, new notices getting pinned up on bulletin boards while old ones came down, maps taking up most of the wall space. At a modest glass-and wood walled-off office, the MP in the lead knocked at a glass-and-wood door stenciled COLONEL W. BLANCHARD.

Pearson's file had filled me in a little on Blanchard—nickname "Butch"—who had a reputation as a "swashbuckling" pilot, rumored to have once returned from a Mexican jaunt in a trainer jet so loaded down with whiskey, the plane crashed to a fiery stop; legend had it he'd fled the scene, then returned to indignantly demand the mysterious pilot be tracked down and court-martialed. Blanchard had been next in line to drop "Fat Man" on Hiroshima, but history had seemed to pass him by—unless, of course, there was something to these flying saucer stories I'd been hearing all day.

Blanchard—husky, dark-haired, dashingly handsome, the "Old Man" as Haut had referred to him— was barely past thirty; he looked up from a desk cluttered with work, framed family photos, humidor, pipe rack and trio of telephones. He waved the MP inside.

"Leave Mr. Heller with me, Sergeant," Blanchard said, in a crisp baritone, "and don't wait around."

"Yes, sir," the colored MP said, and held the door open, nodding curtly for me to enter.

I did. Blanchard gave me half a smile, didn't rise, gesturing to the waiting hardwood chair across from him. I sat, just as the MP was shutting, almost slamming, the door; it startled me, but I'm sure my reaction was no more obvious than Shemp Howard's would have been.

The colonel had the casual look of a man who'd seen combat and didn't suffer bullshit—no tie, sleeves rolled up, but with the authoritative touch of the pipe he was smoking. On the wall behind him were framed photos from the war, Blanchard posing with his plane, with his crew, at the front of a group shot of the 509th; and centrally displayed was an elaborate, and impressive, collection of medals. Also on exhibit, just behind him, was a Japanese ceremonial sword, sitting on a pedestal atop a low-slung bookcase. To his right stood an American flag.

Blanchard said, "Welcome to Walker, Mr. Heller."

"Thanks for inviting me. How is it you know my name?"

Leaning back, he took a couple of puffs at the pipe, then said, "I know a lot about you, Mr. Heller—your war record, including your Silver Star. Honor to have you in my office."

"That's kind of you, Colonel. But *why* am I in your office?"

Now he sat forward. "I understand you've been asking questions around town, about that . . ." He chuckled. ". . . flying saucer flap we had around here, while back."

"It didn't take you long to find that out," I said. "I've only been in town since this morning."

"Well, we pride ourselves on our intelligence here at Walker."

"You talking smarts, Colonel, or spies?"

"Both." Blanchard grinned a winning grin; he had the look of the most popular guy at the frat house. "If you have any questions about that incident, perhaps I can answer them for you."

I blinked a couple times. "You're willing to be interviewed?"

He gestured expansively with pipe in hand. "Certainly. By the way, who is this interview for, Mr. Heller? My understanding is you're working for a well-known journalist."

"I've been asked to keep his name confidential."

Half a grin, now. "Why, does he have a bad reputation?"

"Let's just say he has a reputation, Colonel. You, uh, mind if I take notes?"

"No, no . . . not at all." His pipe had gone out; he used a kitchen match to get it going again—the smoke was fragrant, sweet. Maybe too sweet—like Blanchard's attitude.

Notepad out, pen ready, I asked, "What can you tell me about the incident, Colonel?"

"A local rancher found some debris out on a pasture; with all this saucer hoopla in the air, I'm afraid we jumped the gun." Blanchard shrugged gently, smiled the same way. "Turns out it was just a weather balloon, trailing a Rawin radar target."

"Who authorized the press release?"

"I did."

"On whose authority, Colonel?"

"Mine."

". . . I guess you didn't anticipate the public's reaction."

He laughed through teeth that clenched the pipe.

"I sure as hell didn't. Phones were bombarded; I couldn't even get an open line to make my own outgoing calls."

I kept my tone light as I asked, "Were you reprimanded, Colonel, for 'jumping the gun' with that press release?"

The grin disappeared. "No. It wasn't a big deal, Mr. Heller. We all had a good laugh."

"Who, you and General Ramey? Did Major Marcel find it funny? He was the one who looked like a sap."

"We all thought it was funny," he said tightly. "Is there anything else, Mr. Heller?"

"What about accusations of the military threatening citizens into silence? Cordoning off the Brazel place? Calling the local mortician, asking for small caskets?"

Blanchard leaned back, took a long draw on the pipe, released a cloud of smoke. "Mr. Heller, Roswell's a small town, and this base has a big responsibility. Sometimes the simple people of a farm community can make something out of nothing."

"Mountain out of a molehill?"

"Exactly. This is ancient country, a land of myth, of superstition . . . add to that the kind of gossip that makes any small town go 'round, and you can come up with some really wild tall tales."

I beamed at him, sitting forward. "Well, then, if you don't mind . . . I'll get back to town and see if I can find some more whoppers for this article. I mean, my boss is trying to do something fun, after all, about the saucer fad."

The handsome face went blank; the pipe was in his teeth, but he wasn't drawing on it. "The Air Force would appreciate it if you didn't."

"Didn't what? Stick around, or give my boss the makings of a story?"

"Either. Both."

"If there's nothing to this, Colonel, what's the harm of me staying around, and seeking out some more tall tales?"

Blanchard rose slowly, placed his pipe in an ashtray, and quite dramatically rested both his palms on the desk and leaned across, almost whispering, "You have a distinguished war record, Mr. Heller. You served your country faithfully and well. I'm asking you, as one patriot to another, to leave this be. To pack your bag and leave the Roswell area."

There's a stage out of town at noon. . . .

I shook my head, grinned at him—not as winning a grin as his, I'm sure, but it was all I had. "First of all, Colonel, my war record isn't all that distinguished—not unless you consider a Section Eight something worth framing and putting on the wall. Second, I get real nervous when people talk patriotism. It's like when somebody says they expect you to do the 'Christian' thing."

Blanchard stood erect. "That was not a threat, Mr. Heller. This was an embarrassing incident, and we'd prefer not to have it dredged up again."

"Even if you could have another good laugh over it?"

He sighed, shook his head, wearily. "I had hoped you'd cooperate."

"You mean, go home, and quash this story?"

"Yes." He pointed at me with the pipe stem, emphasizing certain words. "Let me say off the record . . . hypothetically . . . that if the Air Force were presenting a story to the public that did not represent the true facts, in this or any instance, there would be a good reason for it. Having to do with security considerations, and the public good. And I would hope a loyal American would respect the wishes of his government. Loose lips, as we used to say, sink ships."

"Including flying saucers?"

"Mr. Heller, you disappoint me."

I leaned back in my chair and folded my arms. "Say, Butch—did they ever find that pilot who crashed that plane loaded down with whiskey?"

Blanchard blanched. "How did you . . ."

"I pride myself on my intelligence, too, Colonel." I stood. "Can you have somebody give me a lift back to Roswell? Or maybe have your men take me out in the desert and shoot me?"

"I don't find you very amusing, Mr. Heller."

"Sorry—I'm fresh out of weather balloons."

Blanchard picked a receiver off one of his phones, said, "Send Kaufmann over here." Then he hung up, and said, "No MPs, Mr. Heller—a civilian will take you back to town. Now, would you mind stepping out of my office? Step outside the building, in fact. I think I've seen quite enough of you."

The colonel kept his word: no MPs waited to accompany me off the base. My driver was a rather grizzled-looking, brown-haired, square-headed, broad-shouldered civilian in his thirties, in a short-sleeved plaid shirt and chinos. He'd already been behind the wheel, waiting outside, when I'd climbed in the front seat; and we were outside the gate and tooling toward town before he took one blunt-fingered hand off the wheel to offer it in a handshake.

"Frank Kaufmann," he said, in a low-pitched, slightly graveled voice.

His handshake was firm. My straw fedora was at my feet; traveling in the open-air jeep was making my hair stand up, if what I'd been hearing today hadn't already done that.

"Nate Heller," I said, adjusting my sunglasses.

Kaufmann glanced over at me, raising eyebrows that were as brown and wild as the brush streaking by us; his eyes were a light, clear brown and he had a sly smile going.

"Jesse Marcel's friend," he said.

"Now how do you know that?"

There seemed to be a twinkle in those amber eyes. "Maybe it's 'cause I'm in charge of security out at the base."

"A civilian in charge of security?"

He shrugged, still smiling, a private smile. "Well, I wasn't always a civilian. Used to be a master sergeant. During the war I was the NCOIC under General Scanlon."

Noncommissioned officer in charge.

"You must've had a pretty high clearance," I said, "considering the 509th was the only air squadron flying atomic bombs."

"I knew what I was doin'. When I left the service in '45, I was offered my old duties at RAAF, in a civilian capacity, this time. It's delicate, maintaining friendly relations with a nearby community, like Roswell, when you've got top-secret stuff goin' on. The press makes requests, the mayor wants to take dignitaries on tours, and sometimes you gotta say no. Me bein' out of uniform helped smooth that kinda thing over."

"Did it." This guy was striking me as a blowhard and a bore.

Kaufmann chuckled, then lifted a hand from the wheel to gesture toward the desolation around us. "You know, looking out at all this tranquillity, you'd never guess such earth-shakin' events could take place out in these wide open spaces. . . . First atom bomb went off not far from here, at the Trinity test site. Manhattan Project, that was over at Los Alamos. Did you know that when they set that bomb off, a bunch of the scientists thought there was a real chance it'd spark a chain reaction that'd lead to the end of the world?"

"No." I was listening closer now.

"Well, they thought that, all right, and went ahead and set it off, anyway. What does that tell you about scientists? Not to mention ol' Uncle Sam."

"It is a sobering thought," I said, and wasn't kidding.

Kaufmann glanced at me and his eyes had turned as sly as his smile. "You know what they're doin' over at White Sands?"

"No."

"You remember the V-2s, don't you? Them big firecrackers that leveled London?"

The V-2—the fabled buzz bomb—was a rocket, the world's first large-scale one, at that.

"Well," Kaufmann was saying, "over at White Sands, the Air Force is playin' with captured V-2s, and you know who's helping them? You know who's in charge?"

"No."

"Bunch of goddamn Nazis."

"Nazis. Are running the White Sands Proving Ground."

He nodded emphatically. "I've seen it with my own eyes. Smooth son of a bitch named von Braun is runnin' things—he's a 'technical adviser.' He's not the only one, either—more Nazi scientists runnin' around over there than you can shake a stick at. Gettin' kowtowed to, when they oughta be lined up and shot, or maybe hung with piano wire."

My first impulse was to laugh at this nonsense, but then Teddy Kollek's words flashed through my brain: *You can't imagine how many scientists fresh from factories run by concentration-camp labor are on Uncle Sam's payroll, now.*

"They're launching rockets over there," Kaufmann was saying. "Real Flash Gordon stuff. Revamped V-2s. Trying to see how high they can shoot the sumbitches, trying to be more accurate, go further, carry a bigger payload of explosives. Sometimes, instead of TNT, they're loadin' up the noses with photographic equipment, and X-ray, and mice, and even monkeys."

"What for?"

"The Nazis say we're goin' to the moon, someday. Outer space. They talk about it like it's their goddamn religion."

This guy was clearly insane—yet another candidate for the suite next to Forrestal's; I was starting to wish Blanchard had sent me with the MPs, instead. Roswell was looming up ahead, and I was relieved.

And yet I was curious enough to ask: "Why are you telling me this, Frank? This sounds like classified material, to me. . . ."

Kaufmann shrugged, and one eye under one wild eyebrow winked at me. "Some of it is. What the hell, one civilian to another . . . one *veteran* to another. Thought you might like to know what your government's capable of. What our military's willing to go along with. Jesus Christ, goddamn *Nazis!* Hell, I'm of German heritage myself, and it sickens me. . . . You're a Jewish fella, aren't you?"

"That's part of *my* German heritage."

"Well, how do *you* like the idea, Uncle Sam in bed with fuckin' Nazis?" Kaufmann shook his head, sighed heavily. "I'm sure as hell glad this is my last week."

"Of what?"

"Of working out at the base. I've had all I can stomach of the postwar Air Force. Anyway, I got offered a better job."

"Yeah?"

His expression turned proud. "I'm gonna head up the Roswell Chamber of Commerce."

All that smoothing over had paid off.

"Where you staying, Mr. Heller?"

"Don't you know? You seem to know everything else."

Kaufmann grinned at me, a big wide grin, maybe not as winning as Blanchard's but much more real. "You think I'm a bag of wind, don't you? Well, I'll tell you something you probably will believe—Jesse Marcel called me and asked me to talk to you."

". . . You weren't on the list."

He shrugged a shoulder. "I turned Jess down, at first. Didn't want to compromise my job."

"But now you have another job."

"That's part of it," Kaufmann admitted, and this time it was the wild eyebrows that shrugged. "Another part is thinkin' about what a fool they made out of a good man like Jesse. And another is thinkin' about what a fool they're makin' out of all of us . . . the great unwashed American people."

I pointed. "I'm at the El Capitán."

The hotel, just around the corner from Roswell Drug on Main Street, was just up ahead.

Kaufmann gave me his sliest look yet. "I can drop you there . . . unless, of course, you'd like me to take you out to the crash site, first."

"What?" Now the son of a bitch really had my attention. "The Brazel ranch, you mean?"

Making a face, he said, "Hell no, not there; too long a drive, and anyway, there's nothin' to see, all that debris got picked up—they *vacuumed* that damn pasture! I'm talkin' about the saucer . . . and the little bodies."

"Saucer. Bodies."

Kaufmann pulled over, double-parking the jeep in front of the drugstore, turning to grin at me. "Well, here we are, Mr. Heller—Hotel Capitán. Nice meetin' you."

I grinned back at him. "Pretty cute, aren't you, Kaufmann? How far is it?"

"Just about a half hour. You think what I told you so far was good? Wait'll you hear this. . . ."

As we headed north, on the concrete ribbon of 285, into a mostly brown, occasionally green landscape of scrub brush and cactus and sand, under a sky as infinite and wide as the blue eyes of a child, Kaufmann told me a yarn that had me laughing in wonder, even as I wrote it down in my spiral notebook. He was, it seemed to me, one of the following: a raving lunatic; an outrageous bullshit artist; or the witness to something truly extraordinary.

On July 2, 1947, Brigadier General Scanlon of Air Defense Command had dispatched Kaufmann to White Sands Proving Ground at Alamogordo, where radar had detected strange movements, indicating an unidentified object flying over southwestern New Mexico, violating the restricted airspace. With orders to report directly to the general, Kaufmann and two others had, in shifts around the clock, charted the object.

"The blips were just dancin' from one end of the screen to the other," Kaufmann said. "Now, we'd had similar blips back at Roswell, but intermittent—the thing showing up only when it was above the Capitán Mountains. We kept up watch for almost two days. Then late on the night of July Fourth, God decided to serve up His own fireworks show, by way of one incredible lightning storm."

At around eleven-twenty p.m., with the storm at its height, the object on the radar screen stopped flitting, began pulsating, growing larger; finally the object blossomed in "a white flash," then shrank to its original size, dove down and winked out. The assumption was the craft—if that's what it was—had been struck by lightning and possibly exploded, or crash-landed.

"Two other sites—Roswell and Kirtland—were tracking the thing, so the Army techs were able to roughly triangulate the location of what we took to be a crash."

The consensus was that the object had fallen somewhere northwest of Roswell. By a little after two in the morning, Kaufmann had returned to the base, reporting in to Colonel Blanchard, who assembled a small military convoy—the base was undermanned, due to the long holiday weekend—of three jeeps, four trucks, one of them a flatbed, one a crane.

"We took along some of those radiation suits," Kaufmann said, "but we knew it couldn't be what we call a 'broken arrow'—a downed plane with an atom bomb aboard—'cause we had all the planes and the bombs! So radioactivity wasn't really a major concern."

The convoy had headed out 285, which was exactly what Kaufmann and I in his jeep were doing; his story and our location converged, as—near Mile Marker 132—he turned west off the highway onto "an old ranch road," a hard-dirt path, the jeep kicking up a small dust storm.

"Hardest part was," Kaufmann said, "not gettin' stuck—ground was pretty soft, after the rain . . . but these jeeps can drive outa anything."

Soon Kaufmann turned again, near an abandoned ranch house, onto no road at all this time, and suddenly we were cutting across country. At this point, he halted his story to navigate, saying, "Explain the rest when we get there—be easier that way." The jeep jostled along and at one point Kaufmann stopped, climbed out, snipped a barbed-wire fence with cutters, piled back in, and off we went again, driving over the downed fence, bouncing over some fairly rough terrain, making no attempt to avoid rocks, heavy tangled brush or cactus, crushing or burying everything in our wake.

I held on to the side of the jeep, my teeth rattling as I said, "Are you telling me you drove this at night? Braving gullies and barbed-wire fences? How did you know where to go?"

"We followed the glow," he said. "It was a halo of light, beamin' out against the sky. Closer we got, the more the glow seemed to ebb, and fade. . . ."

The jeep was making its way down a gentle slope that gradually became a ravine; then up ahead, perhaps one hundred yards, a forty-foot cliff rose from an arroyo, scrubby green below, thinning to clumps above in a rocky slope that became brown stony ridges.

My guide stopped his jeep and got out.

"Let's walk on down there," Kaufmann said, with a motioning wave, "and I'll show you exactly where the craft was wedged. . . . Look out for snakes."

I was halfway out of the vehicle. "What do you mean, look out for snakes?"

"Rattlesnakes tend to get riled when you step on 'em, is all I'm sayin'."

"I think the jeep could make it down this slope," I offered.

"Just walk careful." Kaufmann was laughing, gently. City folks.

I walked careful. "Had the glow died down by the time you got here?"

"Yes, it pretty much had, but we could see the metal glistening, and we knew then and there it wasn't a plane or a V-2 rocket. . . . When we got here, we actually came out up there, at the edge of the ravine—damn near went over and crashed into the damn crash! But we circled around to where we are now. . . . This is it."

Kaufmann was pointing to a gouge in the sandy ground.

"This is where the craft was embedded—kinda slammed into the sand, got its nose crumpled in the side of the cliff, here. Right off, Colonel Blanchard sent a man in, in a protective suit, to check the craft and the area for signs of radiation. We waited around for the all clear, maybe fifteen minutes, smoking cigarettes and asking each other questions none of us could answer."

"What did this craft look like, Frank?"

"Oh, six feet high maybe, twenty, twenty-five feet long, probably fifteen feet wide. It sure as hell wasn't no damn saucer."

"You said it was."

Kaufmann made a face, waved a dismissive hand. "That was just to get your attention—it's the common usage. . . . This thing was shaped more like a wedge, somewhere between a V and a delta. It had this wraparound window at the front, and the whole thing was split in half, along its side, horizontally, maybe where it got blown open . . . maybe that was where that scattered junk Brazel found come from. Of course, I always thought there was a possibility the Air Force mighta loaded up some of the wreckage here, and carted it over to the Foster ranch, to scatter it around and confuse things, draw the attention away, onto a bogus site."

I wiped the back of my hand across my sweaty forehead under the brim of my straw fedora. "Wouldn't you have known about that?"

"Hell no. I wasn't in charge! Blanchard was. Now, I could see inside the craft—there was control panels and some hieroglyphic-type writing. As for how the thing flew, I didn't see any propulsion system, just a series of cells on the underbelly, quartz-type cells, octagon-shaped, like a beehive. I didn't get that good a look—it was still before dawn, we musta got out here about three a.m.—and we had search-lights from jeeps shinin' down from on top of the cliff. The colonel wanted us to get that craft onto the flatbed and back to the base before dawn, *muy pronto;* daylight, somebody else could stumble onto this mess. Then, of course, we had casualties to deal with."

I was cleaning my sunglasses on my shirt. "The craft's crew, you mean? The 'little bodies'?"

Kaufmann nodded, shook his head, his eyes distant. "There were five of these beings. . . . You know, you see somethin' out of this world, it shakes you up; we were just kind of stunned, kinda stupefied, not saying a word, just staring. Then finally we snapped out of it." He pointed. "One body was tossed up against the wall of the arroyo, flung there; another was half in, half out of the craft. I saw one sitting in-side, slumped over in his seat, dead as hell. They found another one inside there, later, the men that loaded the bodies in those lead-lined body bags."

"That's four—you said there were five."

"Sorry, I'm . . . I mean, I haven't been out here since that night. It's all kinda . . . rushin' back. I didn't mention the one that was still breathing?"

"There was a survivor?"

"Yup. Wasn't in bad shape, neither. He was just sit-tin' on a rock . . . right over there, that boulder by the cliff, there. At first he was kinda cowering, then—when he saw we were trying to help, he got the goddamnedest look on his mug ... almost serene. Like he didn't have a care in the world."

"This world, anyway. What did they look like, Frank?"

The wild eyebrows lifted. "Not like you see in the funnies or the movies. No horns or spiny fingers, and they sure weren't green."

So Mac Brazel had said.

"... They were slim, pale, smooth-looking individuals, hairless, fine skin, silver-type uniforms. Five four, five six ... fine features, small nose, heads kinda too big for their bodies."

"Big eyes?"

"Bigger than yours or mine—kinda slanty, Oriental type...." Kaufmann, hands on his hips, was slowly scanning the landscape; his expression was somewhere between sickened and haunted. "Tell ya what, Nate my friend, I think I had enough of this place. Let's head out. I'll tell you the rest of it on the way back."

That was a good suggestion; the afternoon was fading, shadows starting to lengthen, and on the highway I got treated to one of New Mexico's glorious yellow-red-orange-blue sunsets.

Kaufmann told me that there was concern about the condition of the bodies—one was showing signs of deterioration—and Blanchard's first stop had been the base hospital. A second team had already been dispatched to further clean up and cordon off the crash site. At the base, each of the eight men who—with Blanchard—had been involved close-up with the operation were ushered into the briefing room, one at a time; Kaufmann assumed his instructions from the colonel—that the "retrieval" was "classified at the highest levels"—mirrored that of the others.

Though his participation had come to an end, Kaufmann understood that Hangar 84 at the airfield became the base of operations, housing both the corpses—and the survivor—and the captured crashed craft. Then the craft went on the back of a truck under a tarp to Wright Airfield in Ohio; the bodies—and presumably the survivor—on a flight, first to Andrews Air Force Base at Washington, D.C., then to Wright.

"Why the stop in D.C.?" I asked. Roswell was up ahead.

"Rumor has it, top-ranking Army and Air Force personnel requested a look at the bodies. Also, Truman and Army Chief of Staff Eisenhower . . . oh, and the Defense Secretary."

"Forrestal?"

"Yeah. Isn't he the guy that had the nervous breakdown? I read about that in Drew Pearson."

"Mental problems can afflict the best of us, Frank." Kaufmann grinned at me. "Is that your way of sayin' maybe I'm nuts? Maybe I am."

"Maybe you're still working intelligence and are feeding me . . . what's the word? Disinformation?"

"Why would I do that?"

"You wouldn't. But maybe Blanchard would. To throw me off the scent."

"The scent of what?"

"That's the question, isn't it? You got any proof, Frank? Any pieces of indestructible tinfoil? Photo of a dead spaceman, maybe? One of their silver suits?"

As I'd requested, he was rolling up to a stop at the parking lot where I was keeping my car. "We weren't allowed to keep anything, Nate. Not any piece of information or evidence, not a thing. Any report we made got quickly turned over to an intelligence officer."

"Who, Jesse Marcel?"

"No—those CIC guys."

Counterintelligence Corps.

"Like that guy Cavitt, you mean, who went out to the Brazel spread with Marcel? What became of him?"

Kaufmann shrugged, leaning on the wheel of the idling jeep. "Transferred. I don't know where."

"So where does that leave us, Frank?"

"Leaves you here in this parking lot. I leveled with you, Nate—and you're free to use any of that yarn, as long as you don't use my name. If you do, I'll deny it on a stack of Bibles."

"That's comforting."

"It's like Mr. Ripley says—believe it or not."

I stepped out of the jeep, gave him a little wave, and he gave me a big old grin and big old wave and rumbled off.

I was about to get in the rental, to go driving in search of an interesting restaurant, when I said to hell with it, locked my spiral pad in the glove box and walked back to the hotel.

Bone-tired, I stumbled into the hotel, found my way to the dining room, where I consumed a rare steak and all the trimmings and a couple bottles of Blatz, which seemed to be the local favorite—I wondered if the little men in silver suits liked it better out of the bottle or from the tap. My room was on the third floor, a small clean cubicle that could have been in any hotel, except for the framed print of a desert landscape over the single bed. Caked with dust, frazzled by bizarre information, I showered, standing in the tub, letting the needles try to pound sense into me.

No smarter, but cleaner anyway, I toweled off, and strode naked from the bathroom, wondering whether

I should take in the show at the Chief Theater down the street, or just collapse into bed, where I figured it would take me maybe three seconds to lose consciousness, in which case I might not wake up to take advantage of the back-door date at ten p.m. I had at Maria Selff's place, when she got off work at the base hospital.

Instead, a powerful arm slipped around from behind me, an uninvited guest tucked against the wall outside the bathroom door, a gloved hand settling a chloroformed cloth over my face, changing my plans for the evening.

At least I was right about how long losing consciousness would take.

Fifteen

THE DREAMS WERE VIVID and they were strange and they were compelling but they were also comforting and I not only remembered them upon awaking, I can remember them today, so many years later, as if they were a movie I watched yesterday.

The usual for me, as I suspect is the case for most people, is that I lose my dreams upon awakening, sometimes instantly, sometimes grasping slippery fragments that slide away even as I try to hold on to them, with only the mood of them, their ambience, hanging on, particularly the unpleasant dreams, lingering like a bad taste in the brain, though nice dreams could, on rare occasions, wake you with a smile.

In this dream, I saw someone or something hovering over me, haloed in light, fuzzy and yet distinct, appearing from utter darkness, a small pale person with a big head and big eyes and a silver suit, his features childlike, his mouth tiny but smiling, his speech precise and strangely accented, his words soothing, though later the words were the one thing I could not recall, only that the man—I thought of him as a man, not a monster (or, for that matter, a woman)—was a kind presence, a friendly presence, an unthreatening presence, a real presence, not an imagined one, not some mortician's dream, not my nurse's nightmare, not a disgruntled soon-to-be-ex-employee's wild yarn, and yet at the same time it was all of those, and when that strange thumbless hand with the suction-cup fingertips touched my brow, it was as if a cool cloth had caressed my skin. . . .

When I awoke with a smile, in a bed, in cool sheets, in a cool, dark room, my first thoughts were of this dream, of the strange kind creature and its comforting presence, and I lay staring at the ceiling, fully awake and yet not really aware, luxuriating in the dream's afterglow, like the moments after sex, or a junkie coming slowly down.

And when the thought, the memory, finally broke through—*they fucking kidnapped me!*—I bolted upright, sheets falling to my waist—I was naked but for boxer shorts—the dream still with me but shoved back now, the smile reversing itself, and I sat there for long moments, eyes searching the darkness.

Head clear, body sluggish, my mouth thick with sleep and a brackish medicinal aftertaste—from the chloroform?—I made my way to a window where a fan was whirring . . . not just a fan, but the boxy structure of an evaporation type air cooler taking up the lower half of the bedroom's only window. Above it were blinds, which I drew open, and the night sky revealed itself. Stars and a full moon, too, the latter joining with outdoor electric lighting to illuminate the landscape of what was obviously a part of Walker Air Force Base.

My bare feet were on pile carpeting, and the moonlight revealed the shape of furnishings, a dresser, a few chairs, the bed, of course—and nightstand, with phone and lamp. . . .

I switched the lamp on; its blue parchment shade suffused the room with a gentle pastel glow. As for the phone, it was deader than Roosevelt. Despite that ominous note, I seemed to be in a nicely if modestly appointed bedroom, and the man in the mirror over the dresser seemed to be me, in shorts, looking confused but none the worse for wear. The walls were pale plaster, decorated here and there with framed prints of Southwestern vistas—not unlike the one in the hotel room I'd been snatched from.

This bedroom was, in fact, like a hotel or motel room; if I was a captive, this was an oddly benign prison cell, with any number of objects presenting themselves as the makings of makeshift weapons—mirror-shard knives, chair-leg billy clubs, phone-receiver sap, torn-bedsheet garrotes . . .

Was I in a deluxe jail cell? The window above the air-conditioner unit was fixed in place, unopenable; but that might have been a function of the unit's installation, not an attempt to keep me in. This left me with the room's three doors to try. . . .

The first one led to an empty closet; the second to a bathroom, which had a ventilation fan in the ceiling but no window, and no sign of toiletries on the sink, the cabinet over which was empty. But I did suddenly realize I had to pee, so I took the time to do that, and ponder my situation.

How long had I been here? Since I'd been grabbed virtually stepping out of the shower, I hadn't been wearing a watch; and the one common household item not present in that bedroom was a clock. Rubbing my face with one hand, I felt what I guessed was a day's growth of beard; this indicated I'd been here at least several hours, but—unless they'd taken the time to shave me—the night out that window was the same night I'd been snatched.

How long had I been unconscious, and dreaming that pleasant, weird, possibly drug-induced dream? Did that space creature in the dream represent someone who'd been questioning me, perhaps under sodium pentothal or some other truth-inducing drug?

I flushed the toilet, washed my hands—soap was provided, and a terry towel—and examined my arms and legs and between fingers and toes for needle marks; didn't see anything. The angle was wrong to check my ass out in the mirror, but there was no soreness in either cheek, from an intrusive needle.

Back out in the almost chilly bedroom—the desert air the window unit was churning up was already cool—I went to that final door, put my ear to it, heard nothing, and with a what-the-hell shrug tried the knob, expecting it to be locked.

It wasn't. I entered another darkened room, but light spilling in from the bedroom led me to a standing lamp that I switched on, imbuing a modest living room-cum-kitchenette with a golden glow. Next to the lamp was an easy chair and, man of the house that I was, I sat down, my legs a little rubbery, the alertness of my mind still outdistancing my body, as if below the neck I hadn't quite woken up all the way.

My easy chair matched the frayed blue cotton cushions of the davenport; the furnishings were maple-finish Early American, very homey in a spare modern way, scuffed and nicked from use, maybe even secondhand. Over the davenport, which had the look of a daybed, was a bigger Southwestern landscape, this print depicting a sunset almost as beautiful as the one I'd witnessed from Kaufmann's jeep. A coffee table, scarred with cigarette burns, was littered with a few dog-eared magazines—*Field & Stream, Skyways, Popular Mechanics;* also an ashtray with some spent cigarettes. Since I didn't smoke, I'd obviously had some company.

The only windows in the room were just behind my easy chair, double blinds drawn tight. Opposite the bedroom door was what I assumed to be the front door, to my right from where I sat. Low ceiling, creamy pebble-plaster walls; interestingly, no overhead lighting. This seemed to be that guest cottage Deputy Reynolds had referred to, where Mac Brazel and Sheriff Wilcox and God knew how many other witnesses of the saucer incident had been detained for "unofficial questioning."

So I sat there in my boxer shorts like Dagwood waiting for Blondie to bring him a sandwich and breathed slow and deep and took stock of my situation and myself; the oddly agreeable dream waved at me amiably from the back of my mind, though another part was already wondering why my subconscious found the notion of a space creature pleasing. I rotated my shoulders, rolled my neck, worked my joints, getting the juices going, the blood flowing, like an athlete prepping for the big game.

Then I got up and prowled some more. The drawers in the kitchenette were empty; no spoons or forks, certainly not knives. The cupboards had a few glasses and coffee cups but no supplies; the refrigerator was empty but for a few bottles of Coca-Cola and Canada Dry. I plucked one of the cold Cokes from its shelf and, using a drawer handle for a church key, opened it.

Sipping the soda, I walked to what I took to be double windows, raised the blinds, exposing instead a picture window, unopenable; I touched fingertips to the thing and it was some kind of clear plastic, possibly like what they used in aircraft cockpit windshields—toss a chair at this baby and it would toss the chair back at you. Beyond the plastic picture window were the low-slung barracks-style clapboard buildings of the base, interspersed with trees and bushes; not so much moonlight filtered in as yellow light from a streetlamp on the blacktop artery this cottage was perched along.

I closed the blinds.

Chugging my Coke, puzzling out my predicament, I went to the front door; a man's home was his castle, after all—if he wanted to lower the drawbridge and go out for a midnight pillage, who was to stop him?

"Who" was standing on my front stoop, his back to me: the brawny white-helmeted Negro MP from the jeep, blocking the way like the sentry he was. He glanced over his shoulder at me, like a bull acknowledging a buzzing fly. His face was a beautifully carved tribal mask, his eyes brown and placid and yet very, very hard.

"Can I help you?" He had an intimidating, lower-register Paul Robeson resonance.

"Yeah, how 'bout some clothes and a lawyer . . . oh, and a car."

The helmeted head shook. "I can't let you pass, mister. You're a guest of Colonel Blanchard."

"Swell. I'd like to talk to Colonel Blanchard."

"Colonel's gone for the day. Please move back inside."

And the MP, unblinking eyes fixed upon me, reached out and pulled the door shut.

I backed up a step, grunted, "Huh," took another swig of the Coke, considered my lot in life, and tried the door again—which still wasn't locked.

The MP's head turned slowly, almost mechanically, and his gaze over his shoulder at me oozed barely controlled impatience.

"Mister," he said with the world-weariness only a guy in his twenties can muster, "you got it easy in there. It could go lots harder for you. You prefer the stockade to the guesthouse, I can make that arrangement."

"Can I at least get something to eat?"

"You'll get breakfast in the morning."

The MP half-turned to reach out for the knob again, to slam the door, but instead I slammed the Coke bottle into the side of his head, just under the helmet, across his ear; it didn't knock him out, but sure as shit stunned him, and I yanked him by that arm and flung him like a shot put across the room, where he slammed into the davenport, which slammed into the wall, knocking that framed print off its nail, dropping with a clunk behind.

Now I shut the door.

The MP, who'd somehow lost his helmet on the trip across the room, was sneering at me as he came up off the davenport, blood running from his ear vivid against his black cheek. He moved slowly, with easy, pantherlike grace, crouching low, though even crouching he was taller than I was, and I was six foot, for Christ's sake! It looked like he planned to tackle me, but he was smarter than that: he simply unfastened his holster and got out his sidearm and was raising it, probably not to shoot me, just to cover me and make me listen to reason, but I was past reason, and I swung fast and hard with the Coke bottle and knocked the gun out of his hand, but the bottle slipped out, too, smacking against the plaster wall, taking out a chunk, not breaking. You ever try to break a Coke bottle?

Now he did tackle me, driving me back into my easy chair, but we both went backward, chair and all, ass over teakettle, and he was off-balance enough for me to shove up under him and toss him to one side, where he went crashing into the standing lamp, knocking it down, pulling its plug, sending the room into near darkness.

The MP was getting back on his feet again, but before he could get all the way up, I snatched his helmet off the floor and swung it around and clanged the damn thing off his skull. That dazed him, dropped him to a knee, but my swing had been awkward, the helmet slipping from my fingers and flying someplace. A massive fist arced around and caught me in the side, staggering but not dropping me, and as he was picking himself up, I was picking up that coffee table, magazines spilling, ashtray tumbling, and whammed it into him. The thing didn't shatter, like a chair in a John Wayne saloon fight—the damn thing was maple, and it hurt the big man, sent him onto both knees, this time. So I hit him with it again, across his hunched-over shoulders, and he flopped onto his face, not unconscious, just hurting, with things inside him broken, ribs mostly, I'd wager.

Catching my wind, I found his gun on the floor and, as he was rousing, trained it on him.

"I don't want to kill you," I said, "particularly."

"Shooting an MP is a federal offense." Despite the size of him, despite that commanding Old Man River voice, this fucker was scared.

"So is kidnapping a citizen. Take your clothes off."

His eyes and nostrils flared. "What?"

"Don't worry about it. You're not my type. Take 'em off. Try not to get any blood on 'em."

Grumbling, he got out of his MP uniform and soon we were just two guys in their boxer shorts, with a pile of clothes between us. He had the more impressive musculature by far, but I had the gun. Keeping the .38 trained on him, I crouched to sort through his things, fishing out his gunbelt; his handcuffs were looped on them.

"Turn around," I said, standing, his gun in my right hand, his handcuffs dangling in the left.

He spat on the floor. "Fuck you."

"I can cuff you or shoot you. Pick one."

Doing a commendable job retaining some dignity under humiliating conditions, the MP drew in a deep breath; the blood was glistening on his ear. He was a tough man: most guys wouldn't have to weigh the choice I'd given him. Slowly, he let out the breath; just as slowly, he turned his back to me, and I cuffed his hands behind him.

I left him in the bathtub, his ankles and knees bound with electrical cords I'd liberated from lamps, sticking one of his socks in his yap, shutting him in with the vent fan going (in case he managed to spit the sock out and start in yelling), leaving a chair propped under the knob of the closed bathroom door.

His clothes were too big for me, and I only had one sock, but he was only a half a shoe size or so bigger and the helmet fit fine, not to mention the .38 revolver, which was a perfect fit for my palm, though for decorum's sake I snapped it in its holster before setting out into the world that was Walker Air Force Base.

Bathed in more moonlight and streetlamp illumination than I cared to be, in my oversize one-sock uniform, helmet tipped forward like Bogart's fedora, I walked down the sidewalks with an MP's crisp confidence; at every intersection of blacktops, signs guided me. Up ahead, two noncoms exited a two-story office building, chatting, smoking, heading in my direction; they nodded to me, as they passed, and I nodded curtly back. Up ahead, a pair of MPs stepped out of a barracks, and I cut quickly to the right, moving off the sidewalk onto the grass, hugging bushes, hoping they didn't see me.

Apparently they didn't, as I was able to slip through a row of trees and onto another sidewalk, with hangars up ahead, the landing lights of a plane coming in, streaking through a wire fence in long white fingers, tickling me all over, and revealing another MP, patrolling along that perimeter. Heart pounding, I cut between two barracks, slipping within the safe haven of a row of shrubbery-surrounded trees planted between them, keeping low, almost tripping over two people on the ground.

Backing up, I was unsnapping the holstered sidearm, as somebody was saying, "Shit!"

Not me.

Down on the grass, an enlisted man—actually kid—had been embracing another enlisted man, both with their trousers around their ankles and a hand on each other's, well, gun (as the DI back at boot camp used to say, "This is your rifle, this is your gun, this is for Japs, and this is for fun"). They looked up at me in wide-eyed horror, probably not unlike the expression I was showing them.

"Oh God, oh God," one of the kids was saying. "Please don't turn us in! We weren't doing anything—honest!"

The other kid didn't say a word—he was too busy bawling.

Resnapping the holster, I raised a finger to my lips in shush fashion, whispered, "As you were," and moved on.

Thank God for those signs at intersections, because soon I was headed in the right direction. A black staff car rolled by, slowed momentarily, and I suddenly felt absurd in my baggy uniform, and even as my hand drifted over the holstered revolver, I wondered if I really had it in me to start shooting it out with the Air Force.

Then the car turned left, onto the adjacent blacktop artery, and slipped away into the night. Three

minutes and no further incidents later, faithfully following the intersection signs, I found the building I
was looking for: off by itself, with driveways flowing
in and around for easy access, the long, low, unpretentious white clapboard structure with USAF HOSPI-
TAL over its folksy screened-in porch.

I now had a wristwatch—a Bulova, courtesy of that
colored sergeant—and it was shortly before ten
o'clock p.m., which could be a piece of luck, as ten
was when Air Force nurse Maria Selff's shift ended. I
needed one more piece of luck: for Maria's powder-
blue coupe to be unlocked. There were perhaps
twenty-five cars parked in the front lot, but the sleek
Studebaker, with its short hood and long trunk, was
easy to spot.

The driver's-side door was locked; but the rider's-
side wasn't, and with a quick look around the rather
brightly lit lot, to make sure I was unseen, I opened
the door and slipped into the snug backseat, shut myself in, sitting low, below the wraparound rear windows. My timing was good, because within a minute,
cars began rolling in as new personnel arrived for
shift change. The lot was alive with slamming car
doors and coworker chatter. I kept low and waited.

Not long: within five minutes, she exited the building with two other nurses, chit-chatting as they each
withdrew keys from purses, the other two women
separating off to the left and their own cars, while
Maria headed right, toward me, as I spied her
through the side window, from my backseat slouch.
Clip-clopping in her white nurse's heels, she came
across the parking lot, the generous curves on the
small frame packed into her khaki dress, overseas cap
jauntily cocked, lustrous black hair pinned up.

I ducked down onto the floor just before she got
in, the dome light briefly blinding me before she shut

herself in with me. Before she had started the engine, I sat up—not way up—and said softly, "Maria, stay calm, it's me."

Startled, she turned, eyes wide, mouth open, and I said, "Just talk to me in the rearview mirror—I don't want to attract attention."

She turned away and the blue eyes, round with alarm, stared at me from the rearview mirror. "What are you doing?"

"Waiting for you."

"In the backseat?"

"Well, we did have a date."

Her eyes tightened in the mirror. "Nathan, why are you in an MP uniform? You're scaring me."

"Listen, I'll go if you want me to. I'll try to find a fence without an armed MP walking it, to climb over, and hoof it back to town. But what I want, if you're willing, is for you to sneak me off this goddamn place; I'll just duck down back here, or climb in the trunk—whatever makes you most comfortable."

"I . . . I think the trunk. When I go out through the gate, the guard would see you back there. . . . What's going on, Nathan? Are you going to get me court-martialed?"

"That's a possibility," I said, "and I'll head for that fence if you say so," and I filled her in on my kidnapping, up to and including my escape from the base "guesthouse."

She was shaking her head, and the eyes in the mirror were closed. "I told you . . . I told you I was putting all of us in danger. They warned me not to talk . . . I should never . . ."

I put a hand on her shoulder. "Now, you gotta get hold of yourself, beautiful. We just don't have time, either one of us, to have a nervous breakdown right now. Understand?"

She swallowed, nodded.

"You okay? Got your composure back? Why don't you dry your eyes."

She got a hanky out of her purse and did.

"All right," I said. "Okay. Let's see if I can fit in that trunk. . . ."

Some other hospital personnel on Maria's shift—nurses, orderlies, a doctor or two—were getting their cars; we waited for a clear shot, then we got out, she opened the trunk and I crawled in—just me and a spare Goodyear, in the red blush of her taillights, a big fetus in an MP's uniform. I heard her get back in the car, shut the door, ignition key bringing the engine to life, and the Studey had a smooth ride, as she guided the buggy down the blacktops and glided up to a stop at the front sentry.

I heard some muffled conversation, friendly, male laughter, female laughter—some son of a bitch was flirting with my date!—and then we were moving again, more quickly. My muscles and bones ached, as if I had the flu—or maybe it had something to do with my 190 pounds being stuffed in a car's trunk.

In under five minutes, the Studebaker rolled to a stop. I heard her get out, and then the lid lifted and there she was, Maria, my personal nurse, framed against a starry sky that was the same color blue as those concern-filled eyes in the heart-shaped face under the cute, cocked hat. With her in my life, what was I doing dreaming about space men?

She helped me out of the trunk, and I needed the help, my legs still rubbery, joints creaky as a rusty gate, and I found myself in the alley behind the Mission Revival–style bungalow she rented on Pennsylvania Avenue. We went in the back way and she sat me down at a Formica table in a cozy white-trimmed-red kitchen.

"I'll put some coffee on," she said.

"Please."

"You need anything to eat? There's a couple kinds of sandwiches I can make you . . ."

"No. No thanks."

Maria got the coffee going, then sat beside me; if she looked any cuter in that khaki nurse's outfit I would have done handsprings, or bust out crying. "They'll be looking for you soon, Nathan."

I nodded. "Do you think anyone's connected the two of us?"

She took off her hat, tossed it on the table, began unpinning her shining black hair; her mouth glistened with bright red lipstick. "Other than Glenn, no—and he wouldn't say a word. He'd want to protect me and, anyway, he has to do business at the base, wouldn't want it known he gave you that information. . . . Oh my God!"

She covered her mouth in horror.

"What?" I asked.

"Your spiral pad . . . your notes, *my name,* everyone you talked to, if they took that from your hotel room—"

I shook my head, no, my expression reassuring. "It wasn't in my hotel room; it's locked in the glove compartment of the rental. I doubt they've got it."

"How can you be sure?"

"If they did, we'd have company by now."

I put the gun on the table, where it served as a strange centerpiece; the pageboy once again brushing her shoulders, she looked at the weapon gravely.

I said, "I need to get out of this town—this state. Look, I may still have a little time, before they find that MP, or he hobbles out of that bathroom. . . . I better go get my car. . . ."

She touched my hand. "What if they're watching, what if they're waiting . . . ?"

"I won't go to my hotel room—I'll just fetch my Ford, which is out in the open, in public. They grab me, I'll make a big loud stink." I patted the .38. "And loud noises. . . . I wasn't arrested, remember—bastards kidnapped me. That's illegal, even in New Mexico."

Her eyes narrowed in thought. "Have you considered going to the sheriff's office?"

I smirked, laughed once. "You really think I should go anywhere in Roswell, but here?" I pushed my chair away from the table, stood. "Listen, Maria, you've been terrific . . . but I don't want to get you in a jam—I'm gonna walk over and get my car, and get outa this tinhorn town. I'm not even waiting for the noon stage. . . ."

Now she stood, clutched my MP's shirtsleeve. "In that uniform? You know, they shoot spies for that. . . . Just wait. Have your coffee, first . . . I may have a better idea."

"Maria, I'm running out of time."

The coffee had stopped perking; she went over and poured me a cup. "Cream or sugar?"

"Little sugar," I sighed, walking over to her. "What's your better idea?"

Stirring in a spoonful, she said, "Let me change into civilian clothes, and *I'll* walk over and get your car. . . . Where is it?"

"In that lot on Third Street, but—"

She put the cup of coffee in my hands, walked me over and forced me to sit; weak as my legs were, she didn't have much trouble accomplishing that.

"I'll drive it back here," she said. "I've got a little garage just across the alley, where I usually park the Studebaker. I'll tuck it away in there till you're ready to leave."

I was shaking my head. "Even so, I still need

clothes, and going after my things in that hotel room is out of the question. . . ."

"You're right, that would be too dangerous, for either of us." She looked side to side, as if an answer might be hiding somewhere in the kitchen; then her expression firmed, as if she'd found one. "I have . . . some things here you can wear."

"Your husband's?"

She nodded. "They're in a trunk in my bedroom. May smell a little of mothballs, but they should do you fine—you must wear the same size Steve did, or darn close."

"I can't let you do this," I said. "Too risky. What if you're followed back here, and they find out you were helping me . . ."

"It's no risk, not if we get you out of that MP uniform, and I dump it in a garbage can on my way over to your car. Then, if it comes to that, I simply plead ignorance: how was I to know the Air Force was after you?"

No question about it: she was making sense. Even if they had my notebook, and knew she'd spoken to me on the forbidden "saucer" subject, that didn't mean she knew about my fugitive status.

So I got out of the MP uniform, and bundled it up in brown paper for her, while she changed into a maize-color T-shirt and blue denim slacks and open-toed leather sandals.

"You look like a college coed," I said, handing her the bundle.

Those full cherry-lipsticked lips twisted sideways and she arched an eyebrow knowingly. "You look like a big lug in his boxer shorts."

"That's when I like you best," I said.

"When?"

"When you get out of character. Who'd have

guessed the sensitive waif I met last night could take charge like this?"

Her eyes lowered and her mouth quivered; I wasn't sure whether she was taking offense or letting some nervousness show through. Quietly, she said, "Well, I am in the military, you know."

Then, bundle under her arm, she slipped out the back way, and I sat thinking fond thoughts of her as I drank my coffee.

The trunk in her bedroom provided plenty of choices; I picked out a blue-knit T-shirt, some gray tropical slacks, and some socks with clocks on them. They did smell of mothballs at that, and I laid the clothes out on the dresser, to air out a little, and flopped onto the bed in my shorts, just to rest a wee bit before she got back. I knew I wouldn't fall asleep, particularly after the caffeine in that coffee. But the alertness of my mind fooled me: my weary body had been right all the time.

I was asleep in maybe ten seconds.

Another dream, pleasant dream, of the small pale child/man with the big head and big eyes and silver suit, speaking soothing words, friendly, unthreatening. . . .

I opened my eyes; it was dark and I was under cool sheets again, and someone was hovering over me—not a space creature, an exquisite creature: Maria, tousled black hair, blue eyes, red lips, creamy naked curves, bending down to kiss me on the mouth.

This was not a dream, but it was much, much better, as she buried that lustrous black hair in my lap, fingers fishing expertly in the flap of my boxers and if I really was only the second man she'd ever been with, that first guy had taught her plenty. I made her stop before I came, and she stroked me gently and mounted me and rode me, tenderly, like a child guiding its pet burro up an arroyo, and very soon she came and I came, in a mutual shuddering loss of control. She withdrew me from her, then slipped away, went off to do whatever women do, and, in bra and panties, came trundling back with a Kleenex for me and fell into my arms, whispering, "You must be very tired, very tired, very tired," and I was, I was, I was. . . .

Sixteen

T HE ROOM WAS STILL DARK, but sunlight was finding its way in and around the closed window
blinds; birdies were tweeting and paperboys were
missing porches and milkmen were clattering bottles
and traffic was just starting to flow.

I sat up. I felt incredibly rested; never slept better
in my life, and if I'd been dreaming, whether about
spacemen or pretty girls or an imaginary day at the
racetrack, I had no memory of it.

Hair pinned up under the cocked overseas hat,
Maria was sitting in the kitchen, in her khaki nurse's
uniform, having toast and coffee, looking cuter than
Shirley Temple. And these days Shirley Temple was
looking pretty cute.

"Must be morning," I said.

"Yes," she purred, and her smile was gently wry,
even if her toast was white. "Question is, what morning?"

I pulled up an eyebrow and a chair and sat. "What
do you mean?"

Her lush lips formed a mocking kiss. "Are you hun-
gry, by any chance?"

"Actually . . . now that you mention it, yeah! Rav-
enous."

"That may be because you've been sleeping since
the night before last."

"What? Straight through?"

My private nurse rose and began making me breakfast; she was prepared: a skillet waited on the stove, and—on the counter nearby—two eggs in a bowl, a bottle of milk, several strips of crisp bacon already shedding their grease on a paper towel, toast in a toaster poised for pushing down.

"How do you like 'em?" she asked, an egg in hand.

"Like my brains, scrambled. Maria, tell me I didn't sleep straight through."

She cracked two eggs and started scrambling. "You roused once and wanted to know where the bathroom was. And I showed you. And you used it. And went right back to bed, to sleep."

"God, I don't remember that, at all. They must've pumped a lot of drugs into me, for me to need to sleep it off like that. . . . What about the car?"

"I got it. Notebook, too."

"Any sign of trouble out at the base?"

She shrugged. "I wouldn't know. I called in sick yesterday to baby-sit you. Today I start back on morning shift."

I rubbed my face; heavy beard but not outrageous. "Jesus—we're lucky they didn't put your absence together with my 'jailbreak.' "

She stirred the eggs, adding some milk. "If they haven't connected us by now, they're not going to. But I did have a call from the commanding officer, himself."

"Blanchard! What the hell did he want?"

"I'm being transferred. Remember, I had that hanging over me? The colonel wanted to thank me personally for my 'fine service.' "

"Transferred to where?"

"I haven't received my orders yet."

"Could it have anything to do with . . ."

"I don't think so—this has been a long time coming. Anyway, Nathan, if they knew about us, they'd be here, wouldn't they?"

"You would think. You would think. Maria, I have to go."

"Go sit down. I'll serve you."

I sat, and soon she placed the plate of scrambled eggs and bacon before me, and a glass of orange juice, buttered toast and a cup of coffee. "Where do you have to go, Nathan?"

I began eating; God I was starved. "Not home. I'm going underground for a few weeks, maybe longer— my friends in Chicago will tell me if the heat is on or off."

Her brow furrowed. "What if the heat *is* on? And what if it stays on?"

"I don't know." I took a bite of toast, chewed as I talked; we knew each other well enough for that. "I do have a few friends in high places, and low ones, and I'll call on them, if need be. But I won't make an issue out of this unless I have to. I just want my life back. Maria, I have learned one thing from my investigation, and one thing only: that I do not give a flying shit whether men from outer space crashed near your fair city."

Her expression was blank. "Then maybe your stay at the guesthouse served its purpose. Maybe that's all they were after."

"Then they succeeded. Flying colors."

When I'd finished my breakfast—which was soon—she took the dishes to the sink and ran water over them.

I stood and found a small notepad and pencil by the fridge. "Maria, this is my business number. Call that when you know where your new duty assignment is."

She took the slip of paper, folded it, and snugged it in her breast pocket. Then she slipped her arms around my waist; the blue eyes looked up at me, as if daring me to dive in. "Does this mean you want to see me again, Nathan?"

"Yeah—anywhere but Roswell."

"Aren't you going to kiss me goodbye?"

"Sure ..."

I kissed her, and she kissed back, and it was passionate and sweet and I asked, "When do you have to be at work?"

"Not for a while yet ..."

"How would you feel about hiking up that skirt and taking off your panties and really saying goodbye. ..."

"I think that could arranged," she said with a wicked little smile.

"And please," I said, "leave the little hat on. ..."

"Where shall we ... ?"

"How about one of these chairs. ..."

"Oh my," she said, a little while later, breathing hard, still straddling my lap; me, I was ready for another long nap. "Nathan, that ... that was out of this world. ..."

"I bet you say that to all the Martians."

My car was, as promised, in the garage across the alley. My nurse—her skirt only slightly wrinkled—waved goodbye from the kitchen doorway and, wearing her late husband's clothes, I waved back at her, like she was the little woman and, like a good breadwinner—even if I was unshaven and lacked a lunch pail—I might have been heading for work.

Not preparing to hide my sorry ass.

THREE:

WHITE LIES

WASHINGTON, D.C.
MAY 1949

Seventeen

ONE FINE SATURDAY MORNING in late May, the District of Columbia alive with dogwoods and cherry trees in full blossom, I found myself being chauffeured all about the capital city by a certain skinflint millionaire journalist. During the ride, I was reminded that—despite this city's bewilderingly laid-out street system—the white obelisk of the Washington Monument's position against the washed-out blue of the horizon always served as a massive reference point. Which came in handy, because my chauffeur wasn't taking me anywhere in particular.

We were in the black Buick convertible, which served as Drew Pearson's second office; it was pretty spiffy, right down to its red-leather seats, and the license plate number was a simple 13—the columnist's lucky number.

"I was getting worried," Pearson said, his smile slitting his eyes and sending the well-waxed tips of his mustache skyward, "when your man in Chicago . . . Sapperstein, is it? . . . said you'd be 'incommunicado for an unspecified interval.' "

"That sounded better than 'holed-up someplace,' " I said. "Hey, can't we just park somewhere and talk?"

Pearson was pretty spiffy himself, wearing a gray homburg, dapperly angled and a shade darker than his striped tropical worsted suit, which was enlivened

by a blue tie with a brown-and-yellow bird motif.
How he kept his hat on, in the wind his rapid driving
stirred up, was a mystery this Sherlock Holmes
couldn't solve—glue? Chewing gum? Masking tape?

"Pull over and talk, and be the prey of some lip-
reader?" Pearson asked archly, bulleting through a
yellow light. "I don't think so, Nathan. . . . Besides,
driving relaxes me. Helps me think."

Though I was on the clock, it was Saturday and I
was casually dressed, a brown-and-white checked
sportjacket over a ribbed sky-blue T-shirt. My hat, a
light brown Southwest Flight, was at my feet, or it
would've taken flight, southwest or otherwise.

"Yeah, it helps me think, too," I said. "Like, I think
you're gonna kill us both if you don't slow down."

I had stayed underground—in Vegas, with an old
girlfriend of mine, who worked in the chorus line at
the Flamingo—for three weeks. Checking in on a
daily basis with my office, I learned that no inquiries
about my whereabouts had come from government
sources, or any suspicious sources, for that matter; the
office was swept for electronic bugs and phone taps
every second day—clean as a freshly bathed baby's
butt. Lou Sapperstein—my former boss on the pick-
pocket detail, and current employee, a turnabout I
never ceased to relish—had determined to his satisfaction that neither the office nor my apartment was
under any kind of surveillance.

And, every day when I phoned in, I asked if we'd
heard from Maria Selff about where she'd been
transferred—and every day, no word from her. I had
Lou, pretending to be doing a credit check, call the
Walker Air Base hospital, where he learned the nurse
had indeed been transferred but requests for her
whereabouts would have to go "through channels."

I wasn't too concerned about this; Maria was probably distancing herself from me, in case she and her movements (and even calls) were being monitored. When the time was right, I figured, I would hear from her. Our relationship had been brief, yes, but also intense; and something genuine had passed between us, besides bodily fluids.

With Sapperstein's reassurances that the coast was clear—or anyway, the lakeshore—I'd returned to the A-1 offices in Chicago's Loop. There, somewhat unnervingly, the first phone call for me on my first day back was from a government source, out of Washington, D.C., no less: it was one of Forrestal's Bethesda shrinks, Dr. Bernstein, who had added a second reason for me making the trip, beyond reporting in to Pearson.

"You will be pleased to know," the shrink said, the middle-European accent giving his voice a lilt, "that your former client is doing very well."

"That is good news."

"Is there a possibility you'll be coming to D.C., soon? Mr. Forrestal would be comforted by a visit from you."

"Well, I do have pending business. In fact, I should be there next week."

"Good. Excellent. Call me when you get to town, and I'll see to it that your name is on the visitors list."

And now, five days later, I was back in our nation's capital, with our nation's most feared commentator, aimlessly driving the beautifully paved web of streets in the midst of which the White House sat like a lovely spider. An appointment had been arranged by Dr. Bernstein and I would see Jim Forrestal in his tower room at Bethesda this afternoon, at two.

Pearson had similarly upbeat news about Forrestal to report. "You'll be pleased to hear that your *other* client is on the road to recovery. Gaining his weight back. Truman visited him and pronounced Jim Forrestal 'his old self,' if that's a good thing."

"Would you prefer he stay sick in the head?"

A sneer lifted one waxed mustache tip. "I believe James Forrestal's been sick in his soul a lot longer. I want him to stay out of politics, but rumor is Truman's planning to give him some important government post."

I snorted a laugh, leaning an arm where the window was rolled down. "I doubt that, not straight outa the loony bin. Why don't you lay off the guy, anyway? Jesus, it's fuckin' overkill."

This only amused my dapper chauffeur, who was guiding the Buick around Dupont Circle, as if rounding a curve at the Indy 500. "Still singing that sad song, Nathan? Overkill's a necessity in my business; the public has a notoriously short memory—repetition's the only cure. Anyway, I'm the one you should feel sorry for—I'm the one getting the hate mail."

"Gee, I wonder why. You really know how to please a crowd, Drew—beating on a guy when he's down."

Soon we were on Connecticut Avenue, with traffic heavy enough to keep Pearson's speedometer within reason, in the thick of older buildings and homes converted to charming and probably expensive specialty shops—art dealers, antique stores, boutiques, high-class markets and bookstores.

Just north of M Street, we were paused in backed-up traffic next to a bronze statue in the middle of a grassy dividing triangle, a majestic male figure in academic robes seated in a chair with a book in one hand and a pigeon on his head (the latter not a part of the statue proper).

"Longfellow," Pearson said, noticing me eyeballing the striking statue. "The poet."

"Didn't figure him for a soldier or a politician, not that the pigeons care, either way. Reminds me! Pull over there, would you?"

"Why?"

I was pointing to an open parking space in front of Jefferson Place Books. "I need to pick something up."

"All right, but make it quick—I have a luncheon date, at the Cosmos Club, with Averell Harriman, and you have less than an hour to make your report."

Before long I was back in the convertible, my purchase in a plain brown paper bag.

"*Forever Amber*?" Pearson asked with a smirk and one raised eyebrow. "Or *I, the Jury*"?

"You wouldn't believe it if I told you."

As he pulled back into traffic, Pearson took one hand off the wheel to reach over and rustle at the brown paper bag, and peek in. "Poetry? Nathan Heller?"

"It's a gift—for Jim Forrestal."

"Touching. You must feel terribly guilty, taking money from the villain who put that patriot in the mental ward."

Taking money from Pearson never bothered me other than the small amounts involved—but the son of a bitch was closer than he knew. I'd spoken to Dr. Bernstein again, yesterday afternoon, after checking in at the Ambassador, and he had once more stressed how well Jim Forrestal was doing, though he clearly had reservations.

"Both Dr. Raines and I are in general very pleased," Bernstein had told me over the phone. "There's been a marked improvement in Mr. Forrestal's condition; he's responding well to treatment."

"Glad to hear it."

"His moods of depression are still with him, however—he's fine through the week, but by Saturday and Sunday, he's descended into a state of nervous agitation and anxiety."

"Why is that?"

"Consider it yourself, Mr. Heller—what happens on Sunday night?"

I winced. "Drew Pearson's radio show," I said. "Don't tell me you guys let him listen to it!"

"We don't allow him to listen to the radio at all, Mr. Heller—but on Monday morning, if I do not give Mr. Forrestal an oral summary of the broadcast, he becomes extremely agitated."

"I wish I could convince Pearson to back off."

"Mr. Heller, you touch on the very reason why I want you to see Mr. Forrestal."

"What's that?"

"You just let slip, yourself, that you and Pearson are in contact."

"Well, I, uh . . ."

"One of the perquisites of practicing psychiatry in a military hospital, Mr. Heller, is an ability to do in-depth background research on your patients . . . in this case, I was aided by both the FBI and Secret Service. So I'm well aware that you have a business relationship with Drew Pearson, predating that of my patient becoming your client."

"Okay, Doc, you caught me—but I've never sold either one of them out for the other."

"Still, you're not denying the conflict of interests."

"I always looked after both their interests, to the best of my ability, and judgment."

"I believe you. The problem is this: for whatever reason, Mr. Forrestal thinks very highly of you. You are one of the few associates in his life, business or otherwise, who remain untainted by any of his paranoid delusions."

"That's nice, I guess."

"Mr. Forrestal is progressing very well. However—
I believe he is at a stage in his recovery where news
of what would seem to him a betrayal, by someone he
trusted implicitly—*you,* Mr. Heller—could be very
damaging. Could set him back weeks. Months."

"Well, *I'm* not going to tell him."

"Oh, but that's exactly what you must do."

"What? Are you crazy, too, Doc?"

His voice took on a somber cast. "If Mr. Forrestal
hears this news from anyone but you, the effect could
be devastating. If you tell him yourself—not so much
confess, but explain your dual loyalties, and assure
him of your friendship, and that you have never betrayed him to Pearson, nor would you . . . that is the
only chance he has of accepting, and coming to terms
with, that deception on your part."

"Christ, I don't know, Doc—"

"Think of it as an apology. Make a gesture. Bring
him a gift. You know that he loves to read. Why don't
you bring him a book of poetry? A book of poetry
would be comforting."

"I wouldn't know what to buy."

"A book of poetry would be comforting."

"I heard ya the first time, doc."

"Might I suggest Mark Van Doren's *Anthology of
World Poetry.*"

Which was why, the next afternoon, I'd asked Pearson to pull up in front of Jefferson Place Books to fill
the doctor's prescription. Now, that very volume in a
paper bag on my lap, I resumed my meeting on
wheels with the chief cause of Forrestal's lingering illness, and perhaps the only obstacle to his return to
mental health.

"D'you mind telling me why you went underground for nearly a month, Nathan?" Pearson asked
pleasantly from behind the wheel. We were playing

tag with streetcars on Pennsylvania Avenue at the moment, on our way for our third or fourth look at the Executive Mansion. "Little green men from outer space chasing you?"

"Worse. Big khaki men from the planet earth."

"I don't normally think of you as a coward, Nathan."

"Do you normally think of me as stupid? I don't buck the odds unless I have to."

"This sounds like quite a story."

"Well, I wouldn't stop the presses just yet. I'm not sure you're going to be able to use anything I've come up with."

I started at the end, telling him how my investigation had made me so popular with the Air Force that I'd been invited for a special stay in the Walker base "guesthouse."

"You're going to have to go public about this," Pearson said, his expression grave. Even his mustache seemed to have wilted.

"Why? They kidnapped me, and I got away. It's not like I'm fleeing arrest, and nobody seems to be looking for me."

"If I put this in my column, Nathan, it'll be a life insurance policy: the Air Force will of course deny having done this to you, which will keep them, or any other government agency, from applying the strongarm to you, in future."

"No fucking way do I go public, Drew. They sent me a message, by grabbing me; I've sent them a message, by not reporting it. We'll leave it at that."

"All right . . ." He shook his head, in wonder. ". . . but you must've gotten close to something very big. . . ."

"Yeah, about twenty-five feet by fifteen feet."

I told him the rest of the story, referring to my spiral pad, which I'd brought along, not having written any of this up as a formal report. I went over every witness, from the mortician and the nurse to the insurance agent and the fireman, from the sheriff and his deputy to the radio broadcaster and the rancher, and of course Colonel Blanchard of the frat-house grin and ice-cold eyes. But it was base security chief Kaufmann's tale of a crashed saucer, complete with outer space crew and military retrieval operation, that really got the columnist's attention.

Or was it my matter-of-fact telling of the wild tale that really jarred him?

"Good God, man—you *believe* this stuff, don't you?"

I hadn't actually admitted that to myself, but now I heard my voice saying, out loud, to Drew Pearson yet, "Yes. I think a flying saucer crashed near Roswell—and the government has it in storage somewhere, along with the bodies of the crew."

"And one of these . . . creatures might still be alive? Kept in some secret installation?"

"Yes. These are credible witnesses, Drew, although there are inconsistencies—Glenn Dennis talks about bodies being exposed in the desert sun, torn by predators, while Frank Kaufmann swears the retrieval mission took place relatively shortly after the crash, and before sunup."

"Perhaps other bodies were found later, thrown from the craft, and . . ." We were stopped at a red light; hands on the wheel, he glanced over at me, wide-eyed. "My Lord, will you listen to me, taking this seriously? Do you hear yourself talking, Nathan?"

"I do. And that's the funny thing."

"What is?"

"I'm absolutely convinced that these creatures exist, that a saucer crashed—and yet my instinct is, you shouldn't go with this story."

Someone behind us honked: my chauffeur, this hot-rodder in a homburg, had been sitting through the green light.

Pearson got moving again, not driving so rapidly, now. "But we have testimony from multiple eye-witnesses—"

"None of whom will come forward. None of whom will allow themselves to be identified as anything more than a 'source.' "

Pearson was shaking his head. "You said it yourself: this could be the biggest story of the millennium—and if it isn't, why did the Air Force try to shut you up?"

"Me and how many others, back in Roswell? I wasn't the first one in that 'guesthouse.' "

"You have to talk to Forrestal about this."

"What? Have you gone mad?"

We were rounding the spherical lawn of the templelike Lincoln Memorial, now, and endlessly circled it for the rest of our talk, like a plane never coming in for its landing.

"No," Pearson said emphatically, "you're going to talk to the madman. It comes back to Majestic Twelve, the group Forrestal and Truman created after the Roswell saucer crash."

"Do you have proof that group exists?"

"I have photostats of briefing documents, indicating it does, but I haven't been able to verify them— they're marked 'Majic-12, Top Secret,' which limits my ability to do that."

I smirked at him. "You mean, 'cause you could go to Leavenworth for possessing them?"

A small facial tic, in his upper lip, kicked in. "They may be forgeries. This still may all be an elaborate hoax designed to discredit me . . ."

"Are you important enough, Drew, even in your

own mind, to imagine that all of those people in Roswell are part of a government disinformation campaign to make a sap out of you?"

He frowned, the tic jumping. "*What* kind of information, did you say?"

"Disinformation—government lies posing as the truth. Sort of like when you published that story about Forrestal's cowardice in that jewel robbery."

His eyebrows rose, and so did his homburg. "Then let's suppose it's not misinformation . . . *dis*information, as you put it, black propaganda—let's say you and your Roswell witnesses are right: a saucer crashed in the desert, with a crew consisting of beings from another planet. . . ."

"Let's say."

Pearson's voice grew hushed, like a scoutmaster telling his boys a ghost story around a campfire; he was driving slowly now, as we circled Honest Abe, as if the Buick were running out of gas—but Pearson sure wasn't.

"Now let's think about Jim Forrestal's behavior," he said, "from July 1947 until today, a frazzled individual already suffering from the civilian equivalent of battle fatigue, saddled with a wife herself ill with alcoholism and schizophrenia. Put in the hands of that ticking time bomb of a man—a man charged with the safety of his country—such momentous new information, such a consequential new responsibility . . ."

I laughed, once. "You mean, picture Jim Forrestal as one of the few key members of government who knows we've had a visit from outer space."

He nodded emphatically; the facial tic jumped. "Yes, from creatures whose intentions are unknown to us, and, coming out of this recent devastating war as we have, wouldn't it be natural for Secretary of

Defense Forrestal to consider hostile objectives a likely possibility? Suppose . . . just suppose now, Nathan . . . that Jim Forrestal's paranoia isn't really directed at Mother Russia."

"Maybe he's spooked not by the Reds, but the Red Planet Mars, you mean?"

"Precisely. Maybe the 'they' he thinks are out to get him are little gray or green or silver men. Maybe the invasion he's running in the streets announcing is not from the Soviet Union, but from beyond the stars?"

"Yeah, put that in your column. Go with that. And I'll be visiting *you* at Bethesda."

Suddenly he pulled over, almost opposite the steps up to the memorial. "Nathan, you're going to see Forrestal today, aren't you?"

"Yes."

"Well, never mind the poetry, man! Ask him about Roswell. Ask him about Majic-12."

Eighteen

FOR ALL ITS GRANITE GRANDEUR, the U.S. naval hospital at Bethesda had its cramped aspects; its four wings were rather small, and the floors of its impressive, impractical tower provided limited patient space. The air-conditioned, disinfectant-scented sixteenth floor had a modest capacity of thirteen; only ten patients were currently in residence, however, as the former Secretary of Defense occupied 1618, a large, square double room from which the second bed had been removed, with the smaller adjacent room reserved for doctors and orderlies assigned twenty-four-hour watch on their important patient.

After checking in with the Navy medical corpsman who sat watch outside his door, I found Forrestal seated by the window, draped rather elegantly in a burgundy silk dressing gown with a yellow rope-style, fringed sash, legs crossed, exposing cream-color pajamas and brown leather slippers. All he lacked was an ascot. Smoking his trademark pipe, sitting back in a padded wooden chair, iron-gray hair neatly cut, clean-shaven, arms folded, entirely self-composed, he was staring out the window at a view of the hospital's busy driveway and landscaped grounds.

The room seemed even larger than it was, due to that second bed's absence, and conveyed a sterile emptiness; the walls were a faint peach color, and the sparse furnishings included a writing desk, a couple chairs, a nightstand and a hospital bed, cranked into upright position. A curtain gathered at the wall indicated where the double room would be divided, when not occupied by such an illustrious guest. Forrestal had been here, what? Seven weeks now? So there were no flowers, though on a small table against the right wall countless "Get Well" cards stood like little soldiers.

I'd stepped just inside the room, hat in hand. "Jim? It's Nate."

Still seated, the rather small man glanced my way and his Jimmy Cagney–like face, with its boxing-flattened nose, regarded me blankly for an instant, before the pencil-line mouth broke into the widest smile I'd ever seen him bestow. He almost leapt to his feet and charged over to meet me midway, where we shook hands, his grip as firm as ever.

"Nate Heller," he said. His eyes were bright, his manner ebullient. "I'd been hoping you'd stop by, at some point, on this pleasure cruise."

I tossed the paper bag with the poetry book in it on his nightstand, next to another book, *Peace of Faith* by Fulton J. Sheen.

"You look fine," I told him. "How much more of this resting up can you stand?"

"Dr. Raines says within a month I'll be walking out of here." Forrestal pulled a chair up for me, opposite his, by the window, and we both sat; I noticed the window had been fitted with a heavy steel screen, the security-style that locked with a key. He noticed me noticing.

"That's to keep me from jumping out the window," he said cheerfully, teeth tight around the pipe stem. "That and the 'round-the-clock surveillance. Interesting way to treat a man with symptoms of paranoia, don't you think? Watch him constantly?"

I had to smile. "I hear paranoia is a self-fulfilling prophecy."

His eyes tightened. "True enough, and I have no complaint about the medical treatment I've received, but I do resent, bitterly, the nonsensical extremes these restrictions have been carried to . . . and not entirely for my own benefit, in my opinion."

"What do you mean, Jim?"

He gestured rather forcefully with the pipe. "This is not paranoia speaking, Nate, nor schizophrenia or any other mental disorder. These psychotherapy sessions, which were on a daily basis until recently, served to inspire me to do my own self-analysis of the feelings of persecution that brought me to this room. Do you remember, at the golf course, when we talked briefly about religion?"

"Sure, that I was a Jew but didn't follow the faith, and you'd been raised Catholic and had rejected it."

He sat forward, his eyes intense. "Yes. I believe I've long harbored a guilt, however deeply buried, for rejecting the faith my mother worked so diligently to instill within me. I've wondered if, perhaps, the root cause of my troubles is my break with the Church, that I've been punished . . . or have punished myself . . . for being a bad Catholic. Consequently, I've found myself working my way back to my boyhood faith."

I nodded toward his nightstand. "I noticed the book by Monsignor Sheen."

"I bring this up, Nate, not by way of soul-searching, but to demonstrate that, even with my thinking clear again, I'm more convinced than ever I'm being watched, controlled."

Until he'd made this statement, I'd been feeling good about Forrestal's condition; but now my neck was starting to tingle.

He must have sensed that and his smile was somewhat chagrined. "No, not by Russians, or Zionists,
Nate—by my own government."

Now that I could believe.

Folding his arms again, he sat back, took a few
puffs of the pipe, then spoke with clarity and confidence. "My brother Henry, who's been to visit me frequently, cherishes this rekindling of my Catholicism,
and consequently has asked my doctors to allow a
priest—a Father Sheehy—to visit me. And they have
refused."

"Why in hell?" What sort of doctor denied a mental patient the guidance and solace a visit by a cler-
gyman might bring?

Forrestal arched an eyebrow. "I asked both Dr.
Raines and Dr. Bernstein, and their answers were the
same: reopening the Catholic issue, at this time,
would be too 'disquieting' to me."

"What do you think the real reason is?"

The thin line of a mouth formed the faintest of
smiles. "Can't you guess, Nate? I've always admired
your shrewd, if unschooled, analytical mind."

I thought about it for a few moments, then said,
"You entering a Catholic confessional would risk disclosure of sensitive national security issues."

"Bull's-eye," Forrestal said, eyes twinkling. His
gaze fell upon the steel screen again, beyond which a
sunny May afternoon seemed to beckon. "I could
never bring myself to jump out a window, anyway—
I've always had a mild case of vertigo. And slashing
my wrists would be entirely too messy. I believe I'd
opt for sleeping pills or perhaps hang myself."

"Now you're scaring me."

"A master of the art not recognizing sarcasm?" he
chuckled. "Disappointed in you, Nate. . . . They're
concerned about me attempting suicide? And yet I'm

on the sixteenth floor, when most of the mental patients at Bethesda receive treatment in a one-story wing . . . and they are reluctant to have me rekindle my Catholic faith, a faith that would include the very rejection of suicide as a mortal sin. What do you make of that?"

"There's no paranoia in those suspicions; you'd be nuts not to think that way."

He gestured with the pipe again. "They had my house bugged, too, when I hired you."

"Jim, I had it thoroughly swept . . ."

"The government knew you were coming, didn't they? They knew I'd hired you?"

That was true: the Secret Service certainly did.

Forrestal shrugged. "They took them out. And they would've put them back again, if I hadn't . . . slipped out of control, first."

"You seem fine to me now, Jim."

Nodding, he said, "I'll be all right; I'm pulling out of it. And, to give the bastards credit due them, they are lessening up on the restrictions. I'm allowed to leave this room, visit with other patients, flirt with the nurses . . . and I have full run of the pantry, across the hall. Here, I'll show you—let me play host."

Noting that the Naval medical corpsman was not at his post, I followed the silk-robed Forrestal—who left his pipe behind—across the hall to a much smaller room, a galley-like pantry with a single table, counter and cupboards, and a refrigerator. A pot of coffee sat, steaming fragrantly, on a hot plate.

"Care for a cup?" he asked.

"Thanks. One lump of sugar."

As he prepared the coffee for himself and me, Forrestal said, "This is a rather nice privilege. . . . They call this the diet kitchen, and of all of the patients, I alone have been granted its use—I can wander over and fix myself a snack, pour myself a cup of coffee, as I please. . . . Such are the small pleasures of the incarcerated."

As I sat at the chrome-legged, porcelain-topped table, which was about half again as big as your average kitchen table, I noticed the pantry's single window did not have the tamperproof screen of Forrestal's room; in fact, of the two hooks that fastened it in place, one was broken.

He was asking, "Can I get you a cup of soup, or a sandwich?"

"No, no thanks, Jim. Just had lunch."

Sitting with his cup of coffee, he placed it before him, then patted his stomach, just above the yellow sash. "You should have seen the steak I put away, at noon. It's nice to have my appetite back."

"You look good. You look fit."

"I've been exercising." He sipped his coffee, glanced about the tiny room. "There's nothing wrong with me that not being cooped up here, on the sixteenth floor, wouldn't cure. How I'd like to be outdoors, with friends, visiting an estate, walking in the sun . . . soon, very soon."

"How is Jo holding up under all this?"

The tight line tightened in an unconvincing smile. "Splendidly. She, uh, hasn't been around much—hospitals depress her. I know she'll be sorry she missed you, she's very fond of you." A quiet sadness slipped into his eyes. "She's gone off to Europe, on vacation."

Her husband a mental patient, confined because of his suicidal tendencies, and Jo was off to Europe. Somehow I wasn't surprised.

"My son Michael's over there, you know, in Paris," he was saying. "Mike has a post with the Economic Cooperation Administration. Working for the Marshall Plan."

"How's Peter doing?"

"Very well, thank you—you just missed him. He spent half an hour with me, after lunch; he's living in Morris House, looking after it for me. He's at Princeton, doing very well—just started a summer job as a copyboy at the *Post.*"

His pride in his sons buoyed him; this was the most talkative I'd ever seen Forrestal, and I was relieved to see him doing so well. I hated to forge ahead into troubling territory, but I felt I had to.

"Jim, can I ask about something you mentioned to me, when you were—having your difficulties?"

"Certainly, Nate." He took another sip of his coffee. "I like to think we've gone beyond a client/employer relationship. You were at my side when the chips were down."

Well, that made me feel shitty.

But I asked, "What happened at Roswell?"

His expression froze. Then, slowly, he shook his head. "Nate, I shouldn't have mentioned that to you. That's a delicate, and classified, area."

"I figure it must have something to do with the Air Force," I said.

He said nothing, expressionless, though his eyes were alive.

I had a sip of my coffee, which wasn't bad at all, and pressed on. "You seemed to have, well . . . lost your grip, after Symington rode home with you that last day at the Pentagon. He said he had something important to talk to you about, and, after all, he's the Secretary of the Air Force—"

Forrestal raised a palm, in a stop gesture. "Nate, I'll say only that the defense of one's country sometimes necessitates unfortunate choices." His gaze fell; he was looking at his own reflection in his coffee cup. "I'll go to my grave feeling I betrayed my country; all the laudatory editorials in the world, all the psychiatry, a battalion of priests, cannot assuage that singular guilt."

"I don't understand, Jim. Does this have anything to do with Majestic Twelve?"

He looked up sharply, brow furrowed. "How did you know about that?"

"Someone's leaked it to a reporter I've done some work for."

He was shaking his head. "Majic-12 is a top-secret group, Nate, I won't discuss it. Knowledge of that kind is what makes a . . . mental case like me . . . a security risk. Are you asking on behalf of this reporter?"

"No." And I wasn't. I was asking for myself. I did not consider myself on the clock with Pearson, now; but I wanted to know if what I'd learned at Roswell was real—if my stay at the Walker base "guesthouse" had been due to my getting close to the secret of the century: the visitation of earth by aliens.

So I kept at it, sitting forward, asking the big one: "Do you believe in flying saucers, Jim?"

He studied me with unblinking eyes. "You know that much, do you? Does your reporter friend know, as well?"

"There's been no confirmation."

Now his gaze shifted to that screened window. Rather distantly, he said, "I thought perhaps the Horten brothers had talked."

"Who?"

"They were the pilots and engineers responsible." He shook his head. "We were lucky Hitler was a madman—a difference of a few months, and, hell, forget the V-2s . . . we might have been facing a fleet of saucer-shaped bombers. Imagine a bomber that could take off without a runway! Particularly in a country like Germany, with their runways reduced to rubble by Allied bombing."

Trying to follow this, I asked, "Are you saying flying saucers are from . . . Germany?"

A dry smile tickled the thin lips. "Where did you think they were from—outer space?"

I decided it wasn't prudent to answer that question out loud, anyway not in a mental hospital.

But I did ask, "Then these stories of flying saucers—are they government disinformation?"

"The Communist threat is very real, Nate," was his elliptical response. "It requires deals with various devils. . . . And I still believe there are dozens, perhaps hundreds, of Communist agents and fellow travelers in our government—as I was telling my young friend Joe McCarthy."

"Who?"

His eyes narrowed as he offered me half a smile. "Young senator from Wisconsin. Keep your eye on him. My ability to fight this battle will be limited, now; the presidency is out of my reach, with a nervous breakdown in my history. But other warriors will come forward. I only hope they don't have to make the abhorrent decisions I, from time to time, have had to make."

"What kind of decisions, Jim?"

"You've implied it yourself. With the Reds a plague on the world landscape, dealing with Nazis is a lesser evil." He laughed humorlessly. "Then there's Roswell. To think the Japanese would have engineering minds better than ours—now *that's* insane."

"Wait a minute—are you saying that there are Japs working at White Sands, along with the German scientists?"

Forrestal frowned. "I've said too much. You must promise me you won't share any of this with your reporter friend."

I had a last sip of coffee. "He, uh . . . he's not exactly my friend."

"Well, who is he? Arthur Krock? Marquis Childs? Lyle Wilson, maybe?"

I leaned forward. "Listen . . . Jim . . . there's something difficult I have to get into with you. But first, I want to assure you that nothing we've talked about this afternoon will leave this room."

"I appreciate that. It's been nice to have someone to talk to, someone I can trust, who doesn't have the taint of government."

". . . I'm afraid I have a worse taint."

His eyes tightened. "How is that possible?"

"Oh, it's possible. You just have to understand that I have never betrayed your confidence, and I never will. I've never worked a job for this man that had to do with you. No cross-purposes were involved whatsoever."

And by now the eyes had widened. "You can't be serious . . . *Pearson?*" He popped to his feet, thrust a finger across the table, in my face. "*You're* the goddamn traitor!"

"No! No . . . sit down before someone in the hall hears us. I deserve a fair hearing. Just let me explain."

Forrestal was trembling, his hands turned to fists.

"Please," I said. "Hear me out."

He looked at me for the longest time; then, finally, he sat.

I told him that I'd done a number of jobs for Pearson in the thirties, and that I had stopped working for him, at that time. I had done a few minor jobs since, mostly having to do with the columnist's rackets exposé in Chicago.

"But when we spoke at Chevy Chase," I told Forrestal, "and you wanted me to see if you were being watched, I knew if I told you about my past relationship with Pearson, you wouldn't hire me for the job."

"And you wanted the money?" he asked, bitterly.

"Sure I did. But I knew that if I even mentioned knowing Pearson, you'd read more conspiracy into it, and get even more bent out of shape."

His expression softened. "That's probably true."

"I also knew that I could ascertain the extent of Pearson's surveillance because I'd go right to his office and ask him about it. And, if you'll recall, I uncovered his spy in your house, that maid, who your wife fired accordingly."

Shaking his head, he studied me with dumbfounded disappointment; then he asked, "Why are you admitting this, at this late date?"

"Because I didn't want you to hear it from someone else. One of your shrinks, Bernstein, said it might undo what they've been trying to accomplish here, if your paranoia got fed by finding out I'd . . . betrayed you."

His voice seemed steady again as he asked, "And you're saying you haven't betrayed me?"

"I haven't, and I won't. Listen, maybe I better, uh . . . leave right now. Let you mull this over. You can decide whether you want to talk to me about this again, ever."

"Nonsense." Forrestal sighed, shook his head, even—amazingly enough—smiled. "It took courage for you to admit this . . . although frankly how you can work for that monster is beyond me."

"I don't judge my clients that way. I'm afraid I mostly judge them by whether or not they can afford me."

He managed to chuckle at that. "I'm afraid that son of a bitch found my Achilles' heel. I've never been able to overcome an acute sensitivity to criticism of a personal sort. Rational attacks—even irrational ones—on my policy decisions, my public positions, have never bothered me. But challenge my integrity, or call me a coward, and I'm afraid it shakes me to the core."

"Like that lousy lie about the jewel robbery."

"Exactly. I simply cannot understand this man's fanatical viciousness. What possesses Pearson to pursue me into my sickroom, when I'm no longer even holding public office?"

"You said it yourself, at the golf course—he's a crusader. To Pearson, it's no different than the difficult decisions you've had to make."

"The age-old question," Forrestal said. "Do the ends justify the means?"

"I've always figured it depends on the ends," I said, "and it depends on the means."

"You're a case-by-case sort of individual."

"Yeah, and it's been one damn case after another. Look, Jim . . . you've been very understanding about this. And I've taken up too much of your time."

Forrestal stood. "It was a pleasure seeing you again, Nate, despite this rather bizarre revelation of yours . . . and, while I won't pretend I'm overjoyed by what you revealed about that bastard Pearson . . . I am impressed by your courage in owning up to it."

"Still friends, then?"

"Yes—but no longer a client."

"Fair enough," I laughed. "Oh! I have a gift for you."

"Well, that's very thoughtful."

We walked across the hall to his room and I handed him the brown paper bag.

"I really went all out for the gift-wrapping," I said.

Forrestal smiled, removing the handsome redleather, gold-decorated volume from the bag, then said, "Why, this is too extravagant!"

"I thought maybe you'd find a book of poetry comforting," I said.

He held it in both hands, then flipped through some pages, contemplating the volume with a thin smile. "Very thoughtful of you, Nate. Very thoughtful indeed."

We shook hands and, in an uncharacteristic gesture, he touched my shoulder.

"Thank you for this visit," Forrestal said, surprising warmth in his voice.

"Good seeing you, Jim. See you back on the golf course."

"I'll take you up on that, Nate."

I left Bethesda in a cloud of confusion. If what Forrestal had told me was true, then the flying saucer at Roswell was an experimental aircraft out of White Sands. To some extent that would even account for the government's clampdown, if not quite justify death threats and trips to the Walker "guesthouse."

But how did that explain the detailed, convincing eyewitness accounts I'd encountered in Roswell? And my own, deep sense of conviction that what had happened there did involve a craft from another world, with a crew from the same place? A conviction fueled by recurring dreams of that friendly spaceman . . .

. . . who I was for a change not dreaming about, that night in my bed in my room at the Ambassador Hotel, when the phone rang me awake. I'd been sleeping deep and soundly, after seeking escape from my whirling thoughts with a night out that had included the company of the Yugoslavian lass, Anya, the bebop of Louis Jordan and the comic antics of Tim Moore at the Howard Theater, and a late dinner at the Water Gate Inn.

After clicking on the nightstand lamp and blinding me, Anya, blonde hair pleasantly tousled, handed me the receiver. I glanced grumpily at my watch, and said thickly into the mouthpiece, "It's two-thirty a.m. This better be good."

"Actually, it's bad, Mr. Heller," a businesslike second tenor intoned. "This is Baughman, and I'm over at Bethesda. How quickly can you get here?"

Anya batting her blue eyes at me, I sat up and said to the chief of the Secret Service, "Give me a reason and I'm on my way."

"James V. Forrestal committed suicide here, forty minutes ago. You were his last outside visitor. Is that sufficient reason?"

I felt it was.

Nineteen

No RED LIGHTS FLASHED, no scurry of activity indicated that an event with international repercussions had taken place within the looming white tower; no ambulance out front to cart a dead body away—after all, this facility had its own morgue. One-stop shopping here at the National Naval Medical Center at Bethesda, Maryland, which—not being in the District of Columbia proper—fell within the jurisdiction of the Montgomery County Sheriff's Department, a few bemused uniformed officers of which could be seen loitering in the parking lot and in the lobby.

But on the sixteenth floor of the hospital tower, the only uniforms on view were those of the naval medical ensigns and a few naval nurses. The investigation into the death of James V. Forrestal was strictly a plainclothes affair, an apparent mingling of Secret Service, FBI and possibly even CIA.

The plainclothes agent in the lobby (he didn't identify his branch) who had allowed me onto the elevator must have walkie-talkied ahead, because Chief Baughman himself was waiting for me as the elevators opened onto the sixteenth floor.

Though he had surely once again been called in from home, Baughman was a considerable distance from the Hawaiian shirt of our first meeting. The

lanky, fortyish, poker-faced Secret Service chief with
the piercing gaze wore a double-breasted blue tropical worsted with a red-and-blue striped tie against a
white shirt—appropriately patriotic. He showed no
signs of middle-of-the-night awakening, in contrast to
my casual clothes of earlier today (actually yesterday—this was Sunday morning, now) which I'd
tossed back on, the brown-and-white sportjacket
over a blue T-shirt. The Southwest Flight fedora was
pushed back on my head.

Baughman offered me a hand to shake, which I
took and shook, even as we started walking slowly
down the relatively short hallway toward room 1618.
Even without a mysterious death, the world of a hospital at night is an eerie one, the corridors dimly
lighted, the cleaning staff leaving their mark by way
of slick floors and antiseptic smells, as the rubber-
soled shoes of nurses and orderlies take careful footsteps, so as not to disturb patients sedated and asleep
in their rooms, their deep breathing providing a wall
of ambient sound.

"Thank you for coming, Mr. Heller," Baughman
said, in that hushed manner reserved for churches
and after-hours hospitals. "I want you to understand
that we're not going to ask you for an official statement. That may come later."

"Am I a suspect?"

"Of what?"

"You tell me. Forrestal's murder, maybe."

Down a hallway at the left was the nurses' station,
where a number of plainclothes officers gathered in a
small lounge area.

Baughman was matter-of-fact. "I told you on the
phone, Mr. Heller. The former Secretary of Defense
jumped from the pantry window. This is a suicide."

"Did anybody see him jump?"

We were nearing the short hallway between 1618 and the diet kitchen; next to the diet kitchen was the single room that adjoined Forrestal's double one via a bathroom—the single room where supposedly either a medical corpsman or a doctor had been on watch, twenty-four hours. Baughman stopped, so we could speak without being heard by the handful of plainclothesmen bustling about from room to room.

"No one saw him jump," Baughman said, almost whispering. "But we've completed questioning of Lieutenant Dorothy Turner, a duty nurse on the seventh floor, who heard a loud crash around one-fifty a.m. She called the alarm and within minutes the body was found, on the roof of a third-floor passageway connecting this tower to one of the wings."

"A thirteen-story fall."

"Yes. The body was, uh . . . rather badly mangled, I'm afraid. Landed facedown, sprawled amongst some drying mops and buckets . . . apparently they'd been cleaning off the roof."

"Lucky for them they hadn't finished."

"Forrestal was found in his dressing gown, with the sash of the gown knotted and wrapped tightly around his neck."

"Well, that sounds to me like somebody strangled him with it, which isn't suicide in Chicago unless you pay off the right cops."

Baughman frowned at that, just a little, then said, "Apparently Mr. Forrestal tied the other end of the sash to the radiator and when he jumped, the sash slipped undone. The fact that he meant to hang himself and fell accidentally to his death, instead, makes it no less suicide."

"Yeah, well it does sound like the Dutch act, at that."

Baughman sighed. "At least death came instanta-
neously. That's what Dr. Brochart says, anyway."

"Who?"

"The Montgomery County coroner. He agrees
with our verdict."

"I thought verdicts were a jury's job."

Baughman ignored that; a hint of emotion broke
through the professional mask. "Funny—poor bastard's wristwatch was still ticking, hadn't been broken
in the fall; but his face was so badly crushed, he
wasn't identified until a bed check turned him up
missing."

"What about the 'round-the-clock observation he
was supposedly under?"

"We're about to interview the two medical corpsmen who were on duty, one who went off at midnight, and his replacement, who was on duty when
this happened. The other member of that ' 'round-
the-clock watch' we're also going to interview; he's a
staff psychiatrist named Deen who slept through the
whole thing."

I frowned. "Raines and Bernstein were Forrestal's
doctors, was my understanding."

Baughman nodded. "Raines is the primary physician and Bernstein is consulting. This fellow Deen is
just one of a number of staff shrinks who take turns
standing watch; he's not actively involved in the
case."

"I assume Raines and Bernstein have been notified."

Another nod. "Bernstein lives just fifteen minutes
away—should be here at any moment. Raines is in
Montreal for a week. Attending a psychiatrists' convention."

"You're kidding."

"Wish I were, Mr. Heller. He left Wednesday;

seems he felt Forrestal was making such nice progress, both doctor and patient could use a little break from all this rigorous therapy."

"Well, they do say psychiatry is an inexact science."

Pretty much on cue, Dr. Bernstein stepped off the elevator back down the hall from us, looking casual in a studied way: dark brown button-front sweater over a yellow shirt with the top button buttoned, no tie and brown slacks, the dark colors emphasizing his nearly albino coloration, that blond hair going white, the invisible eyebrows over light blue-gray eyes, and handsome features right out of an Arrow shirt ad.

"That's Bernstein right there," I told Baughman.

The psychiatrist approached us and we met him halfway, as he introduced himself to the chief of the Secret Service. Hands were shaken, Bernstein nodding his acknowledgment of my presence.

"Chief Baughman," Bernstein said, "this is a tragedy not just for Mr. Forrestal's family, but for America."

The body wasn't even cold yet, and this guy was writing press releases already.

Baughman and Bernstein had already spoken on the phone, and what followed was the second half of what was obviously an already in-progress conversation that I sometimes had a little trouble following.

"If all the signs pointed toward your patient's imminent recovery," Baughman said, "what do you think happened here?"

"It's my opinion," the psychiatrist said, with somber authority, his arms folded, "that Mr. Forrestal was seized with a sudden fit of despondence, probably very late this evening—perhaps he awoke from a troubling dream, and found himself in a state of melancholia . . . such a seizure is extremely common in severe depression cases."

Baughman said, "If that's the case, Doctor, why was your patient allowed these privileges? Including that pantry with the unguarded window?"

"This facility doesn't subscribe to the view that psychiatric patients ought to be thrown in a dungeon." Bernstein sighed, shrugged. "We had reached a point where certain privileges had to be extended to the patient, to make him feel our confidence in him . . . to give him confidence that a full recovery was possible. We did this, frankly, even though certain suicidal preoccupations might still be present."

Baughman twitched a non-smile. "I don't mean to tell you your job, Doctor, but that sounds a little risky to me."

"Chief Baughman, calculated risks of therapy are an accepted part of the practice of modern psychiatry."

What a pompous ass this guy was; everything he said that wasn't a press release was a goddamn lecture.

Baughman was asking, "What I read to you over the phone, Doctor, do you consider that a substitute for a suicide note?"

"Most definitely—there are many examples of indirect suicide notes on file, Chief Baughman, as I'm sure you know. Now, of course, I must remind you that Dr. Raines is the primary physician on this case."

"Of course."

Bernstein smiled, and it was a dazzler; he really would have been a handsome devil, if he'd some color in his face and hair. "I just wanted to offer my services, as a sort of substitute, until he returns. By the way, I've already spoken to him, by long distance, and he's made arrangements to return by air."

"Glad to hear that." The Secret Service chief gestured toward me with a thumb, like he was hitchhiking. "I'd like to speak further with you, Doctor, but first I need a few minutes with Mr. Heller."

"Certainly." He half-bowed. "I'm at your service. I'll wait at the nurses' station."

"If you would."

Bernstein nodded curtly and turned down the hall-way at left, moving toward the agents clustered at the waiting area across from the duty nurse's desk.

"Covering his ass already," I said.

"There'll be a lot of that in this case," Baughman said, with a humorless laugh. "Listen, before you and I talk, I need to interview those corpsmen and the sleeping shrink. Care to sit in?"

"Love to."

We began walking again, Baughman saying, "We'll talk to this boy who worked the early shift, first. He was close to Mr. Forrestal—of the three corpsmen assigned to him, this kid was his favorite—and the boy's been quite upset. I'm hoping he's composed enough to speak to us, now."

Self-composure was exactly what Navy Medical Corpsman Edward Prise seemed to be trying to maintain; looking like the sailor he technically was, in his white uniform with its dark neckerchief, the corpsman sat erect in Forrestal's padded wooden chair, which had been yanked out into the middle of the dimly lighted double room. Towheaded, ruddy-cheeked Prise, in his early twenties and looking impossibly young, had a glazed expression, the whites of his blue eyes red with crying; he was turning his bucket cap in his hand like a wheel.

Baughman, his tall thin frame looming over the boy, stood with hands on hips; though his voice was almost kind, the Secret Service chief's presence was surely intimidating as he asked, "What can you tell us about tonight, Edward?"

Another plainclothesman, presumably Secret Service, took notes while Baughman conducted the low-key interrogation. There were three plainclothes agents in the room with us, and, again, FBI and/or CIA may have been among them; no one clued me in.

"Bad luck, sir," the boy said. "Terrible bad luck. Normally we watch . . . watched . . . Mr. Forrestal on eight-hour 'round-the-clock shifts. The shift change is usually at nine p.m., but we had to double up tonight, sir."

"Why is that, son?"

"My usual replacement picked Friday night to go absent without leave, sir, and get drunk on his butt; he's in the brig, and now we're shorthanded. So this new fella, Bob Harrison, just a hospital apprentice, is not attuned to the . . ." The boy looked for the right word. ". . . subtleties and hazards of this particular situation, sir. He didn't know Mr. Forrestal, and Mr. Forrestal didn't know him. So I was concerned, when I went off duty, sir."

"Strictly because of your replacement's inexperience?"

"That wasn't the only thing. Mr. Forrestal had seemed in good spirits today, and real energetic, but also, this evening, he seemed restless. He refused his usual sleeping pill and sedative, saying he wanted to stay up late and read, tonight."

"The patient had leeway to do that?"

"We don't force-feed medication, sir. That's hospital policy. I did notify, or tried to notify, Dr. Deen of my concerns. He was sleeping in that adjacent room, you know? Dr. Deen wasn't happy I woke him up, which was typical."

"Of Deen?"

"No, sir, he's not better or worse than any of them,

frankly, sir. None of these doctors like to get advice on their patients from enlisted corpsmen. I stuck around, after midnight, for maybe half an hour—I just had a bad feeling. But, finally, I left—you know how it is, sir. Against regulations to just hang about."

Baughman nodded. "Your watch was over and custom, and discipline, dictated you go about your business elsewhere. You did nothing wrong, son."

Now Prise began to cry; quietly sobbing. "I . . . I went back to my room at the barracks, but I couldn't sleep. Musta tossed and turned for a good hour. Finally I just got dressed and was walkin' across the hospital grounds, to the canteen, for a cup of coffee, you know? And all of a sudden there was this big commotion, yelling, running, alarm bells . . . and I just felt sick to my stomach. I knew what happened. Somehow I just knew."

Baughman put a comforting hand on the boy's shoulder. "It's all right, son. It's all right."

"Mr. Forrestal, he . . . he was the most interesting man I ever met, a great and famous man. I was going to go to work for him, after he got out. He said I'd be his 'man Friday,' you know, chauffeur, valet and all." The corpsman shook his head. "It was a once-in-a-lifetime opportunity, out the window . . . my one big chance."

Baughman looked at me, said, "Let's go next door," and nodded toward the bathroom that connected the rooms. But he paused in the john, with both doors closed, to ask me what I made of Prise's story.

"Nothing sounds fishy there to me," I said. "Kid is sincere enough. Of course, I think his tears are more for his future than his pal Forrestal."

Baughman nodded. "Let's see what this other boy has to say."

Corpsman Robert Harrison, another impossibly young kid, dark-haired, skinny, said, "Tell you the truth, I was supposed to check on him every five minutes, but he got irritated with that. So I cut it to fifteen."

Baughman was again doing the interrogating while one of another trio of plainclothes agents stationed in this room took the notes. "You came on at midnight?"

"Yes, sir."

"And he was still awake?'

"Yeah, well—at one-thirty, he was asleep, or seemed to be. When I looked in on him at one forty-five, he was up, sitting at his desk, writing . . . not writing exactly, copying something from a book."

I wondered what that was about. The only two books in the room I knew of were that Catholic tome by Monsignor Sheen and the poetry anthology I'd given him.

The kid was saying, "I told him if he was having trouble sleeping, maybe he should have a sleeping pill . . . sodium amytal is what we use."

The corpsman apparently wanted to let us know he knew his stuff, even if the psychiatric patient he'd been charged to watch had jumped out the window.

"But Mr. Forrestal refused the pill," the boy said. "I went down to check with the floor nurse about it, but she was away from her desk. So I woke Dr. Deen up, right here in this room, and he wasn't happy with me. Told me if Mr. Forrestal didn't want the sleeping tablet, he didn't have to take it."

"When did you check on Mr. Forrestal again?"

"I didn't wait any fifteen minutes, that's for sure! I stepped it back up to five . . . it was one-fifty. And Mr. Forrestal's bed was empty. I woke Dr. Deen up, and we looked for him, and we saw the screen in the

pantry was took out, and looked out the window
and . . . well, he was down there, but they'd already
found him. We were kinda shook up, me and the
doc—just sat down at the table there, in the pantry.
Figured, you know, it was obvious who he was. But I
guess the patient got messed up pretty bad in the fall,
and some nurse came up to do a bed check and we
told her it was Forrestal who fell . . . or jumped."

". . . Thank you, Robert." Baughman turned to the
other agents. "Anyone have anything else?"

Baughman may not have been including me in that
question, but I asked, "Robert, what was Mr. Forrestal copying?"

"I don't know. Just something out of some big red
book."

My book of poetry. Was this the "substitute" for a
suicide note Baughman mentioned to Dr. Bernstein?

"We found what he wrote," Baughman said to me.
"Let you have a look, later." He turned to the note-
taking agent. "Show Robert out, would you? And
bring Dr. Deen in?"

The slender, handsome young doctor who had
slept through Forrestal's journey out the pantry window did not look like he'd be getting any more sleep
tonight. Anguish was etched in his pasty-white face,
the blueness of his night-duty beard giving him an
unwashed look; his dark hair was uncombed and his
eyes were wide and haunted. A sleeve of his white
jacket hung loose, torn away from the shoulder.

"How did that happen, Doctor?" Baughman asked
his seated interview subject, nodding at the sleeve.

"I tore it loose."

"How?"

"Yanked on it myself."

"Why?"

Deen swallowed. "When I saw that corpsman,

Prise, step out of the elevator . . . he was coming up to see what happened, you know, in the brief bedlam after the body was discovered." He shook his head. "The look the kid gave me . . . accusing look . . ." He lowered his head and covered his face with a hand.

"That's okay, Doctor . . ."

He raised his head; his face was slick with tears. "Nothing's okay. Why did I tear off my sleeve, when I saw that kid who'd tried to warn me, looking at me? Because I couldn't reach my heart."

Baughman asked him the pertinent questions, and the story the doctor told mirrored and corroborated those of the two corpsmen.

"I don't think I was negligent," he said, wearily, "not really—not when both Dr. Raines and Dr. Bernstein told me the patient was close to full recovery. But that won't make this any easier to live with."

A while later in the hallway, Baughman said, "Getting the picture, Mr. Heller? It's not a murder, it's a suicide."

"If you say so."

Baughman smiled at my misgivings, saying, "I tell you what—let's take a look at the crime scene. I believe you'll quickly concur with our findings."

He led me into the tiny diet kitchen, where a plainclothes photographer—apparently just finishing up—was loading up his gear, and a white-jacketed technician was also closing up his kit, which sat on the porcelain tabletop where, not so long ago, Forrestal and I had sat, in friendly conversation.

The screen had been removed from the window and rested against the wall, at the left of the radiator under the window yawning open onto, and letting in, the cool night.

"No usable fingerprints on the sill or the screen," the white-jacketed technician told Baughman; he was a bald, bespectacled guy of maybe thirty, with a flatly expressionless voice. "Smudges only. Same for the radiator, and the wall. But that would be expected, considering."

"How about the sill outside?" Baughman asked.

"Sorry. Nothing. But did you see the scuff marks, on the concrete?"

"No." Baughman moved to the window and I tagged along. He leaned way out, studying the concrete below the window. Pulling back in, he nodded toward the window, inviting me to have a look. I did. Scuff marks and scratches on the concrete indicated Forrestal, in the process of trying to hang himself, may have changed his mind and tried to climb back in, to safety, to no avail. The view out this window—unlike the pleasant, bustling one of the hospital's driveway from room 1618—was bleak: a small, dark utility building and weedy overgrown vacant lots.

"Did you dust out there?" Baughman was asking the technician.

"As best I could. But if the guy was flailing out there, slappin' and clawin', it's unlikely he left a clear print of any kind. I suppose we could put a ladder up, from that roof below, and see what we come up with."

Baughman thought about that, then said, "Thanks, Frank. Maybe we'll do that, in the daylight. . . . You're done here, then?"

The photographer had already slipped out.

"That's your call, Chief," the fingerprint man said. "Other than the ladder routine, I'm fresh out of ideas."

Baughman nodded, and the technician left.

We were alone.

I said, "Close the door, Chief, would you? I don't want us to be overheard."

He did. We sat at the table; I was where Forrestal had been seated that afternoon, Baughman in my chair.

"Don't you find some of this troubling?" I asked.

Baughman grunted. "Whole thing's troubling."

"A nurse who steps away from her desk at just the right moment? A doctor who'd rather sleep than attend a patient? A suicidal patient, at that, kept on the sixteenth floor? Whose windows, overlooking the front of the hospital, have security locks in his own room, but who has access to a pantry, overlooking nothing, with a window screen you just have to look at hard to open?"

"Mr. Heller . . ."

"For Christ's sake, call me Nate."

"Nate." Baughman dug a pack of Camels out of his breast pocket, offered me one, which I declined, while he found a lighter in his suitcoat pocket, firing one up, saying, "My friends call me 'Hughie,' and this is a suicide. Open and shut."

"The only thing open and shut about this case is that fucking window. You've got a floor nurse, a corpsman and a doctor simultaneously out of action, either away from their posts or sleeping like a baby. Maybe that was arranged so somebody could drop by Forrestal's room after visiting hours, and find him alone, unprotected. How do you know somebody—either a hospital employee, or somebody from the outside, hospitals have notoriously poor security, even military ones—how do you know somebody didn't accost Forrestal, either catching him in the pantry or dragging him over there, strangling him with the cord of his robe, tossing him out of the window, then taking the elevator, just a few steps down the hall, to freedom?"

Baughman exhaled some smoke. "All right, Nate.

Let's play it your way. Are you saying that one of those young men—Prise, Harrison, or Dr. Deen—is a part-time hired assassin? Whichever one it is, he's an excellent actor, wouldn't you say?"

"Come on, Baughman, this is a naval hospital, a military installation, professional killers for Uncle Sam are treated here every day. Anyway, I didn't say it was one of those three . . . I admit, none of them seem likely. . . ."

"Neither is your scenario." He drew in some smoke, let it stream out, saying, "I do not see how a killer could have sneaked in, skulked around, strangled Forrestal, tossed him from the window and slipped out unseen. The quarters on this cramped floor are just too damn close. That nurse or corpsman could show back up, anytime. And the doctor's sleeping in a room literally next door to this pantry."

I held up both hands, palms out. "All I'm saying is, don't be too hasty, writing this off as a suicide. This begs for a full and thorough investigation. Why don't I see any Bethesda police detectives here? Or state police, or even sheriff's boys?"

Baughman shrugged. "This hospital is a U.S. naval reservation. There will be no local police investigation. And our investigation is almost to a close."

I rolled my eyes. "Then you're not going to like what I have to say at the inquest. For one thing, the man I spoke to in this very room was about the least likely candidate for suicide that I can think of, based upon the conversation we had."

Shaking his head, Baughman said, "There'll be no inquest, Nate. Coroner Brochart has ruled this a suicide."

"Is that legal?"

"Legal enough."

"You from Chicago originally, Hughie? By the

way, why am I here, if I'm not a suspect? You haven't asked me a thing about Forrestal's behavior, his demeanor, today."

He gestured casually, cigarette in hand. "Two reasons, really. I did want your insights, where the crime scene was concerned . . ."

"Which you've ignored."

". . . and I wanted to ask you about the book of poetry."

"What?" I sat forward; this interested me. "You mean the book of poetry I gave Forrestal, this afternoon?"

"Yes. He was apparently quite touched by the gift, and mentioned to young Prise that his friend Nate Heller had given it to him."

"Why is that significant? Is that the book he was copying from?"

Baughman nodded, put out his Camel in an ashtray, and said, "Come with me."

Room 1618 was empty now, the agents in the hall, no more interrogations being conducted, unless you counted the occasional questions Baughman was asking me.

The writing desk next to the nightstand, the bed next to it rumpled from Forrestal's last night of on-and-off-again sleep, had on it the red-leather gold-trimmed *Anthology of World Poetry*. Two sheets of cheap paper and a fountain pen were next to the book, and written on the foolscap in Forrestal's rather cramped hand were the words of a poem he'd copied.

"What poem is this?" I asked.

"It's marked with a red-ribbon bookmark," Baughman said, picking up the volume, opening it, holding it in one hand like a hymnal he was about to sing out of. "Sophocles. Called 'The Chorus from *Ajax*.' "

"I'm more a limerick man, myself. What sort of poem is this?"

Baughman offered a brief half-smile. "Kipling's about as poetic as I get. Fortunately, one of my agents, who has more refined literary tastes than the two of us, was familiar with it. He says it's a 'brooding' poem, in which the warrior Ajax contemplates suicide."

"Really."

He nodded. "All about how desirable death is, how inviting the grave. . . ."

I read Forrestal's copied version: " 'Better to die and sleep. . . . Worn by the waste of time—Comfortless, nameless, hopeless grave' . . . Well, it's not Johnny Mercer."

Baughman smiled gently at me, but his eyes were hard and serious. "That's what had me wondering, Nate. What possesses a 'limerick man' to pick up a book of poetry as a gift? Did Forrestal ask you to buy that particular book for him?"

Forrestal hadn't, but somebody had.

I looked further down the sheet of foolscap: *No quiet murmur like the tremulous wail/Of the lone bird, the querulous night,* and there it stopped.

"Is this the whole poem?" I asked.

"No. Forrestal stopped midway—actually, in mid-word."

"No he didn't. It's right here: 'night.' "

Baughman shook his head, no. "That's the first half of 'nightingale.' "

I frowned. "Forrestal stopped in the middle of the word 'nightingale,' got up, went across the hall and killed himself?"

Nightingale . . . nightingale . . . why was that ringing a bell?

"Apparently," Baughman said. He hefted the red-

and-gold volume. "So why this book, Nate? Was this Forrestal's idea or not?"

"No," I said. "I, uh . . . just knew he had high-class tastes, that's all. The thicker the book, the bigger the words, the more he liked it. . . . You figure this was his suicide note."

"That's our opinion. And you heard Dr. Bernstein second it."

I shrugged. "I sure wish I had more information for you, Hughie."

He touched my sleeve, tentatively. "Listen, Nate— I would appreciate it . . . and I'm sure the President would appreciate it if . . . when you're interviewed by the press—as I'm sure you will be, having been the last outside visitor to see Mr. Forrestal—that you keep these, uh, contrary thoughts about his suicide to yourself."

"Now who's covering their ass."

Baughman had a penetrating gaze and it was cutting right through me, at the moment. "Will you be discreet, Nate? The President appreciates your role in alerting us to Mr. Forrestal's mental condition."

"Fat lot of good it did any of us."

"Well, just the same, Mr. Truman asked me— tonight—to personally convey to you those thanks."

"Yeah." I put on my hat, snugged it into place. "Well, tell him 'you're welcome,' but I'm starting to wonder if I should've voted for Dewey."

Exiting the elevator into the lobby, I was experiencing a sick exhilaration. I knew something that Baughman didn't: I knew that Dr. Bernstein had recommended that fatal book of poetry. And I even thought I knew why . . . pieces falling into place in my mind like a puzzle assembling itself.

My brain was racing, and my body compensated by slowing down. In fact, I was walking in such a daze that I almost didn't recognize her, up ahead of me in the lobby, chatting with several other pretty nurses as she exited into the parking lot.

Nonc as pretty, though, as Nurse Maria Selff—herself.

Twenty

Out in front of the hospital, the quartet of nurses, one of them my Maria, had—before going their separate ways to their separate cars—paused on the sidewalk, at the edge of the parking lot, for an end-of-shift gabfest, exchanging girlish laughter and, no doubt, gossip. Maria was right in there with them, her lovely Dorothy Lamour–like features animated, her gestures too, a giddy Maria I didn't really know.

But then I didn't really know her, did I?

The lustrous black hair was again tucked up under an overseas cap, only now her petite, curvy frame had been poured into a white naval uniform, in exchange for the khaki Air Force number. And as she laughed and talked, she was lighting up a cigarette—a very self-assured young woman, the frightened waif of Cloudcroft nowhere to be seen.

The pretty nurses were standing over to the right as I exited the hospital, my fedora snugged down, head lowered as well, and I cut sharply left, walking across the driveway toward the parking lot, away from the well-lighted entrance, into the shadows, skirting pools of lamppost light. There was no way I could be certain, but I felt fairly confident she hadn't spotted me.

My plan, initially, was to get to my car while keeping an eye on her—right now she was still gaily chat-

ting—and watch her walk to her vehicle and then tail
her. But to avoid bumping into her, I'd entered the
parking lot on the opposite side from where I'd
parked; and in making my way across the dimly
lighted lot, not terribly far from my own car, I noticed
a sleek powder-blue coupe, a Studebaker . . .

. . . with New Mexico plates.

When she pitched her cigarette, shooting sparks
into the night, and got into the car, her keys out and
ready to insert in the ignition, I sat up in the backseat
and said, "We have to quit meeting like this."

Her eyes were enormous in the rearview mirror
and the red-rouged mouth opened wide, possibly to
emit a scream, and I slipped my left hand around
from behind her and clamped down over those wonderful lips.

"No scream," I whispered into her right ear; she
was still using Evening in Paris perfume, I noted.
"You're not a helpless woman, Maria, it wouldn't become you . . . besides, do you really want to attract attention? You might not like what I have to say to the
authorities. Or Drew Pearson."

She was breathing hard, but her eyes had gone
back to their normal condition—merely huge, a new
coldness in their long-lashed, deep blue loveliness—
and I removed my hand.

"You going to behave?" I asked her.

We were looking at each other in the rearview
mirror.

"Are *you?*" she gasped, her breath still coming
hard. Her lipstick was smeared, the lovely mouth a
gaudy wound.

I wiped the red off my palm onto the back of her
car seat. "Give me the keys."

She handed them back to me—a Studebaker key-
chain with a number of keys on it.

"Slide over," I ordered.

Maria scooched over onto the rider's side, looking guardedly back at me, not in the mirror this time, as I said, "I'm gonna get out and come around and get behind the wheel. No funny business or it's gonna be at least loud and maybe messy."

That was when I showed her the nine-millimeter in my fist. Her eyes got wide again, momentarily, and she nodded.

Soon I was behind the wheel, slipping the nine-millimeter back into its shoulder holster.

"Normally I don't carry this unless a job requires it," I said pleasantly, patting the snugged-away automatic, "but ever since I got grabbed at Roswell, I been skittish."

The smeared mouth worked up a tiny sneer. "Have you now?"

"You're a beautiful woman, Maria. Is that still your name? Or are you somebody else, at Bethesda? I noticed your branch of the service has changed."

"It's Maria," she said, and ever so subtly, she shifted gears into vulnerability, putting some quaver into that mellifluous alto. "Nathan, why are you treating me like this? I told you I was being transferred. I haven't contacted you because I didn't know if it was safe."

"You figure it's safe, now?"

"Maybe not. They could be watching this very moment." Her brow furrowed; eyelashes fluttered. In the near-dark of the car, her creamy complexion had a ghostlike radiance, recalling the Lodge, and Rebecca—fond memories of phony passion.

She was saying, "I . . . I thought it was unusual when they stationed me here, and strange, too, how they had the paperwork all ready to go, to transfer me from the Air Force to the Navy—"

"It's not that I don't admire how fast you are on your feet, or anyway on your cute fanny; but we've moved past the stage where I'm a fucking idiot you can manipulate like a dog chasing a flashlight."

She thought about that, drew in some air and, as she let it back out, her carriage changed again, the defenseless girl replaced by the self-confident woman.

Her voice seemed a little lower, less musical, as she asked, "What stage are you at now?"

"Not quite sure. Homicidal maniac, maybe. Pleasure of finally figuring out what the hell's been going on, though, is helping keep my anger in check. Which is good, 'cause I do some of my best work, in a cold rage."

"If you're trying to frighten me," she said, a little quaver in the voice, possibly not faked, "it's working."

I shrugged. "Well, I wasn't really trying, but that's probably a prudent response. Probably wise to keep in mind the fucking Marines kicked me out for mental instability."

Trembling just a little, she reached tentatively toward her purse, on the seat between us. "You mind if I have a cigarette?"

I put my hand on her purse, and looked toward the hospital; nobody else seemed to be coming out. "Is this the end of shift? Is this parking lot gonna be flooded with people?"

"No. My friends and I were scheduled for extra hours. What about that cigarette?"

"I'll get it for you." I opened the purse—no guns or knives or anything, just lipstick and compact and Kleenex and so on; plus a half pack of Chesterfields. Found a book of matches in there, too, and lifted the Chesties to my lips, plucked one out for myself and handed them to her. Lighted her up, then me, off the same match.

"Let's roll the windows down," I said, waving out the match, sucking smoke into my lungs, "so we don't suffocate. Enjoy some of this nice cool night air . . . but let's keep our voices down, shall we? Keep it cozy, and private."

"I thought you didn't smoke," she said, rolling down her window.

"I don't, usually." I blew a perfect smoke ring, then put another one inside it. "Only time and place I ever smoked was in the service, on the Island . . . you know—Guadalcanal. Now when I crave a smoke it's . . . at odd times. Those rare occasions when civilian life mirrors battle conditions."

"Now you are trying to scare me," she said, but sounding not at all scared. "Trying a little *too* hard, maybe." And she blew smoke out her nostrils, cutely contemptuous, the world's prettiest dragon—or Dragon Lady.

"I mean, you're familiar with that kind of neurotic behavior, right, baby? You know what a Section Eight is, you're acquainted with battle neuroses. I figure you're probably working as a psychiatric nurse, here at Bethesda . . . though I bet you stayed away from the sixteenth floor today, knowing I'd be there."

She scowled at me; even her scowls were appealing. "Why the hell should I know that?"

"Actually, I'm surprised you worked at all today. Of course, that's probably why you took the night shift, knowing I'd be around to see Forrestal, this afternoon."

"I worked night shift this week," she said tightly, plucking some tobacco off her pink tongue, "because that's how I was assigned. From what I hear, James Forrestal committed suicide. What do you know that I don't know?"

I blew another smoke ring. "Not much of anything, I'm sure . . . including that he was murdered."

The smeary mouth made a disgusted half-smirk. "Don't be more stupid than you already are. That man was a suicidal case and he stepped out a window; happens every day." She took off her overseas cap and began unpinning her hair.

"Make yourself at home."

She arched an eyebrow at me. "You don't mind if I get comfortable, do you?"

"Strip, for all I care."

Shaking her head, the lush blackness of her hair tumbling to her shoulders, she said cattily, "You've lost that privilege."

"Tell me, Maria—were you really married? Was there a 'Steve'?"

Smoothing her pageboy with a palm, she grunted a small laugh. "Why, you think I planned ahead and put a trunk of old clothes in my bedroom, just your size, so you could make your getaway?"

"Maybe. It's no less tortuous than some of the other bullshit you people pulled on me."

Folding her arms and resting them on the considerable shelf of her bosom, she gazed out at the parking lot, the shadows and pools of light separating us from the well-illuminated entrance.

"There was a Steve," she said, then glanced at me with half-hooded eyes. "And you don't look a goddamn thing like him."

"But he was my size."

"I can think of one place he was bigger."

Now I grunted a laugh. "He really die at Dresden?"

Shook her head. "Pearl Harbor. He went down on the *Arizona*."

"Well, jeez—why'd you change that story? That's a good one."

She still wasn't looking at me, staring out the windshield instead. "It was felt I needed to be more . . . freshly widowed."

"To sucker me, you mean? I think you went to too much trouble, baby. With your looks, I'd've believed just about anything you told me . . . hell! I did."

"You are a little gullible, at that."

Smiling, shaking my head, I said, "This afternoon, Forrestal told me about his Achilles' heel, which was his pride, I guess. . . . Me, I'm a dick with an Achilles' heel, all right, or is that a heel with an Achilles' dick?"

That actually made her smile. She said, "Is it all right if I freshen my lipstick?"

"Why, you want to take another stab at me?"

She looked at me with both eyebrows arched, this time, and gestured to the clown-smear of her mouth. "Do you mind?"

I fished the tube of lipstick out. "This doesn't shoot poison gas or anything, does it, Mata Hari?"

Maria smirked, snatched the lipstick from my hand, turned the mirror to where she could see herself. "Ugh," she said, looking at herself. "Give me a Kleenex, would you?"

I gave her one and she cleaned off her mouth and reapplied glistening bright red lipstick on the full, sensuous lips. Satisfied, she put the mirror back in place, folded her arms across her bosom again and looked at me like a bored genie.

"What exactly do you hope to accomplish, Nathan? Who are you going to go to? The police? The press? And say what?"

"That Forrestal was murdered would be a good start."

Now her expression turned impatient. "You *are* insane. I told you that was a suicide."

"You almost sound like you believe it."

"I do believe it, because it's true. Look—Nathan . . . I'm not really at liberty to confirm or deny your suspicions about me. . . ." And now, surprisingly, she worked up what seemed to be real indignation: "But I will say this—if you think I'm working against the best interests of my country, then you are sadly—"

"I know what you are."

"You do."

"Sure. You're an undercover agent."

"Very funny. Working for Russia, d'you suppose? Or the Chinese Commies, maybe?"

I nodded toward the hospital. "I'd say you're working with Dr. Bernstein in that big white building over there."

She made a face. "Why should I deny that? It's not classified information; it's not top-secret. I'm a nurse assigned to the Psychological Research and Development Department."

"Which is of course a CIA operation; experimental mind control, via drugs, shock therapy, hypnosis and God knows what else."

Now she looked at me with new respect—and genuine alarm. Her voice was hushed: "Nathan . . . sometimes it's dangerous to know things."

"No kiddin'. Ask Jim Forrestal." Despite the open windows, our smoke was wreathing us, now. "Okay, let's see how much I do know. . . . How about we start with your part in an elaborate disinformation scenario? Designed to cover up the crash of a strange aircraft in the desert?"

"Is that what you want me to admit? That flying saucers are real?" Her expression was blank now, but her eyes danced with the hope that I'd veered off onto the wrong track.

"Sure they're real," I said, laughing at her, "they're

just not from outer space—at least not the one that went down after the Fourth of July, near Roswell. That was a top-secret, experimental aircraft, of an advanced design, courtesy of our Nazi pals at White Sands."

The blood drained out of her face, and the panic in her widened eyes was very real—the concern in her voice definitely not artifice. "Nathan, listen to me—if any small part is left of how you felt about me, know that I am *not* lying to you, and listen to me, *hear* me: you need to just walk away from this."

I flipped my spent Chesterfield out the window. "I think the scientists involved are probably the Horten brothers, and of course von Braun . . ."

She gripped my arm. "Jesus Christ, Nathan, stop it! You don't know what you've gotten yourself into . . ."

My eyes swung onto hers and locked them. "Do you, Maria? Know what *you've* gotten into?"

Nervous, for the first time vulnerable in a real way, she lowered her gaze, not able to stand up to mine. "I told you . . . I can't confirm any of your suspicions about me. Don't ask me to."

"But you're a good American, right? A patriot?"

Her chin jerked up and her eyes flew to mine. "I like to think I am."

"Who just happens to collaborate with Nazis?"

Her voice was barely audible as she said, "That war is over. We're in a new one."

"Lesser of two evils, huh? The Communist threat is so perilous to the American way of life, it justifies climbing in bed with just about anybody—Japs, Nazis . . . me."

"Trying to hurt my feelings, now, Nathan?" A tiny smile formed as she popped her cigarette, which she'd smoked down to the last inch, out the window. "Don't be naive. That doesn't become you."

"You're the naive one, Maria, if you're *really* buy-

ing Forrestal as a suicide. If you're not lying about
that, then somebody in your little group is cleaning
house without permission."

Her eyes tensed. "Explain."

I nodded toward the hospital. "Why don't we let
him do the explaining?"

A rather distinguished-looking individual in a
brown button-up sweater was exiting, a blond man so
pale his face seemed to glow as he stepped away from
the well-illuminated entrance and moved briskly
across the driveway into the relative darkness of the
parking lot. Dr. Bernstein—apparently finished with
his interview with Chief Baughman of the Secret Service—was heading into the lot, off to our left.

We watched as he got into a '49 Cadillac, a dark
blue Coupe DeVille sedan; apparently even government doctors were well paid. He started the engine
and turned on his lights; they streaked across us like
prison searchlights as he pulled out of the lot—but
we had ducked down.

Sitting up, I started up the Studebaker. A small,
strong hand clutched my forearm.

"You're going to tail him?"

"One of the tricks of my trade, baby."

Urgency colored her tone. "He might recognize my
car. Listen . . . I know the way he goes home. I can
take you another route."

"What if he gets there before we do?"

"We want him to," she said emphatically. "He lives
on a very quiet street, on a cul-de-sac. We don't want
to beat him home, trust me."

"Trust you. . . . I love you dearly, Maria, but if you're
fucking me over, I'll shoot you without blinking."

She studied me for a moment, swallowed and said,
"I believe you would, at that, Nathan. . . . Let's go—
I'll take you to him."

Twenty-one

I WASN'T SURE I WANTED TO KNOW why Maria had been to Bernstein's house before; but I had more important questions to ask as I tooled south on Highway 240, heading back toward the District of Columbia. At after four in the morning, traffic was light, and an alternate route was a good idea—it would not have been an easy tail job.

"Is Bernstein married?" I asked her.

"He was. He lost his wife in the war."

I smirked. "What, Dresden?"

"Actually . . . yes. They didn't have any children. He lives alone."

"I'm liking this. I do hope you're not lying. Any guard dogs? Alarms?"

"I'm not lying, and there's no dog, no alarm."

"Good. Now describe the neighborhood, and the layout of the house—quickly but in detail."

She did, interrupting only to guide me through the shade-tree-rich suburban streets of the Bethesda area. Soon we'd turned off Fairfield Drive onto a quiet lane where a wooded area had been developed for housing. In the yellow glow of streetlamps sat half a dozen interchangeable new homes on either side, those anonymous boxy white cookie-cutter clapboard dream houses that were popping up these days like toadstools in every spare patch of suburban real estate. Their slightly sloping, generous lawns were golf-green immaculate, their yards stingily dotted with baby trees, while behind them loomed father forest, part of which they'd displaced.

Bernstein's house, rather isolated on the cul-de-sac, although the smallest house in the little development, was no exception; like all of these homes, it had an attached two-car garage, and we were half a block away from the darkened house when he drove the Caddy up inside. Maria touched my arm, signaling me to stop and wait, and I did, and we watched him pull down the garage door. Soon a light switched on inside the house, creating a warm glow behind the drawn curtains of the living room.

Cutting the lights well before I got there, I guided the Studebaker up the gentle slope of the driveway, gliding to a stop.

"What now?" Maria whispered.

"Now," I said, withdrawing the nine-millimeter from under my arm, "you drop in on the doc."

She gave me a sharp look. "What's my excuse for being here?"

"Don't worry about it," I said. "It's not gonna get that far."

She clutched my sleeve again. "Nathan . . . don't underestimate this man. He . . . he's capable of terrible things."

"Concentration-camp-type things, you mean? Or is he just a strict boss?"

Then we were standing on his front stoop, a few cement steps up from the lawn, and the nurse was ringing the doctor's bell and I was standing with my back to the house, against the outer wall, just to the right of the door, covering up the street numbers and mail slot. The nine-millimeter, in my right hand, was tucked behind me.

The door opened, and Bernstein, in that clipped precise middle-European-accented English, said, "Why, Maria—what are you doing here at this late—"

That was all he got out before I bulled my way in, grabbing onto Maria's arm with my left hand, yanking her along—not really trusting her, after all—and sticking the nose of the automatic, clutched in my right fist, into the bastard's neck.

"Shut the door, Maria," I said, "then come around where I can see you."

She shut the door and scurried into view.

"I see you don't keep *shabbes,* Doc," I said, digging the snout of the nine-millimeter into his neck, dimpling it; he was lifting his chin, looking down at me with unblinking blue-gray eyes. "Electric lights, driving after sundown—but then, that's right, you're not Orthodox, are you?"

"Mr. Heller, what in—"

"That's all right, Doc. Neither am I."

I withdrew the gun from his neck, gave him a push—not a shove, I'm no sadist—to back him off from me, a ways; he put his hands up, without being asked, and that pale well-chiseled face of his had gone white as milk, only his expression was curdled. Keeping the automatic trained on my reluctant host, I took the place in, the living room, anyway—checking to see if Maria had been truthful about the layout. To the left, an archway leading (she'd said) to the bedrooms and a TV room; just behind and to the right of Bernstein, an archway into the kitchen. So far, it seemed, she'd played it straight.

We were in the largest room in the house—cream-color plaster walls and a Chinese blue pile carpet, and a modern living-room suite with medium-blue bouclé overstuffed sofa, matching easy chair and blond modern occasional pieces. Still, the place was underfurnished— Bernstein was a bachelor, after all—and the living room in particular didn't look lived in, like a display room in a furniture store, only a little less homey. Nothing of the person living here showed.

"Nice digs, Doc—you're really enjoying the all-American good life, great job, Cadillac, nice new house . . . that wonderful postwar world they promised us fighting men, looks like you wound up with it. Congratulations."

Bernstein's voice was calm, soothing; he patted the air with his upraised palms. "Mr. Heller—you've obviously had a relapse of your battle neurosis. You've fixated upon me for some reason, and I would suggest—"

"If I even suspect you're layin' a posthypnotic suggestion on me, you son of a bitch, I'm going to repaint these walls red. Guess how."

His voice remained soothing, reasonable. "Can we talk about this, whatever it is?" He craned his neck to look at his nurse. "Maria? Can you explain?"

"I'm his hostage, too," she shrugged, but her hands were on her hips, not in the air.

I nodded to a mirror with birds painted on it, over the sofa. "Gee, with your Zionist leanings, Doc, I'd figure you'd have a painting of Palestine on display, or maybe a big autographed picture of you and Ben-Gurion. I mean, you are the guy that suggested I embrace my Jewish side."

"Obviously Mr. Forrestal's death has unsettled you," he said gently, the invisible eyebrows raising. "I only want to help you, Mr. Heller—why don't you just put down the gun . . . after all, I'm unarmed, I'm in no way a threat to you . . . and we'll talk."

I pointed with the automatic, toward the archway just behind him. "We'll talk in the kitchen, Doc.

Come on, Maria—we're all going to sit down, like one big happy family."

The kitchen was small and blindingly white, closed white window blinds, white dinette set with chrome legs and white-and-chrome chairs, white cupboards, sparkling white Westinghouse refrigerator and gas range, with only the black-and-white speckled linoleum floor for relief. A shining steel electric percolator and toaster sat on the white countertop, but otherwise the kitchen had that same unlived-in look as the living room.

This was not a home; it was a place to hide.

I had Bernstein sit with his back to the countertop while I sat across from him, the stove behind me, my arm resting on the tabletop, nine-millimeter trained on him. Maria sat to my right, and both of them I directed to sit with their hands folded on the tabletop. The three of us sat there like we were waiting for Mom to serve us something.

His fingers interlocked prayerfully, Bernstein—his complexion seeming less albino-like in contrast with the harsh whiteness of the kitchen—asked, "Are you ready to tell me what this is about, Mr. Heller?"

"Sure, Doc—why don't we start with Roswell?"

"Roswell," he said. He pretended to think about that, shrugging. "And what is Roswell?"

"My intelligence may be limited, Doc, but don't insult it, okay?"

His mouth twitched, or was that a sneer? "Have I treated you disrespectfully, Mr. Heller? I'd prefer you dispense with the 'Doc' cuteness. My name is Dr. Bernstein."

"No it isn't. I don't know what it is, but it sure as hell isn't Bernstein—though speaking of cute, that Jew routine of yours sure was. The Star of David tie tack—nice touch, Doc."

His nostrils flared; the gray-blue eyes showed no fear, just an icy cast. "Gun or no gun, I won't stand for this. My name is Joseph Bernstein and I'm a Jew . . . unlike you, Mr. Heller, a proud Jew, and this is some bizarre case of mistaken identity on your part. If necessary, I can get you the documentation to prove who I am."

I smiled at Maria, whose eyes—like those of a spectator at a tennis match—were moving from me to Bernstein and back again, as our conversation bounced along on its merry way. "I'm sure you can, Doc," I said. "I bet you have a better pedigree than a prize-winning poodle. I'm curious, though—as a member of the master race, does this Zionist masquerade sicken you, or amuse you?"

A sneer, this time, no question. "This *farce* sickens me."

The nine-millimeter in my fist remained trained on him.

"And please, as our little talk progresses, Doc, let me save you some time—spare me about how you weren't really a Nazi, you were a man of science, caught up in winds of political change not of your choosing. Serving science and mankind, as best you could, under unfortunate circumstances. Hating Hitler, much as you now love Uncle Sam. One word of that shit and I just fucking shoot you—clear?"

Now, finally, a little fear was melting the icy eyes; he swallowed thickly. "You're a very sick man."

"Well, why don't we pretend I'm on your couch and you can have a listen to my crazy story. And it's a crazy story, all right. Seems some Nazi scientists were working on a project at White Sands involving a flying-saucer-like vehicle. Actually, it was shaped more like a wedge, and I'm just piecing this together, but I understand, during the war, you Germans were trying to build a saucer-shaped bomber, that could lift off vertically, since all your runways were shot to shit; and this project grew from that wartime research. Now somehow, at White Sands, for some reason, Japanese engineers and pilots were also involved . . ."

Bernstein's mask slipped; my mention of the Japanese startled him. He clearly didn't expect me to have such esoteric information.

". . . possibly because their knowledge, combined with their small stature, made them ideal pilots. And, since Uncle Sam is willing to collaborate with Nazis, why not with Nips? Fair's fair, isn't it? Anyway, there was a crash, maybe the craft got struck by lightning; seems to have been a midair explosion, over the Brazel ranch, scattering some debris, with the vehicle crashing, or crash-landing, some miles away."

Those eyes of his didn't blink much—the icy-gray eyes fixed on me like a cobra looking at a mouse; it would have been unsettling, if I hadn't had the gun.

I went on with my tale: "Colonel Blanchard and his boys found the craft with the crew mostly dead, with maybe one left alive. In the darkness of the night, some of the witnesses apparently took the craft for one of those new-fangled flying saucers they'd been hearing and reading so much about—the Japanese crew, in their silver flight suits, maybe with their heads shaved, maybe with swelling around their eyes . . . traumatic hematoma can cause that . . . must have looked pretty damn strange. Like little men from outer space, in the dark, next to their 'flying saucer.' How do you like my story so far?"

"Delusions like these, Mr. Heller, can get a man committed."

"I'll bet. You could probably even arrange a little shock therapy, huh, Doc? Now some of the witnesses knew they weren't looking at spacemen, recognizing a Jap when they saw one, puffy eyes or not . . . and some of the fringe players didn't really see much at all—Major Marcel just found some weird debris, that p.r. guy Haut just issued the press release as ordered, Maria's mortician sweetie just had some phone calls for small caskets, then got the bum's rush when he dropped by the base hospital. Maria here was the one who 'saw' the autopsies and the weird corpses. That's where the black propaganda campaign kicks in."

Bernstein shifted in his chair, but knew enough not to unfold his hands. "Mr. Heller, if this were true, it would be classified material, *top-secret* information, and a wise man would walk away—right now. I might be willing to forget this intrusion . . . even including you threatening me with a gun."

"Well, that crashed aircraft does represent a threat of exposure of top-secret technology, all right; but that wasn't the big worry. The upper echelons of our great democracy—for example, an advisory panel called Majestic Twelve, including one James Vincent Forrestal—shrewdly deduced that the public's reaction to the government collaborating with both Nazis and Japs would have been a public relations disaster. Nazi scientists retooling V-2s, Japs test-piloting U.S. experimental aircraft—this stuff doesn't go over big with families that haven't gotten over, yet, losing sons and fathers at Bataan and the Bulge."

His lips pursed in a smile as he pretended to be amused. "So now, Mr. Heller, you're suggesting the federal government concocted the 'flying saucer' hysteria themselves, to cover up testing of experimental aircraft?"

"That I don't know. The saucer hysteria may have been a natural by-product of a nation exiting a catastrophic world war, and needing something new to be afraid of. Maybe the government fueled that hysteria for its own purposes; I just don't know. But I do know, with so much talk of flying saucers in the air—so to speak—it provided the perfect cover-up for the Roswell crash."

An invisible eyebrow arched. "Paranoid schizophrenics, Mr. Heller, see conspiracies everywhere they look. Tell me, have you been hearing voices?"

"Actually, I have: yours. But I don't want to get ahead of myself, Doc. You see, the brilliance of this cover-up is that it substitutes a fake cover-up for a real one . . . leading people to believe that what the government is trying to hide is evidence of flying saucers and outer-space men. You feed, and feed off, the rumors that a flying saucer crashed in the desert; this plays into the witnesses who didn't see much, or didn't see anything, and probably a handful—perhaps Kaufmann—who misidentified the Japs as Martians or whatever. Still others, who saw the Japanese pilots and knew damn well what they were seeing, were warned and threatened into silence. Some of those who saw too much—Sheriff Wilcox, Mac Brazel, again maybe Kaufmann—were taken to the Walker base 'guesthouse,' and this is where you come in, Doc—and you, Maria."

The mention of her name made Maria visibly uncomfortable.

Bernstein's expression took on an air of patronizing disgust. "I've never been in Roswell in my life."

"You were there last month, Doc," I said. "But we'll get to that. You, or somebody like you, managed that guesthouse, where—using a combination of drugs, hypnosis and what-have-you—you manipulated real memories into false ones. You worked your mind-control magic on them, Doc, the flying-saucer scenario being similar enough to their real memories to take hold. A few players like Maria, here, are meanwhile injected into the mix, disseminating disinformation, and lending credence and richness to those false memories various witnesses are 'remembering.'"

Bernstein nodded toward Maria, curtly. "If Nurse Selff was an active player in this ridiculous 'disinformation scenario' of yours, what was she doing still working as a nurse at the Walker base, almost two years later?"

Maria smiled a little, her expression challenging me to get it right.

I shrugged. "Maintenance. Keeping an eye on the witnesses. Making sure your experimental methods had taken root and held, Doc, and keeping an eye out for anyone—like me—who might come snooping around. That's my guess, anyway. Or maybe she's just a nurse who occasionally gets pulled in on intelligence jobs. Care to enlighten me, Maria?"

Her expression suddenly rather sullen, Maria shook her head.

"Hey, well I'm doing pretty well on my own, wouldn't you say, Doc?"

"I'd say you're delusional; almost certainly a paranoid schizophrenic."

"Sorry to hear that—that's what Forrestal had, and look how he ended up."

"You might want to keep that in mind."

I gave him the most awful grin I had in me as I kept the gun trained on him. "Good for you, Doc. Getting cute like that's the first step, in coming out from behind your mask. Where was I? Ah—the other brilliant thing about the saucer cover-up is that the witnesses—and their tampered-with memories—will fall into the lunatic fringe, and any reporters who cover the story—like Pearson—will look like saps. I mean, I've figured out what's going on, but I still can't be sure who's a disinformation disseminator, and who's a mind-controlled witness. Can't tell the players without a scorecard, but then, of course, in the end it doesn't matter."

Bernstein's voice was both soothing and condescending as he said, "A symptom of your illness, Mr. Heller, is the inability to differentiate between speculative fantasy and hard reality. In short, fascinating as this may be, it is as preposterous as, well, flying saucers . . . and there's nothing here you can prove, and if there were, who would you prove it to?"

"I've proved it to myself," I said. "To my own satisfaction. The certainty is in my head and my gut. I have no doubt that you worked your sick magic on me. I left Roswell, having heard ridiculous stories about spacemen from all sorts of people, Maria included, yet came away with a strong conviction that what I'd heard was true! After my stay at the guesthouse, I believed in flying saucers, all right; I even had a sort of vision of a pale, benign spaceman, in my dreams, soothing me with his suction-cup fingertips. But then it finally occurred to me, Doc . . . I admit to being a little slow on the uptake, here . . . but outer space creatures don't usually have German accents."

Bernstein didn't have anything to say to that—no perfect clipped English response at all.

Now Maria was looking Bernstein's way, as she said, "Mr. Heller says that Forrestal was murdered."

"That's his most ludicrous statement yet," Bernstein snorted. "Why would the upper echelons of the United States government murder a celebrated former Secretary of Defense?"

I said, "The government didn't kill Forrestal—you did, Doc . . . or rather, we did, you and I."

He laughed, once. "Did you help me, or did I help you?"

"James Forrestal was a threat because he was feeling guilty about sanctioning our government's collaboration with Nazis; further, he was genuinely mentally ill, and capable of either disintegrating in public, or going public with what he knew, neither of which was particularly desirable. Jim Forrestal was one of your classic men who knew too much, a nightmare of a security risk. Various steps were taken, including leaking forged Majestic Twelve files to Drew Pearson to throw the press off the trail of the real Majestic Twelve, which apparently had to do with saucer experimentation via Nazi collaboration, not unidentified objects from outer space. But however you cut it, Forrestal had to go—not in the government's opinion, though I'm sure there will be as much relief in private as there is mourning in public. No, this was your call, Doc, protecting your own Aryan ass. Exposure of the extent of our government's Nazi collaboration could lead to a second series of Nuremberg-like trials; your cushy new life, your Caddy, your house, your prestigious position, it would all go up like so much smoke out an Auschwitz chimney."

"Nurse Selff," Bernstein said, his tone temperate, the gaze he gave her radiating reasonableness, "please know these are the ramblings, the ravings, of a very diseased mind."

"Like me, Maria," I said, "you were this bastard's unwitting accomplice. You were still working the Roswell disinformation project, not realizing the good doctor was putting the Forrestal kill in motion."

Bernstein snapped, "I was nowhere near that hospital when Mr. Forrestal took his life!"

Gun steady on him, I said, "Neither was I, Doc, but we killed him together, just the same."

Confused, Maria asked, "How is that possible, Nathan?"

"The doc here was well aware that I was a veteran of hypnosis therapy, that my battle-fatigue amnesia had been cured by hypnotherapy, in fact. So he knew I'd make a good subject, easily controlled, by a combination of, well . . . sex—that's, uh, your role, Maria . . . and of course a visit to the base guesthouse. Either before or just after my guesthouse stay, back at Bethesda the doc prepped Forrestal to be receptive to posthypnotic suggestion; how exactly the doc achieved that, narcosis, hypnosis . . . well, he's the magician, not me."

Maria asked, in a hushed voice, "What do you think happened to you in the guesthouse?"

"Well for one thing—and this much you do know, Maria—I was a guest at the base longer than I'd been led to believe . . . don't play dumb, baby, that doesn't become you, either. You told me, when I fell asleep at your bungalow, that I'd slept straight through, losing a day . . . but really I'd only slept through that one night. Right?"

Chagrined, she nodded.

"You even gave me a posthypnotic suggestion yourself, didn't you, Maria? Per the doc's instructions, when you said, 'You must be very tired, very tired, very tired.' "

"That is true," she admitted, sending an accusing glare Bernstein's way.

"That had nothing to do with Forrestal," he told her emphatically.

I shook my head. "It had everything to do with him, Doc. You had, what, a day, a day and a half to work your magic on me, in that guesthouse? *Including giving me the posthypnotic suggestion to buy that book of poetry for Forrestal.* I vividly remember,

Doc, you repeating the phrase on the phone, twice: 'A book of poetry would be comforting.' As if that wasn't enough, you advised me to tell Forrestal that I, his trusted associate, had been secretly working for his nemesis, Drew Pearson, making a damn good case for that being a good idea, while in reality anticipating that my disclosure would help create in Forrestal the right suicidal mind-set."

Now some desperation had found its way into Bernstein's voice and his demeanor, as he turned to the nurse. "Maria, do you realize how preposterous all of this is? Do you see now that Mr. Heller is suffering from a complete mental breakdown?"

Maria said nothing.

I said, "Funny thing is, Doc, after I looked the crime scene over? I figured somebody had sneaked in and murdered Forrestal . . . and I was right: *I* did. I was the murderer who sneaked into Bethesda to kill Forrestal—I just didn't know it. I didn't know that that book I handed him was as lethal as poison gas."

Bernstein said, flatly, "Forrestal threw himself out a window. Nothing changes that."

"Yeah, I gave Jim Forrestal my thoughtful gift, that book of poetry, and I must've also passed along a posthypnotic suggestion to him—when was that, Doc, when I said, 'I thought you'd find a book of poetry comforting,' something like that? Anyway, thanks to the doc's manipulation of my meager subconscious, I passed on the posthypnotic suggestion that made Forrestal get out of bed in the middle of the night, read that uplifting suicide poem you'd programmed him to read, Doc—and when Forrestal hit the crucial, guilt-inducing word—*nightingale*—he followed doctor's orders and got some fresh air, trying to hang himself but succeeding instead in just throwing himself out the pantry window."

Maria frowned, the big dark blue eyes tensed with curiosity. "Why 'nightingale'?"

"Well," I said, "in the original German, it's *Nachtigall*, right, Doc? A guy named Teddy Kollek told me about it—you ought to get together with him, Doc, with your mutual interest in Palestine. Anyway, Operation Nightingale was a particularly ugly act of collaboration that Forrestal approved, subsidizing Ukrainian anti-Communist guerrillas who during the war were a Nazi execution squad, responsible for the mass slaughter of thousands of Jews. Not a bad guilt trigger for a man who felt he'd betrayed his country through such associations."

He sat erect; chin up. "My name is Dr. Joseph Bernstein. As a Jew, I deeply resent these implications and accusations."

"You know, Doc, as a guy who fought in the trenches on Guadalcanal, as a half-assed Jew myself, I find you just about the lowest-life piece of shit it's ever been my misfortune to encounter. But what I really resent, Doc, what really annoys me, what really puts me in a bad place right now, is being used as your murder weapon. Jim Forrestal hired me to find out if somebody was trying to kill him; and, like everybody, I told him he was crazy. Then I wind up helping the guy who wanted him dead make that happen. Funny, huh? Ironic, even."

I lifted my arm from the table and leveled the nine-millimeter at Bernstein's head.

"Probably a tactical error on your part, Doc," I said, "making a murderer out of me."

Maria reached over and touched my shoulder, gently. "Nathan—don't do it."

"Don't tell me I've convinced you that the doc, here, has been a bad boy. . . ."

"Yes you have. I believe he's been a very bad boy

indeed. If you leave this to me, Nathan, I'll handle it. The government will handle it, clean up their mistake—discreetly, but decisively."

I shook my head. "Can't do that, baby—but here's what I will do. I'll take the doc into custody right now—citizen's arrest, if you will, of a war criminal."

"All right," she said guardedly. "But what then?"

"Then you and I, Maria, will hand his ass over to Chief Baughman of the Secret Service. I'll tell Baughman my story and you'll corroborate it. What do you say, baby?"

But she didn't answer; she didn't have a chance to.

Bernstein lurched across the table with a savage suddenness and in less than an instant his hands latched onto my fist, which clutched the nine-millimeter, swinging the gun's muzzle away from himself, one of his hands tightening around the trigger and trigger guard and the gun went off, in Maria's direction.

The bullet caught her in the forehead and I saw the terrible immediate emptiness in the dark blue eyes as the back of her head emptied in a horrible spray of red and gray and white, and I screamed in horror and reflexively loosened my grip on the gun, for a fraction of an instant, and then she had gone backward in the chair, sprawled onto the floor, vacant eyes staring up at the ceiling, red spreading in an awful pool on the linoleum, and the nine-millimeter wasn't in my hand, anymore.

Bernstein was seated across me, and now the nine-millimeter was in his hand, and leveled at me. . . . Only he didn't shoot.

"Sit down, Mr. Heller. Relax."

Slowly, I sat back down.

"There are advantages to knowing the ways of the human mind," he told me calmly. "If I had struggled with you for this weapon, I might be dead now. But by helping you squeeze the trigger on the lovely . . . late . . . Nurse Selff, I created the only circumstance that would cause you to loosen your grip on that gun, however momentarily."

I said nothing, wondering why I was still alive.

"You're wondering why you're still alive, aren't you, Mr. Heller? Maybe I'd like a few moments to gloat. You certainly subjected me to enough humiliation."

"Gloating can be dangerous."

The dazzling white smile flashed in his pale handsome face. "Yes. Look where it led you. Now you've helped me kill two people. We make quite a team. Or I should say, 'made.' "

"Better kill me with the first shot."

The scorched odor of cordite was mingling with the smell of blood. I didn't dare look at her, afraid of what the rage might make me risk; I needed just the right opportunity. . . .

"I appreciate the friendly advice, Mr. Heller. I must admit, you displayed a remarkable ability to gather disparate information and form an unlikely, albeit largely accurate, whole. There are tiny aspects you've misunderstood, or gotten incorrect—but yours is an extraordinary, if limited, intellectual capacity."

"Fuck you, you sick bastard."

"You were right before—I'm not a Nazi. I was a party member only because it was a political necessity; all of us, von Braun and the rest, were ushered into the SS only as a formality . . . I wore the uniform a mere handful of times, at official functions."

"Too bad. I bet you looked spiffy as hell. What else did you do as a political necessity? Suck off Adolf?"

The psychiatrist shook his head. "What a sad, pathetic man you are. Do you really think it was my choice to see Jew and Russian prisoners treated as subhumans? But once these creatures were marked for death, their destinies decided by those above me, why not use them for research, for the furtherance of science, and medicine? Why not give these pitiful martyrs some purpose for having lived and died, some meaning to otherwise meaningless existences? The things we discovered, because of having disposable specimens, will make life better for all the rest of us, and our children, and their children."

"You should be getting that Nobel Prize in the mail any day now." I grinned at him, and it unsettled him, I could see. "You're trying to figure it out, aren't you?"

"Figure what out, Mr. Heller?"

"How to stage this. How to kill me. It's got to look right to your superiors. If they think you murdered Maria and me to cover something up, you'll have some fancy explaining to do. I mean, there'll be suspicions about Forrestal's convenient exit, already. How do you explain two corpses in your kitchen?"

His mouth formed something that was half smile, half sneer. "Maybe the bodies won't be in my kitchen. Maybe you'll drag Nurse Selff out to my garage and put her in the trunk of my car."

I nodded at the wisdom of this. "Yeah, then you could shoot me, push me in there, dump us both somewhere. Maybe make it look like a murder/suicide ... lover's quarrel. Not bad for a beginner, Doc."

Bernstein stood. Gestured at me with the gun. I came around the table, on the side where Maria wasn't, and he stood facing me, leveling the gun at my chest, maybe eight inches separating us.

"You know, Doc, you may know a lot about the human mind, but you don't know jack shit about guns."

"I know how to squeeze a trigger."

"Not with a broken finger you don't."

And I grabbed the muzzle of the nine-millimeter and twisted it, hard; his howl of pain as his trigger finger broke, jamming against the metal trigger guard, was music to my ears. But he hadn't let go of the weapon, so I jammed the slide back.

Then his hand loosened and I snatched the gun away as he fell to his knees, clutching his hand, the finger bent at an impossible angle.

"You see, the Browning nine-millimeter is a recoil-operated weapon, Doc. Everything has to be locked together for it to fire, everything has to be lined up perfectly—kind of like the human brain."

By grabbing the nine-millimeter's slide and pushing it back, I'd made a jammed weapon out of it. So I slapped its magazine, racked the slide and the weapon was good as new again. Ready to fire. But I had a better idea.

Bernstein sat on the floor, grasping his hand, whimpering, tears streaming down his face.

Kneeling at an angle that kept the fallen, sniveling psychiatrist in view, I took the opportunity to spend a moment beside my beautiful Maria. The vulnerable girl, the hard-as-nails woman, nurse, spy, lovely even in death, even with the black-and-red dime-size pucker in her forehead; I closed her eyes, kissed her cheek and whispered, "Forgive me."

Then, rubbing the tears out of my eyes, I stood. "Jeez, Doc, we're both crying. Real couple of he-men, huh?"

Bernstein, cheeks flushed—funny, his face finally had some color in it—looked up at me, the icy eyes red and blinking. "What . . . what now?"

Keeping the weapon trained on him, I moved to the stove, dropped open the door.

"Now, Doc?" I shrugged, walking back to where he sat, shivering with pain. "Now I'm going to embrace my Jewish side."

The barrel of the nine-millimeter caught him across the forehead, knocking him out, and I dragged his unconscious form over like a bag of grain and shoved the top half of him into the oven.

Then I turned on the gas.

Twenty-two

On a clear, sunny morning in May, after a nineteen-gun salute, the boom of howitzers playing bass drum to the Naval Academy Band's rendition of Chopin's "Funeral March," the Old Glory–draped caisson bearing the casket, drawn by seven gray horses, accompanied by an honor guard made up of all three services, wound its way up the serpentine drive of Arlington National Cemetery.

There, on the Wednesday following his fatal fall, James Vincent Forrestal received full military honors at a ceremony attended by President Truman, the cabinet, an array of Congressional leaders, the diplomatic corps and several thousand friends and associates. A crowd of interested citizens numbering at least four thousand stood behind a velvet rope at the end of the white marble amphitheater, in the chapel of which the President, Vice President and pallbearers including former president Herbert Hoover, Generals Marshall and Eisenhower, Bernard Baruch and Forrestal's friend Ferdinand Eberstadt, attended the service itself, with Bishop Conkling from Chicago presiding.

Jo Forrestal did not attend. She and her sons Peter and Michael, young men in their early twenties, both of whom had echoes of their father in their faces, waited a few hundred yards away, at the gravesite, for a ceremony reserved for family, relatives and close friends.

I'd been invited—by Eberstadt—and was among this fairly small group. Forrestal, of course, had been physically rather small, and the size of his casket reflected this, and was little bigger than a child's coffin—like the coffins the Air Force had tried to buy from Glenn Dennis at the Ballard Funeral Home in Roswell.

The air was sharply cool, almost cold, and I stood at the back—immediate family seated on folding chairs, no tent—as Bishop Conkling read from First Corinthians. The little casket was lowered, and the sons threw in the symbolic clumps of earth. We were on an oak-studded knoll overlooking the tranquillity of the gray blue Potomac and the panorama of government buildings beyond.

A slender, fragile, elegant-looking pale figure in mesh-veiled, stylish black (had Mainbocher designed her a funeral gown?), Jo Forrestal—looking more than ever like Charles Addams' creation—drifted among the gathering of friends and relatives with her sons in attendance, making introductions when necessary. I shook hands with both boys, who had appropriately shell-shocked expressions.

Jo said to me, "You should have felt at home here today, Nate."

"Well, uh, yes, you mean with Bishop Conkling presiding . . ."

"No, I mean Jim got a regular Chicago-style send-off, don't you think?"

She took me by the arm and walked me a few steps away from her boys; I couldn't smell any drink on her, but then I never could—vodka was kind to the breath, after all.

"I don't quite get your drift, Jo . . ."

Her eyes glittered under the veil; her voice had a brittle edge. "All the pomp and goddamn circumstance, flowers and brass bands, it's like when your syndicate big shots take one of the boys for a ride, right? Got to have a big show, after the bump-off—to feel less guilty, and fool the gullible fucking public. You must feel at home."

"Now that you mention it," I said, "it's not the first time I've been at this kind of affair."

She touched my sleeve with a black-gloved hand. "Jim liked you. I'm sure he didn't show it, but you were one of his favorites. He felt you were a man's man . . . sometimes he felt his . . . intellectual pursuits were less than . . . I don't know . . . manly."

"You and Jim turned out a couple of handsome boys."

"Nate, you may not believe this, but Jim and I loved each other, in our way. I will never forgive those shits for . . ." And she slipped a hanky-in-hand up under the veil and caught a sob.

"Jo . . ."

". . . never forgive them for sending me out of town. When they killed him. Do you know how that made me look? 'Mrs. Forrestal was in Paris when her husband fell to his death.' Cold, heartless bitch. They're the cold, heartless ones. I told the cocksuckers—you can have your gangster's funeral, but I'll have no part of it."

"You better keep those thoughts to yourself, Jo."

She smirked beneath the veil. "Why, 'cause I'll be the next lunatic they stick on the sixteenth floor, near an open window?"

". . . Yes."

She thought about that for a moment, turning her gaze toward the Potomac. From this knoll on the heights of Arlington, we could see in the distance on this clear morning the great dome and the magnificent white marble temples of our nation's capital.

"Funny, isn't it?" she said. "What men in public life will do, in the name of the people."

Then I walked her back to her sons, who stood at the graveside, standing, heads lowered, at the edge of where the casket had been lowered. That was when it occurred to me: this was the first time—in all the years I'd known them, in the various jobs I'd done for our late Secretary of Defense—I had ever seen Jim and Jo Forrestal together.

The suicide of Dr. Joseph Bernstein—no surviving relatives—was buried in the back pages, with no mention that he had been one of James Forrestal's psychiatrists, in fact no mention that he had worked at the Naval Medical Center at Bethesda. Nobody, not even Drew Pearson, picked up on the amazing coincidence of the two interrelated suicides in one night.

Nobody questioned me. Whether they suspected me or not, who can say? I had wiped my fingerprints from the few surfaces I had touched in Bernstein's dream house, and had driven Maria's Studebaker back to the hospital parking lot, wiping it clean of prints. No one seemed to have seen me leave the car there, and get in my own and drive away.

The biggest risk had been leaving the bullet that killed Maria behind; it was lodged, no doubt, somewhere in the woodwork of that house, having traveled at close range through her brain. If anyone had thought to check with the Chicago police department, or probably the FBI—who had that thick file on me, remember—a ballistics match to my weapon might have been possible. The nine-millimeter was a gun I had carried since my father's suicide, and it had left its own fingerprints, here and there.

I wasn't worried about it, not when the newspapers carried no word of Maria's death. She had vanished, like a magician's assistant. Bernstein, in that half-assed way, got mentioned; a psychiatrist was too high-profile to just disappear. A nurse was far less significant. She could do a vanishing act.

That gave me the worst nights, thinking about the family she must have had, somewhere. We never spoke of it, but hell—even I'd had a mother and father. What lie had the government told them about their daughter's death? Where, if anywhere, had her remains been interred? Not on an oak-studded knoll in Arlington, I'd wager.

The only conversation I had with a government official bearing at all on Forrestal's death was a rather oblique one with onetime Capone nemesis and former Secret Service chief Frank J. Wilson, the evening before the big funeral. The meeting—he'd asked to meet me for a cocktail in the Ambassador's High Hat Cocktail Lounge—was ostensibly a social one; but soon it revealed itself as business, pertaining to Wilson's consultant role with the Atomic Energy Commission.

Chatting over beers, Wilson and I sat in a back booth, with the privacy only a boisterous public place can provide. In his dark blue suit and dark-rimmed glasses, and with that stern cleft-chin countenance of his, he didn't look much like a guy out for a night on the town.

"You should know that the Commission is aware of your inquiries at Walker Air Base," Wilson said, "and in Roswell. . . . I understand you were poking around for Drew Pearson, about that so-called flying saucer crash."

"That's right."

"We'd just as soon not see any further attention

drawn to that. The incident had its flurry of press interest, at the time, which has long since died down."

"Since when is the Atomic Energy Commission concerned about little green men?"

He twitched a smile, sipped his beer. "I can clear some things up for you—if you'll agree to keep quiet. You can't give this to Pearson. Not to anyone, Nate—not your priest, not your best girl."

My best girl had been recently shot and killed, and lately everybody had been reminding me I was a Jew; so none of that seemed a problem.

"Okay, then, Frank—just between us girls."

He held his glass of beer with both hands, as if it were something precious, leaning forward, ever so slightly. "Obviously, that was no flying saucer. There's a top-secret project . . . no, that's not quite right. Actually it's classified Top Secret A-1, the same national security rating as the Manhattan Project."

My forehead frowned and my mouth smiled. "And you're telling me about it? In the cocktail lounge at the Ambassador Hotel?"

"I'm not going to tell you in detail. But the material Major Marcel recovered *was* debris from a fallen balloon."

"Weather balloon, yeah. Hell, like Daffy Duck says, 'That's no military secret.' The government's been peddling that sliced baloney since two hours after the saucer story broke."

Wilson shook his head, no; his expression grave, his voice hushed. "This isn't a weather balloon . . . it's not one balloon at all, but a train of as many as twenty-three balloons, a massive affair designed to climb to high altitudes, for intelligence-gathering purposes."

"Okay," I said, as if accepting all that. "If the Atomic Energy Commission is involved, then I can probably guess the kind of intelligence-gathering you're talking about."

"You probably can. As for some of the descriptions you no doubt heard, of the strange debris, this balloon train included a very sophisticated new aluminum material, with rubberized backing."

"Which accounts for the tales of crumple-proof metal from outer space. What about these so-called hieroglyphics people say they saw?"

"That's a funny story." And Wilson smiled, having cued himself. "Apparently the radar reflectors were contracted from a toy company, who used some tape they had on hand for reinforcement purposes—with flowers, diamonds, circles, other childish designs . . . 'hieroglyphics.' As for the unbreakable 'beams,' they were balsa wood treated with a special-formula glue."

I sipped my beer. "That is a funny story, Frank. Almost as funny as trained Army Air Force personnel mistaking that stuff for a crashed flying saucer."

His eyebrows climbed his endless forehead and then made the long trip back down. "That I can't explain, other than that some of these materials were sophisticated, and differed greatly from the run-of-the-mill balloons that would have commonly come down in the Southwest, which those Air Force people would have immediately recognized. . . . And that's all I can say, Nate—other than, as a friend, to ask you to try, to the best of your ability, to quash Pearson's interest in the Roswell story. It might draw . . . unwanted attention."

The implication, of course, was Soviet attention; and my assumption was that these balloons were gathering the data that, oddly enough, Major Marcel at SAC was lately interpreting and collating, regarding whether or not the Russians were engaging in the testing of atomic weapons.

I went along with this, though I've always wondered whether straight-arrow Frank Wilson had knowingly passed disinformation along to me. The only way that train of weather balloons might have been involved in the Roswell crash was if that experimental aircraft codesigned by Germans and Japanese had collided with it—which I supposed was a possibility.

Nonetheless, as Wilson had requested, I did dissuade Pearson from pursuing the Roswell tale, informing him that I believed the accounts were riddled with disinformation, and that Majestic Twelve, while it might well exist, did not seem to have been formed to investigate saucers from outer space.

"Was somebody trying to make a sap of me?" Pearson asked over the phone, the afternoon after Forrestal's funeral.

"That may be the intent, or possibly just a happy by-product of concealing the real purpose of Majic-12."

"Which is just one of the many secrets—and sins—Forrestal took to the grave with him."

The bitterness in Pearson's tone didn't surprise me; he had taken terrible blows to his reputation—and to his list of subscribing newspapers—by the blame others in the press were heaping on him; it was widely implied that Pearson, via his hounding, had "murdered" Forrestal. The *New York Times* pilloried Pearson for overstepping "the bounds of accuracy and decency," the *Washington Post* spoke of the columnist's "below the belt blows"—and this in Pearson's home paper. (Many years later, Jack Anderson—who would take over the "Washington Merry-Go-Round" column and distinguish himself as Pearson's successor—would say with regret, "Our hand was surely in this tragedy.")

"Tell me, Drew," I asked him, just curious, "do you feel you bear any blame at all for Jim Forrestal's demise?"

"It was the Navy's fault—if they'd taken proper precautions, he'd be alive today."

"There's some truth in that," I admitted. "But I thought maybe you could at least scrape up a little pity for the poor bastard."

"Sorry, no. This was a man who spent all his life thinking about only himself, trying to fulfill his great ambition to be President of the United States. Anyway, is a public official immune from criticism or investigation, for fear his health might be impaired by the process?"

"You know, Drew—I know why you hated him so much, if you're interested."

"I didn't hate him! . . . Why?"

"He reminded you of you."

"That's a despicable thing to say. You know better than most people what that man was capable of, to see that his point of view prevailed."

"That's what I'm talking about. You two're the original ends-justify-the-means twins. There's only one thing Forrestal has over you, Drew, just one little thing . . ."

"And what would that be?"

"He had the decency to go out a high window."

Well, I didn't get any jobs from Pearson for a while, after that. But we did reconcile, when in later years he mellowed some, as his power dwindled. He accomplished many good things with his muckraking style, including paving the way for modern investigative journalism. One of his many positive accomplishments was to follow up my lead on our government's collaboration with Nazis, exposing the likes of Luftwaffe Major General Walter Schreiber—

who had been involved with medical experimentation on concentration camp inmates—forcing the Nazi general to flee from our shores in 1952. Toward the end of Pearson's life, when he was receiving accolades for his long, illustrious career, the Forrestal case was dredged up and he suffered another round of criticism, dying of a heart attack in 1969.

James Forrestal's legacy was probably more lasting than Pearson's. The headquarters of the Defense Department bears his name; 1954 marked the christening of the USS *Forrestal,* the nation's largest cant-deck aircraft carrier; and in 1975, Princeton University designated its corporate research park the Princeton Forrestal Center. More significant was the role of this paranoid schizophrenic as an architect of the Cold War—based largely on false, inflated data from an East-Bloc-countries-based Nazi spy network with whom our government was now collaborating—and in inspiring Senator Joe McCarthy to seek out the largely nonexistent Communists supposedly riddling our government. McCarthy himself, in 1952, credited Forrestal as the one who had alerted him to the "existence of traitors in high government positions."

I liked Jim Forrestal, and as was the case with Pearson, the guy was a dedicated servant of the public who did a lot of good, particularly toward the winning of the Second World War; but there would have perhaps been better things to bequeath the nation he loved and served than Nazi collaboration, the Cold War and McCarthyism.

Caught up in the pressures of McCarthyism, his popularity eroded, Harry Truman left office largely unheralded, though with his position in history secure as the first (and at this writing only) U.S. president to use the atomic bomb in war; historians rate him a good to great president, a perception that had long since become evident by his death in 1972.

Teddy Kollek—who had fled to Canada from U.S. prosecution in April of 1949—was elected Mayor of Jerusalem in 1965, a position he held for twenty-eight years; much of the face of modern Jerusalem, it has been said, is his doing. His efforts toward tolerance for minority groups in his city, including Arabs, alienated some of his constituents, and his last two mayoral campaigns failed, despite efforts by such Hollywood supporters as his old friend Frank Sinatra. In 1991 he established the Jerusalem Foundation to help further aesthetic and cultural development of his beloved city.

Jo Forrestal was in and out of clinics for the rest of her life, for alcoholism and mental problems. In the first years after her husband's passing, she traveled constantly, and lived for a time in France, Ireland and Jamaica, finally landing in Newport, Rhode Island, selling Morris House in 1951. She also maintained an apartment on Park Avenue in New York, and backed several theatrical productions in Newport as well as writing a play of her own, *Democracy,* never produced. Sporadic reports of her bizarre behavior continued until her death in January of 1976.

The Forrestals' son Michael distinguished himself with service in the Kennedy White House, returning to law practice after the assassination; his life was devoted to improving understanding between the United States and the Soviet Union. Unmarried, he died of an aneurysm in January 1989, at sixty-one; he was chairing a committee of the governing board of Lincoln Center, at the time. Brother Peter worked for his father's old firm, Dillon, Read, then for Ferdinand Eberstadt's company (Eberstadt died in 1969, leaving a personal estate of fifty million). Peter shared his mother's love of and skill with horses, but also shared her love for, and lack of skill with, alcohol. He died at fifty-two of an abdominal hemorrhage due to heavy drinking, leaving behind a bride of a year, pregnant with a daughter he never knew.

Many of those I met on the Forrestal/Roswell job are gone—including two class acts of law enforcement, Frank J. Wilson and Hughie Baughman—and others I never saw again and couldn't tell you what became of them, like the two medical corpsmen, Prise and Harrison, and the doctor who tore his sleeve, Deen.

But Roswell . . . that was another story.

For many years, the incident at Roswell—despite the historical significance of the Air Force issuing a press release announcing the recovery of a flying saucer—rarely received even a mention in the voluminous UFO literature of the late forties and on through the seventies.

But in 1978, Stanton Friedman—a nuclear physicist with an interest in UFOs—followed up a lead that led him to Lieutenant Colonel Jesse Marcel, retired, who had spent his post-military years running a television repair shop in Houma, Louisiana. Marcel told Friedman the same story he'd told me back in 1949—a story he had apparently told no one since—and a Roswell floodgate opened.

A cottage industry of books by Friedman and others blossomed, with scads of television documentaries, in which Marcel and other witnesses—like Glenn Dennis, Walter Haut, Frank Joyce and Frank Kaufmann—came forward, becoming celebrities in UFO circles, even television stars, with the many appearances they made. Marcel's son, a physician and pilot, with memories of the samples of strange "saucer" debris his father had brought home in '47, joined in with his own recollections, taking over as family TV spokesman after his father's death in 1986. These were solid citizens, clearly not kooks, and their reminiscences carried weight.

Some potential Roswell witnesses, however, received their fifteen minutes of fame posthumously.

Mac Brazel died in 1963, though relatives and neighbors told his story to researchers and on camera. His son Bill Brazel reported his father had been held by the Air Force for eight days in the base "guesthouse."

Colonel William "Butch" Blanchard remained tight-lipped on the subject of Roswell, in public at least, though friends reported he'd said, when asked about the supposed saucer, "I'll tell you this, what I saw I'd never seen before." Shortly after the incident, he was promoted to general and, at the time of his death in 1966, was Deputy Chief of Staff of the Air Force.

Sheriff George Wilcox did not run for reelection and his family considered the saucer incident to have gravely affected his health and outlook. Wilcox passed away before the renewed interest in the saucer crash; but family members, including his wife, Inez, came forward with tales of death threats from the military.

The daughter of fireman Dan Dwyer, Frankie Rowe, told of the strange debris, scraps of which she had handled, and claimed that her father (part of a fire department crew called to the crash site) had described "aliens" being loaded into body bags. She also tearfully recounted death threats to her father and herself by sinister figures from the government.

The resurgence of Roswell interest caused the Air Force to do something remarkable: they contradicted their previous explanation of the debris found on the

Foster ranch with a thick official report in 1994, admitting the weather balloon story had been a cover-up for Project Mogul—which in 1947 had been classified Top Secret A-1. This—the third official explanation (first a flying disk, then a weather balloon, now Project Mogul)—was the intelligence-gathering balloon train described to me by Frank Wilson in 1949. An experimental attempt to acoustically detect suspected Soviet atomic explosions and missile launchings, Mogul utilized acoustical sensors, radar reflecting targets and other gizmos, all of which were attached to a train of weather balloons over six hundred feet long.

The flaw in this explanation—which I've never heard anybody point out, including the "UFOlogists"—is that Project Mogul would be the very device gathering information for Major Jesse Marcel at SAC in 1948 and '49. Unless Marcel was part of a decades-spanning disinformation campaign—which seems very unlikely, considering his burst of UFO TV fame in his elderly years—this indicates Marcel, in the new job he'd been transferred to from Roswell, would have likely discovered that the strange debris he'd found in '47 was from one of the devices gathering information for him in '48. And he would not have spoken to me in 1949, nor a horde of Roswell researchers in the late seventies and early eighties, from the point of view of a man still bewildered by what he'd found on the Foster ranch.

The Project Mogul explanation, of course, didn't speak to the many witnesses—Frank Kaufmann, Glenn Dennis and a number of others who came out of the woodwork in the eighties and thereafter—who spoke of the second crash site, the wedgelike aircraft and the alien crew.

So the Air Force rolled up its sleeves for a fourth

official explanation. In 1997, in perhaps the most tortuous piece of logic to arise out of Roswell yet, the
Air Force explained that the alien bodies that had
been seen by witnesses in 1947 were crash-test dummies dropped by the USAF starting around 1952.
Seems the residents of Roswell were simply confused
about the time frame.

The Air Force insisted that "Maria Selff," the nurse
Glenn Dennis claimed to have known (and of whom
others had memories), never existed; memories of
aliens were probably confused recollections of Captain Dan Fulgham's injury in a 1959 balloon gondola
accident, from which the captain's face became
swollen; and furthermore the mortician's claim that
he'd been bullied by a black MP was impossible, because no black sergeants were stationed at the air
base during that time period.

Majestic Twelve reared its head in 1984 when documents similar to the ones Pearson had received (I
never actually saw them) were delivered anonymously to a UFO researcher, Jamie Shandera. On a
roll of 35mm black-and-white film were copies of the
letter from Truman to Forrestal, and a "briefing document" supposedly prepared for President-elect
Eisenhower. Tops and bottoms of pages were
stamped TOP SECRET/MAJIC EYES ONLY. The list of
Majic-12 members included Forrestal, with mention
that, after his death, he had been replaced (he was
MJ-3) by General Walter Bedell Smith.

Majestic Twelve (or Majic-12), according to these
documents, was "a TOP SECRET Research and Development/Intelligence operation responsible directly
and only to the President of the United States," and
the briefing papers described the crash of a saucer-
like craft near Roswell and the recovery of "four
small human-like beings."

To true believers, the Majic-12 papers were the Holy Grail found; for professional UFO debunkers, the material was an obvious hoax. Both sides mounted impressive arguments, but those in the know recognized the extensive inside knowledge and expertise in military documents that would have had to go into such an elaborate fabrication. A few small voices cried, "Disinformation," largely unheeded. The Majestic Twelve files remain a hotly debated topic among believers and debunkers alike.

Perhaps because my inquiry into Roswell had taken place almost two years after the various events that composed the "incident," none of the researchers or documentary filmmakers sought me out, at least not until the pending fiftieth anniversary of the crash in 1997 raised interest to a fever pitch. A freelance journalist from Davenport, Iowa—Matthew Clemens—had run across a mention of me in a Roswell-related FBI memo unearthed by the Freedom of Information Act, and tracked me down (by phone) at my Coral Springs condo.

"You talked to the eyewitnesses," Clemens said over the phone, sounding young and eager, "in a contemporary time frame—everyone else who interviewed them did so thirty years after the fact, or more."

"Yeah," I said, sounding like the cranky old man that I was. "So?"

"So, did you uncover anything, back then, when memories were fresh, that the latter-day researchers haven't?"

"I don't know. I haven't read any of the 'latter-day researchers.' "

"Mr. Heller, I'm going down my own path, here, and I need to talk to somebody knowledgeable, somebody who was there, but who doesn't have an agenda."

"What do you mean, an agenda?"

"Well, guys like Walter Haut and Glenn Dennis, they're caught up in it, now. Haut's a longtime Roswell Chamber of Commerce guy, and both of 'em are involved with running a UFO museum there! I mean, it's become the town industry."

"So what road are you going down, Mr. Clemens?"

"I've been digging for information on the Nazi presence at White Sands, which was nearby. You know about Operation Paperclip, don't you?"

"Putting Nazi scientists on the U.S. payroll. Got us to the moon."

"Yeah, it did. We had . . . let me check my notes . . . seven hundred and sixty-five of 'em working for us, scientists, doctors, technicians; at least half, maybe as many as eighty percent of 'em, were Nazi party members and/or SS men. Of course those guys claim they only joined the party and SS because they couldn't get research grants, otherwise."

"And you think this has something to do with Roswell, Mr. Clemens?"

"Yeah, at first I thought the 'saucer' was one of these refurbished V-2s . . . you know, maybe the 'aliens' were monkeys; von Braun was obsessed with manned flight, you know. But I'm onto something better, something bigger. You ever hear of the Fugo incendiary bomb?"

"Yeah."

"Really?"

"The Japs launched unmanned high-altitude balloons, with bombs on 'em, hoping to explode them in our Pacific Northwest."

"I'm impressed, Mr. Heller. The hope was to ignite forest fires, and deny lumber to the war effort. And of course, the effort was a bust. But new evidence indicates the Japanese may have been working on a second-generation Fugo, with kamikaze pilots to target them. That never got off the drawing board."

"So you think the Roswell crash was a Fugo balloon?"

"No. I think it was a VTOL."

"And what would that be, Mr. Clemens?"

"A vertical-takeoff-and-landing aircraft. These German brothers, Walter and Reimar Horten, designed them—first for the Nazis, then for us, after the war. See, the German runways were shot to hell, and something that could lift off without a runway might have won the thing for them, and Hitler and his crowd would be carved on Mount Rushmore, right now. Also, the VTOL was the Reich's only shot at trying out their new jet-engine propulsion system."

"So was the Roswell crash a balloon or a, what? Vertical-takeoff whatever?"

"I think it was a combination of both, a hybrid craft utilizing Fugo lifting technology and a Horten-designed lifting body."

He had just explained the balloon debris found on the Brazel ranch, and the aircraft discovered north of Roswell.

"Well, Mr. Heller? What do you think of my theory?"

"Son," I said, "it'll never fly."

And that ended my one and only interview on Roswell.

I have finally broken my silence, including admitting a murder, confident that the United States government will not come to Florida looking for the old man making these absurd statements. The true believers will discount my tale—part of me hopes they'll label it "disinformation"—and the debunkers will reject it, too, because they didn't think of it.

As I write this, a new millennium approaches, and

Roswell, New Mexico, has three UFO museums (retired mortician Glenn Dennis is the president of the International UFO Museum & Research Center). The town of fifty thousand also has bus tours to various impact sites, and numerous shops selling T-shirts, dolls, puppets, spaceship earrings, bumper stickers and UFO hats. More than five million earth dollars a year, of late, have been pumped into Roswell, where its annual summer UFO celebration—with rock concert, "Best Alien" costume contest, laser light show and film festival—has attracted as many as 150,000 tourists.

The town's new motto: "Crash in Roswell."

No one seems to care about the space program anymore, that trip to the moon the Nazi scientists helped us make; we're more interested in watching science-fiction movies on our Japanese-designed video equipment. But, of course, everybody's interested in Roswell, and why not?

Something strange happened there.

I Owe Them One

Despite its extensive basis in history, this is a work of fiction, and liberties have been taken with the facts, though as few as possible—and any blame for historical (and/or geographical) inaccuracies is my own, reflecting, I hope, the limitations of conflicting source material.

Of all the subjects I've chosen to explore to date in the Heller "memoirs," the Roswell incident is perhaps the most written about, outdistancing even Amelia Earhart (*Flying Blind*, 1998), Huey Long's assassination (*Blood and Thunder*, 1995) and the Lindbergh baby kidnapping (*Stolen Away*, 1991). Whether this fact is remarkable or absurd, I leave to the reader's judgment.

But—as with the disappearance of Amelia Earhart—books on this subject tend to display the bias of the authors/researchers. Many of the debunkers will accept no evidence tending toward extraterrestrial phenomena; many of the believers will accept any evidence. Both approaches are, as is obvious even to a B– biology student like me, bad science.

This does not deprive the best Roswell books of their entertainment value or make them less than worthwhile; it does demand that readers approach these works with a combination of skepticism and open-mindedness. I am prepared to be attacked by both sides, incidentally, because the theory expressed in this book is unlikely to be accepted by either the debunkers or the believers. And while I do not put this theory forth as anything more than a reasoned, reasonably informed alternative solution, it is a result of a trip down a research road fraught with the potholes of contradictory and frustrating evidence.

The best-known of the believers is probably my fellow Iowan Kevin Randle, and he alone of the pro-UFO crowd seems to make an attempt to hold the evidence to somewhat rigorous standards. He regularly revises his opinions, based on new facts, and has debunked some of his own star witnesses—a rarity in UFO circles. At this writing, Randle's most recent thoughts on Roswell can be found in *The Randle Report* (1997); his earlier book-length works on the subject are *UFO Crash at Roswell* (1991, with Donald R. Schmitt) and *The Truth About the UFO Crash at Roswell* (1994, also with Schmitt). All three of Randle's well-crafted books were useful in the writing of this novel.

Another pioneer (mentioned in the narrative), and the key defender of the Majestic Twelve documents, is nuclear physicist Stanton Friedman, who contributed research to the first book-length work on the subject, *The Roswell Incident* (1980) by Charles Berlitz and William L. Moore. Friedman's books *Crash at Corona* (1992, 1997, written with Don Berliner) and *Top Secret/Majic* (1996) were extremely helpful to this project. Anyone interested in Roswell needs to read both Randle and Friedman.

Two excellent books that attempt, with some success, to debunk the incident are *The Real Roswell Crashed-Saucer Incident* (1997) by Philip J. Klass, and *The Roswell UFO Crash* (1997) by Kal K. Korff. These were vital sources in the writing of this novel, particularly useful in trying to sort through the muddled chronology of events (and supposed events), although the extent to which Klass and Korff disbelieve at times rivals the absurdity of the believers at their most naive. Incidentally, inconsistencies in the various Roswell authors' chronology have been resolved in this book in favor of whatever the hell the narrative needed.

The Roswell File (1997) by Tim Shawcross is the closest attempt I found to examine the incident in an objective fashion; while Shawcross appears to be in the believer camp, he presents negative evidence, which he discusses with an open mind, as opposed to the professional skepticism of Klass and Korff. A similar approach—but with a wider-ranging view of the UFO phenomenon—is taken by Jim Marrs in *Alien Agenda* (1997); and yet another objective look is provided by a former teacher of mine (at the University of Iowa in the early seventies), C.D.B. Bryan, in *Close Encounters of the Fourth Kind: Alien Abduction, UFOs, and the Conference at MIT* (1995).

I relied heavily upon a wide-eyed believer's account of the incident, the lavishly illustrated *Beyond Roswell* (1997) by Michael Hesemann and Philip Mantle, which thoroughly explores Majestic Twelve and may be the most fun of any of these books, assembling a coherent narrative out of the various, sometimes incredibly dubious, evidence. *The Roswell Report: Case Closed* (1997) by Captain James McAndrew is the United States Air Force's second published report on the incident, and was extremely useful, and less tainted by bias than the Klass and Korff books, but at the same time less credible, particularly considering that this is the government's fourth official explanation of the incident.

Roswell articles I consulted include "Roswell or

Bust" by Bruce Handy, *Time* (June 23, 1997); "50 Years After Roswell" by Dawn Stover, *Popular Science* (June 1997); and "Roswell—50 Years Later" by Jim Wilson, *Popular Mechanics* (July 1997)—the latter in particular helping me fine-tune my "solution." *The Complete Roswell Encyclopedia,* a one-shot magazine published by Steve Harris, was another valuable resource. Various Internet articles, including Troy Taylor's "The Lodge—Cloudcroft, New Mexico" (which details the legend of the hotel's ghost), were helpful, as well.

In addition, I screened numerous Roswell documentaries (about half of which seemed to be hosted by Jonathan Frakes), including *Alien Autopsy (Fact or Fiction),* directed by Tom McGough and written by Robert Kiviat and Tom Seligson; and viewed the 1994 TV movie *Roswell,* an entertaining, somewhat fanciful adaptation by Arthur Kopit, Paul Davids and the film's director, Jeremy Kagain, of the first Randle/Schmitt book; Forrestal is a secondary character in the melodrama, which hints that the former Secretary of Defense was murdered because he planned to tell the public about the aliens who were coming to invade the earth.

With very few exceptions, the characters in this novel appear with their real names, despite receiving varying degrees of fictionalization. A number of minor characters—Deputy Reynolds and Della Brown, for instance—are fictional but have one or more real-life counterparts. A liberty I've taken has been to have such witnesses as Glenn Dennis and Frank Kauffman—who did not come forward until many years later—discussing their experiences in 1949.

The romantic relationship between Glenn Dennis and Maria Selff is cited in many references, but—in more recent interviews, anyway—Dennis himself has begun to deny it. Furthermore, "Naomi Maria Selff"—which may be a Dennis-invented pseudonym for a woman whose existence some researchers doubt—is heavily fictionalized in this story. Perhaps the major liberty I've taken is depicting the nurse's presence at Walker Air Force Base in 1949, when Glenn Dennis recalls her being transferred within days of the July 1947 incident. Dennis also claims that Selff was transferred to England and mail to her there was returned to him marked "deceased," and that he was later told by mutual friends she had died in a plane crash. If Maria Selff actually ever existed— and researchers have for many years tried diligently to find her, or even proof of her existence—there is no evidence to suggest the intelligence work (or lively sex life, much less the violent death) I have invented for her in this novel has any basis in reality.

While Heller's fictional interviews with Kaufmann, Dennis, and other witnesses such as Walter Haut and Frank Joyce are based upon actual interviews and statements these real people have given researchers over the years, their characterizations in the context of this novel should be viewed as fictionalized, and no negative reflection on any of these individuals is intended. There is, for example, no reason to think that Kaufmann in real life revealed the top-secret and/or classified material the fictionalized Kaufmann shares with Heller in this novel.

Dr. Joseph Bernstein is a fictional character, representing the very real influence and activities of Nazi scientists and doctors within the postwar U.S. government. In this novel Bernstein—in discussing patient Forrestal—occasionally utters sentiments similar to those spoken by Forrestal's real psychiatrist, Dr. George Raines, who is not an onstage character in this book (though referred to); Bernstein is in no way a reflection of, or for that matter a fictionalized version of, Dr. Raines.

My portrayal of James Forrestal was influenced by two excellent biographies, *Driven Patriot: The Life and Times of James Forrestal* (1992) by Townsend Hoopes and Douglas Brinkley; and *James Forrestal: A Study of Personality, Politics and Policy* (1963) by Arnold A. Rogow. *Driven Patriot* provided much of the background used to develop my unflattering, but I hope sympathetic, portrait of Jo Forrestal. Also helpful were *The Death of James Forrestal* (1966) by Cornell Simpson, a conservative conspiracist's take on Forrestal's "murder" that provided many wonderful details unavailable elsewhere; *The Forrestal Diaries* (1951), edited by Walter Millis with the collaboration of E. S. Duffield; *James Forrestal* (1951) by Frank P. Leslie, an affectionate monograph by a Princeton classmate; and *Men of the Pentagon: From Forrestal to McNamara* (1966) by Carl W. Borklund.

My characterization of the perplexing Drew Pearson was drawn from material in numerous sources, including the first-rate, pro-Pearson *Drew Pearson: An Unauthorized Biography* (1973) by Oliver Pilat; *Drew Pearson: Diaries 1949—1959* (1974), edited by his stepson, Tyler Abell; and an anti-Pearson diatribe, *The Drew Pearson Story* (1967) by Frank Kluckhohn and Jay Franklin. Perhaps the most enlightening material, however, came from Jack Anderson's wonderful *Confessions of a Muckraker* (1979, written with James Boyd), which of course influenced the (somewhat fictionalized) Anderson characterization in this book, as well.

The whimsical portrait of Teddy Kollek—which may have little to do with the real man—is nonetheless drawn from the following sources: *For Jerusalem:*

A Life (1978) by Teddy Kollek with his son, Amos Kollek; *Every Spy a Prince* (1990) by Dan Raviv and Yossi Melman; *Friends in Deed* (1994) by Yossi Melman; *Return to Zion* (1987) by Bodie Thoene; and numerous Internet articles.

My longtime collaborator, research associate George Hagenauer, searched out books and newspaper and magazine articles on topics including the Bethesda naval hospital, CIA mind control, the birth of Israel, the U.S. government's recruitment of Nazis and much more; he also played advance scout, reading many of the Roswell books and sending me toward only the most worthwhile among them. Articles George uncovered included a 1942 *Scientific American* article, "The Progress of Science—National Naval Medical Center" by Commander Frederick C. Greaves; "Citadel of Navy Medicine" by Sidney Shalett, *New York Times Magazine,* April 18, 1943; "Spare Parts of Human Bodies" by Milton MacKaye, *The Saturday Evening Post,* December 23, 1950; and "Pools of Healing," *Time,* August 22, 1955. George, your engraved silver cup is in the mail (stay away from the windows).

Three other good friends helped with research matters: writer Joe Collins (no relation), who dug up material on V-2s and other experimental rocketry, and provided last-minute weapons training; booking detective Lynn Meyers, who located an elusive Forrestal monograph, among other things; and my right-hand man on my film *Mommy's Day,* Steven Henke, who shared his research and thoughts relating to his own in-progress documentary on early rocketry (and the German scientists involved therein), not to mention providing a copy of the FBI's annotated Majestic Twelve documents (every page is boldly marked "BOGUS").

Additional books that aided in the writing of this novel include *Blowback* (1988), Christopher Simpson; *Capitol Hill in Black and White* (1986), Robert Parker with Richard Rashke; *The Man Who Got Capone* (1976), Frank Spiering; *New Mexico: Off the Beaten Path* (1991), Todd Staats; *Operation Mind Control* (1978), Walter Bowart; *The Search for the "Manchurian Candidate"* (1979), John Marks; *Smithsonian Guide to Historic America: The Desert States* (1990), Michael S. Durham; *Stuart Symington* (1960), Paul I. Wellman; *Trading with the Enemy* (1983), Charles Higham; *Treasury Agent* (1958), Andrew Tully; *Truman* (1992), David McCullough; *The United States Secret Service* (1961), Walter S. Bowen and Harry Edward Neal; *Virtual Government* (1997), Alex Constantine; *Washington Goes to War* (1988), David Brinkley; *Washington Lowdown* (1956), Larston D. Farrar; *Where I Stand* (1966), Hank Greenspun with Alex Pelle; *Winchell* (1971), Bob Thomas; and *World Without Cancer* (1974), G. Edward Griffin. As has often been the case in the past, various WPA Guides were extremely beneficial, specifically those for the District of Columbia (both the 1937 and 1942 versions) and New Mexico (1940). And I would especially like to acknowledge the lively *Washington Confidential* (1951) by Jack Lait and Lee Mortimer.

I would again like to thank editors Joseph Pittman and Michaela Hamilton for giving Nate Heller and his creator the opportunity to enjoy the classic Mickey Spillane Dutton/Signet imprimatur; and of course Dominick Abel, my friend and agent, who went to bat for his author with characteristic tenacity, courage and loyalty.

With the magic of her patience and love, my talented wife helped me through this particularly harrowing race to make deadline in the midst of a chaotically busy year, protecting and advising me as only she can. Nate Heller has many women, and so do I: but mine are all named Barbara Collins.